A Dom Is Forever

Masters and Mercenaries, Book 3

Lexi Blake

A Dom Is Forever
Masters and Mercenaries, Book 3
Lexi Blake

Published by DLZ Entertainment LLC

Copyright 2012 DLZ Entertainment LLC
Edited by Chloe Vale and Kasi Alexander
Print ISBN: 978-1-937608-11-8

Acknowledgements

This book wouldn't exist without the enormous support of my friends and family. Chloe Vale worked tirelessly editing and keeping me in check—a job all on its own. This book is as much hers as it is mine so if anyone has complaints, they should probably go to Chloe. Also thanks to the amazing Kasi Alexander for a great edit. The lovely Fiona Archer served as my Brit speak coach. Thanks to Liz Berry for her tireless support. Thanks to Sheri Vidal for letting me know I'm not insane and for her great work with Lexi's Doms and Dolls, and to Leah Christensen for setting up the group. And a very special shout out to Riane Holt, the pickiest beta reader ever. You made this a much better book than it was before.

I also want to thank my husband and Shayla Black, the two people who accompanied me as I explored and researched one of the greatest cities in the world—London. This is my love letter to London and its people. And I promise to stand to the right from now on.

Prologue

Dublin, Ireland

Liam opened his eyes slowly, praying the world was actually coming to some sort of violent end. The ground beneath him didn't seem quite solid. It was moving, spinning, and along with it went his stomach.

He groaned. No apocalypse. Just a bloody fucking hangover to end all hangovers. He'd gotten pissed the night before. Little flashes came back. He and Rory in the pub. They weren't going to have more than a pint. How had everything gotten away from him?

Liam sat up, his head pounding. Early morning light poured through the small window above him. Early morning or late afternoon? He forced his eyes to focus on the completely foreign room.

Feminine colors and frills dominated. He'd gotten laid? *Fuck.* He should remember that. He turned slightly. Yep. He wasn't alone in bed. Blonde hair. Nice legs, from what he could tell. She seemed to be a stomach sleeper.

He scrubbed a hand across his face. Maybe he should just sneak out. Where the hell was his brother?

His tongue felt thick in his mouth. How the fuck much did he drink last night? He hadn't intended to drink more than his pint and have some roast and potatoes.

Fog clouded his head. Something was wrong. He

wouldn't have gotten pissed during a mission. Sure the mission was almost over, but he still had to meet with the handler and then on to the really dangerous portion. Not that getting in good with the Russian mafia hadn't been dangerous, but this arms dealer they were meeting represented the end of the game. They would take down the mysterious arms dealer and hand back the bearer bonds. God only knew where all that mob money would go from there. MI6 most likely. His mother would turn over in her grave. Pure IRA, she was, but he was a man of the new world, and that included working with the bloody Brits. They paid well, and the truth was their fates were somewhat tied together in this new freaking world. Their economies were joined at the hip. The world was a smaller place than when his mother had cursed the Brits.

He stretched, trying not to wake the woman next to him—the girl he'd apparently fucked without having a single memory of it. He got to his very wobbly feet and stopped, forcing himself to focus on her. He should remember something about her. Anything. A hint of a smile. A flirtatious word.

Nothing.

Where was the pack with the bonds? Rory had them last. His head throbbed. They needed those bonds. They were the proof that they came from Leonov. The arms dealer they had been trying to locate would only accept the bonds and no other payment. They were screwed if someone had taken them. The arms dealer would disappear, and he'd peddle his uranium elsewhere.

Dirty bombs. It's what that fucker Leonov had been trying to put together for his clients. Leonov was an arms dealer himself, but he was small-time trying to move into the Middle East. He and Rory had spent a year of their lives chasing this guy and finally they had brokered the deal. G2, MI6, and very likely the CIA, had a plan to use the bonds Liam and Rory had taken off the Russian mobster to complete the deal and learn the name of the arms dealer who offered the uranium.

And that was above his fucking pay grade, as his American friend Ian would say. He just needed to finish the job and get home for some well-deserved R&R. He had six weeks coming to him. Six weeks to rest and eat and fuck and get rat-arsed drunk. Not necessarily in that order.

He felt like a dirty bomb had gone off in his bloody brain.

He sighed. He should at least wake her up and say good-bye. Hell, maybe she could make him a spot of breakfast. He could use some sausage. Might settle his rolling gut.

And she could tell him where the fuck Rory was.

He leaned over and touched her shoulder.

Cold skin met his touch. So much colder than a simple chill. With dawning horror, he rolled her over. Deep blue lines surrounded her throat, slender tendrils that marked the place where her oxygen had been cut off. She'd been strangled and not by meaty, masculine hands. The bruising was too perfect. Rope, he suspected.

Then he saw it. A line of rope likely thirty feet in length because that's how he bought it. Jute. The type he used in Shibari.

He hadn't killed that girl. He would never harm a submissive. He wouldn't play when he was drunk. Panic started to overwhelm him. He picked up the rope. It had to be his. The young woman wouldn't just have jute lying around. It had to have come from his pack.

What the hell had happened? Questions started to pound

3

through his head like waves crashing on a rock.

His phone. It was lying on the floor. He picked it up. He needed Rory. Had they split up in search of a little tail? He wouldn't put it past his brother. Rory was a wild one, and he could get into trouble faster than anyone Liam knew. He pressed the number one. It was fitting. His younger brother was number one in his life. Liam was the one who had talked Rory into following him into the Defence Forces. He'd thought the Army would do his younger brother a bit of good, and he'd been right. When G2 had come calling with a bit of undercover work, Rory had followed him again. Rory was damn good at this job. He was finally turning out to be a man Liam could be proud of.

The call went straight to voice mail. *Fuck.*

"Rory, I need you to call me. God, please wake up, brother. I'm in a mess. I don't remember what happened but I woke up in bed…" What the hell was he doing? He knew bloody well better than to leave an incriminating message on his brother's voice mail. He shook his head as he looked for his pants. "Just call me."

He dressed as quickly as he could. Boxers, dark wash jeans, socks, boots. He found his shirt rolled up in the corner of the overly frilly dead girl's room. How the hell old was this girl? It didn't matter now because she wouldn't age another second. She would be forever stuck in this pink and white room, a purple collar of damage around her throat.

His hands shook as he pulled the black T-shirt free. Why was it wet? Had he spilled beer all over it?

Why couldn't he remember?

Blood. It stained his hands as he let the shirt drop. His shirt was soaked in blood.

He stared at it for a moment. Blood? There wasn't a drop of blood on the girl.

He reached for his jacket, zipping it up. He found his bag lying on the dresser, open as though he'd just left it there for a moment. The only thing missing was his rope and a knife. His stomach churned in a way that had nothing to do with the alcohol from the previous night. Where was that knife?

Who should he call? The police? G2? The Irish Intelligence Agency would love the fact that a soldier had gotten into this ball of shit. He wasn't an intelligence agent. He was sort of a contractor. He'd been hoping he'd be asked to join up after this.

No one was going to want to hire him when he ended up in jail. *Fuck. Fuck. Fuck.* What had happened? Why couldn't he remember?

He dialed Rory's number again. *Wake up, you bastard. I'm in trouble.*

He clutched the phone to his ear, but a sound from another room called to him. Trilling. Familiar.

Rory's phone was ringing. Inside the house. The next room. And he still wasn't answering. Liam's heart pounded as his mind sought all the reasons his brother wouldn't answer. It was a bloody short list.

Liam stepped outside the dead girl's room and found himself in hell.

Chapter One

London, England
Five years later

Liam watched the girl with the dark hair walk into the light. Girl? She was a woman in every sense of the word. Avery Charles was twenty-eight years old, but from what he'd pieced together she'd likely lived through enough crap for two lifetimes. So why did she still look so bloody innocent?

The woman in front of him wasn't his type. Not even close. She was too soft, too curvy, too much. Too serious, quite frankly. He preferred young women who just wanted a good time. But something about her drew him in. Maybe it was her background or the way her skin practically glowed when she walked into the great rotunda of the British Museum. She did it enough. She was here almost every day, and he'd stalked her, watching her move from room to room, studying each exhibit before her lunch hour was up. She would glide from the dark corners of the museum into the brilliant light of the atrium to purchase a sandwich she would eat before heading back to the Tube and work again.

And every day she would stop when the light hit her face. She would move from the dark, hushed rooms of the exhibits into the stark brilliance of the white marbled center of the museum. She would tilt her chin up and bask in the light as though taking a moment to soak it in.

Liam never left the darkness.

"Is that the mark?" Ian Taggart asked, his voice low.

He didn't need to be so silent. The museum hummed with activity, but his boss was a cautious man. Paranoid, but then when everyone really was out to get you, it wasn't paranoia. It was smart.

"Yes," Liam replied, his voice equally low. "Avery Charles. She works for Molina. She became his personal assistant six months ago."

She was his primary target for the moment. It had been easy to gather data on Molina. He was a public figure. Within minutes of confirming that Thomas Molina, philanthropist, was somehow involved with the rogue CIA agent his firm had been tracking for months, he'd had a full dossier on the man. Molina was considered a bit odd. He'd been injured as a teenager in a riding accident. He'd had several spinal surgeries and had been left with legs that never functioned properly again. He disappeared for many years, living a life of seclusion after his parents had passed away.

He was now in sole control of a huge multi-national company, but preferred to spend his time on a charity operation called United One Fund.

It had been easy to find Molina. His personal assistant had taken more digging.

"Do we know if she has any ties to Black?" Somehow Ian managed to make the question sound like a threat. "Sorry. Nelson. We should call the devil by his real name. Does she have any ties to Eli Nelson?"

That was the big question of the day. What was seemingly sweet Avery Charles, who had never had so much as a parking ticket, doing working for a man who did indeed have ties to Eli Nelson, rogue CIA agent? "I doubt it. If I had to place a bet, I would bank money on the fact that she's just the personal assistant of one of the world's leading philanthropists. She's got a do-gooder vibe I can feel from here. It makes me a little nauseous."

It made him a little horny, but there was no way he was telling Ian that. And no way to explain it because she just wasn't his type. No way. No how. Well, she wasn't his type now. He'd given up on soft, voluptuous women for a reason. They fucked with a man's mental capacities. Nope. She wasn't his type now. It was just that he hadn't gotten laid in a while. That was the only explanation.

"Alex is looking into Molina. He's running financials on those charities of his." Ian frowned as he looked around. "I don't like it."

Ian Taggart didn't like charities? There was a surprise since the man was practically a charity in and of himself. Liam knew he was alive today based on the man's sense of charity. "From the press surrounding him, he's practically a saint."

Ian smiled, though on him it was more a predatory baring of teeth. "I don't believe in saints. Sinners. Now, I can believe that." He sighed as he looked back in the atrium. Avery was ordering a sandwich and a cup of coffee. "Have Adam and Jake moved in?"

Ian's eyes shifted around the big room, constantly seeking a threat.

They weren't carrying. He felt a little naked without a gun. It was too dangerous in such a public place, and they weren't exactly here in a formal capacity. That was his fault. Everyone on the team had tried to talk him out of coming back to Europe, but it had been years. He'd changed. Perhaps it was past time to face his demons and honor his brother's memory.

After he'd taken down Eli Nelson.

"They moved into her building last week. We were oh so lucky that her neighbor decided to leave town for a while and was forced to sublet the place." Liam kept his eyes on Avery as she paid seven pounds fifty. She smiled at the bloke in front of her. How did the woman smile like that, bright and open after everything that had happened to her? She smiled as though she'd come through that crucible and could still have a full heart in her body.

Of course, it could all be an act.

"I think you'll find Adam and Jake are paying enough to well compensate the lady," Ian explained. His body went on alert, shoulders squaring. "Who the fuck is that? I thought you said she didn't have a boyfriend."

Liam felt his eyes narrow as Avery greeted the tall blond man. He was obviously British. It was all there in the cool cut of his suit and the deeply pretentious way the bugger air kissed her cheeks. He had to bend over because Avery was short. She was short and curvy, and the Brit bastard was looking down her shirt.

"I haven't seen him before," Liam said. A solid week of following her around and he hadn't once seen her even look at a man who wasn't carved of marble and brought back to London from some far-off place during the days of British Imperialism. The only man he'd seen her with was her boss. She would wheel him around St. James's Park twice a week, settling a blanket around his unsteady legs before making the jaunt. Molina could walk with the aid of a cane, but the millionaire used a wheelchair on those walks of theirs.

Ian was already taking pictures with his phone. It had been adapted for Ian's own use. High resolution, super focus. Any picture Ian took was immediately forwarded to headquarters for a little turn through Adam's facial recognition software. They would have the bugger's name and life story within minutes.

Why the hell did he want to kick the blond bloke's ass? Days of watching Avery Charles and going over and over her tragic story had made him protective. She'd been through a lot. And the young Liam, the Liam he'd been before he'd lost his brother, would have been all over her.

Still, it was a bad idea to get protective of a woman who just might be involved in international terrorism.

She sat down at one of the long tables, blond bastard following her. He curled his tall body into the seat across from her as she began talking animatedly. He reached out, cradling her hand in his, but she almost immediately pulled away, grabbing her coffee mug.

No sex there. No intimacy. She was awkward, unsure about his physical affection.

"He's not the boyfriend." Ian almost certainly saw what he saw. Ian was a master at reading body language. Likely because he was an actual Master. And that was why Liam wanted Ian to see her in person.

"What's your take on her?" Liam asked.

Ian had been watching her for two hours, since she'd gotten off the Tube at Holborn. Liam had been following her path for days, and she took the same trains without fail. She left the offices at Charing Cross and bought a bottle of water. Switched from Bakerloo to the Picadilly Line and got off at Holborn. From there it should have been a quick walk up New Oxford to Bloomsbury and the museum, but Avery seemed to always find a way to stroll and look at whatever minutiae caught her eye. And she often had a camera. One day she'd spent twenty minutes taking pictures of tulips in street boxes.

It was maddening. Boring. Dull as dishwater. And he'd started to wonder if she was seeing a world he didn't see.

Ian leaned back, taking out the museum map he'd bought and pretending to study it. "I think she's intriguing. Given what I know about her background, I would have expected someone a little more broken than she appears to be."

Yes. That was the problem. Most women who had lost what Avery had lost would bear the marks like scars. It would be there in their eyes, but Avery's were a clear, crystal blue. "It has been ten years since the accident."

"That kind of pain never goes away." Ian's lips formed a grim line, and his eyes closed momentarily. When he opened them again, his face was a careful blank. "She lost her husband and her baby in an accident. She nearly lost the use of her legs. It might have been ten years since the accident, but I assure you, she feels it every day. Or maybe not. Maybe she's not capable of love. I've met people who weren't."

"She works for a charity," Liam pointed out. He didn't like the cold way Ian was talking. Ian hadn't been the one watching her day in and day out. Ian hadn't been the one to see how she stopped and talked to people on the street and how she'd helped a lost kid. She'd hugged him and held his hand while everyone else just walked on by as though it wasn't their problem.

Ian shrugged. "I worked for a vegetarian restaurant once while I was undercover. Didn't mean I didn't find animals awfully tasty. She's getting a good paycheck from Molina. He's paying for her apartment. Are you sure she's not fucking him?"

"She goes home every night and she goes alone. Unless she's fucking him at the office, I sincerely doubt it." She

11

wasn't the type. Was she?

"I just find it odd that Molina could afford anyone and he picks her." Ian folded his map. "Come on. Until we're ready to send someone in, we need to keep our distance. Let's get back to the club. Eve should be in town by now. Her flight was coming in this morning. And I want to see if Adam figured out who the blond guy is."

Ian started to walk away. It was like the big bastard to think Liam would just follow along. But he did, because they needed to clear something up. Liam kept his mouth shut as they walked out the Russell Street entrance and into the light of day.

"What do you mean 'someone,' Ian?"

Ian never broke stride. "'Some' as in being an undetermined or unspecified one. 'One' as in determining the specified some."

Bastard. "You're talking like you haven't decided who's going in after the girl."

"Adam and Jake are doing the neighbor thing."

"Yeah, and that's not going to get us anywhere. She's not going to invite her neighbors to come to lunch at her office or to sleep at her place."

"Adam and Jake are pretty damn good at breaking in." Ian turned toward the Tube station. "Ask Serena. She'd love to tell you that story. We're lucky they married her and she didn't sue the holy fuck out of us. Seriously, it's one of the only good things that came out of that op. They got a collar around her throat and a ring on her finger. Presto, lawsuit disappears. And people say BDSM isn't good for a man."

None of which answered the question. "Don't you try to replace me. This is my op. I found the connection between Nelson and Molina. This is mine."

Ian stopped. A long moment passed. "I don't know that

you're right for this girl. We might only get one shot to put someone in her bed, and she's just not your type."

"It's my op. I'll handle it." He wasn't sending someone else in. "Besides, who the hell else are you going to get to play the boyfriend role? Adam and Jake are off the market. Sean quit. Are you planning to romance the girl?"

Ian frowned again. "Alex asked about it."

Motherfucker. "No. You can't be serious. Eve…what about Eve?"

Alex and Eve were divorced and had been for years, but there was no doubt in Liam's mind that Eve still loved her husband. Ex. Even he couldn't keep it straight. Alex had been a bloody monk since the divorce.

"Alex is trying to move on, and that includes taking one for the team. You're right. We're low on males who don't mind a little play with their work." Ian growled a little, his frustration evident. "Damn it, I don't want to do shit like this. I don't like having to fuck for information."

No one with half a tablespoon of morality did, but sometimes it was necessary. Eli Nelson was a danger to everyone on Liam's team. If Liam's instincts were correct, he might be a danger to everyone in the world. Nelson had already attempted to sell state secrets to China. Balanced against all the danger, hurting Avery Charles's feminine heart was the lesser of two evils. "But this case is different. This is Nelson, and we won't get anywhere if we try to play by the rules. He wouldn't hesitate to fuck anything he had to in order to get the information he needs. We can't either. There's too much at stake."

Ian settled the baseball cap he was wearing over his head, pulling out the Oyster card he'd bought earlier. Liam found his own. The little card was the gateway to the Tube and the easiest way to get anywhere in London. "I left the

Agency because I didn't like the man it was turning me into, but I'll admit that I need to get Nelson. I need it. Until I see that man six feet under, I won't be able to rest. He nearly killed my brother, and he used my team to sell this country out. The Agency hasn't done shit to bring him in, so I'll do it myself. Which is precisely why I'll handle the girl. Send me her file. I'll make contact tomorrow."

He reached out and grabbed Ian's arm. "No, you won't. It's my bloody fucking op, and I'll take the girl."

Ian's eyes went positively arctic as he looked at the hand on his sleeve. "Watch it. Your Irish is up."

Fuck all. Liam took a long breath and forced himself back into his bland Midwestern accent. He'd perfected it over the years because it was better camouflage than his real accent. For the first several years he'd worked at McKay-Taggart Security, only Alex and Ian had known his real voice. He needed to pull it together. "Sorry. It's hard being surrounded by it."

"Yes. A damn good reason for you to be at home."

Liam had heard this argument about a million times. "I understand the way this city works better than anyone on the team, and I still have underground contacts. My op, Ian. And my mark."

Ian's voice got low, his mouth firming to a stubborn line. "Just see that the reason you're staying is the op and not the girl. What I didn't say before, but you've almost certainly picked up on, is the fact that she seems amazingly innocent and is very likely to be submissive. You know the signs. She's been painstakingly polite and she defers to everyone. When the museum docent talked to her, her eyes slid right to the floor. She's a sub and a sweet one at that. A dangerous combo for men like us. I'm not stupid, Li. The reason you hang out with club subs is that they're hard core and just looking for some fun. That woman in there is not looking for a good time. She's serious, and this can only end one of two ways. One, she's dirty and you'll feel like shit because you'll send her to jail or a grave. Two, she's clean as a whistle and you break her heart because if she's as innocent as she looks, she'll have to fall for you in order for you to get into her bed. And you'll feel like shit. You've worked backup for years. Are you really ready to take the lead?"

He'd been a pussy for years, hiding behind his teammates and letting them take all the real risks. Sure he'd gotten shot at on occasion, but running the op meant taking responsibility for the health and safety of everyone involved, and that included Avery Charles if she was an innocent bystander.

"I'm ready."

Ian nodded. "Then it's your op. But the minute Nelson rears his head, I take over."

Ian pressed through the turnstile. Liam took a deep breath. One hurdle over. Now he had to figure out the best way to get close to Avery Charles.

It didn't help that the very thought of sliding into her bed got his dick hard. Yeah, he couldn't lie to himself. She might be some sweet, innocent thing, or she might be hiding something dirty beneath all that sugar.

Either way he knew exactly what Avery Charles was. She was trouble. Luckily he was a man who could handle a little trouble.

* * * *

Avery smiled at Simon Weston. He was a very nice man, and she was so deeply uninterested that she had to fight back a yawn.

And that really wasn't a nice way to think. He'd been nothing but polite to her. She forced herself to focus in on him. Simon was very sweet and often made her laugh, but they were in completely different departments so they hadn't had occasion to spend much time together.

Though he seemed to try to be around her. It was a mystery.

"I was telling Jason the other day that he simply had to try the new Indian place in Soho. The fish curry is amazing. Nothing like I got when I went to Bangalore, but it's the best you can get in London." Simon leaned forward a little. "You know we could go there for lunch one of these days. The food here can't be great."

It was overpriced, and she often had to scarf it down on her way back to Charing Cross, but nothing could compete with the views. She'd spent her hour looking through the Elgin Marbles rooms, carefully reading every placard, amazed that she was looking at the very same work that had decorated the Parthenon. She almost teared up thinking about it, but Simon Weston didn't seem like a man who would understand that a bunch of ancient marble could fire her imagination. It pointed out to her that while she had many fascinating conversations with her very intellectual boss, she was lonely. Thomas was into economics and business. Though he tried, she could see his eyes glaze over the minute she started talking about art. Simon was the same way. And she was drifting. What had he said? Oh. The food. "It's okay. A sandwich is a sandwich, though I've come to really love salmon and cream cheese."

She had a bit of a distracted brain.

Simon's fingers drummed along the table. "Rumor has it you come here every day."

She stopped, hands in mid-motion of bringing her sandwich to her mouth. "There are rumors about me? Gosh, you guys must be really bored."

She was the dullest thing in the world. Her great and grand scandal was forgetting to recycle on occasion. Well, that and the fact that everyone assumed she was sleeping with her boss. Which she wasn't.

Simon grinned. He was quite adorable. He was tall and lean and had Hollywood-actor good looks, but he also seemed a bit calculating. She couldn't figure it out, but there was something in the way he looked at her that made her feel like he was sizing her up and making decisions based on some matrix in his head. "Well, life at United One Fund can be quite boring, but with the boss in town, it's picked up considerably. We've never met the big guy in person, you know. And meeting his lovely assistant was even better."

Avery set her sandwich down, completely unable to figure out how to handle the problem of Simon Weston. He was a lawyer and had been with the company for almost a year. Like almost all of the employees of the Fund, as they liked to call it, Simon had taken a pay cut to work for a foundation known for its good works.

He was obviously a good man. So why did she think he had ulterior motives for pursuing her? Nothing in his manner told her he was attracted to her except his words. And why did she think she should follow her instincts? She didn't have any. She barely knew how to function in the dating world. She knew next to nothing about men. Her only experience had been Brandon, and he was a distant memory now. When she thought about her husband, her memories were of a happy, sweet smile and the awkward way he'd loved her. They'd been so damn young. He was a ghost, and her memories were starting to fade. She was practically a

17

virgin again.

Except virgins didn't miss their babies.

Avery took a long breath and forced herself back into the moment. The moment was everything. Forward. Always forward.

She was well aware that every woman at the Fund thought she was completely insane for turning the tall, lean blond god of a man down. It seemed to be yet another reason for the rumor that she was sleeping with Thomas.

Her new neighbors were easier. The two Americans who had moved in after Mrs. Elenora Pettigrew had decided she needed the country air were perfect. They were gorgeous. Simply divine. They were easy to talk to. Well, Adam was. Jacob seemed to grunt a lot, but he was friendly enough. She could look at them all she liked because they were also gay.

At least she thought they were. She was confused here in England. No. They were Americans. They were gay. Straight American men didn't wear pink polos with skinny jeans.

It would be easier if Simon was gay.

"I'm not gay." Simon's huffed words pulled her out of her head.

Damn it. Had she said that out loud? "What? I asked 'what did you say'? Sorry. I missed it."

He stared at her for a moment as though trying to decide if she was for real. She gave him her best dumb smile. She didn't have to pretend. She felt really dumb. Socially awkward. She'd spent so much time alone, she sometimes talked out loud. It had worked when she was in the hospital and rehab for years at a time. No one questioned the insane woman who talked to herself. In the real world, she was odd to say the least, but she'd somehow managed to find a weird place for herself here in London.

Simon's flushed face turned back to perfectly charming. "I was saying the Fund's been more interesting with you around."

"Is it because I routinely pratfall and tumble down the stairs?" Her leg gave out at the oddest of times. The staff had taken to calling her the Amazing Falling Woman. She gave regular shows at nine and noon. Everyone was welcome.

Simon frowned. "I don't think that's very amusing. You have a bad leg. People shouldn't comment on it."

She sighed. Why was he here when they were so obviously not suited? He was very proper, and she was a walking *Three Stooges* movie. "It's the reality of the situation."

"If the staff is making fun of you, I shall talk to Molina and have them fired."

Yes, this was the heart of the problem. Half the time she was sure what Simon felt for her was sympathy. The other half she wondered if he wasn't trying to move up the chain by getting close to the boss. "They're not making fun of me. They're helping me to laugh about it. It's funny, Simon. I can be talking about the most serious subject in the world and sounding deeply intellectual and then I'm on the floor. Sometimes it takes a few steps for the person I was talking with to realize I'm no longer with them. It would be different if they were letting me lie there and laughing at me. They help me up."

He sat back in his chair, his jaw a mulish line. "Still, I don't know that it's a laughing matter."

If she couldn't laugh, she would cry, and she was so tired of crying. It felt good to laugh. It felt good to work. It felt good to explore a whole world she'd never imagined she would see.

And lately she was wondering if it would feel good to explore more than museums and parks. She'd started to wonder if she could explore intimacy. But she knew damn well she wouldn't be exploring it with Simon. Though he was truly a handsome man, with broad shoulders and lean muscle, there was no heat in his eyes when he looked at her.

And she needed to be wanted.

She decided to change the subject. "So you needed me to look at something?"

He nodded and reached into his briefcase. "Sorry. You didn't answer your phone and this just came up. It's a potential donor, but he wants to meet with Molina. We all know that you're the one who gets to decide who meets with Molina. It's a substantial donation."

He passed the file to her. Two million and change. Yes, that was substantial. She glanced at the name. Lachlan Bates. She had no idea who that was. Molina was a bit of an introvert. There were only a few people he regularly met with. A few friends, like the one he'd come to London to see. She thought it rather funny that her very prissy boss made time once a week to meet his friend at a fish and chips place on the Thames beside the Tate Modern. She would have guessed Thomas wouldn't eat anything so common as fish and chips. He was a caviar and *foie gras* kind of guy.

Simon pointed to his file. "He claims to be a self-made millionaire. Something about software or something."

"I'll take a look at the file and talk to Thomas about it. It's odd, though. Usually donations this large go through Monica. I'm surprised it got on your desk." She rarely dealt with actual donations, and it wasn't Simon's department at all.

He shrugged. "It just showed up on my desk with some

other paperwork. Probably a mistake. I thought you would be the person to handle it. You're the only one who calls him that, you know."

She was well aware that Thomas Molina was misunderstood. For some reason the staff was completely intimidated by him, but he was sweet with her. Perhaps because of that wheelchair he would one day be confined to. She'd spent her time in one. They understood each other when it came to the pain of struggling just to walk. "It's his name. I won't wear it out."

Simon stared at her. "I don't get Americans sometimes. Come along. Let me walk you back. Perhaps I can convince you to have dinner with me."

She had the best excuse in the world. Thank god for new neighbors. "I can't. I promised to meet some friends for dinner."

She'd agreed to help the new guys find some places. Adam and Jake claimed to be completely lost. Jake had been transferred by his American corporation to their London offices, and Adam wasn't sure what he was going to do. Maybe he would like to do tourist stuff with her. She had Fridays off, and she was planning some day and weekend trips. It would be fun to have a companion.

If he didn't figure out what a complete freak she was, she might make a friend.

Her small flat in the Financial District used to be Thomas Molina's brother's place. Now it was hers while they were in London. Thomas had generously offered her a room in his townhouse, but she'd needed a little space. After so many years alone but surrounded by people, she needed some independence. And she'd found some great places to eat. She was rather excited to share her finds with the new hotties.

21

"And I lost you again," Simon said with a long-suffering sigh.

"Sorry. I drift. I will handle this. Thanks for bringing it to my attention. We need all the funding we can get with the new Congo plans." The Congo was on the verge of civil war or a spiral into the domesticity of true democracy. The Fund intended to help ensure the country had everything it needed to take the right path. Fed people were happy people. Educated people tended toward democracy. "I'm sorry about my plans tonight."

"Of course," Simon said. "Perhaps another time. At least let me escort you back to the office. You can explain to me the fascination this place holds. I can see a day or two, but you've been coming here for a while now."

"And I could take another two months and still not see everything." She wrapped her sandwich up. It could wait until she was back at her desk.

She began to follow Simon out of the light of the grand rotunda. Tomorrow she would visit the Egypt Galleries. And maybe she would find someone to talk to. Like that amazing-looking guy she'd seen here a couple of times. Tall, dark, and gorgeous. He seemed to be just as obsessed with the British Museum as she was. And today he'd even brought a friend. A blond Viking of a man.

He'd been beautiful, but nothing like the dark-haired man. She'd been thinking about him all week. Two chance glances at the same man and she was having dreams about him. It might not even have been the same guy.

Maybe she should stop reading those damn romance novels. They were giving her crazy expectations.

She followed Simon on to the train and thought about her green-eyed mystery man.

Chapter Two

Liam walked through the very unimpressive doors of The Garden. There was nothing about the Chelsea club from the outside that would give away the decadent playground that was inside the bland-looking, six-story building. From the outside, it could be any office space. There was no signage, no neon lights marking the way. If a patron wanted inside The Garden, he had to know the way, and he better be approved by Damon Knight, the owner and resident Dom.

"Ian." Damon stood behind the front desk talking to the hostess. She was already dressed in fet wear for the evening. The perfectly young and fresh sub was exactly his type. Skinny with nice tits and more makeup than any single woman should ever wear. She couldn't be past twenty-two, so why did she seem so much older and harder than Avery? And why the fuck couldn't he get that woman out of his head?

Damon Knight stood almost as tall as Ian, his shoulders broad and wide and his body still fit from years of time served in Britain's Special Air Service. He was an old friend of Ian's. Apparently ex-commandos-turned-Doms stuck together.

Liam just had to hope Damon wasn't also working with MI6. Liam couldn't imagine that Britain's version of the CIA wouldn't love to sit him down and have a talk about what had happened in Dublin all those years ago.

Not that he would have much to say since he didn't bloody remember what had happened.

He'd been on the run for years, but now he'd walked right back into the lion's den.

"Damon." Ian held out a hand, shaking the ex-SAS soldier's. "Thanks for hosting us."

"No problem." Damon's accent was cultured, not a hint of cockney or country in there. He was pure Oxford bred. "I'm happy to have you. All of you. More of you than I expected."

The last was said with a broad grin, as though the man was thrilled at the prospect of a little chaos.

Ian's brow furrowed, a sure sign that he wasn't happy. "I told you to expect Eve. And this is Liam O'Donnell. He's running the op. He's the one who found the connection between Molina and Eli Nelson."

Damon turned to Liam, holding out a hand. Would the big guy want to shake his hand if he knew he was likely considered a traitor by his government? Liam didn't miss a beat. He shook Damon's hand. "Nice to meet you, O'Donnell. Your crew is in the meeting room. And I've offered everyone who has rights at Sanctum the same rights in The Garden. Feel free to enjoy the club. Especially that pretty little brunette your boys brought with them. From what I understand, she's a bit of a celebrity. Siobhan back there says her books are all the rage."

Ian's face went cold. "They wouldn't."

Liam bit back a laugh. Someone was in serious trouble. "Oh, I bet they would. They just got married, Ian. I would bet little Serena didn't like her boys heading off to Europe without her."

"I'm going to kill them." Ian strode into the dungeon and toward the lifts. Liam followed, Damon's laugh echoing through the big room.

The Garden was very different from Sanctum, the club Ian owned in Dallas. Sanctum was a dungeon, and it looked that way. The Garden was pure theater. It was one of the most unusual spaces Liam had ever been in. There was a large hole in the dead center of the building, a massive skylight that allowed light to fill the space. The big dungeon was decked out as a decadent, wild garden, with vines and dark plants seeming to permeate the walls. Liam didn't really look, though. He was on a mission, and a bunch of night-blooming flowers weren't really his thing. He did see a couple of clever scene spaces. St. Andrew's Crosses dominated one wall, and there was a space with plush spanking benches. Damon Knight seemed to thrive on the drama of his dungeon space.

Ian jabbed at the lift button, his impatience seeming to grow by the minute. Liam followed him into the lift.

The idea of having Master rights at the club was something to be grateful for. He would need the outlet. Spanking a lovely sub would be a good way to unwind at the end of the day. Maybe Siobhan needed a partner. He could get into that.

The lift walls were glass. Liam stared out and down as they rode up to the fourth floor. He could see the dungeon below him.

A sudden vision of Avery Charles among the winding vines assaulted him. Her luminous skin would make her look like a pearl among the dark plants, like a flower blooming in the gloom. He'd mostly seen her in the sun. Would she illuminate the darkness?

The lift doors opened, and Liam was startled out of his vision. He was getting to be as bad as his friends. He felt a grin light his face because those friends of his were about to get their asses kicked. Ian looked like he was out for blood.

The fourth floor looked more like an office space. Liam stepped out of the lift and it was like he'd been transported back to the real world. He followed Ian toward the boardroom.

Liam pushed open the door to the meeting room. The boardroom was brightly lit with an expensive looking conference table and chairs. High-tech computer equipment sat on a desk in the corner, and a big projection screen covered the far wall.

Adam Miles sat at the desk fiddling around with the equipment. Alex McKay looked over his shoulder. No problem there. And then he saw Jacob Dean. Jake was in the corner quietly talking to a pretty brunette. Liam felt a smile cross his face. That brunette wasn't supposed to be here. She wasn't anywhere close to being a member of the team. *Thank god.* Ian would crawl out of his backside now that he had a new target.

"Jacob Dean," Ian began in the icy voice that must have scared the crap out of every soldier he used it on. "Do you want to explain to me why your wife is in my boardroom when she should be safely back in the Lone Star State?"

"I told you this wasn't the way to tell him," a low, feminine voice said. She didn't try to hide her amusement as she rose gracefully from her seat. Eve St. James. Liam couldn't help but smile. The resident shrink had a calming presence about her. Eve was gorgeous, with sleek blonde hair and a lovely face that was always perfectly made up. She was the very picture of serene, competent femininity. She winked Liam's way. "I think I told you both you should hide her and pray Ian never found out."

Jake pushed Serena behind him as though Ian would attack at any minute. "Now, Ian, we need to talk about this."

Adam got up, scrambling away from the desk to put his own body in front of Serena. Did they really think Ian was going to kill the girl? "She had to come with us."

Ian crossed his arms over his massive chest. "Oh, I would like to hear this one. Has Serena been surgically attached to one of you? Has she developed a medical condition in which she must be around one of her Masters or she'll die? Submissivitis?"

"Ian, we just got married. You can't expect us to leave our wife behind," Adam argued.

"Oh, really? Because I did."

Liam stood beside Ian, only mocking his ultra-alpha stance a little. Maybe a lot. "Would you like to let me know how you're going to explain little Miss Sunshine to our mark? I thought you were doing the gay thing as your cover."

"Our cover is solid." Adam pointed down to his pants, a ridiculously tight pair of denims that molded to his legs. "Look, jeggings. Trust me, there's no worry on that front."

Jake grinned. "They didn't have any in my size. Guess guys as big as me don't wear jeggings."

An arm crept around Adam's waist. "I think you look hot, babe. And I'm not exactly staying with them, you know, Ian. I have a very nice hotel room in Kensington. That's on the whole other side of the city."

"There's nowhere in London that's not a couple of Tube stops away. You are getting back on a plane tonight," Ian said.

Jake and Adam started to puff up. Serena moved from between them and faced down Ian herself. Or rather faced up. She was a good foot shorter than him.

"I'm not going home."

Ian growled.

27

"Fine. I'm not going home, Sir." Serena stood her ground even though she flinched just a little. "I might be pregnant."

Ian's eyes flared. "Then why were you drinking vodka tonics the last time I saw you?"

"It's too early to tell." Serena's eyes were wide with a hint of mischief in them.

"Oh, I can tell, Serena," Ian shot back. "I can walk outside right now and find a stick for you to pee on."

That was Ian. Always a giver.

"Back off, Ian." Jake pulled her back.

"Not when she's disrupting the op," Ian replied.

Serena's eyes rolled in a way that would ensure her ass was red at some point in the day. She was an awfully cute little brat. "I'm not going to disrupt anything. And I'm not leaving. We're trying to get pregnant. I can't get pregnant if my husbands are on a different continent. And before you offer to ship their sperm via UPS, you should know that I intend to do this the old-fashioned, traditional way."

Yes, Serena Dean-Miles was so traditional she'd married two men. Well, legally she'd married one, but the other had come along for the ride. "Serena, you have to stay in Kensington. You can't come to Jake and Adam's place. I don't even want you within a mile of Liverpool station."

Avery's apartment was in a building just across from the station. She was conveniently situated between a fast food joint and a pub called Dirty Dick's.

Serena turned to him, her eyes bright as though she recognized a reprieve when it was offered to her. "I promise. I won't go near that part of the city. I'm working on a book. I'm on a hard deadline, so it's very unlikely you'll see me at all. I'll just send them a text when I'm ovulating."

Adam grinned. "We tag team on the baby making. It's

my sperm's turn next time."

Ian groaned. "God, I did not need to hear that."

Liam didn't understand the impulse to create a tiny human thing that would be utterly dependent on him and require hours of upkeep. Simple. That was the only way to live, and that meant avoiding hairy entanglements like children. He could barely maintain friendships. "Can we move on to the actual work portion of this evening?"

He wanted the rundown on the blond asshole who'd been hitting on her. She'd obviously known him. He didn't need competition. He needed to be the only thing little Avery thought about. He needed to find a way to become her obsession.

Serena's eyes lit up, and she ran for her notepad. Liam groaned. If he let her stay, she would inundate the whole team with questions and then later this little meeting would undoubtedly show up in one of her books.

"Jake and Adam, no civvies allowed." Liam didn't want to become one of her bloody heroes. They inevitably lost their balls to some girl.

Serena looked up. "What? Come on. I just want to take a few notes."

Adam simply picked his sub up and started for the door. "You've pushed them enough, love. Time to go and wait for us to be done. You knew we were working. I'm taking you back down to the dungeon."

She pouted up at him. "Yeah, but I thought I could watch."

"Not this time, baby. Sit out in the club and don't pester Master Damon with questions," Jake said as his partner opened the door.

"But he seems so interesting." Serena's voice faded as Adam carried her away.

"We'll be lucky if Damon doesn't toss us out on our arses, as he would say." Ian growled right before throwing himself in the chair at the head of the table. "Reports, people."

"He's in an awesome mood." Eve opened her arms and hugged Liam. "How are you doing?"

There was a speculative look in her eyes as she gave him a once-over. There was no denying that look. It was the look a shrink gave her prized patient. Sometimes Liam thought Eve used his case as a way to escape her own problems, but he didn't begrudge her. She kept his secrets and he kept hers. They had settled into a nice friendship. "I'm fine."

"Are you sure?" Eve touched his shirt, smoothing it down. Sometimes Eve could treat him like a child in need of soothing and mothering. Perhaps because she'd heard him cry out like one.

"He said he was fine, Eve. You don't have to baby him." Alex stared at them, arms crossed over his chest. Alex stood almost as tall as Ian, though he had a leaner frame. He looked just as fucking mean, though, as he stared at Liam.

Because Liam knew what Alex thought. Alex thought Liam was sleeping with Eve. Alex didn't understand that the time he and Eve spent together had nothing to do with sex. Alex was brutally jealous and a simple conversation could clear it up, but it really wasn't Liam's problem. Alex didn't need to know that he was seeing Eve on a professional basis. That's what the whole term "client-patient confidentiality" meant, and he wasn't going to feel guilty about it. He just wasn't.

"I think I can ask questions on my own, Alex." Eve's voice was frosty cold, and she turned away from Liam, crossing the room and taking her seat again.

Fucking hell. He didn't want to give a shit. Eve was his bloody therapist, and Alex didn't need to know a thing. He could think what he well wanted. It didn't mean anything to Liam. He didn't care. The mission was the only thing that mattered.

Yeah, he was going to keep right on telling himself that.

Adam walked back in the room. He twisted a dial on the wall and the lights dimmed. Liam took his seat. It was showtime.

"So who's the blond guy?" Liam asked.

Adam jogged across the room, clicking on the remote in his hand. "Okay. I got the lowdown on this guy. Simon Weston. Thirty-five. Single. So very British. He's a lawyer. Cambridge law. Top of his class. Joined a small, top-of-the-line firm right out of school. He's the second son of the Duke of Norsely. Financially he's a winner. According to what I could track down, he's worth roughly ten million pounds. He did some time in the Royal Air Force because apparently that's what Weston males do."

So he was rich and had titled relatives. Nice. "What's he doing chasing after Avery Charles?"

Liam could hear the edge in his own voice. The fucker should be dating some available pop star. What was he doing with a slightly overweight brunette who was so fucking soft she practically melted in the sunlight?

"He left Hanover and Giles last year to join the United One Fund. He now heads up the legal department of the charity. He doesn't have anything to do with Molina's for profit businesses."

"So he's a do-gooder?" Eve asked, her pen tapping against the table.

"I don't know. He seems very eager to get close to his new boss. This was taken a couple of weeks ago. The

31

London staff threw a surprise welcome party. It was all suitably posh. Apparently Molina has never visited the London offices before." Adam clicked the remote and a picture of Simon and Molina came up. Simon was sitting in a chair at what was obviously a banquet table, and Molina stood beside him, leaning on his cane. Molina was a dark-haired man with a round face and a dour smile. While Simon Weston was in a tuxedo, Molina was professorial in slacks and a tweed blazer. He looked very much the intellectual philanthropist.

What was that man doing meeting with Eli Nelson?

"It's odd actually," Adam explained. "In Cambridge he was quite involved in conservative party politics. He wrote several published essays decrying the Labor Party, including complaints about the amount of foreign aid Westernized countries dole out and a long-winded argument against the dole itself. He doesn't like dole."

"Keep the jokes to a minimum. So what happened to turn the boy into a bleeding heart?" Ian stared at the screen.

"No idea," Adam replied.

"Maybe it was a girl." Jake leaned forward, his hands on the table. "If you're really worried about this guy, we can dig into his dating history. We all know that falling for a girl can make you do strange things. Things you wouldn't normally do. Things you never want to do again."

"Serena talked us into trying tofu. It did not go well." Even in the low light, Liam could see the look of glee on Adam's face.

"I'm allergic. I have to be." Jake shuddered a little.

Yeah, Liam didn't understand that. He wasn't going to try something nasty because a woman asked him to. "Simon doesn't have a criminal record?"

"None. But I wouldn't necessarily hold a lot of faith in

that," Jake replied. "His father is titled. That still means something around here, and it certainly means something in the small town Simon grew up in. It would be easy to cover up youthful indiscretions."

"But not major problems," Alex said. "The tabloids around here love a good 'royal screws up' story. Seriously, we think we have intrusive reporters in the States? They have nothing on the Brits. I found three stories about the Weston family in recent tabloids. Two were concerning the marriage of his older brother, the heir to the title, and one about his mother's new recipe book. The family seems clean."

"Okay, so let's ask some questions of our British friends, starting with Damon." Liam glanced at Ian. "Will he have a problem putting some feelers out about this guy?"

"Damon was excited when I asked him to help us," Ian said, settling back in his chair. "Apparently he's finding club business isn't as thrilling as getting his ass shot at. He'll be fine asking around."

"All right then, let's move on to the reason for this meeting. Adam?" Liam waited as Adam clicked the remote, and Avery Charles's face filled the screen. He studied her for a moment. It was a shot he'd taken himself while following her in St. James's Park. She was smiling slightly, a mysterious look. A little Mona Lisa smile. Her dark hair hung to her shoulders in a cascading wave. *Fuck.* What was he thinking? Cascading wave? Her hair was brown, and she was mildly attractive in a bland sort of way. She was a little chunky. Her boobs were probably *C* cups, and they were natural because they sagged a little.

"Pretty girl." Alex was staring at the screen, obviously contemplating Avery. Yeah, Liam didn't like that.

"She's also been through a lot," Eve murmured,

carefully avoiding looking at her ex-husband. She glanced down at her notes. "Avery Charles was born Avery Adamson and came from a fairly wealthy family. She was the only child. Her parents died in a plane crash. She was sent to live with her aunt who went through most of Avery's trust fund."

"Cinderella." Adam sighed. "Sorry, I was telling Serena about her, and she said Avery reminded her of Cinderella."

Ian reached over and slapped Adam upside the head. It was one of his patented moves. "Don't talk about the case with your wife, asshole. Do you understand the word 'confidential'?"

"Ow, one of these days, Ian." Adam rubbed his head. "And I know, but all this information was public. It didn't seem wrong to talk to her."

And Liam had discovered that Serena could be very observant. "What did she think?"

Adam looked Liam's way. "She guessed that any relative who would use her ward's college money to buy designer clothes for her own daughter probably wasn't very nice to Avery. Avery got married very young. Barely eighteen. She was trying to escape."

"Her husband was a kid from her high school. Brandon Charles," Eve continued.

"How was her trust set up?" Ian asked.

Eve passed Ian a copy of the file. "It came to Avery at the age of twenty-five or if she got married. Otherwise her aunt had full control and use of the fund to raise Avery."

So she hadn't married for love. She'd married to get her trust fund. Calculating. Liam would do well to remember that. "So she marries on her eighteenth birthday. I wonder if she made a deal with this Brandon kid."

"If she did then it involved consummation of the

marriage. She had Madison Rachelle Charles eight months after they'd eloped. At that point there was roughly one million dollars left in a trust fund that should have been in the fifteen million range." Eve shook her head. "I would have tried to save it, too. I would have found the first guy willing to marry me and run with it. The trust wasn't very well set up, but then Avery's aunt was a lawyer. She knew how to work the system."

"So the aunt sets up the trust fund in a way that she gets to use it free and clear?" That didn't sound particularly fair. "Why would her parents do that?"

"Her father was the last of an old-money line. He preferred his charity work over everything else. By the time the money came to him, the industry that had created the money was gone. He wasn't a particularly good caretaker. He spent millions on various charity projects," Alex explained. "And when it came to lawyers, he likely figured his sister-in-law was family and wouldn't harm him. As far as I can tell, this whole group is very naïve."

"Tell me about the accident. The car accident," Ian corrected. "Is there any way the aunt was involved? She had to be mad she'd lost the money."

They were getting off topic. Liam needed to steer it back to the case at hand. "They were driving home late one night and got into a high-speed collision with a sixteen-year-old. Brandon died instantly. The baby died a few days later. They were both on the passenger side. Avery was driving. Her spine was damaged in the accident. She was in a coma for several months. The sixteen-year-old was put on trial, but the case got tossed out over some tainted evidence."

She'd woken up one day and her world was gone. Liam knew how that felt. Did she wonder where they were? Did she wonder sometimes if it had all been a terrible mistake and they were out there somewhere in the world wondering why she didn't look for them? Liam knew what it meant to not have an inch of closure in the death of a loved one.

"Rough." Ian leaned forward, looking at the file Adam had prepared. "So this was ten years ago? How long before she walked again?"

Eve frowned. "She was in and out of hospitals for years. She would spend time with Brandon's mother in the beginning, but something happened and the Charles family seems to have cut off all communications with her by the time she was twenty. I haven't figured out why yet. She still sends flowers on her mother-in-law's birthday, but they get sent back."

Avery had no one in the whole world. How had that isolation affected her? Had it turned her bitter under that seemingly sweet exterior?

"She met Thomas Molina's brother in her last rehab hospital," Eve continued. "She underwent an experimental surgery two years ago after being accepted into a medical research study the year before. She was lucky. She was walking again within eight months of the surgery. She met Brian Molina last year. He was rehabbing a knee replacement at the same facility she was at. They formed a friendship."

"Sleeping together?" Ian asked.

Liam took over. He knew that file as well as Eve. "Doubt it. She was fragile at the time. It doesn't look like they had anything beyond a friendship. When Thomas Molina decided to get out of his house and into the world, Brian recommended Avery for the job of assistant and companion. Despite her lack of skills, she was hired to be the assistant to one of the world's leading philanthropists. Brian died shortly after she was hired. Drug overdose."

Avery wasn't fragile now. She was strong enough to take a lover, yet it seemed she hadn't. There was nothing in her manner with Molina that led him to believe they were truly intimate. Molina was likely interested, but Avery seemed oblivious.

He would have to make sure she wasn't clueless when it came to him. Not at all. She would be very, very aware of him.

"The troubling part is the missing money," Adam said.

"Missing money?" Liam hadn't heard about missing money.

Adam turned his computer around to show the screen to Liam. "I ran her financials last night. She should have still had that million from her trust fund. Insurance and then a research fund paid for her medical care and expenses. So where's the money? Over the course of several years she depleted the trust. Every withdrawal was in cash and was exactly nine thousand, nine hundred, and ninety-nine dollars."

The amount stayed below the bank's reporting regulations. Anything over ten thousand would have been reported to the government. Someone was being sneaky. Someone didn't want records of where she was putting her money.

"Give me the full report." It looked like Avery Charles wasn't quite as innocent as she looked. She was like everyone else. She had her secrets.

Liam intended to discover every single one.

* * * *

"Do you know a Lachlan Bates?" Avery polished off the last of her sandwich as her boss walked in the office.

She was sure he'd been trying to get to his desk for a good twenty minutes. When he refused to use his chair, he inevitably stopped to talk to everyone on the way from the lift to his office. Lift. She'd just thought lift instead of elevator. She was becoming so European.

She wished she had someone to send postcards to.

"Did I lose you, dear?" Thomas stood at her desk, leaning heavily on his cane, an amused look on his face. He had his cane in his right hand and a tablet in his left. He used the tablet the way most people used a laptop. Though his legs were frail, his fingers and hands weren't. She'd watched them fly across the virtual keyboard before. She couldn't text without feeling graceless.

She sighed and refocused. "Sorry. I was thinking about something."

"You were thinking about Lydia and Frank Charles, weren't you?" Thomas had always been brutally observant. Avery sometimes wondered if the man could read minds. "You get that wistful look on your face when you think of them. I wish you would allow me to reach out to them."

She shook her head. "I'll keep trying. Eventually perhaps they'll forgive me." Probably not, but she wasn't going to ask her boss to intervene. He had enough to deal with on his own.

Thomas winked at her. He looked a little older than his thirty-nine years, as though pain had started to wear him down. He was an attractive man, but the tightness around his eyes always made her wonder how he managed the daily pain. His upper body was fit and strong, but his lower body seemed thin under his slacks. She'd never actually seen his legs. Even on the hottest days, he wore heavy slacks. He kept them completely hidden. She could understand that. She remembered how it felt to not be able to use her own legs. "If anyone can work that miracle, it's you, Avery. You understand they have nothing to forgive you for. You're trying to do good in the world. I admire you greatly for it."

But her in-laws would never understand why she'd done what she did. "Thank you." It was time to change the subject to something happier. "Apparently this Lachlan Bates person wants to do good in the world, too. To the tune of two million dollars."

Thomas's brown eyes widened. "Two million. That's a nice round sum. Who is this guy? I've never heard of him."

"No idea. Do you want me to work up a dossier on him?" Thomas liked to know where his money was coming from. He'd turned down a few large donations in the past because he didn't like his fund to be used for political capital. She glanced down at the notes Simon had given her. "And it's not exactly a round sum. The donation is for two million, one hundred and fifty thousand, five hundred and three. What an odd amount. Do you think it's a percentage thing?"

Sometimes religious donors gave a percentage of their income.

Thomas stopped, put down his tablet and reached out for the folder. "That is odd, but not utterly out of the ordinary. It is likely a percentage for his religious beliefs or more likely for his taxes, depending on where he actually lives. I'll take care of this, dear. Don't worry about it. I need you completely focused on the Black and White Ball. It's only a few weeks away."

It was their biggest European fund-raiser of the year. It was precisely why they were in London. She was organizing a huge event. Her palms sweated a little just thinking about it. She wasn't elegant. She wasn't even very social. What was she doing planning a party for a thousand European socialites?

"Calm down." Thomas touched her cheek. He was very affectionate with her. He was always encouraging and supporting her. He'd become something of a father figure. "You're going to be fine. You're just coordinating. The caterers and designers have impeccable tastes. Follow their lead, but don't be afraid to let them know what you want. All right?"

"Yes, sir. As a matter of fact, I need to go down and talk to the florists. I want to make sure we corner the market in London for white tulips. The event planner tells me they're all the rage right now. Of course the event planner isn't trying to stay in budget." The event planner was a lovely man named Sascha who spoke with a thick New York accent and favored neon tuxedo coats. She'd been worried at first, but his style was refined and elegant outside of his personal wardrobe choices.

She stood, grabbing her bag. It was a bright day outside, one of few. She really wanted to walk in the sunshine, not be cooped up in the office. "Are you sure you don't need anything? I could put this off."

He shook his head. "Not at all, dear. Go. Enjoy the afternoon. You are instructed to not come back to this office until at least Monday morning." He picked up the tablet, nestling it against the Lachlan Bates file. He started to shuffle toward his office. "And we're only here a few more weeks. If you don't get through the British Museum, you won't get to see the Tower or the National Gallery or tour Churchill's war offices. We won't be back in London for a while. I wouldn't want you to miss a thing. And the Eye. Make sure you take a little trip. View's spectacular. Go on now."

She caught him, giving him an impulsive hug. He

seemed surprised for a moment. His arm wound around her, hugging her tight. "You're too good to me, Thomas."

He pulled away. "No. The world has been unkind. I'm exactly what you deserve. Now go and have fun."

She winked at him as she made her way into the glorious London afternoon.

* * * *

Thomas Molina stood by the window doing what he loved to do most in the world—watch Avery's ass sway as she walked. There was a sweetly sexy gait to her walk that got his cock hard every time she walked in a room.

So sweet. So innocent. So fucking naïve, but he intended to use that innocence to his advantage.

Patience. She required patience. She'd touched him on her own for the first time today. She wrapped her arms around him, and her breasts had brushed his chest. He'd hugged her before, but she'd initiated the affection this time.

What he wouldn't do to be able to slam her on his desk and shove his cock deep. He wanted her more than he'd ever wanted a woman. She was rapidly becoming his obsession.

She disappeared around the corner. It was for the best since if he did haul her into his arms and toss her on the desk, it might give away his game.

When he was sure his office door was locked, he shut the blinds and let the cane dangle from the side of his desk. Fucking cane. Fucking wheelchair. He didn't need either one, but Thomas Molina's disabilities came in handy from time to time. Too bad the poor old boy was in the ground thanks in part to his own dear brother who had seen a good opportunity when it offered to bankroll his partying ways.

Brian Molina had been a hopeless drug addict. He'd hid

41

it pretty well, but he'd do anything for another hit. Even kill
his brother and allow someone else to assume his identity
for perfectly nefarious reasons. It was really too bad that
Brian had finally met the needle that didn't love him back.
One dose of pure uncut China White and there were no
Molinas left to claim he wasn't exactly who he said he was.

He'd been Thomas Molina for years. The poor cripple
had been so isolated and secluded no one had questioned
him at all when he'd taken over the United One Fund. A
little weight gain. A lot of plastic surgery and he'd become
wealthy and powerful and deeply interested in the plight of
people in war zones.

Yes. He liked war zones. War zones were the perfect
retail grounds for what he liked to sell. Guns. Mines.
Grenades.

Now bio weapons. Yes, that was the wave of the future.
A good bio weapon could wipe out a population and leave
the infrastructure standing, waiting for the victors to take
over. He was the bloody motherfucking pimp daddy of
warfare. And he had the perfect shipping system. No one
checked United One Fund's shipments. No one thought to
question the saint of the Western world.

He smuggled weapons into war zones under the veneer
of lending aid to all the children.

Fuck children. He didn't want them or need them,
though lately he had started to believe that Thomas Molina
would do well with a wife. Sweet, naïve, been-there-before
Avery wouldn't even question why he left the light off when
he fucked her. She would believe him. She wouldn't
question him because he'd become Thomas Molina in every
way.

And all with the help of the finest institution known to
man. The bloody CIA. Well, maybe not the whole CIA, but

with the help of one righteous bastard of an agent, he'd gone from pathetic errand boy to running a black market weapons empire.

It was supposed to be a get-rich-quick scheme. The trouble was, he'd found he rather liked the game. He liked being Thomas Molina. He liked the wealthy parties and the elegant gatherings. He liked the way Avery looked at him.

He couldn't fool himself. He'd fallen under her spell. There was something about her that simply called to him. He would have the little fool all to himself, but she wasn't going to change his plans.

It would be best, however, if she had no ties to her past life. Her continuing obsession with gaining forgiveness from her former in-laws kept her too much in their world. And he would definitely prefer she have no family beyond him when he finally brought her into the fold.

A quick phone call and it was done. He had to remind them every now and then of just how much Avery had hurt them. The wounds ran deep, but it was good to open them back up every now and then. The last thing he wanted was for Avery to get close to anyone but him. He would take her with him all over the world, never staying in one place more than a month or two. She would be forced to cling to him. The travel would bond them together. Eventually he could even "find" a cure for his ailment and be normal around her.

But first he had to deal with the Lachlan Bates situation. He opened the folder and picked up the small scanner from his desk. His personal files were more important than anything else. The scanner immediately sent the file to his tablet, and then he would lock up the original at his town house.

Lachlan Bates wasn't a man, but a code. He had a shipment going out next month. Lachlan Bates was the carefully selected code for a new buyer. The amount of the donation was code for the type of arms, number of each type, and country of delivery. In this case, the buyer was very interested in Thomas's large shipment of P90s and several other high-priced items.

It was perfect. It meant his next shipment would be full. It meant he would be bringing in about ten million.

Taking over Thomas Molina's life had brought him a nice stash of cash, but turning his charity into an arms retailer was going to bring him what he truly craved. Power.

He would have the power, and he would have the woman he wanted, too.

Avery was sweet, perfectly innocent.

It was up to him to see just how much he could corrupt her. He looked forward to the job.

But first he had to deal with the problem of Eli Nelson. Fuck but he wished the former CIA agent hadn't gotten exposed. The man was quickly becoming a pain in his ass.

And Thomas didn't like pains in his ass.

Chapter Three

The next day, Avery stared at the mummy in his glass case, but her mind kept flitting to other things. She thought about her dinner the night before. Adam and Jake were such a cute couple. She hated to admit it, but she'd enjoyed hearing American accents again. Adam had made a heavenly dinner, and she'd briefly forgotten how lonely she was. She was trying not to think about it today.

The Egypt Gallery held many wonders, some as lovely as the Greek and Roman rooms, but the mummies were definitely interesting in a less aesthetically pleasing way. She was standing in a room with a person who had lived centuries before. Millennia. A deep connection to a distant past. She was being fanciful, but it was her day off. She could let her mind do that wandering thing it so often did and not be worried she would screw up a big deal like the one with Lachlan Bates that Thomas had taken off her plate. It had been odd. He usually didn't like to take care of things himself. He had told her on many occasions that he'd hired her so he didn't have to talk to people.

But she was relieved he was taking more of an interest in their donors. Maybe it meant he would be more sociable. And it wasn't like he never talked to donors. He'd pulled three files from Monica's desk this year, all over a million dollars.

She let it go. She wasn't going to think about work

today. She was going to spend the afternoon staring at mummies.

She really wasn't in Kansas anymore. Not that she'd ever actually been in Kansas. She was from New York, but it seemed an appropriate thing to say. Think. Unless she'd actually said it out loud. Avery glanced around, but no one was looking at her like she was a crazy person. Her impulse control issues were much better hidden in big cities. No one noticed the girl who talked to herself when there were so many actually real crazy people walking around. Just earlier in the day she'd had a conversation with a man on the Tube who believed he was Henry the Eighth and wanted his Tower back.

Yes, she should go see the Tower of London. Definitely.

Mummies. She forced herself to concentrate. She felt a smile cross her lips. It was so much nicer when her rambling thoughts were about mummies and historical sites than bedpans and whether or not her legs would ever work again. Or where her baby was now that she wasn't in her arms.

"It can't be all that bad. I don't think he minds being stuck in here."

Avery started, a deep voice pulling her from the edge of a very dark thought. She turned on her heels and, as any sudden movement was likely to do, her weak leg buckled underneath her. She started the long trip to the ground, except this time she was headed straight for the ancient, probably priceless, mummy. God, she was going to set off all kinds of alarms and get kicked out of the museum and maybe out of England, and then she would have to find a new job and who would want a woman who'd been arrested for molesting mummified corpses?

And just like that, she stopped. Two big arms wrapped

around her, lifting her away from the oncoming chaos. "You okay?"

Without even thinking about it, her arms drifted up and around his neck, fingertips brushing warm, deliciously firm skin. The dark-haired man she'd seen before, the one she'd fantasized about last night, held her in his arms. Curly, midnight-black hair and emeralds for eyes. He was dressed for sin in a black motorcycle jacket and a T-shirt that molded to his very well-defined chest. Did he have to buy them one size too small? Did he have to walk around like a big old gorgeous man cupcake when she'd been on a diet for so long?

"Lost the power of speech? Well, that guy's ugly mug would do that to me, too."

She'd thought for sure he was British. She'd fantasized about a lyrical accent coming out of his mouth, but no, his voice was pure Midwestern American. And she should say something since the man was still standing there holding her like she was his virgin bride or something. Virgin. She wasn't. Unless it grew back after too many years of vaginal disuse. *God, say something, Avery.* "I'm so sorry."

His lips curled up in a flirty little smile. She couldn't take her eyes off him. He was the single most beautiful man she'd ever seen. Even if that smile didn't quite reach his eyes. "I think I'm the one who should apologize. I didn't mean to startle you. It just seemed like it was time that I should talk to you. I've been following you around for days. We seem to have the same tastes in museums."

He'd noticed her, too? That was odd. She typically blended into the background, when she wasn't falling down. She was well aware she wasn't a great beauty. She wasn't horrific, but she fell into a bland attractiveness that usually required a forceful personality to go along with it in order to

47

be truly pretty. She wasn't exactly aggressive. She was more a "watch from a distance and dream" kind of girl.

There was no distance between them now. None at all. She could feel the heat of his body against hers, the hardness of his form. How long had it been since she'd been held? Touched? Nothing for years that didn't include a therapist massaging muscles to keep them from atrophying. Her mother-in-law hadn't touched her once since she'd discovered what Avery had done. No more motherly hugs. Even the few friends she'd had back home had treated her like she was fragile. No touching allowed or someone would break Avery. Gorgeous Green Eyes didn't seem to think she would break. His arms were tight around her body, cradling her to his chest.

"Can I put you down? Do you think you can stand?"

She felt herself flush. She was making a complete idiot of herself. He'd only reached out because she'd fallen. Again. Would she ever again feel like she had control over her body? "Yes. I'm fine. I'm so sorry for the whole nearly killing a mummy thing."

He set her on her feet, holding her until he seemed sure she was steady. He smiled down at her, definite amusement in his eyes. They seemed so much warmer now than a moment before. "I think he's already dead, sweetheart. Now on the other hand, you nearly gave the security guy a heart attack."

She gasped and looked around. Sure enough, there was the museum employee in his suit coat with his walkie-talkie at his side. His face was slightly flushed, but he'd taken his place again.

"Think nothing of it, ma'am. Women faint dead away at the sight all the time." The security guard winked her way.

Avery gave him a smile. "Well, maybe Egypt is too

much for my constitution. I think I'll just go have some lunch and fortify myself against the sight." It was really time to retreat. Deep breath. Confident smile. She turned back to the hottie. That's what all the girls back in the New York offices called someone who looked like Green Eyes. Hotties. They were right. She could really use a fan. "Thank you so much for the save."

"Not a problem." He seemed to be waiting on something.

It was an awkward moment, but then much of her life was made up of them. "Good-bye."

She turned carefully and hoped she could make a graceful exit.

"So what sounds good? I think there's a fish and chips place across the street." Hottie kept pace, not that it was hard for him. He was so much taller. He probably took one stride to her two slightly awkward ones.

She stopped. He was doing the flirting thing. Why? He was obviously out of her league. She wasn't good at stuff like this. He was far more gorgeous than Simon, and she couldn't figure out why he was pursuing her beyond the obvious career implications. This guy didn't even know her name. She decided to try to be polite. Maybe he just felt sorry for her. "Thank you for the offer. I really can make my way. Thanks so much for the save."

"You're welcome," he replied, not moving at all. He simply stood in front of the stairs, blocking her way. "You don't like fish and chips? You do know you're in England, right?"

"Yes, I know I'm in England." Flustered. He was making her flustered. "I like fish and chips just fine."

He smiled broadly. "Excellent. I could use a pint. I need some fortification before we get back to the mummies, too.

Seriously, these are some ugly dudes. Why would anyone want their body to last this long? I want to immediately be cremated."

"It was part of their religion. They needed a body if they were to go to the afterlife. I'm pretty sure they didn't imagine they would end up in a museum thousands of miles away with tourists ogling them." She started to make an argument about tolerance for other religions, but that was really beside the point. "I didn't ask you to go to lunch with me."

He nodded, leaning out of the way so others could come into the hall, but still blocking her advance. "Yes, you forgot to. I admit it was a little rude, but I've decided to believe that you were just a little distracted after your near miss with old Tut back there."

"That wasn't King Tut."

He shrugged. "Yeah, I'm not enormously big on Egyptian history. So we've decided that you're a little distractible and it totally affects your social skills, but luckily I'm a very focused guy and I can be polite enough for both of us. I can teach you how the polite world works." He held out a big hand. "Lee Donnelly. I work in construction back in the States. I just finished a huge renovation job back in Dallas and gave myself two months off to come visit some friends here in London. This is the part where you shake my hand and tell me your name and what you do."

"Avery Charles." He'd kind of put her in a corner. There was nothing to do except take his hand. She quickly found her own hand completely wrapped in his. Warmth flooded her system. He had strong hands, callused and rough from work, but so nice to touch. Lee. She liked that name. It was solid and masculine and simple. "I'm the personal assistant to a man who runs a charity fund."

He nodded at her like she was a slow learner who had finally caught on. "See, that wasn't so hard. And do you live here in London?"

She kind of wanted to run away, but she had the sudden sense that he would follow, and he would be so much faster. She was caught. Trapped. So why shouldn't she enjoy the afternoon with the most beautiful man she'd ever met? There wasn't any harm in it. She spent so much time alone that it would be nice to have a meal with a handsome stranger, and he was obviously at loose ends. He probably felt as out of place as she did and was just looking for some company. Despite the fact that the employees of United One Fund were friendly, no one asked her to have lunch with them. They had their own cliques and friendships, and it would be that way everywhere she and Thomas went.

What could it hurt to make a friend? He was probably just looking for someone to buy him lunch. It might be nice to have someone to talk to.

"I'm from New York," she replied, allowing her shoulders to come down from around her ears. Now that she'd made the choice to get to know him, she found herself eager to ask him a few questions. "Are you from Dallas?"

"Not originally, though I've spent the last several years there. Wow. It's getting late. Time flies when you're having fun." He moved out of the doorway, his hand moving in a graceful gesture. "Let's go grab some grub as they would say in my neck of the woods. I'm starving."

She followed him out of the museum, hoping all the while she wasn't making a mistake.

* * * *

51

Liam followed her to the door of her building.

"Thanks for escorting me home." She flushed beautifully in the early evening light. People rushed up and down Bishopsgate Street, but she seemed to have a core calm inside her that made her stand out from the frantic London pace.

He was surprised at just how protective he'd gotten in the last five hours. Avery moved with caution when she was thinking about it, her every step well thought out and intended to keep her on balance. But when she stopped thinking, there was a sweet grace to her steps, a sway to those curvy hips that had him entranced.

She was utterly unlike any woman he'd ever met. Smart. Sweet. Kind.

Was it all an act? He rather thought not so the question was just how she'd gotten involved with a man who was in business with Eli Nelson.

"What happened to your leg? It's your right leg, isn't it?" He'd waited all through lunch and the hours they'd spent at the museum for her to bring it up. Most people enjoyed talking about their past pain, holding it up as some sort of excuse for all things in their lives. Not Avery. She hadn't mentioned it once. All he'd gotten out of her the whole time they had walked through the museum was that she'd been born in New York. She didn't have siblings, and her parents had died when she was young.

No mention of her crappy childhood. No mention of everything she'd lost.

She flushed, biting that bottom lip of hers. Fuck, he liked her lips. If she'd put a gloss on them, it had come off hours ago. The pretty pink color was all her own and the bottom lip was pouty and plush. When she ran her tongue over it, his cock hardened in response. "I was in an accident.

A car accident. It kind of affected my legs. I'm still a little weak on the right side, hence all the near misses. I'm not usually so clumsy. I try to keep my pratfalls to once a day."

But she'd been distracted. He'd made a careful study of her over the last week. She was right. She usually wasn't so clumsy. She usually made her way with careful resolve, but she'd been animatedly talking all afternoon as though having a companion to tour with was a special treat for her.

She was lonely. He could use that.

The trouble was, he was starting to think he was lonely, too. He'd enjoyed the afternoon with her far too much. His previous years' worth of dates had consisted of picking up some willing young thing and topping her for a while before he fucked her and sent her on her way with cab fare.

He hadn't spent a lazy afternoon with any woman just looking at art or weird dog statues. And yet he'd found himself staring at the big marble dog someone in ancient Greece had carved thousands of years ago and listening to Avery's chatter about the clean lines and perfect construction, and all he had been able to think about was the fact that maybe he was as stuck as that dog. Maybe he was carved from marble, unmoving, unchanging, and had been ever since that day he'd lost his brother.

It was stupid, but five hours with the woman and he'd relaxed more than he had in years.

But he had a job to do. "I've had a few accidents in my time. Working construction can be hell on a man. Sometime I'll tell you about the hole in my back. Man versus nail gun. Nail gun won."

He fully intended to tell her that fabrication once he got her horizontal. There was no way to miss the bullet wound he'd taken during his SAS years, but the nail gun was a convenient lie.

Her eyes widened. "That sounds horrible."

He shrugged. "Yeah, well, I got a body covered in scars, but then who doesn't? If you don't have a few scars, you haven't really lived."

She blushed again, her whole face turning red. If he had to bet, he would say she couldn't lie to save her life. "I know how that goes. Thank you so much for the nice day. It was good to have someone to talk to."

She was right back to where they'd been before lunch. Wary. Cautious. For a few hours she'd been open and smiling. At one point, she'd even held his hand as a wave of people came off the Tube at Holborn. They'd been standing by the tracks, chatting about all the places she wanted to see and the things she wanted to do while she was in London, and the Tube doors had opened, busy Londoners rushing past. They'd almost been separated. Her hand had come out, seeking his, a nervous look in her eyes as though the crowd frightened her.

He'd been taken over by the oddest emotion. He'd pulled her close as the crush engulfed them, his left hand covering the back of her head and pulling her into his chest.

And now she was dismissing him without so much as another date? That wasn't going to happen. "The day isn't over yet."

She frowned. "What do you want from me?"

He hadn't expected that. He'd expected a coy invitation to come inside or a little angling for another date. "I like you."

"You don't really know me, and I'm not blind. There are far prettier women just walking down this street. I've been thinking about it all day, and I can't figure out what you want. If you would please tell me, I'll see if I can give it to you."

He stared at her for a moment, trying to figure out her game. "What are you talking about?"

She sighed as though trying to find a way to say what she wanted to say. "I don't have a lot of money but if you need some, I can give you a little."

He crowded her, anger starting to take root in his gut. What exactly did she think he was? "You tell me what you're talking about and you do it now, girl."

Damn, but he'd almost lost it and gone into his Irish accent.

She trembled a little as he backed her up against the building. Her eyes flashed from right to left, looking for a little help, but everyone ignored her. Liam was counting on that. It was a big city. Unless she just flat wanted to scream for help, everyone would ignore their little scene. It was time to start showing the sub who topped whom.

"You have an idea about me, Avery, don't you?" He was well aware his voice had gone deeper than she'd heard all day. It was the voice he used when training a sub. Hard. Unrelenting. Dominant. "Put it in plain English. I'd like to hear it."

"You're scaring me." She put her hands up as though that could possibly stop him.

"And I think you're insulting me." He came up with two ideas she could possibly have about him. Both of them insulting. Neither of them right. "Correct me if I'm wrong, but do you think I'm indigent and need a handout?"

She huffed, her eyes on her hands. "No. Obviously not. You're very well dressed. You obviously have money."

So it was door number two. "And you think I get it by hustling women out of cash. You think if you invite me upstairs, you're agreeing to have sex with me for money. Tell me something, little girl, just how much would I have charged?"

The sub thought he was a hustler, did she? The thought didn't sit well. Somewhere in the back of his head he knew he should be laughing this off, but it just made him angry. She was so sweet and innocent, and he was just a nasty, disgusting brute. It hit way too close to home.

"Does it help if I thought you would be worth a lot, and I was worried I didn't have the money?" Those big eyes looked up, wide and slightly afraid, but there was a hint of sass to her words.

He pressed his advantage, crowding her until their bodies came together. "Well now, Avery. If a man is going to get accused of being a prostitute, the very least you can do is accuse him of being an expensive one. And no. I wasn't going to charge you, but I was damn straight going to get in your pants."

"I don't think that's such a good idea," she started.

But he was done talking to her. Talking to her all day had just made her think he was so dumb he couldn't find work that didn't involve his dick. The fact that she was his work and she definitely involved his dick didn't matter. All that mattered now was making a damn good impression on the lady.

Before she could get another word in, he swooped in, lowering his head and pressing his lips to hers.

He'd already planned their first kiss. He'd viewed it like a coach planning a football play. He'd gone over every instant in his head, each move meant to gain maximum trust from Avery. Gentle. Soft.

All that careful planning was blown straight out of the water the minute his lips touched hers. He was overwhelmed with the need to dominate. His hands came up, tangling in that soft cloud of hair and forcing her head back so he could take her mouth. His lips pressed to hers, molding over that bee-stung bottom lip. He sucked it into his mouth, drawing his tongue across it. So plump and firm. He wanted to suck on it and give her a little nip. Yeah, she might like a little bite of pain. God knew he did.

"Open your mouth for me," he demanded. He could force her to do it, but he wanted her submission. He wanted her willing. He fully intended to walk away, but he wanted her hot and desperate first. He wanted her thinking about him all fucking night long.

"I don't think..." She sounded breathless. Her hands were still on his chest, but she wasn't pushing at him. In fact, her hands were moving against his chest almost restlessly. "God, I need to stop thinking."

She turned her head up, and it was all the invitation he needed. He took her mouth, those sexy lips opening for him. His tongue surged inside, and she was every bit as sweet and hot as he'd thought she would be. He slanted his mouth over hers, coaxing her tongue with his.

She was still for a long moment, utterly motionless in his arms, but then her tongue slid along his almost shyly as though she'd forgotten somewhere along the way how to play this particular game, but she was willing to try.

Her arms drifted up, and he could feel her lifting herself on her toes, throwing herself into the kiss. Pure lust pounded through Liam's system as she opened herself to him.

This. This was what he'd wanted since the first moment he'd seen her. This sweet, perfect harmony that flowed between them. There was no wall up now, no wariness. It was like she'd been in the Tube station when she'd been afraid to get separated from him. She clung to him like he was her lifeline, like he was the only thing between her and being utterly swept away.

And he liked it. He'd never wanted a clingy woman. He didn't have anything to offer them. It was why he chose women who knew the score, who knew that it was all just a fun game and the only thing that they could ever get out of him was momentary pleasure.

Avery didn't even know what the game was called.

And it didn't matter. In that moment, all that mattered was that she was submitting and he could get inside her. Once he was inside her, he would have her. He would make damn sure if she was involved in this mess that she picked the right fucking side to come down on. She would do it because he would wrap her in so much pleasure that her loyalty would belong to him and him alone.

He pressed his cock against her belly so there could be no doubt what was going to happen between them. He didn't want her money. He wanted her body and her secrets. Yes, he would settle for those.

Her arms tightened, and he could feel her breasts thrusting up against his chest as her leg startled to tangle with his. Control. He was losing his, and it seemed she wasn't far behind.

And then her leg buckled, her whole body sagging.

Liam tightened his hold and kept her upright, but the moment was broken.

And he'd damn near fucked her right on the street in front of Liverpool station for all to see. The bloody police station was not a block away, and he was nearly going at her in public. What the fuck had just happened?

He'd almost forgotten everything.

"I'm so sorry," Avery mumbled.

The plan. He'd had a plan before he'd lost his damn mind. She'd insulted him. She'd tried to put walls up. He'd blown past them, but sometimes to get through a wall it was best to go under it instead of drilling straight through. He wanted Avery's walls to crumble so badly she couldn't put them back up again. "Are you sorry for falling or for calling me a whore?"

She gasped, the sound very nearly sending him into apology mode, but this was the plan and he was going to stick to it. He didn't apologize.

"Is there a problem here, Avery?"

Fucking Adam. He stood by the door to the building, a grocery bag in his hand. He looked on with concern on his face.

Avery pushed away, sniffling a little as she did. A sheen of tears pooled in her blue eyes and that lower lip trembled slightly. Fuck, how had he ever thought she was plain? She was stinking gorgeous, and it hit him straight in the gut to watch her cry. "No. Not at all. I'm fine. I was just saying good-bye to my…friend…uhm, to this guy I met."

But for a moment today, it had felt like they were friends. Just for a couple of minutes, he'd stopped being an agent and felt like the Liam he'd been before he'd lost Rory.

But he was an asshole agent, and he needed her to get close to a man who might or might not be a terrorist. No matter what happened, he couldn't forget that. She was a job and nothing more. He'd put out his hook and baited it with sex, but a little guilt couldn't hurt.

"Think about that when you go to sleep tonight, sweetheart," he growled her way. "I wanted you. Not money. You, and you treated me like crap. Sweet dreams."

He turned and forced himself to walk away. The next time he saw her, he would have the high moral ground, and he would use it to his advantage.

He got on the Tube, hoping and praying the next battle wasn't far away.

Chapter Four

"Do you want to talk?" Adam asked as he swiped the key card to the door. "What just happened?"

What had happened? Avery wasn't exactly sure except that she'd totally screwed up, and she'd do just about anything to apologize to the poor man. He'd been perfectly lovely, and she'd been horrible and suspicious. "I think I just accused that man of being a prostitute."

That man. She was trying to distance herself. His name was Lee.

Adam nearly dropped the bag he was carrying. "Are you serious?"

Avery nodded.

"Holy shit balls. Why didn't I get here sooner? All I saw was the two of you going at it in the middle of the street. Had you like settled on a price or something? Come on. Let's get inside and go up to my place. You look like you can use a drink."

She could use more than one. She turned to see if she could find Lee in the crowd, but he'd disappeared down the escalator into the cavernous Liverpool station. He wouldn't have been held back by her bad leg this time. She'd been very impressed with how patient he'd been. London was a fast city. Unlike the States, almost no one viewed an escalator as something to ride. It was a tool to get a person to their destination that much more quickly. She'd nearly been trampled on escalators many times before since she couldn't move fast.

Lee had simply moved her to the right and stood behind her, an arm around her waist to balance her against the rushing commuters. "Always stand on the right," he'd whispered to her.

And she'd brutally insulted the man.

"He's gone, Avery. Come up with me," Adam offered. "You can tell me all about it while I cook some dinner."

Or she could go and hide in her room and eat a nasty microwave dinner. No. If she'd proven anything to herself today, it was that she needed to be more sociable. Maybe then she would learn when it was proper and right to accuse someone of trying to seduce her for cash.

She followed Adam inside. The concierge looked up from his desk. The building was a mix of residences and condos purchased by large corporations for employees to stay in. The concierge was used to an ex-pat community.

"Nice day at the museum, Miss Charles?" He was dressed in a perfectly pressed suit.

She nodded. "Yes, thank you, though I fear it's time for me to move on. Perhaps you can suggest some more excursions for me tomorrow?"

He nodded. "Absolutely. I'll keep you right entertained, miss. Mr. Kelly, welcome back. Hope the market was good."

"Absolutely," Adam replied as he pushed the button to the elevator. He escorted her inside and soon they were on the seventh floor and he was opening the door to his and his partner's flat.

Avery had only known Jake and Adam for a brief period of time, but she already felt completely comfortable with Adam. He had a way of putting a woman at ease. She

61

didn't have to worry about why he was interested in her, or if he was interested in her, because he flatly wasn't. He was into his boyfriend, though they weren't the most demonstrative couple. In fact, last night as she'd sat on their terrace, she could have sworn she'd glimpsed them punching each other, but it seemed friendly. Maybe guys were just guys whether they were gay or straight.

Jake was talking on the phone as she entered, his voice hushed. He was a hottie, too. Jacob was all beefy American male while Adam fit in with the well-dressed and mannered Europeans, though there was no doubting the man worked out.

Neither of them was quite as beautiful as Lee. Had she made a mistake? Should she have gone after him?

She'd never been kissed like that. Not in her entire life. It was like the whole world had melted away and nothing mattered or was even real except for him. She'd clung to him, wrapping herself around him, trusting him to hold her up. She'd made a baby with her husband, but nothing had prepared her for Lee's kiss.

She was still shaking just thinking about it.

"Hey, babe," Adam said, dropping the bag on the counter. "Guess what? Our little neighbor found a boyfriend and then accused him of whoredom, but not before she sampled the goods."

Jake's jaw dropped a little. "Are you serious? How did he handle that?"

A long look passed between them. Adam seemed to be holding in a smile. He started pulling out a bottle of wine. "Not well from the looks of it. He seemed a little out of control if you ask me."

"Nice," Jake shot back. He had his hand over his phone. "So you need to talk to Avery here and make sure she's okay, right?"

Avery shook her head. "I'm fine."

"She's on the verge of tears," Jake said, staring at her. "Oh, verge broken. Honey, you're crying. You need a glass of wine and a shoulder to cry on. Why don't you tell Adam what happened? He's good at fixing bad situations. He gets himself into them so often."

She didn't miss the quiet finger Adam shot his partner's way, but he was all smiles when he turned to her. "I can help."

"So it's settled," Jake said. "You take care of Avery and I'll take care of that other little project we have going on."

Adam went red. "You son of a...yes, dear. I suppose you should handle that now. I need to get dinner on. Yours might be poisoned."

But Jake was talking into his phone again, utterly ignoring Adam. "Yeah. I understand, boss. No problem. I can be there in twenty. No, he's got some work to do. He won't be coming with me. He won't be coming at all."

Adam closed his eyes briefly, but when he opened them, he smiled her way. "Come on, sweetheart. We can soldier on without Jake. Have a glass of wine. I've been assured this Chianti is perfect. Sit at the bar and keep me company while I cook."

Jake was out the door with a little wave.

The truth was Jake made her a little nervous. But still, she had the feeling something had just happened between the two men, and she hoped she wasn't the cause. "I can go back to my place."

Adam was back to his perfectly polite self. "Not at all. The little task Jake is taking care of only really needs one of us. I would rather hear about what happened to you today."

She took a sip of the wine. It was rich on her tongue.

Her tongue. She'd felt out of control when his tongue had slid against hers. "I met this man today."

Adam took a drink before he pulled out his cutting board and set himself to slicing veggies. "I could tell. What's his name and why did you decide he was a member of the world's oldest profession?"

"His name is Lee Donnelly, and he seemed to like me," she tried to explain.

"And that makes him a hustler?"

"Guys don't like me." She was blushing again. "I haven't had a date in ten years."

"You're kidding." He stopped in mid-chop. "Why?"

She shrugged. "No one asked me."

There was more to it, but she didn't want Adam's pity. Well, she didn't want sympathy past the whole "she couldn't get a date to save her life" thing. That was pathetic enough.

"I don't understand that, Avery." Adam went back to the celery. "What's wrong with the men in New York?"

"I think they like prettier girls." And girls who hadn't spent most of their adult lives in hospitals. And girls who hadn't been in deep mourning for years.

"We need to work on your self-esteem, sweetheart." Adam looked at her thoughtfully. "You're pretty. You just don't know it. And you don't dress for your body type."

She glanced down at her somewhat shapeless sweater and jeans. "It's comfortable."

"Yeah, well, comfort doesn't always equal sex appeal. And a V-neck sweater would be just as comfortable, but it wouldn't cut your torso off the way that crew neck does. You're a *C*-cup, right?"

He seemed to know a lot about boobs for a gay guy. She was a thirty-six *C*. "Yes. Why?"

"Because your boobs are too big for a crew neck or for

64

those turtlenecks you wear. You need some skin to balance them out. And your skin, by the way, is quite lovely. You should show more of it. And I would buy some jeans with a little bling on the backside. You have a nice butt."

"I do?" She hadn't really taken much stock of her butt except for the fact that she'd been forced to sit on it for years. "I thought it was a little big."

When he grinned like that, she almost wondered if there wasn't some bisexual in there. It seemed an insult to women everywhere that he slept with men. "Not at all. Men like a little junk in the trunk, if you know what I mean. Well, straight guys do. I think it's fair to say that your hustler was into you for something other than cash. Did he get you to pay for lunch?"

"No." Lee had been very insistent on taking care of the bill. She'd reached for it, and he'd stared her down until she'd passed it to him and then he'd jovially taken care of it. "And he paid for coffee later, too."

Adam looked thoughtful as he selected another tomato to dice. "Okay. So most hustlers want the female to pay for everything. They don't tend to treat their customers. Their customers treat them. And besides, one would think that a hustler would be better dressed."

"He was dressed just fine." He'd looked very nice. Super nice. Hot. God, she'd pushed that guy away. What was wrong with her?

Adam snorted lightly and shook his head. "There was a stain on his jeans. I doubt he noticed. A hustler would have noticed. It looked like paint or something. He should have been wearing slacks. Slacks are slicker."

"He said he worked in construction." His hands had been callused and rough like he worked with them all the time. Like he did exactly what he said he did.

"Ah, then he probably knows and doesn't care. He probably got it while he was working, and like lots of straight guys, doesn't give a crap because they still fit. Again, a hustler would have been dressed to kill. He was like dressed to maim maybe. Actually, he's not really all that hot. Are you sure you like him? He seems a little like a douchebag to me. You know the kind who goes around kissing women who don't belong to him. Do you want me to punch him the next time we see him?"

"He's not a douchebag." Now that she was out of the situation, she could look at things a little more clearly. He'd been nice all afternoon. He'd been a wonderful companion and he'd taken care of her, and she'd repaid him by insulting him horribly. "He's a nice man. I just don't understand what he sees in me."

Adam put down his knife and sighed. "I don't think dinner is in the cards tonight. I think you need to start looking at yourself in a different way or you're going to push away every guy who tries to make a pass at you." He stopped. "You want some guy out there to make a pass at you, right? I'm being so very in the box right now. Do you like girls, sweetheart? Because it didn't look like it when you had your tongue down his throat."

"Okay, ewww." She had to laugh. It had not been halfway down his throat. It had been just the right amount of distance inside his mouth so their tongues could rub against each other in a way that had very nearly made her melt. "I like guys. I just don't know that I'm ready. I was married."

"I thought you hadn't dated in years. How old were you?"

"Barely eighteen." She'd been so young and so very, very stupid, but her short marriage to Brandon was a bittersweet memory, a pure time in her life when she'd been loved and taken care of and the whole world seemed like it might go right for once.

Adam whistled. "That's young. How long have you been divorced?"

"I didn't get divorced." She hated this conversation. Maybe this was precisely why she'd been fine with avoiding friendships. They were costly and uncertain, and she wasn't sure she was truly brave enough to reach out and open herself up. And she wouldn't know until she tried. She couldn't blunder through life hurting people the way she had today. If she did that then she should have just stayed in that car and died with Brandon and her precious baby. She owed them more than the life she'd been living. "Brandon died."

She couldn't bring herself to mention Madison. He didn't need to know about Madison.

"Sweetheart, I am so sorry to hear that." Adam's hand covered her own, a warm reminder that he was there. It held her in the present when her thoughts would normally drift to the past.

That was what a friend could offer, she finally realized. That was what Lee had maybe been offering. Perhaps not long term, but not a lot in her life had lasted for more than a little while.

"Thanks, but it was a long time ago."

"And you haven't dated since then?" Adam asked.

Somehow the pity in his eyes wasn't so horrible now. Maybe it wasn't pity and she should stop thinking about it that way. Maybe what some people offered was empathy, and that was a gift. Connection. Pain could connect people. When it was shared and understood, maybe friends could help lessen the pain. "Not once."

He frowned, but his eyes widened questioningly. "Uhm, so if you haven't dated then I'm going to assume the obvious. Right?"

She could totally guess what the obvious was. "No sex."

"Oh, honey, that hurts. We need to get you laid." Adam grinned. He was adorable when he grinned. But he didn't make her heart pound the way Lee did. Lee had the sweetest dimple. Just one, on the right side of his face.

Stay to the right, love. She'd felt so protected when he'd sheltered her, like he was a bulwark against a world that insisted on intruding.

"I have some friends here I can call," Adam offered. He put a hand up. "To date. Not to sleep with, unless you want to."

"I want him." Lee had been the one to reawaken all her female parts. Even before she'd spoken a word to him, she'd fantasized about him.

Adam frowned. "Are you sure? Because I know this guy who is way nice and doesn't seem like a douchebag. Seriously, I can have him over here in like twenty minutes. He'll be so much easier than the angry guy with paint on his jeans."

But she liked the angry guy with paint on his jeans. "I want him. At the very least I want to find him so I can apologize."

And see if he might think about kissing her again. Probably not. She'd probably wrecked that, but she had to try. She couldn't let it go. She would regret it, and she had more than enough to regret in this lifetime.

"Do you have any idea how to find him? You said he was a tourist, right?" Adam asked. "Did he tell you what hotel he was staying at?"

She thought about their lunchtime conversation. He was staying at a friend's place in Chelsea. That wasn't helpful. They had talked about all the places they wanted to see.

He'd been a bit specific. "He's going to the Tower of London with a friend of his tomorrow morning."

He'd invited her along. At the time she'd wondered if it wasn't one more way to get some mysterious something out of her. It had been an offer of friendship…maybe more.

Adam shoved the veggies into the trash.

"Hey, weren't you going to use those?"

"I was," he agreed as he washed his hands. "I was going to make a lovely pasta primavera the way my friend back home taught me. It's one of Jake's favorites, but he's likely eating pie as we speak. Sweet, sweet, creamy pie. Yeah. He'll likely steal my slice of pie, too, because he can be a greedy bastard. So he gets no dinner tonight."

She was deeply confused about the whole pie thing. "I think he might get full if he eats too much pie."

"Oh, he never gets enough of this pie. This is a forever pie. He'll just keep eating on that pie as long as it takes. Fucker." He gave her a brilliant smile. "But you and I are going shopping, and we'll end our makeover session with a brilliant meal. I am going to prove to you just how gorgeous you can be. Come on, Avery. Do you trust me?"

He held a hand out.

New clothes? Maybe makeup? It wouldn't mean a thing if she didn't really want a new life.

"Yes. I will go with you." She felt a smile steal over her face. Maybe Lee wouldn't talk to her again, but the way he'd kissed her made her think he really was interested. It was crazy to think, but she had to give it a shot.

He was the most interesting thing that had happened to her in years. She'd made the decision when she'd taken the job with Thomas that she would try new things. At the time that had meant museums and tourist sights and job-related things.

But she wanted to try sex. Sex with a beautiful man who could make her feel again. It wouldn't be forever. It wouldn't even be for long, but just for a little while she could feel wanted and loved.

Just for a little while.

"I'm ready to go if you are, sweetheart. Let's take the town." Adam seemed ready to throw himself into a little fun.

And so was she. She'd screwed up royally, but she had a plan. She would face Lee, and she would know one way or another. No more hiding.

She was going to owe Adam. Maybe she would make him a pie. He seemed to really like pie.

She followed Adam out into the night, ready to start again.

* * * *

Liam walked for hours, ignoring the impulse to go right back to Avery's flat and get her on her knees at his feet, begging for his forgiveness. He would eventually give in, but not before she'd begged a little. Then he would show her just how forgiving he could be. He would start with a spanking. A sub should always be disciplined, but that wasn't the point of this spanking. It would be to get her hot and needy. Only when she begged him would he break down and give her his cock, thrusting inside what had to be a tight, hot pussy and bringing them both some fucking relief.

Yeah, he wasn't going to do any of that.

After making certain he wasn't being tailed, he made his way back to The Garden. He needed to file a report. What the fuck would he write down? Caught subject before she caused a national incident. *Forced subject to eat fish and chips. Nearly fucked subject on the street.* Yeah, that would go over really well. Ian would love that one.

Damon stood at the front desk, talking to a couple of men. A Dom and his male sub from the looks of it. The thinner man had a leash trailing from the collar around his throat. Damon nodded them in when he caught Liam's eye. A broad grin bloomed over the bugger's face, and Liam had the sudden revelation that Damon had been brought up to speed on everything that had gone on today. The tiny wire he'd been wearing had captured everything he and Avery had said, and he'd had backup on him at all times.

Fucking Alex, who probably couldn't wait to tell everyone what had happened.

"I am in the presence of a real-life fancy man," Damon said in that oh so upper-crust accent. "Is Ian not paying you enough?"

He gave the wanker his happy middle finger. "Fuck off. Where's Eve?"

She was the only one who wouldn't give him hell.

"Li," Ian called out as he opened the door that led back to the locker room. "Nice to see you've decided to join us. I was worried for a minute that you had found another career. How's tricks?"

"Fuck you, too, Ian." He'd screwed up. He wasn't sure how because she'd seemed so happy right up until he'd tried to get an invitation inside. He'd been so sure she was wriggling on his hook and he could reel her in.

Fuck all. What if she wouldn't see him again? What if he'd blown his shot to get into her bed? Would Ian send Alex in? Would he go in himself? The thought wasn't a pleasant one. A vision of Avery in bed with someone else assaulted him. The man in that bed was going to be him.

"I know I fucked up."

"You moved way too fast for her," Ian said, sobering a

little.

He was used to fast women. He fucked most of the women he dated before he knew their last names. And suddenly that seemed empty. Cold and lonely. "She seemed to be responding."

Ian sighed and started walking toward the lifts. "Come on upstairs. Eve said she was expecting you. Damon, if you don't mind taking a look at those files I sent you?"

The big Dom nodded. "Not a problem. I'll let you know if I see anything out of the ordinary."

Liam followed Ian, his brain scrambling as he tried to put together a decent argument that might keep him in the game.

"I have Damon looking into all the files Adam managed to pull on the United One Fund employees," Ian explained, pushing the button for the lift. "He's got a good eye. He might find something I missed. It's just Alex and Eve staying upstairs on the fifth floor. I rented a place here in Chelsea in case you need to produce your friend's place."

It was all part of the elaborate setup to make Avery believe he was just another tourist.

"Yeah, I don't think I'll need that now. How long did it take him to tell you just how badly I'd fucked up? Did he send you the tape immediately or just give you a rundown?" Bitterness welled inside him.

Ian turned, a surprised look on his face. "Are you talking about Alex? Alex hasn't told me shit. He hasn't submitted the tape or the report yet. Jake, on the other hand, called from Serena's and had a great time telling us how Avery thought you were in the flesh trade."

"Fucker." Jake was supposed to be his friend. Of course, Liam probably would have done the same damn thing.

"Alex is professional. It's all he has left." The lift dinged and Ian got in. "When are you going to let him off the hook?"

Liam had to squeeze inside. Lifts in Europe were a little like cars. Small, sleek, not built for overgrown men. "What do you mean?"

"He thinks you're sleeping with Eve."

"That ain't my problem, mate." He winced. He had to stop doing that. He'd been too relaxed for too long. He had to stay in character even when they were alone. He forced his Irish down. "What happens between me and Eve isn't his business."

Ian's hand shot out and the elevator stopped. "He loves her."

That was plain to see. "But they're divorced, and she doesn't seem to want to go back to him."

Ian growled a little. It was his default state. "I fucking hate this shit. He's my best friend, and he's about to make a horrible mistake. If he starts dating again, everyone's going to get hurt. See, this shit didn't happen in the Army. It was neat and clean in the Army. Your buddy had your back and the only thing coming at it was a bullet or an IED or some shit. Women are way more dangerous."

"How about the Agency?"

Ian stopped, his mouth turning down. "Nothing's neat and clean in the Agency. You should know that."

He'd worked for some European intelligence when he'd been SAS. He likely would have been recruited into intelligence if his life hadn't exploded. Liam sighed. He owed Ian. "I can tell him, but that doesn't mean he's going to believe me."

"I know." He pressed the button and the lift began again. "I don't suppose you want to explain why you're spending your nights with Eve, sometimes not leaving her place until two or three in the morning?"

Liam turned to Ian. "What the fuck? You got a tail on me?" He sighed. "Damn it. Tell Alex he's got to stop stalking her. That's some creepy shit."

"He isn't stalking her. After she joined the company, Alex and I agreed to certain security protocols where Eve is concerned. She left the FBI under some very rough circumstances, and there are a couple of people out there who would love to see her hurt or dead. She wouldn't agree to a bodyguard."

"Ah, so you have the doorman in her building vet everyone who comes and goes." He remembered the doorman who took the night shift. He was big and burly and had the look of former military about him. Yeah, he could see that. "And Alex saw the report about me and leapt to an improper conclusion. We're not fucking, Ian."

He didn't owe his boss the story. He didn't owe Alex. So why did his mouth open and the truth pop out?

"Eve's been putting me under hypnosis."

The door opened to the fifth floor, but Ian held it there. "You're trying to remember what happened that night, aren't you?"

Liam stared straight ahead. "For all the good it's doing me."

"Are you ready for this? You've stayed away from that case for a very long time." Ian's face closed off.

"I need to know for myself. Do you know what it's like to have your whole life change and you can't bloody remember why?" It ate at him. He'd been able to shove it down for years, but it was bubbling to the surface like an angry whirlpool threatening to take him down. He had to know.

A long sigh came from Ian's chest and he nodded. "Just be careful. Sometimes these things don't turn out the way we want them to. I just hope you remember that the past is the past. Eve's in the second room to the left."

Liam started to walk out. "Thanks. And feel free to tell Alex I'm not shagging his ex. As far as I can tell, she's not shagging anyone. She lives like a well-dressed designer nun."

"And Liam. You didn't fuck up. Adam texted me. He's out shopping with Avery so she can look pretty when she searches for you tomorrow. You mentioned that you were meeting a friend at the Tower. She plans to be there."

His heart rate surged. *Fucking A, yes.* She'd taken the bait. "Good."

He hadn't scared her away. She still wanted him, and now he was in the power position. She would feel guilty, and he would use that to push her where he wanted her—straight into bed where he could figure out her secrets.

And decide if he was going to protect her or throw her to the wolves.

He walked down the hall and knocked on Eve's door. He'd been thrown to the wolves once. He'd survived. He wasn't sure Avery Charles would.

Eve answered the door, allowing him in. It wasn't long before he was back, back in hell.

* * * *

Five. He counted five bodies on the floor. Not exactly the floor. Two were draped over the floral print couch. Nasty thing. Like something a kid at university would pick up at a second hand store and drag back to his first flat.

Her. He saw a picture of the dead girl he'd woken up

75

next to on the wall. She was smiling with her proud parents on either side. Her skin wasn't chalky, and there was no rope around her throat.

Time had slowed down. He knew he should be panicking, but something made him stop. Look.

"What do you see?" Eve's voice asked.

"Bodies. Blood." Liam could hear her voice, but he was in the moment. He could smell the stench of the wharf coming from the open window. It confused him. He hadn't been close to the water. The pub he'd been at had been on the edge of the city. He was supposed to meet with intelligence at noon to debrief. He was supposed to show his contacts the bonds and get the go-ahead to meet with the arms dealer.

"I don't have the bonds," he heard himself saying.

"No, you don't. Rory has the bonds. Do you see Rory's pack?" Eve's calm voice kept him tethered.

"No. I just see them. The dead ones. Fuck, why can't I remember?" It was the story of his life. The most important twenty-four hours of his life and all he could remember were bits and pieces, broken shards of a nightmare. The truth was buried somewhere in his head.

"Don't panic." Eve's tone was firmer now. "Don't lose the thread, Liam. Remember that you're really here with me. You can come back at any moment, but it's safe for you stay there."

It didn't feel safe. This little flat had turned into a body dump. No one bothered with rope on these victims. They all had their throats slashed, their heads tipping back to make ghastly, bloody perversions of smiles.

Someone had enjoyed his work. He'd reveled in it.

"Stay where you are, Liam. Don't move the memory forward. Tell me what you see. Not the bodies. I know you have that memorized. What else do you see?"

He forced himself to look past the blood. It coated the furnishings, soaked the rug. Anywhere he stepped, he would get it on him. He looked at the small table in front of the couch. It was littered with crap, but the mirror caught his eye. It was an old mirror with a pink plastic handle, but it was the residue on it that really made him think.

"I see evidence that someone was snorting coke. Eve, I've never touched that shit in my life. SAS would have my ass. They check from time to time and almost always before and after a mission like this. They might do it under the guise of a checkup, but everyone knows what they're looking for."

He'd never so much as smoked a joint. He wouldn't have just snorted a bit of coke for fun. Rory was another story. Rory was spontaneous. Sometimes too spontaneous. He was impulsive, and it was important to keep Rory grounded or he might lose him.

Take care of your brother, Liam. He needs you. He could still hear his mother's words even under hypnosis. They had become a part of his life. They had become his shame.

"Stay with me," Eve said.

He took a long breath. This, Eve had explained, was like a painting and he was in the center, merely observing. He could control the memory, slow it down or force it to speed up. He was safe as long as he stayed in control. "I don't remember any of these people. Not even little flashes of them when they were alive. There's a bill from the pub lying on the floor. That must be where we met them, but we're miles away from there. Miles from the inn we were staying at."

"I want you to stay calm now, Li. I want you to let the

77

phone ring again. I want you to find Rory for me."

This was the moment when he inevitably lost control and the memory took over. This was where his brain always shut down, and he came out of the hypnosis screaming.

But something was different. He felt more settled, calmer. He could do this.

The phone rang. He hated that sound, but he allowed it to ring. It trilled, pointing the way to something he didn't want to find.

"You have to follow it, Li. It's okay. This happened years ago. It can't hurt you now."

She was wrong. This would always have the ability to devastate him. This was his failure in life. Still, he let that ring fill his head. He stood there for a moment as time sped up. He concentrated on remaining in the moment. He felt the phone in his hand, the way his fingers seemed to struggle to hold it. His knees felt weak and nausea churned in his gut.

And that smell. Blood and the wharf. Someone had left a window open. In the distance, he could see the docks. He could hear the sound of water churning. Were they right on the water?

Liam forced himself to turn. Voice mail came on again. Rory didn't have a personal message. It was just a computerized voice requesting that he leave a message and then a long beep.

But he'd heard the ring long enough. He hung up his phone and saw it. What he didn't want to see.

Rory's boots were on the floor. They stuck out just past the edge of the couch. Something was wrong with those boots. It was something about how they were sitting on the floor. His brain couldn't quite handle the input. Why were the boots wrong? He shook his head. The boots could only mean one thing.

His brother was laid out on the blood-soaked floor.

"Rory?" His voice sounded smaller, younger. A boy calling out for his younger brother. *Please get up. Please.*

Nothing. No movement. The boots were still, as though someone had painted them there and they weren't actually real. As though they were nothing he could reach out and touch.

And the ringing began again.

His phone. Someone was calling him.

Don't answer. Don't answer. Don't answer.

Panic welled up. Fire seemed to flare from the corners of his eyes. Control. He was losing control. *Don't answer.* He stared down at the phone. Bad things would happen if he answered that phone.

"Wake up, Li. Come out of it."

Liam focused. He was in Eve's room. Fuck. He wiped the sweat away. It was dripping down his brow and into his eyes. He was standing up. He'd been lying down. Confusion. He hated the feeling. One minute he'd been back there hearing that phone ringing and the next he was here doing god only knew what.

"You were trying to get out the window, Li. You seemed very intent on throwing yourself out the window." Eve was out of breath, her normally perfect clothes askew. There was a fine tremble in her hands.

"Did I try to hurt you?" Fuck all. It was the last thing he wanted to do. Eve was his friend. She was trying to help him, and if he hurt her he would never forgive himself. Hadn't he hurt enough people he cared about in his time? Why wouldn't he ever learn?

She shook her head. "No. You did not. Liam, you didn't hurt me. You were just trying to get out the window for some reason. I had to stop you, and it was a near thing." She took a long breath. "I think you're close to something."

Yes. He was close to losing his bloody mind. He scrubbed a hand through his hair. "I got further this time."

Eve reached out, taking his hand in hers. "You were much more in control for longer. It will get better. But next time I think we should invite someone with a little more upper-body strength to sit in."

He gave her hand a squeeze and then backed away. "I don't think so."

"Why? Li, Ian wouldn't judge you for something that happened years ago. If I know Ian, he probably knows more than he's saying. He wouldn't have brought you on board if he didn't trust you."

"If Ian knows something, why wouldn't he bloody well tell me?" Ian didn't know a thing. He couldn't possibly. If he knew, Ian would have told him. Ian was the one damn person in the world he trusted completely. Ian had saved him when all evidence was against him.

Eve found her way back to her chair on shaky legs. "If Ian didn't think you were ready he might have kept it from you. I'm not saying he knows a damn thing, Li. I'm just saying that he likely looked into the incident even if you asked him not to."

He hadn't. Liam had looked into it himself, calling on a few people he trusted, but all he'd been able to discover was that he and Rory were missing and considered dead.

And all he remembered about the whole bloody affair before Eve had started her therapy was waking up in the water with blood on his hands and the memory of those boots. He'd been able to remember the dead girl and Rory's body and that the bonds were gone.

He'd woken up face down and nearly drowning with no recollection of how he'd gotten there. One minute he'd been staring at his brother's boots and the next he'd been in the water.

After he'd gotten out of the water and realized just how fucked he was, he'd called Ian Taggart.

Eight hours later, he'd been on a plane to the States.

Liam sat down, making a few decisions. "If Ian knows something, then he had a reason to keep it from me. He probably didn't think I was ready to know. He was the one who helped me find the building I'd been in, and he was the one who found out it had exploded that very morning."

Eve leaned forward, intelligence radiating from her eyes. "I think you knew the building was going to explode. That's why you were trying to get out tonight."

"Well none of us bought the newspaper's explanation of a gas leak," Liam said. "I tried to run down ten leads and they all ended in nothing. No one had any idea where the bonds had gone. If they were used, it was with complete discretion. The arms dealer we were trying to take down mysteriously vanished off the face of the earth."

"You've never told me why you didn't contact your SAS group and attempt to explain what happened."

That was easy. "I don't know what happened. Not really. I think someone drugged my drink and after that it's all hazy. They think I died. I thought it best to leave it at that. I tried for the first couple of years to figure out what had happened and then little by little I just gave up. I think there's a part of me that has always wondered."

"Li, you did not kill that girl."

Her face still haunted him. He'd found out her name much, much later, but it was her face that came to him every night. "It was my rope. What if I did it in a drug-induced haze? What if I killed them all?"

"If you killed them all then you would know where the

bonds were. It's too coincidental. You were set up as the fall guy. Someone stole the bonds and you were supposed to be arrested, but they'd done their job too well. The SAS decided you died in the blast, too. They likely think the bonds were destroyed, and they might have been."

Liam doubted it. Why blow the place up? It didn't make a lick of sense. None of it did. "I got a phone call that night."

Eve nodded. "Yes. This is the furthest we've been. We've never made it past finding Rory's body before. That phone call sent you running for the window. It could explain how you ended up in the water. We need to know what it was about and who made it. You need to go under again. Take a few days. Do your job. Don't think about this. When you're ready, we'll try again, but I need some muscle to back me up if you try to take a header again, Li. I know you want answers, but I won't let you kill yourself to get them."

He stood. He was done for the night. He needed a pint or twelve to get the vision out of his head.

The dungeon was down below. He could burn away the memories in some sub's body, driving in and out until he could finally sleep.

Eve followed him out of the small room she'd taken over as her office. "Tell me something, Liam."

He turned, weary and ready to get to the part of his night that didn't involve reexamining his nightmares. "What?"

"What did you think of the Charles girl? Your first instinct. Is she involved with Eli Nelson?"

A vision of perfect blue eyes assaulted him. She'd been so shy at first, but when she'd given in she'd wrapped herself around him like she couldn't get enough, like he could never give her enough to fully satisfy her. Like she would want him for the rest of her days.

"If she's involved, she has no idea who he is. I think I could walk into a room where she was holding a smoking gun with a dead body on the floor and I would look around for the killer. She's innocent." After the day he'd spent with her, there was no doubt in his mind. She wasn't capable of making a decision that might hurt someone.

Eve nodded as she opened the door to let him out. "That was my assessment, too. My profile is of a very courageous young woman. She's been through a lot, Li. If she's innocent, then why would you put her through more?"

Because he wanted her so badly he could still taste her on his fucking tongue. Because the minute he'd thought about her again, all those wretched visions had fled and he'd only been able to see her. Because she was different. "Just because she's innocent doesn't mean she doesn't know something. She probably doesn't even know she knows something."

"Adam could find out without a sexual element. He can be her friend. A friend's betrayal can be much easier to get over than a lover's. Especially since I doubt she's had many of those. You do intend to sleep with her, I assume."

He was going to sleep with her. He was going to drown himself in her until he couldn't see straight. "I'll try not to hurt her, but I have to get close. Have you thought about the fact that if this gets dangerous, she'll need someone to protect her?"

Yes. He could make it sound noble. He could hide the fact that he was a greedy fucker who wanted to use her to forget himself. Eve didn't need to know that.

She sighed as though realizing she couldn't win this battle. "All right. Just remember, she's still fragile. She doesn't need to lose more people she loves."

Avery wouldn't love him. She would come to him for

something she hadn't found. Sex. Pleasure. Submission. But she wouldn't love him. He wasn't lovable. She would figure that out soon enough.

He closed the door behind him only to feel eyes on his back.

Motherfucking Alex. He stood not ten feet away glaring at Liam.

"You know, this is pathetic, McKay. You've turned into a second-rate stalker." He would brush past the bugger and down into the dungeon. He would fuck the first pretty brunette he could find.

"I'm just worried about her." Alex's whole body seemed to sag. He shook his head and turned down the hallway. "She's a hell of a woman. Treat her right."

Fuck. Fuck. Fuck.

Alex stepped into the elevator, and Liam jogged to catch up. He got in and pressed the floor for the bar.

"I'm going to buy you a pint. You're going to listen to me, and you're going to stop looking at me like I'm the playground bully who took away your favorite toy. I'm not sleeping with Eve. She's my therapist, and if you laugh, I reserve the right to kick you in the balls."

He was deeply amused by Alex's shocked stare.

He couldn't sleep with anyone else. He only wanted Avery. Maybe confession was the better alternative. He'd heard confession was good for the soul.

And beer. Lots of beer.

Chapter Five

Avery looked at the magnificent white building in front of her. The Tower of London. She stood at the western entrance staring up at the sight of numerous historical executions and wondered how she ever thought she would find him here. A throng of tourists moved around the ticket office. The Tower was huge. She would never find him, and they hadn't exchanged phone numbers.

She felt like an idiot. She was standing there in too-tight jeans and a sweater that formed a deep *V* that pointed right at her breasts, and she hadn't seen hide nor hair of Lee. It was probably for the best. She looked silly. She couldn't pull off the sexy look. Adam had to tutor her on how to put on makeup. She still wasn't sure she looked good.

Tears pooled in her eyes as she clutched her purse. She'd screwed up royally, and she wouldn't get a second chance with Lee. He would forget about her, likely already had. He would find a woman who didn't have a wall built around her. She was a little like the Tower. Surrounded by walls, unwilling to let anyone in or out.

She'd dreamed about him the night before. She'd dreamed that he hadn't kissed her in the street. He'd kissed her in her bedroom. He'd held her and touched her, and she hadn't been afraid. She'd been aggressive. She'd given as good as she'd got. She'd been woman enough for him.

She'd woken up in a hot sweat, still able to feel his

weight on her body, holding her down. He'd pinned her, forcing her to take him, but she'd loved it.

And it wouldn't happen because she'd been such a pathetic idiot.

She glanced around. It was the right time, but there were just so many people. Maybe if she stood by the ticket booth she could find him. Unless he'd bought tickets somewhere else. There were a lot of tourist packages to be had in London.

With a heavy sigh, she walked over to the ticket booth and waited. It was penance of a sort. She would give it a half an hour and then go. Or maybe she would just buy a ticket and spend the day here. Alone.

Her cell phone rang. She pulled it out knowing exactly who it was. No one but Thomas called her, though she'd given Adam her number.

Her in-laws had the number too, though they would never call and she knew it.

"Hello, Thomas."

There was a warm chuckle on the other end of the line. "How is the museum today?"

He'd had to listen to her talk about the British Museum and all its wonders for days now. As they'd taken their walks through St. James's Park, he'd asked about all the rooms and been a perfectly polite companion. He had to have been bored out of his mind. When she'd asked if he'd like to come along, he'd always found a business excuse. "I'm making a change this weekend. I'm at the Tower."

"Very nice, dear. I'm glad to see you're branching out. We won't be in London forever. We need to move on to Dubai soon."

The Dubai offices were where UOF coordinated much of their relief programs for Africa and Asia. Thomas insisted

86

on being very hands-on. She'd been told he would take a lot of meetings in Dubai. Many more than he took in London. He had only taken three donor meetings since they had crossed the pond.

Three meetings. And they hadn't been the biggest donors. What had made Thomas take those meetings? What really made her boss tick? It was a question she'd wondered about more and more, ever since his brother had died. Brian had been the one to introduce them. She'd only really known him for a few months, but he'd been very nice. She'd stood at Thomas's side at the funeral.

She was still waiting for his inevitable breakdown. It would come. No one was so strong that he could lose a brother and not cry.

"I'll be ready. Besides, this is a yearly trip, right? We'll be back in London next year."

His voice went low, slightly intimate. "We will, Avery. We're settling into a nice routine, you and I. Next year I'm going to schedule in some free time so I can see the sights with you. I don't know that I like you running around London on your own."

Who else would she run around with? "I've had a lot of fun."

"I know you have, and I've enjoyed watching you bloom," he said. There was a silent moment before he spoke again. "I was wondering if you were a little lonely today. Perhaps we could have lunch. I'm afraid the Tower would be a bit much for a man of my age."

She couldn't help but laugh a bit. "You're not much older than me."

"Oh, not in years, dear, but in all the other ways that count, I'm an old man. I have to meet that Bates fellow on Monday, so that means I won't be back in the office until

Tuesday. Why don't you come over and keep me company?"

She sniffled a little. It didn't look like she had anything better to do, and Thomas did sound lonely. Perhaps she could help him prepare for the meeting with Bates. It was odd. He usually kept her close to his side, but he always insisted on meeting the donors he chose to meet alone. Her boss had some weird peccadilloes, but then the rich really were different. "Well, I don't think my friend is going to show up, so I guess I could stop by for a while and let you decimate me at chess."

"A friend? I had no idea you were meeting a friend. Is it Theresa? She seems nice enough."

Theresa worked in promotions and outreach for the UOF. She was ten years older and spent all her free time with her husband and five kids. "No. It's not Theresa."

She could hear his disapproval over the phone. "Well I hope it's not the younger girls, Avery. They can be rather wild. I don't like the thought of you getting involved in their antics."

Sometimes he sounded like an overprotective father. "It's no one from the office. It's a man I met yesterday at the museum, but it doesn't look like he's going to show up."

There was a long pause. "I had no idea you were looking for male companionship."

What was wrong with Thomas? His tone had gone positively glacial. "I wasn't really looking. I sort of fell into him."

"Well, it's probably best he didn't show up. Men take advantage of women like you." His voice went right back to silky smooth. "So I'll be expecting you in twenty minutes or so? I'll have chef make a nice luncheon."

His words sort of faded into the background because

Lee was standing right in front of her. There was no mistaking him. He was staring at her, the heat from those emerald eyes nearly scorching her. She couldn't tell if he was still flaming mad or happy to see her. She just knew that she was so very aware of him.

Her heart sped up. Was this lust? Love at second sight? It didn't really matter because she felt something for the first time in forever. She'd fooled herself that she was fine, that she was over the tragedy and starting to live again, but everything she'd felt had been echoes of real emotion.

This was what she'd missed for years. Heart-pounding desire at the very sight of him.

"I have to go, Thomas. He's here." Even to her own ears, her voice sounded breathy.

"What? Avery, we should talk about this. What do you know about this man?"

She knew that he'd gotten tired of waiting. Lee stalked the distance between them.

"Hang up the phone, Avery," he said in a deep voice that brooked no disobedience. Yeah, she kind of liked that, too.

"I'll see you on Tuesday, Thomas. Sorry I can't make it for lunch." She hung up the phone and looked up. He was invading her space, forcing her to tilt her head up to look at him. It was a blatant show of alpha male dominance. He was bigger. He was taller. He was stronger. "Hi, Lee."

His dark hair was falling over his forehead as he stared down at her. "Did you decide you could afford me?"

Tears filled her eyes. Damn it, she'd told herself she wasn't going to cry. "Are you going to make me regret coming here?"

If she had to, she would make her apology and then leave. It had been a dumb mistake, but she hadn't meant to hurt him.

His eyes softened slightly, his hand coming out to touch her hair. He brushed a loose strand away from her face. "Why are you here?"

She could totally save face. She could apologize and walk away and then she never had to know if he would reject her. He could be perfectly relegated to fantasy. She would be safe. She could make her way to Thomas's place and spend the afternoon playing chess and having tea, and she would never know if Lee might have changed her life.

"Because I want you to forgive me for being so afraid."

He looked down at her chest, blatantly eyeing the valley of her breasts that were oh so visible because Adam had convinced her the V-neck sweater was a good idea. "Is this new look for me?"

"I wanted to be pretty." If he laughed at her, she would likely break down.

A brilliant smile crossed his face, like the sun coming out from behind the clouds. "You can't not be pretty, Avery. You're beautiful. And you're forgiven. Tell me something, sweetheart. Did you come here to just be my friend? I made it very plain what I want from you."

Sex. God, he wanted sex. "I'm nervous. I don't really know you."

"Then you should get to know me."

"You're going to leave. You'll go back to the States."

"Not for a while. I'm here for a couple of months and then we'll see. Avery, I'm not going to push you. Let's go do some sightseeing, and we'll see where things go. I like you. Let's consider today a date and take it from there. Can you trust me that far?"

He backed off, and she could breathe again. "Yes. I would like to spend the day with you."

She wasn't sure she could pull off the whole brief hook-up thing, but she could go on a date. *God.* She was on a date. He reached out and took her hand, threading his big fingers through hers. Warmth spread across her skin.

"Come on. I want you to meet my friend. His name is Ian. Don't let him scare you. He only looks like he eats small children for breakfast."

Avery followed him. Her day was definitely looking up.

* * * *

Thomas stared down at the phone in his hand, an unholy rage threatening to take over.

What the hell did she think she was doing? Had she picked up some local? Or some bloody fucking tourist?

He should have insisted she stay here with him, but no, he'd sent her to the tiny flat Brian used to use because he wasn't ready to make his play. In Dubai, he intended to meet with some doctors who could use "inventive new therapies" to strengthen his legs. He'd also scheduled some plastic surgeries of a most unusual variety. Thomas Molina had several spinal surgeries over his miserable life. The lack of scars hadn't mattered until he'd decided to take Avery into his bed. She would be looking for scars and thin legs. He had to have a reason they were stronger than they looked. The whores he paid didn't give a shit, didn't even realize who he was.

Who he was supposed to be. *Fuck.* Sometimes it got jumbled in his head. He needed to get rid of the fucking cane so he could be a man again.

He was sick of the cane, and god he hated that fucking wheelchair. He was a man. He was a brilliant man who'd killed his way to the top, and the fact that he couldn't just

91

throw down Avery was starting to chafe. She should be in his bed, begging for his cock.

He should be her god.

Maybe she wasn't as innocent as he'd thought.

Who was this fucker?

Molina took a long breath. He hadn't gotten where he was by being impulsive. He also was a brilliant judge of character. Avery was sweet and lonely, and he'd waited too long to make his move. He'd put it off because dealing with Eli Nelson was harder now that he'd left the Agency.

Nelson was a danger to everything he held dear. Nelson was also necessary to the Lachlan Bates deal.

Ten million was too much to push aside because his dick wanted to play with someone he didn't have to pay.

He forced himself to calm down. If he called back, he could lose her. He had to play the supportive boss. He'd been right in the first place. He needed to cull her from the herd. He needed her alone and vulnerable.

This was a long game, and he was damn good at long games. Patience had gotten him to where he was. Patience and the willingness to destroy anyone who got in his way. Even his own family. Taking care of some tourist would be a breeze.

He'd purposefully squashed her friendships here in London. A word here and a word there and suddenly no one invited her to lunch, and she was perfectly free to spend her afternoons with him. It would be even easier in Dubai. She would feel much more isolated as a woman in a Muslim country. He would make sure the people around her were friendly enough, but they would keep their distance. She would be alone, and she would feel the need to have a man protect her.

But it wouldn't hurt to figure out who this fucker she

was seeing was before he killed him. A man in his position couldn't be too careful. The last thing he needed was some dumbass intelligence agent bumbling in and fucking everything up.

He pressed a button on his desk, and within seconds his door opened.

"You rang, sir?" Malcolm was dressed impeccably in a three-piece suit. On paper, he was Thomas Molina's driver. In truth, he was so much more important. Malcolm was his enforcer. Malcolm had been with him since the day of his rebirth. He did have Eli Nelson to thank for that.

"I need you to find Avery and follow her."

Malcolm's expression never left the blank, bland facade he wore even when he was slitting a throat. "Should I kill her, sir?"

Again, he was forced to hold his temper. "No. She's got a boyfriend."

"Will wonders never cease?"

"I don't need your sarcasm." Malcolm had made it clear he didn't understand his attraction to Avery, but then the man had no use for innocence. As far as Molina knew, Malcolm's grand love was his SIG Sauer and his bank account. "I need information on the man. I have a trace on her phone. Call her if you need to find her, but as far as I know, she was visiting the Tower of London this morning. I don't want her to know she's being watched."

"And what should I do with this boyfriend of hers?" Malcolm asked, his eyes finally glinting slightly as though he was sure what was coming.

"Get me information and then you can handle things as you see fit, though you will make sure Avery is left out of it." Yes. He liked this plan. Avery would be more vulnerable, and she would turn to him.

He'd been her boss and her friend for months. This fucker had just shown up. She would turn to him. No doubt.

He nodded toward the door, sending Malcolm out.

This man Avery was meeting had an "end-by" date. He just didn't know it.

And when he died, Avery would turn to her friend. She would be in his arms in no time.

Calm settled over him. He was getting far too emotional. Malcolm might not understand, but Molina was self-aware enough to know what Avery's appeal was.

He'd sold his soul long ago, but he was still able to appreciate true innocence and purity.

He just wanted to corrupt it. It was his final frontier.

When he had Avery in his bed, he would twist that pretty soul until hers was just as dark as his own. It would be fun. He would do it with pleasure and a good deal of pain— both emotional and physical. Her tears would feed his soul.

Molina pulled the file on "Lachlan Bates" and got back to work. He whistled a little while he did it. After all, work was fun.

* * * *

Liam was ready to kill Adam. He was the one who had convinced Avery to walk around with her boobs on display. He looked across the table and would swear he could practically see a nipple. He'd followed her up and down medieval prison rooms and past the crown jewels, and all he could think about was the fact that every man walking around the Tower was staring at her breasts.

And her bum. Yesterday she'd worn perfectly respectable jeans that hadn't hugged her every curve. Those jeans yesterday hadn't sported little diamonds on her cheeks that just begged a man to find out how much treasure was buried beneath.

"So where did you say you were from, Avery?" Ian asked in an absolutely flawless London accent. There was just the faintest hint of working class in the way he rounded his vowels.

Avery smiled at him, leaning on the table. She'd barely had half a glass of wine, but her face was already flushed and she'd relaxed, her hips brushing his in the booth.

"I'm from New York originally, but now I kind of live out of my suitcase," she explained. She'd seemed a little wary of Ian at first, but it hadn't taken her long to warm up. She'd teased both him and Ian about how difficult it had been for them to fit into the Tower's narrow staircases and small rooms. The Tower hadn't been built for bulky men.

This was what Ian had been waiting for. There was no question in Liam's mind. He'd been waiting for a break so he could get her to talk about her job. A knot of guilt twisted in Liam's gut, and he rather wanted to go back to the hours when they'd just been tourists enjoying their time together. He'd been to London many times, toured the Tower, but seeing it through Avery's enthusiastic eyes had been a novel experience. She'd wanted to see everything. She'd stood on the yard where Anne Boleyn had walked, and he could see her mind wandering, likely imagining what it had been like to have her hours numbered, trapped inside.

"So what exactly do you do?" Ian asked.

"I'm kind of a Girl Friday. I assist my boss with the running of the charity."

"United One Fund," Liam offered. "The way she explained it yesterday, it's a relief fund."

"We go into war-torn or disaster hit countries and offer food, water, all the necessities. We also offer microlending.

95

We'll give out small loans of as little as fifty to a hundred dollars, and it helps women in Third World countries start businesses and begin to support themselves and their children. We work with a couple of medical charities, too."

She was a believer. It was right there on her face. Avery Charles believed she was saving the world in some small way. Liam had thought that once, back in his SAS days. Back before he'd found himself in a dingy, blood-soaked hellhole.

Avery might believe, but Liam had his doubts. If her boss was so very angelic, what was he doing meeting with Eli Nelson? And what did Nelson want with a humanitarian organization?

"So the organization is based in the States?" Ian asked. To an outsider, it would seem to be a very polite question. Just a friend asking all the trivial things of a new girlfriend. But Ian Taggart already knew the answers to his questions. Most of them, anyway. He wanted to trap Avery in a lie.

Seemingly of their own accord, Liam's fingers brushed against hers. Ian wouldn't catch her in a lie. She didn't know how to lie.

"I wouldn't say based exactly. There are small offices all over the place. The London office is one of the biggest, but Thomas is planning on spending most of the rest of the year in Dubai. From there we'll tour a lot of Africa."

"That's interesting." And potentially very dangerous. Thomas Molina would be a target of kidnappers and any number of troubles. "Does your boss do this every year?"

She shook her head. "Oh, no. This is brand new. Up until a couple of years ago, Thomas ran everything from his place in upstate New York. He was very isolated. He had a childhood accident that caused his legs to be very weak."

"So Molina just one day decided to see the world?"

Liam asked. It was odd. Liam had read a couple of reports that hinted Molina was agoraphobic.

"I guess so," Avery replied. "He seems to really love it here in England. We go for walks in St. James's Park, and he has this place he loves to eat at. It's got a view of the Thames and St Paul's Cathedral. He meets a friend there every now and then. It's all very mysterious. I keep his appointment book, but he never asks me to put down a name. Just that he's having lunch there and shouldn't be disturbed. I kind of think it's a woman. I have to admit I'm a little curious."

It wasn't a woman Molina was meeting. It was Eli Nelson. And he would love to know when that next meeting was going to take place. The booth they were in was small. Liam decided to make it a little smaller by taking up more space. He put an arm around the back of the booth and scooted close to her, his fingers brushing her shoulders.

She leaned into him, accepting the affection. But his move had shoved her hips right up against her purse.

"Why don't you put that monstrosity over on Ian's side of the booth? He isn't doing anything interesting with half his seat."

Ian grimaced. "Well we can't all get to London and find a girl in a matter of days. I've been here for years, and I'm still bloody alone. Some of us work more slowly."

From what Liam had heard from Alex last night, Ian had already slept with a couple of subs. He was plowing his way through The Garden the way he did back at Sanctum. Always with a contract, never for more than a night or two. "Yeah, buddy, you're going to die alone the way you're going."

Ian shrugged. "At least it's peaceful. And hey, I can now say I'm dating Avery's bag."

Avery handed it over. Ian settled it to the side, giving the big black bag plenty of space, and the minute Avery turned her head, Liam watched him palm her cell phone. It was buried in his pocket before Avery could look back.

Ian slid from the booth and stretched. "I'm hitting the loo. Be back in a minute."

Copying and tagging her phone was the first line of business today. They would pull down all the data she had and then place a small tracking device in it so they could locate her. They would dupe the phone and the number so when Avery received a call, they could listen in. Liam didn't have a single reservation about doing it. It was a clear invasion of her privacy, but it was also the best way to protect her if her boss was dirty.

But it required that the subject not realize her phone had ever been taken.

"Maybe I should follow Ian's lead. I think I'll try to find the bathroom and fix my hair. I got a little windblown," Avery said.

And naturally she would take her purse and check her phone. She was a creature of habit. She routinely checked her phone for messages. He had to break that routine.

He turned slightly in his seat, his arm curling around her shoulders. "Stay with me for a minute. I haven't gotten you alone all day. I'm glad you came to find me today, Avery."

Her eyes went wide as she looked up at him, but he watched her make a decision. She forced herself to relax, letting her body cuddle close to his. "I almost didn't. I was afraid you wouldn't talk to me."

"Somehow I think I would have been back at your doorstep in a day or two. I was a little miffed that you thought I was a hustler, but when I calmed down, I realized I hadn't told you the whole truth about myself. I came on strong. It's kind of a part of my personality. I thought about it all last night. Maybe you were picking up some clues I was giving you, but you came to the wrong conclusion." Honesty worked at times. Honesty would keep her sitting right where she was until Ian had found Alex and they'd gotten the job done. Alex had been shadowing them all day, waiting for a chance. "I'm certainly not a hustler, but I do have some…proclivities you might want to know about before you make the decision to become involved with me."

She bit into that gorgeous bottom lip, the sight going straight to his cock. "Proclivities? What do you mean? Are you bi?"

He shook his head. "I'm one hundred percent hetero, sweetheart. But I do like to spank my partners from time to time. Nothing harsh. Maybe a little flogger play. I like to be in charge of the sexual side of my relationships."

Her whole body flushed, the blush rushing across her like a tidal wave. Yeah, he had her attention now. "You're a sadist?"

Ah, the uneducated. He'd been around Grace and Serena for too long. He'd forgotten there were women who didn't understand BDSM. It seemed they all read the novels these days. "No. I'm not a sadist. Well, there's a tiny bit of it in there, but I never cause my submissives more pain than they want. I'm a Dom. Do you know what that means?"

"I've heard the term before. Some of the women in the office were talking about fetish clubs and Doms." Her voice was just breathy enough that he was sure she'd been intrigued. It was up to him to get her even more curious.

"Ian belongs to one of those clubs," Liam said. "And I belong to one back in the States. I'm a regular there, though I don't have a full-time submissive. I play around. I train other Doms and some couples. I'm certified in Shibari and all forms of suspension play."

Her eyes went round, and a sexy little smile lit her face. "Certified?"

It was time to make her comfortable. "Yes, certified. Safety is very important, and so is proper form and protocols. Especially when playing in public. In private, with someone I care about, it's not so formal. It's more intimate, and we can make up our own rules."

He could see the pulse on her throat racing. Her breathing was a bit shallower than before.

"I don't know, Lee. I'm not very experienced."

"But you're not a virgin, either." He'd never prized virginity. He'd lost his own at the age of fifteen to a woman in his block of flats. He didn't expect a woman to come to him without a little mileage of her own.

She looked down, her eyes darkening slightly. "That was a long time ago, and there hasn't been anyone since."

Fuck. Eve had told him she thought Avery hadn't had many lovers, but she hadn't had sex in ten years? He'd spent his twenties fucking his way across three continents, and she'd been a bloody nun. He found his role slipping a little. His curiosity about her wasn't an act. It was real and visceral. "Why?"

Her head came back up, but there was a sadness in her eyes. "A lot of reasons."

He let his arm tighten and pulled her close. He followed his instincts. He might be a son of a bitch, but he was a good Dom. A good Dom knew when a sub needed comfort. *Fuck.* What was wrong with him? He wasn't a cuddler. Alex McKay was the Dom every sub ran to for cuddles and a shoulder to cry on. Liam was the Dom subs ran to for a good flogging and a meaningless fuck, but holding Avery felt so right. Her softness practically blanketed him. "You don't have to tell me."

She frowned for a minute and then her head found his shoulder, her hand lying across his chest. "I was in and out of hospitals for a long time after my accident. I guess I was in recovery for years. Not that people in hospitals don't have sex. Seriously. They do. A lot. But I didn't."

He knew the story, but hearing it come from her somehow made it more real. "So you had surgery?"

"A bunch of them. I spent a couple of years in nursing homes." She shuddered a little.

Nursing homes. Sad dank places that smelled like piss and shit and death. He couldn't imagine her stuck in a bed, shoved away and forgotten. "Why the hell did they put you there?"

She settled in, hugging him closer as though physical contact made the story easier to tell. She hadn't seemed to mind his gruff question. "I didn't have anyone to take care of me. My parents were gone. My husband and, well, my husband died in the accident. I didn't have siblings. I was alone, and I couldn't take care of myself so insurance paid for a nursing home for a while. It wasn't so bad."

She was trying to calm him now, her hand brushing across his chest as though he was the one who needed the comfort. And he kind of did.

"Where were your husband's parents? His family should have been yours after you married him." Family should stick together. He didn't have a family anymore, but if Rory had been married, he would have bloody well made sure his wife was taken care of.

"They were older when Brandon was born. He was their only child. They were devastated after Brandon and…well, they were wrecked after Brandon died. They came to see me, but they couldn't take care of me. It was okay. It was

101

good to have visitors every now and then."

Someone as sweet as her should have had visitors every day, should have had someone in the world who would step up and take some fucking responsibility. He could already see she was a caregiver. Hell, she tried to help people she didn't know. He couldn't imagine she hadn't done it all her life, so where were all the people she'd helped when she needed them? Where had her fucking aunt been? But she hadn't told him about her aunt so he couldn't call her on it. It was hard to keep straight what Lee knew and what Liam knew. "How long was it before you got out of the home?"

"I was in and out for a couple of years. But then I qualified for this experimental surgery. It was perfect because the doctors and hospitals involved had grants to cover the costs of everything, and I didn't have to depend on insurance anymore. And within a year, I was walking, really walking again. I met this man named Brian Molina and he introduced me to Thomas, my boss, and now I'm seeing the world and I have a whole new life. I guess those years feel a little lost to me. I was closed down. I wasn't ready for any kind of relationship."

And the hesitance in her voice told him she might not be ready now, but he was going to push her. She was on the edge. He couldn't play it cool with her. With any other woman, he would pull back, let her come to him. He would allow her to pursue so she understood that he could take her or leave her and all the proper expectations could be set.

But this was a job. And when he'd sat up half the night thinking about her, he'd realized he didn't even want to treat her with his usual careful distance. He wanted to get her close.

Deep in the night, he'd acknowledged the fact that he wanted this time with her. He would walk away when it was over, but he was going to enjoy her while she was here. Just for a few days, he wouldn't be the righteous bastard he'd been for the last ten years. He was going to indulge in the man he might have been. Open. Caring. Worthy of someone like Avery.

He tilted her head up, bringing her face to meet his. Adam had apparently taken her to a makeup counter. She'd put on makeup, but it only enhanced her already sweet features.

She wasn't the most beautiful woman he'd ever seen. Not even close. He'd been with so many lovely women, younger and thinner. So why did she call to him? Why had he sat up all night with an aching cock and a guilty conscience?

He shoved the conscience aside. It was an unwanted intrusion. And the aching cock wouldn't go away until he'd had her. Which he intended to do very soon.

"We can take this as slowly as you want, but I need to put my cards on the table. I want to be honest with you." God, he was a bastard, but it was kind of the truth. He wanted to be honest with her. He simply couldn't. "Any sexual relationship with me is going to involve Dominance and submission. I can play it vanilla for a while, but not forever. I need control."

That wasn't a lie. He couldn't handle being out of control. He'd been a bit of a control freak before the incident that took his brother's life. He was so much worse now.

"Vanilla?" Avery asked, humor in the tilt of her mouth.

Yes, he'd spent way too much time in clubs. He'd forgotten some people didn't understand the language. "That's the kink term for plain sex. The type that doesn't involve bondage and a promise of submission."

"So what does the sub get in return for all this

submission?"

That was easy. "Multiple orgasms."

Even in the low light, he could see the way her pupils dilated. She was sexually aroused by all the talk. "Well, I have to admit I never really liked vanilla. I'm more of a strawberry girl."

Thank god for that. He leaned over and brushed his lips against hers, reveling in the soft feel of her. Everything about Avery was soft and feminine. He let his hand come up to sink into her hair. She'd put it up in a ponytail, but he liked it down and long. It was best to begin as he meant to go. Teaching Avery to submit to him, to obey him in certain circumstances without question, just might save her life. Yeah, that was how he could justify it. He pulled the ponytail out, the soft brown tresses tumbling past her shoulders. "Wear your hair down for me. I like it long."

She shivered a little. Her mouth played along his. She was getting bolder about being affectionate. "I guess I can do that."

He tugged just a little on her hair, fisting it lightly. "You'll do it to please me. You'll do it because I find it sexy and beautiful."

Her voice was soft, just a little shaky. "Yes. I will." There was a stubborn tilt to her chin. "Do I get to make any demands? I know I'm supposed to be the submissive one, but I might need things, too. I don't think I like the idea that you just control me, but you get to do anything you like."

"Ah, but that's because you don't understand the power exchange. Note that I used the word exchange. Listen, there are as many different ways to practice BDSM as there are people who practice it. I like to play. I like to know that my lover will turn to me when she needs something. I'll want to protect you. And I like to give you what you need. It makes me feel good. It makes me feel necessary." He hadn't thought about it before. He'd first investigated the lifestyle because he needed a way to focus Rory and teach him control. His brother had enjoyed the power, but not the obligations of a Dom, and Liam had found a place where he fit. He'd enjoyed it for its honest communication. But now, he meant everything he said. He suddenly wanted to be necessary to this woman. Even if only for a little bit. "So tell me what you need. This won't work if you don't talk to me."

She sighed. "I've really only had one relationship before. Brandon and I were so young. I don't guess we really talked about stuff like sex." She flushed, the pink in her cheeks doing nothing to mar her prettiness. "It's hard to talk about this."

"No, it's not. It's simple. It's natural, baby. How will I know what you need if you don't tell me?"

Avery seemed to struggle to find the right words. "Well, I need to know you're with me. I'm not stupid. I know this isn't like forever or something, but while we're…what did you call it?"

Sex. She was talking about sex. She was talking about fucking and taking his cock until he was balls deep inside her and he couldn't see straight, and the word he would use seemed brutally inadequate. "Play."

"While we're playing, I would like to know that I'm your only playmate. I know that sounds old-fashioned. I might not be up with the times…"

He cut her off because he was going to make that so simple on her. "Avery, I can promise you this. If you come to my bed, if you submit to me, then you're the only one there. For however long this lasts, I'm yours. You want to know how I practice?" Fuck, he hadn't really practiced before. He'd just poked his head in for a little fun, but his beliefs seemed to be coalescing, forming something real and tangible. He'd never needed a real code before, but now it was easy to know what he wanted. "It's a two-way street. I want you, Avery, and not in a random hook-up way. I want to know you. I want to explore you. For however long that lasts, I will only be with you. If you're mine, then I'm fucking yours, too."

God, he really meant it. What the fuck was happening to him? He'd come to London and lost his fucking mind.

"Okay."

It couldn't be that simple. God. She needed a damn keeper. "What are you saying?"

"I want to try."

He wanted clarification on that. "You want to try what?"

There it was, that deep flush. "You know."

Yes, he knew, but he wasn't going to let her off the hook so easily. She was going to be his. For a brief time, she would belong to him and he would have everything he wanted, and he wanted her to start talking dirty. Yes. He wanted to teach her, to train her to accept pleasure so she would expect it. "No, I don't know. You'll have to be plain."

Avery blushed a little. "I want to be intimate with you."

So sweet. So polite. So not happening. "That sounds like you want me to get into my pajamas and exchange secrets with you. I'm not your girlfriend, Avery. Tell me what you want. That's lesson number one. Communication and honesty are the keys to the relationship I want. I need to hear you say plainly what you want."

She hesitated, but only for a moment. He wasn't surprised. Deep in her heart, she was a brave girl. She'd faced so much and still was open with her heart. Damn, but he didn't understand that. "I would like for us to sleep together."

"I'm not very sleepy." He wasn't going to let her get away with anything.

She groaned a little in obvious frustration. "You know that's not what I'm talking about."

"Yes. I do. So say what you want."

"I want to have sex."

"So clinical. I'll have to think about that."

"I want to make love."

"Sweet, but not what I'm looking for."

Her face crinkled into the cutest pout. "Damn it, Lee. I want to fuck."

Just like that he was primed and ready. She'd said fuck with such a sweet little heat, her eyebrows forming a *V* over her face as though the entire incident had offended her polite sensibilities. She would learn there wasn't room for politeness between them.

He growled just a little. "I want to fuck, too, baby. I want to fuck all night long."

He pulled her in hard, slamming her chest against his. He wanted to cup them, feel their weight in his hands, pluck at the nipples until they were hard little points begging for his mouth. His lips covered hers, and he was thrilled at the way she responded. She flowered open beneath him, welcoming his kiss. He wanted to spread her wide, forcing her to take his cock to the root. He would fuck her hard so she couldn't remember another man, so he was branded on her body. He would fuck her pussy. He would take her ass. He would feel the heat of her mouth around his cock. And when she was sore from his fucking, he would still want her. He would just lube up her breasts and make another hole for his dick.

There wouldn't be an inch of her body that wasn't

coated in his come.

He slid his tongue inside. She'd become accustomed. He didn't have to remind her to open her mouth to him. She was so submissive. She followed his lead. Her arms wound around his neck. He loved that, too.

He knew some Doms who merely wanted their submissives to be vessels. Ian, himself, simply offered pleasure, and that only came with perfect submission. Ian wouldn't allow a sub to put her arms around him. He made it very clear to the submissives he slept with that all he offered was his cock and a night of orgasms. Liam had been that way, too, though he'd never gone so far as to not allow a sub to touch him. He didn't want any aggression, but Liam needed to know Avery wanted him, too. "You taste so good, baby."

She slid her tongue over his. Yes. She was so cautious, but he was getting under her skin. He could feel it. He wanted it. She'd slid under his before he'd said a single word to her. She was a sweet little flower winding her way through his desolate garden, bringing a little life to him.

It didn't matter that they were in a pub. He wanted to lay her out and take her. Only after he'd penetrated her would he really know that he was in control. Years had passed and she hadn't taken anyone, but she would take him.

He was a low-life bastard motherfucker, but she would let him inside, and just for a few minutes, he would feel like a king. His cock throbbed. He wanted to press himself against her, but the damn table was in the way. He pulled her close, trying to shift her so she could sit in his lap. He wanted her to straddle him so she could feel just what she did to him.

"Should I leave?"

Avery was startled out of the moment. She pulled away

from Liam at Ian's words. *Bastard*. He could have given Liam another couple of minutes. *Fuck*. He wouldn't be satisfied with minutes. He wanted hours. Days. Months inside her. But he couldn't let Ian know that. He had to play it cool.

He sat back, leaning against the back of the booth. "Anyone ready for some food?"

Ian's eyes narrowed. There was a flat set to his jaw that told Liam he wasn't happy about something, but he patted the bag beside him. He'd done what he could with the phone, but he obviously wasn't thrilled with the outcome.

And Liam didn't care. It was time to ditch Ian. It was time to start claiming his place in Avery's life. It was time to claim his place in her bed. God, his cock was so fucking hard. He needed to get himself under control.

"I think I should head out," Ian said. "It's been a blast, Lee. And Avery, it was so nice to meet you. I hope to see you around."

"At the club?" Avery asked.

Fuck. Yeah, he probably shouldn't have mentioned that.

Ian's face went slightly cold. "The club?"

Liam shrugged. "I want to be upfront with her."

Ian's lips thinned. "It's supposed to be an underground club, Lee."

Ian was going to kick his ass, but Liam had to go with it. "Well, I want her to be underground with me. I have full rights at The Garden, do I not? I can bring a sub with me. I've read the contract."

Ian sighed. "Yes. You can bring a sub, of course. Thank you for informing me that you might bring a sub. It will make it easier to be prepared to meet your needs."

Or in other words, he was happy Liam hadn't just shown up and thrown the whole club into complete panic because he'd walked in with their mark.

But he intended to walk in with their mark because she needed it. And he needed it, too.

Ian gave him a brief nod. "See you later, mate."

He shoved out of the booth, and Liam found himself alone with Avery. Finally. He turned back to her. Every pore of her skin was flushed, but she looked up at him, her eyes clear.

"So, Avery, are you in or out? If you want me to walk you home and leave you on your doorstep like a gentleman, I will do it. But if you invite me in, all the rules change."

She hesitated but only for a moment. "Come home with me."

He took her hand and led her out into the night.

Chapter Six

Avery fumbled with the keys to her flat. Her hands were shaking. The wine she'd imbibed had managed to break through a layer of her inhibitions, but now she'd found a whole new strata of worries as she realized she was here. There was no more wine and conversation to hide behind. There was just an empty apartment.

Except it wouldn't be empty once Lee walked in. It would be full of superhot man and a woman who hadn't had sex in ten years. Somehow she thought Lee had probably had sex in the last decade. Crazy, kinky sex. Dominant sex. Bondage sex.

Why wasn't she running? She should be running, right? She wasn't in his league. He was so much more attractive than she was. He was into crazy sex stuff and she was absolutely inexperienced. She was overweight. How was she going to get naked with him?

How was she going to hide the fact that she'd never been particularly sexy? She had no idea what to do.

Open the door. She should open the door. It really was the first step. The problem was the second step. The second step might take her off the ledge, and who knew how far she had to fall. A long way. The question was could she survive that moment when she hit the concrete at a hundred miles an hour? Did she really know what she was doing?

Did she really know what she wanted?

"I could open the door for you if it's really that hard." Lee's deep voice brought her out of her thoughts, her fears.

She winced. How long had she been standing there? "Sorry." She tried to concentrate on getting the door open.

Before she could turn the key, he pulled her around, pressing her back to the door. He invaded her space, taking up all the air and leaving her lungs in a hazy, breathless state.

His chest bumped against hers. "You are easily distracted. I need to give you something to focus on."

He leaned over and brushed his lips against hers, his tongue coming out and lazily tracing her bottom lip. He swiped his tongue across her lips and then she felt his hand fisting in her hair, pulling her back as he surged into her mouth. What was he doing to her? She felt that kiss deep inside. It skimmed along her lips, lighting up her skin and finding its way to her breasts, her nipples peaking, moving lower.

What did she want? Oh, she wanted this.

She dropped the keys as her hands drifted to touch his chest. Even through the cotton of his shirt, she could feel how muscular he was. Every inch of him was hard and perfectly cut. He towered over her, making her feel small and delicate. She let her arms wind around him, pressing up to plaster herself against him.

He held her head, dominating her mouth while his left hand made its way to her backside, cupping her cheek and pulling her closer even as he pushed her against the door. She was trapped, and it felt so good. Out of control. She'd been out of control before, but that had been a terrible thing. This was a roller coaster ride, and she wanted to know where it led.

Lee pulled away, his gorgeous face flushed and hard.

112

"Let's go inside. I'll handle the whole key thing."

He knelt down and grabbed the key, opening the door in one swift move.

And she was right back to nervous as she followed him in. She wasn't good at sex. The only experience she'd had had been with Brandon, and they had gotten pregnant their first time together. She'd been married a month later, and the pregnancy had been hard. They had lived with his parents for a while. It had been weird to try to have a sex life while she felt sick and tired and his parents were in the next room. By the time she felt good enough again, they had a baby and then everything had gone to hell.

She was practically a virgin, and he was a man who went to sex clubs.

What was she thinking?

She followed him inside and locked the door behind her. She was alone with him. Maybe if she just got through this first time, it would be okay. The kissing part was nice, but she knew the actual sex would be something she just endured. It was okay because she really liked the kissing and the holding afterward.

Her hand found the light switch, illuminating her small flat. There was only one bedroom, and Lee was standing next to it.

"Come here." His voice was velvety smooth, making her heart race. He'd taken off his jacket, tossing it over the small leather sofa.

She hadn't had many visitors. Thomas never came to her place. No one at the office seemed to want to be more than casual friends besides Simon. She hadn't had girl friends over. It felt odd to not be alone.

"Are you changing your mind?" Lee asked. His face was a polite blank, all emotion gone. He stood there, his shoulders set and she just knew that if she turned him down, she wouldn't see him again. Not because he would walk out but because she would never have the courage to try again.

"No." She wanted him. She just didn't want for him to know how scarred her body was or how much cellulite she had. She didn't want him to realize she wasn't really capable of having one of those crazy screaming orgasms that women in movies seemed to have. She wasn't that girl, but if she kept the light off and made the right sounds, maybe he would think she was fully functional.

She was only going to be in London for a short time longer. This wasn't forever, but she wanted him for however long they had. He'd been so open and honest. That was what she needed in a man. She hadn't told him everything. She'd left out parts of her tragedy because she wanted him to see her as a strong woman he could partner with. If he knew about Madison, he would just see her as an object of pity. A childless mother.

What if he saw her C-section scar? Maybe she was changing her mind.

"Come on." He held out his hand.

She knew she should run, but she just kept moving toward him, her hand floating up as though there was some invisible tether pulling her along and binding her to him.

A slow, sexy smile crossed his face. "You look like you're going back to the Tower to stay as a resident."

Yes. She could believe that because this whole episode could put her right back in the prison of her solitude. Now that she was here with him, she realized just how lonely she'd been. There had been no one to hold her hand, to protect her body with his. Her father had been wonderful, but he'd died. Her husband had been just a child really with no chance to become a loving man.

Lee was the first time someone had shielded her. It was the little things that drew her in. He made sure he was the one who walked next to the street. He made sure she found a seat on the Tube and then loomed over her like a bodyguard.

Lee was the first time she'd felt safe in years.

This had to work.

She let him pull her close, reveling in the feel of his body against hers. Safe was only one of the things he made her feel. Her body came alive the minute he touched her. "Kiss me again."

His face went slightly hard, and his voice was a low growl. "Ask me nicely."

Was this part of the games he liked to play? "Please kiss me."

"Let's start with the rules. You'll call me 'Sir' when we're playing."

She could do that. It was actually a little sexy. "Sir, will you please kiss me?"

"With pleasure, sweetheart." His voice went silky smooth when he was happy. He lowered his lips to hers and took over.

She loved this part. She'd been kissed before, certainly, but never like this. This was a long slow devouring of her mouth. Lee didn't just peck and poke and then move on. He settled in like he could kiss her for hours, days, like he never wanted to stop. Over and over again his mouth took hers, their tongues moving in a fluid dance, and it was so easy to forget everything except him.

He came up for air, those green eyes practically glowing in the dim light. "Do you want another drink? Do you have anything in the kitchen?"

Nope. She wasn't ready for company. "I have some bottled water."

"Tomorrow we'll get some beer and some Scotch. I like a Scotch before dinner. We'll have to figure out what you like." His hands never stopped moving. He was always stroking her somewhere as if he simply couldn't stop himself. "So why don't we sit down and talk about how this is going to go?"

She couldn't stand another minute of talking. Why couldn't he just attack her and be done with it? That cold feeling in the pit of her stomach was back. She would feel better once this whole thing was done and she knew she could please him. Sex wasn't so hard. She just had to show him she wanted him and let him have her. That was easy. Then she would feel better.

Unless he took one look at her so not-perfect body and ran for Scotland. Lights out. That shouldn't be a problem.

"I don't want to wait." Boldness was required. She went on her toes and kissed him again.

He stood there for a moment, but then his hands found her backside and he hauled her up. "Fuck, I shouldn't let you do this to me. There's a way to handle this, but if you can't wait then neither can I."

His fingers gripped her cheeks, pulling her up so her pelvis rested against his. She could feel the hard line of his erection. He did want her. He rubbed that thick part against her. Big. He was really big, way bigger than Brandon had been. She whimpered a little.

"Hush," he said, his voice like gravel. "You can take me. You were built to take me."

She wasn't so sure about that. He was a Mack Truck, and she was kind of worried that her girl parts were more in line with a Prius, but it didn't matter. She didn't give a damn about the penetration part. That was the part she had to get through to get to the good part, the part where he was happy and held her all night long.

"I'll make sure you're ready. Just follow my lead." The words skimmed across her skin. So tempting. She could just follow him and everything would be all right.

He opened the door and led her inside her tiny bedroom. The bed dominated the room leaving only a little space for a wardrobe and a nightstand. She might be the only person in the world who came to London and thought the living space was bigger than she'd been used to, but hospital rooms would do that to a girl.

"Where's the light, baby?" Lee asked.

She didn't answer him. She really didn't want that light on. The ambient light that filtered in through the window shades from the busy street below was bad enough. She couldn't put her body on display. It wasn't pretty. She let her hands do what she'd wanted all along. She touched him. His chest, his arms. Steel covered in soft, warm flesh. She pulled at the bottom of his T-shirt.

"Damn it, Avery. I'm trying to play this first time your way, but you should understand that after this, I'm in charge." He pulled the shirt free and tossed it to the side.

She still wasn't completely sure what he meant. Panic was threatening to take her over. Her mind wouldn't stop racing. Even when he kissed her this time, she couldn't stop thinking about the fact that she wasn't wearing anything pretty under her clothes. She was wearing spandex underwear and a minimizer bra. He had to be used to women who wore lingerie. She wasn't that girl. When Adam had tried to get her to buy something frilly, she'd laughed and refused because she had looked ridiculous in it. She had looked like a fool.

God, she was sick of looking like a fool.

Poor sick Avery. Poor girl, the universe must be against

her. It would have been better off if she'd died with them. What kind of life can she have now?

She'd heard the whispers. They were imprinted on her brain.

Lee's hands were on her sweater, pulling it off. Would he think her breasts were okay? They were already sagging a little. Her nipples were too big. They weren't small and tight and perky.

Concentrate, Avery. This is going to be fine. You'll get through this. You can do this.

She shook a little when he unclasped her bra. Her breasts bounced free. Yes. Definitely saggy. God, she was only twenty-eight. Shouldn't they still be really firm?

But they had nursed a baby. Her baby.

Lee's hands played at her breasts, tweaking the nipples while he kissed her neck.

She winced a little. He was rough.

Lee pulled back. "Did I hurt you?"

"No." It hadn't been bad. She tried to get close to him again, but he moved away.

"That shouldn't hurt, Avery."

"It didn't."

"Yes, it did."

She sighed, thinking about grabbing her sweater again. She hated being exposed. "It wasn't bad. Just be a little gentler."

He stared at her. "This is about as gentle as I get. I'll get a whole lot rougher, Avery. I wasn't worried that I'd done something wrong. That was a little minor stimulation that should have been pleasant. Your nipples are sexual zones. But you have to be in a certain mood. You're not in that mood, are you, Avery?"

It felt like an accusation. "I'm fine."

"Then take off the rest of your clothes and let me feel your pussy. I can tell in two seconds flat if you're ready for sex or not."

She reached for the sweater now, hauling it up to cover her breasts. "Why are you being like this?"

He stood up, reminding her just how big he was. He was a tiger in a small cage, predatory and restless. "You want me to throw you down on the bed and get this over with, don't you?"

"Would that be so bad? I'm not pushing you away. I'm offering you sex."

"No, you're offering me a quickie. I don't particularly like quickies. And worse than that, you're offering me a quickie where I take from you and give nothing back. I'm beginning to suspect you don't think very highly of me. First you decided I was a hustler trying to play you for cash, and now I'm a man who just fucks and doesn't care about his partner's pleasure."

The room had gone icy cold, and it was all coming from Lee. He seemed to have grown an inch or two, and if he'd opened his mouth and suddenly had fangs, it wouldn't have shocked her. He was a predator, and she was a fluffy little bunny who might make a nice snack.

"I understand. I won't bother you again." She needed to get him out of here. It had all been an enormous mistake. She wasn't ready for any of this. She wasn't a sexy woman. She'd had her shot at a relationship and it had died in that car, the light of her life snuffing out with Brandon's and Madison's.

Maybe the nurses had been right. Maybe it would have been better to die.

Lee huffed a little. "You aren't the woman I thought you were."

Yeah, she got that a lot. "You should go."

"Not until I've had my say." He reached for his shirt. "You're lying down. If that's because I'm not the one you want, then that's perfectly fine, but you should have the courtesy to me and to yourself to say it."

"It's not that."

"Yeah, that's what I thought. You're giving up. You're letting fear rule you. That's not a way to live. It's a way to exist until the inevitable happens. Is that how you live your life, Avery Charles? You just want to float through until you die, never taking a chance because it might not work out?"

How could he say that? A little kernel of anger sparked through her system. She didn't deserve that. She was well aware that the best thing to do would be to just walk away, to shoo him out of her apartment. Why should she care that he thought she was a doormat? But she did. "I lost the use of my freaking legs, Lee. I didn't float through my twenties. I spent them on a fucking hospital bed fighting to learn to walk again."

"That's what I want. That's the girl I saw. And you curse at me all you like. I'm keeping track of it for later punishment."

And what the hell was up with that? Righteous anger burned through her. "Punishment? You don't have any right to punish me. And I can curse. I choose not to most of the time, but don't think it doesn't go through my head, asshole. I was trying to give you something. I was trying to give you my body."

"That's where you fucked up, little girl. I don't want your body. I want your soul. I want your everything. And I definitely want your orgasms. I want them all. I'll be a greedy bastard, savoring them and hoarding them all for myself. You wanted to give me your body? I can buy that on a street corner, sweetheart. You're the one who's being selfish now."

"How is it selfish to offer to have sex? I don't understand what you want." She was coming down from the high of her anger. She hated this feeling. Her emotions were bouncing around like a Ping-Pong ball.

"You weren't really offering me anything of yourself." Lee backed off slightly, his voice softening just a bit.

"What do you want from me?" She was truly at a loss. And she wished she'd kept her bra on.

He pulled the sweater out of her hand and reached over and turned on the light. "First off, I want you to stop hiding yourself from me. You're the one making this tawdry by pretending it's dirty and not worthy of the light of day."

"I didn't mean it that way." She was just trying to make things go smoothly.

"Yes, you did. Tell me you really want me." His voice had gone positively gentle. His hand cupped her cheek, forcing her to look up at him. God, he was gorgeous. No man should have those sensual lips.

"I want you." She wanted him so badly. She just didn't trust that he could possibly want her.

"No, you don't, but you will." He stepped back and tucked his shirt in. "We're going to do this my way. We tried yours and it didn't work, so I'm taking control. I should have done it in the first place. If I thought you had some, I would tell you to change into fet wear, but you don't happen to have a corset and some PVC hiding in that closet, do you?"

"I don't know what PVC is," she admitted, her heart aching a little. "I don't think this is a good idea, Lee. I don't think I can be what you need. I'm not experienced, and what experience I have wasn't very good. Don't get me wrong. I loved my husband, but the sex wasn't spectacular. I think I'm just one of those women who can't be sexy. I was trying to please you, but I couldn't."

Even in the dim light, she could see him staring, assessing. "And I think you're one of those women who can't stop thinking long enough to let her body take over. Look, Avery, the sex you've had happened with a kid. Was your husband older than you? More experienced?"

She shook her head. They had both been virgins.

"Then you have no idea what it can be like. I look at sex differently than most people. It's an exchange, and it should be good for both parties. I don't want you to spread your legs and let me have you because you want someone to hold you. If you want me to hold you, ask me. I want you to spread your legs because you can't wait another single second for my cock. I want that pussy ripe and ready and weeping for a big dick to split it wide and have its way. I want your nipples to peak because I walk into a room and you remember every dirty thing I can do to them. I want you to want me. I can make you crave me. I don't want some drive-by fucking that gets me off and I forget it five minutes later. I want to fuck all night long. I want to feel it all the next day because my cock got so used to being deep inside your body. If that's what you want, then get dressed in the sexiest thing you own and agree that I'm the boss when it comes to sex." He turned and walked out. "I'll give you five minutes to decide. I'll be waiting in your living room. If you really want me, you'll dress exactly how I've told you to dress and you'll present yourself to me for inspection. And Avery, no bra and no underwear. You won't need them."

The door closed behind him, and she had to remember how to breathe.

She wasn't sexy. She wasn't orgasmic.

But what if she could be? Lee hadn't been right about everything, but he had a few points. He'd told her he wanted to be in control and then she'd tried to make all the decisions. He had more experience, but she'd decided she knew best. She hadn't listened to him.

He wanted control. He wanted her to really want him. She didn't understand, but if she ever wanted to understand, she had to try.

She'd taught herself how to walk again. That had been an enormous mountain to climb. Why was she so scared of this? She'd faced worse, but she was cowering in her boots over not wearing underwear and a bra? She'd lost so much. Was she willing to lose this, too?

What was she really risking? She might look dumb. She could end up with her heart broken, but at least she would have proven it still worked.

She'd come across the ocean to change her life—to have a life. What was life without a few risks?

She got her phone out and sent a quick text to Adam letting him know she was home and who she was with so if she was serially murdered, at least they would have a starting place for where to find her body.

But she was going to do this because she felt safe with Lee. And because she wanted to finally understand what it really meant to want someone.

* * * *

Liam forced himself to be patient. Why had he given her that fucking ultimatum? What had he been thinking?

He'd been thinking about how he wanted the relationship to go. He hadn't been thinking about the fucking op. He'd been thinking about what he needed and

123

the idea of her not wanting him the way he wanted her. His cock had been hard for days thinking about taking her, but he'd felt her arousal. It was a pathetic thing compared to his.

She just didn't understand what they could do. She was like a virgin.

God, he didn't do virgins.

But he wanted to do this one. The minute he'd figured out what the problem was, he'd gone into overdrive. If he'd thought he was hard before, realizing that Avery had never had an orgasm sent him into "I took two Viagra" territory.

He finally had something to fucking offer her. He wasn't cut out for long term. He was a fucker of a boyfriend. Hell, he hadn't been a boyfriend since he'd groped around with Katie Reilly during his *A* level years. After that, it had been the Army and the SAS and then working with intelligence. Women had been comfort, nothing more.

Then he'd gotten his brother killed and nothing could comfort him. He'd finally settled down and found a little place for himself at Sanctum, but he wasn't anyone's boyfriend.

But he was good at getting a girl off. He was fine at knowing how and where to touch a woman so she was panting and begging for it. And he sure as bloody hell knew how to use his cock. He could teach her that her body was built for pleasure. He could give her that.

If she took him up on his offer.

Minutes ticked by, and he wondered how the fuck he was going to salvage this. And he hadn't even planted the bugs he was supposed to plant. Ian was going to kick his ass.

Alex would have to try if she kicked him out. He couldn't stand the thought of Alex's hands on her. Alex would be gentle. Alex would treat her with courtesy. Alex wouldn't have told her it was his way or the highway.

"Is this all right?"

He turned, surprised she'd been able to sneak up on him, but then his mind hadn't been on the mission in days. His mind and his dick had been in perfect harmony, focused on her.

She stood in front of the tiny bathroom wearing a denim miniskirt and a tank top that should be illegal. Oh, it would look perfectly fine on someone else. On a woman with smaller breasts, it would look sporty. On Avery it looked lascivious, like she was just waiting for a man to rip it off her so he could suck those breasts in his mouth, getting her nipples hard, her pussy wet.

She fidgeted, trying to pull the skirt down. "I usually wear it with leggings. Well, I actually bought it yesterday. A friend told me it looked nice, but I think it's too short."

It was far too short, and it qualified as fet wear. He was going to have to buy Adam a beer. *Smart bugger.* "Let me see. Turn around."

She bit into her bottom lip, but she turned slowly, allowing him to see the skirt from the backside.

"Stop," he commanded. She likely would have just kept going until she'd made a complete circle, but he wanted to look at her ass. He groaned a little. Her backside was round with nice-sized hips that flared from her waist led to a truly spectacularly juicy ass.

All of his life he'd adored full-figured women. He'd denied himself for years, opting for skinny little young things because they didn't make his mouth water like this one did. Those barely legal women had wanted one thing from him—a good time. They hadn't moved him. They hadn't made him want to sink inside and never leave.

"Bend over." He wanted to see just how kind Adam had been. She hesitated. "This won't work if you don't obey me."

Her eyes widened. "I don't know that I like the word 'obey.'"

How did he put this to her in a way she could understand? BDSM could seem weird and foreign, but it made sense to him. "Think about it as a rule. Look, do you have directions you have to follow in order to get the outcome you want? Like building a desk or something? Do you follow the directions? Do you obey the rules?"

"Yes."

"Why do you think there aren't rules to how sex will work? You didn't want to talk to me about what you wanted. You pushed me into the room so I wouldn't turn on the light because you knew damn well I would push back on that, didn't you?"

She stayed where she was. "Yes. I don't want you to see me. I don't look like one of those girls in a magazine."

He groaned, the sound coming from deep in his chest. "Those girls in the magazines are airbrushed and way too thin. The camera adds pounds so those girls are so skinny I wouldn't be able to fuck them for fear I would break them. I want a woman, Avery, not some tiny freaking thing whose waistline only proves she doesn't eat. I want a woman who can take me. I want a woman I can hold on to. So bend over because I want to see your ass. I want to look at it because I've been dreaming about it for days. It's hot and round and so fucking juicy I can't stand it. Get me hot, Avery. Show me your ass."

It took her a moment, but she bent over, her spine curving. The skirt twisted up until he could see plainly that she had complied with his edict about the underwear. Her round, curvy ass cheeks peeked out from the ridiculously high hem of her skirt. Sweet cheeks. So fucking pretty.

126

"That's beautiful, love." Fuck, his cock was dying, and he couldn't just do her yet. He needed to push her boundaries. He needed to make her howl, and he couldn't do that by just shoving his cock in.

He let his fingertips find her thighs. The minute he touched her, she gasped and stood straight up.

"Did I hurt you?" He knew the answer to the question. He'd startled her because she wasn't expecting it, but she needed to learn here and now that he would touch her any way he wanted to.

"No." She was shivering, but it wasn't cold in the room. The room was nice and toasty warm.

"Then bend back over. I'm only going to touch you, Avery." He couldn't expect her to act like a trained submissive. He had to be patient and teach her what he wanted. Later, if she reacted like this, he would place her over his knee and she would feel the flat of his hand on her ass. Fuck, his cock loved that image.

"This is weird, you know," she said, but she was complying.

"Weird is in the eye of the beholder." He let his hand skim along her thighs. Soft, sweet skin. "I think it's weird how vanilla people just jump into a bed and fuck and don't ever relish the moment, don't talk to each other about what works and what doesn't. So many people just expect sex to happen, but really great sex takes work, like everything in life. You have to talk to your partner. If you were working on a project with a partner, you would talk to him, wouldn't you?"

"Yes." Her voice came out on a little gasp. "But you make it sound like this is work. I'm having a hard time thinking about sex as a project to manage."

He barely touched the cheeks of her ass, just a little

tickle on her flesh, and her muscles clenched. "Only because you don't take it seriously."

"I take it very seriously," she shot back.

"No, you take the choice of your partner seriously, but not the sex itself. The sex itself you view as something you have to give up to get to what you really want, and that's companionship and affection. You can't buy those with sex, Avery. Those will come or not, and it doesn't mean a damn thing to any man. Not really. He'll take sex from you even if he doesn't particularly like you. He'll take it because you offer it up so easily. Again—not the relationship, but the sex. You're offering me easy sex. Sex where I don't have to work, but I want to work because I do like you and I do feel affection for you. Do you understand?"

"You think I should ask for more."

"No, I think you should demand more."

"That doesn't sound very submissive, Lee."

He sighed as he touched her cheeks one last time and backed away. "You can stand up now." He sank back on her sofa. It would do for what he wanted. For what she needed. "Come sit in my lap."

She moved a little awkwardly, trying to pull the skirt down. "I can't get it down far enough. If I sit in your lap, it's going to ride up."

"Sit in my lap, Avery." He let his voice go hard and was happy to see her respond. She did what he wanted, though she took her sweet time doing it, trying valiantly to keep as much denim between them as possible. She settled in, holding herself up.

And that wouldn't do. One little pull of his hand and the skirt was bunched around her waist.

Avery shrieked a little, but he kept her where he wanted her. "Lee, you don't understand. I'm...I'm going to ruin your pants. God, I need to go clean up."

"Oh, is my baby's little pussy finally getting wet?" He put his hand on her knee.

She tried to cross her legs. "Yes, and it's a lot. It feels very messy."

He could smell her now. Bending over and presenting her ass had done something for her. So had dirty talk. Yeah, he could talk dirty. "Messy is good. I want that pussy dirty and ripe when I start to eat it."

Her skin turned the prettiest shade of pink. "How can you just talk like that?"

"Like what?" He cupped her knees. "Stop shutting me out. Start talking to me."

She relaxed a little, her knees falling apart and giving him access. "It's the dirty talk. No one's ever talked to me that way."

"And you don't like it?" His hand crept up, and he wondered if she would lie to him. She obviously liked it. He could feel the heat of her pussy. Her pretty eyes dilated when he started spouting a little sweet filth.

"I like it. I wouldn't have said I would. I don't like to hear a lot of cursing, but when you say it, it sounds different."

"Because we're in a safe place. Baby, there's a huge difference between some construction worker yelling out about how nice your tits look and me telling you how I want to get my mouth on those same gorgeous tits and never leave them. There's no disrespect in me telling you just how much I want to fuck your little pussy."

"I don't know why."

He didn't pretend to misunderstand her. He knew damn well what she was talking about. "We have to work on your self-esteem, baby. I want to fuck you because you make my cock hard. I want to fuck you because I'm pretty sure you're going to be the sweetest fuck I've ever had. You're going to be like sugar on my cock. I'll be addicted to that little bit of sunshine after a while and no other pussy will do. But this is where I play the Dom card, Avery. I'm trying to go slow with that, but if you start in on yourself again, I will spank you. I hear one more word out of your mouth about how this body isn't sexy and you'll place yourself over my lap and take twenty. Do you understand?"

She shoved her head into his shoulder with a little cry. Her body shook.

He'd scared the hell out of her. His heart threatened to crack. He'd fucked up again. He'd misjudged her. He'd been so certain of her natural submissiveness, but what if she couldn't handle it? He should have played this vanilla. He'd taken the chance because he wanted her so fucking badly. Liam, not Lee. Not some fucking construct he'd come up with for his undercover work, but Liam, the screwed-up man he was needed her on a level he'd never known existed.

And now she would kick him out for being a brutal bastard.

Her face came up and instead of tears, he saw laughter and a pretty pink flush. She was laughing, her lips curling up in the sweetest smile. "Lee, you're making me crazy. I think I'm a freak because that getting wet thing happened again when you started talking about spanking me."

Her laugh filled the air for the first time all night, and it looked like she was having some fun. Fun with herself. Fun with him.

"Spanking can be very erotic," he said, tightening his hands on her, pulling her back in. "It can also hurt like hell."

Her voice was deeper, more intimate than before. Her eyes came up, questioning him. "How would you know?"

It was time for some real honesty. He felt himself smile as he stared down at her. It felt so fucking right to have her in his lap. Like she belonged there. "I told you, baby. I'm trained. You don't get trained at Club Sanctum without trying everything out. How can I know how to spank a partner if I haven't been spanked myself?"

She cuddled up against him. "I wish I'd been there to see that. I'm trying to imagine you lying over someone's lap. I'm glad you tried it. It doesn't seem fair that you would just get to make all the rules and hand out all the discipline if you didn't know what it felt like."

She'd relaxed a little, but her legs had come together again and he wasn't having that. "Keep your legs spread, Avery. I want access to your pussy. While we're playing together, your pussy belongs to me."

Her face tightened, but she spread her legs. "Why do you call it play?"

"It's what we call intimate scenes. I'm not a Dom twenty-four seven. Some Doms are, but I want a partner, not a slave. I want to be in charge of sex, and I want any woman I'm deeply involved with to come to me when there's trouble. Do you understand?"

That was important. It was part of his cover. He needed to become her lover so when the shit hit the fan, and it would, she would turn to him and let him take care of her. He needed her to not hesitate. He needed her to turn to him, to trust him.

She didn't even know his name. She had never heard his real voice.

A bright smile crossed her face. "I do understand, but you should know I lead a very boring life. I don't know how much you're going to have to save me. Nothing ever happens to me." She frowned. "Except for car accidents. I

131

probably shouldn't drive." She gasped a little, one hand covering her mouth. "I can't believe I just joked about that."

He wasn't supposed to know what a breakthrough that was, but he felt it. She'd likely never joked about it before, but she had with him. She'd felt safe enough to joke with him about the worst thing that had ever happened to her. A deep affection curled in his gut. She was so sweet, and she trusted him. She shouldn't. He was a bastard who was lying to her every moment they were together, but she trusted him and that meant something to Liam.

"How about I promise to drive?" His hand was on her upper thigh, just inches from that pussy. He could feel her heat. It nearly singed his fingers. "I think you'll find I'm quite good at being in the driver's seat."

"I'm a little scared." She stared up at him, honest desire nearly ripping him up.

He had to get control of himself. "There's no reason. Let me take care of you. Let me take control. I promise I won't steer you wrong."

"You really want me? You're being honest?"

He was lying through his teeth about everything but the part where he wanted her. He wanted her like he wanted his next fucking breath. He fucking needed her. "I am. I won't lie to you, baby."

He would lie to her every day of their relationship because it was the only way to protect her. He would tell her what she needed to hear. He would tell her he was a man who could love her with an open heart.

She never needed to know that he didn't have a fucking heart.

He pressed his lips to hers, savoring just how good she felt. "Let me have you."

She never needed to know how he really viewed her.

How Liam and not Lee viewed her. Liam viewed her as payment. Her sweetness, her innocent caring, was payment for every inch of pain he'd endured. He had sacrificed, and she was his reward.

His prize was a few days, a week at most, where he got to love her, to sink himself deep inside her innocence and pretend he was worthy.

"Let me have you, baby," he whispered against her lips.

Her arms drifted up, surrounding his neck. "Yes."

Liam took her lips and claimed his prize.

Chapter Seven

Avery was in a slow descent to madness. Lee kept kissing her, his hands so close to the center of her body. She'd never thought of her vagina as her core, but it was blatantly obvious now that it was the place from which all feeling ran.

Her pussy, god she was thinking of it as her pussy, was wet. Ripe. Ready. She'd never wanted the way she did now. She'd never really understood what the word want meant until she'd sat down on Lee Donnelly's lap and spread her legs.

"I want to touch you. Tell me your pussy belongs to me tonight."

His voice somehow had a straight line to her pelvis. What was that fluttery feeling she kept getting? She should be more cautious, but every damn word he said made sense to her. Honesty. Communication. Trust. All words that made her feel safe.

Her pussy had never really belonged to anyone. She hadn't really cared about it. It hadn't been a part of her body that mattered. Her legs had been the center of her world, but her girl parts had been fairly useless.

Until his hands had skimmed along her skin. Every inch of flesh lit up under his fingers. What had he asked? Her brain felt like mush. Her pussy belonged to him? "Yes."

It was easy since no one else had ever really wanted her

pussy. It had been hers for years by rights of being on her body, but she hadn't done anything interesting with it. She hadn't thought about it. Lee brought it out in her so it was easy to answer him.

The air in her lungs fled as his fingers invaded. He split her labia, his fingers pressing her pussy wide and swirling all around. He pinched at her clitoris making her squirm and want more.

"Tell me what you like," he demanded.

He didn't ask. He commanded and it did something for her. He wanted to talk. He wanted to know what got her hot. How did she tell him that what got her really hot was him? All he had to do was walk into a room and her temperature rose, her interest flared.

"I love it when you kiss me." She adored the way his mouth moved on hers. Kissing before had been sloppy and something to endure to get to the part where she was held. He'd been right about that. All she'd wanted at the beginning was for him to hold her, but that was changing. Her legs were splayed, and it felt good. His fingers played in her pussy, and she wanted more.

He didn't move his hand. It stayed right on her pussy, but his lips descended, covering her own. His tongue gently played at her lower lip, and she opened her mouth, willing him to come inside. She'd never been kissed the way Lee kissed her. When she'd been kissed before it had been messy and awkward, but Lee inhaled her. He made her feel like she was a delicious treat to be savored.

He made her feel sexy.

His fingers, so gentle before, became firmer, more forceful as he stroked her pussy. He split her labial lips and dipped inside.

"That's where my cock wants to be, love. It wants to be

right there on the precipice, waiting to delve inside." He stroked around her entry, making long, slow circles, drawing out her arousal. "Can you feel it?"

She gasped as a single finger stroked inside. She'd had actual real sex but nothing so erotic. Lee had been right. She'd used sex in an attempt to gain love and affection, but now what she really wanted was sex. Dirty. Nasty. Filthy sex.

She wanted to ride that finger and see where it took her. Her hips seemed to move of their own accord as though they were magnetically attracted to his hand.

"Who's in charge of this?" Lee asked, his mouth against her ear. Warm breath covered her skin, making her shiver and want more.

She didn't even think. Her whole brain was focused and centered on that finger. He'd put the image in her mind. His cock. Hard male flesh. His finger massaged all around her pussy, but she wanted more. She needed to get it inside. "You are. You're in charge."

The words pushed out, but she didn't care. All she cared about was getting that finger deep inside and finally knowing what all the fuss was about. She'd read novels and seen movies where sex seemed to be the end all be all of existence, but she'd never had a glimmer of understanding until now. She pushed her hips down, trying to trap him, to force him to shove his finger deep.

She nearly cried out when he withdrew that finger completely.

"I'm glad you agree, love. Now hop up and take off the rest of your clothes. I want to see you."

She blinked a couple of times before she processed what he was saying. "But I was so close."

A sexy little smile curled his lips up. "No you weren't,

but you will be. Avery, trust me. I'll give you what you need. Now give me what I need. I need to see you."

He wasn't seeing enough of her? Her pussy was out for him to see. Why did he have to push it? Most men would have just shoved her skirt up and had their way with her, but no, Lee Donnelly had to make a huge production number out of it.

Because it was important. Because sex should have meaning beyond having an orgasm and falling asleep. Because he took it seriously.

She finally figured it out. Yes, he was looking for pleasure, but beyond that he was looking for something more. He was looking for a connection. He was looking for trust and honesty, and she wanted all those things, too. This whole night could have been a forgettable and likely regrettable fling, but Lee seemed intent on teaching her something. That she mattered. That what she wanted mattered, and she shouldn't accept less so she had to take what he wanted just as seriously.

"Talk to me, Avery." Serious green eyes pinned her. He wouldn't let her get away with anything, and that suddenly seemed sexy to her.

"I'm afraid when I take my clothes off that you won't want me anymore."

He groaned and put his forehead to hers. "Damn it, baby. We have a lot of work to do. You were in an accident, and you're worried I won't like the scars, right?"

"Yes, though they mostly faded. I'm also worried about how big I am. I'm not pencil thin, and my breasts sag. I have stretch marks." She hadn't really thought about those. They told a story, those stretch marks and the way her breasts hung, and he wouldn't be able to avoid the C-section scar that split her body in a curve above her pelvic bone. Would he ask? Would he know what it meant? Would it mean a thing if she didn't tell him? "I had a baby when I was eighteen."

She hadn't told anyone about Maddie. Thomas had only found out because he'd run a background check on her before she was hired. She'd kept that part of her life utterly secret, but sitting on his lap with her body warm and his arms around her, it seemed wrong to withhold it. That was what she was doing, she suddenly realized. She was withholding. She was using the knowledge like a wall to keep herself safe. No one had to know the real Avery Charles and then no one could really hurt her, but suddenly it also seemed like no one could really connect with her, either. No one could love her.

His face softened. "What happened? Was it the accident?"

Those hands, so dominant and intent the moment before, now stroked and pulled her close. He was fluid in his comfort, moving from predatory sexual male to protective and open in an instant. He'd said he would give her what she needed. And what he seemed to need was her trust. "I don't want to talk about it tonight, Lee. Please. I'm not trying to shut you out. I just don't want tonight to be about the past."

He sighed. "I'll have the story, Avery. I'll have all your stories in the end, but we'll play this your way tonight."

She nodded. He'd given her something, and it was time to return his kindness. She scooted off his lap. Just moments before she'd felt sexy and powerful, and now she was right back to awkward and ungainly. And her pussy was really wet. Should she clean that up?

"Hold on." Lee looked ridiculously decadent sitting on her little couch. It was far too small for him, but he inhabited the space like he owned it. "Don't touch your skirt yet. I like it like this. You look like you hiked it up for your Master so he could play with you and get you ready for a nice long fuck. Your pussy is awfully pretty. Why did you start shaving? Most women who aren't having sex wouldn't bother."

He was staring at her pussy. It was so weird and so hot. "Surgeries. I had a few in that area and they always shaved me. I hated the way it felt when it started to grow back."

Sometimes shaving her girl parts was the only time they were ever touched.

"It's beautiful." His thumb came out, and he slowly swiped down the center. His thumb was covered in her juice and without a single obvious inhibition, he sucked it into his mouth. "You taste so fucking good, baby. Has anyone ever eaten that pussy? Has anyone ever put their mouth on it and made a meal of you?"

Yes, this was what she needed. She needed to sink into the moment, letting it crowd out all of the tragedy of the past. She'd lived there for so long, and she didn't want to tonight. She wanted to be in the moment and the moment meant Lee. "No. No one's ever touched me down there with his mouth."

Lee sat back, crossing his legs. "I thought not. We'll get to that. Now take off the clothes. I'm not asking you to do this because I'm trying to decide if I want to sleep with you or not. We're going to fuck, baby. That's a foregone conclusion. I'm asking because I want to see you naked."

"I didn't think you were asking at all," she muttered, her heart racing a little.

"Excellent, then you're learning. Take off your clothes. This is what we call the presentation. A good submissive will present herself to her Master, showing him exactly what she's offering him—her beautiful body and her trust that he can take care of her."

He wasn't giving her any way out. He was saying all the right things. Could she really trust it? He was almost too good to be true, but good things came around so rarely in her life that she was going to risk it. She was going to grasp the moment with both hands, and if it all fell apart later, she would find a way to forgive herself. She pulled the tank top over her head and placed it on the chair behind her before working on her skirt. Her hands trembled slightly as she worked the button and undid the zipper. She pushed the skirt off, her hands touching the scars on her right leg, but he'd already seen those. He didn't seem bothered by them.

All the while he sat back, silent, as though waiting for a show to begin. She folded the skirt, but her eyes were on him. She'd felt his erection before while she sat on his lap, but it tented his jeans and there was no way to miss just how long and thick it was. That had to be a trick of the light. He couldn't be that big. He couldn't be that aroused.

"You're gorgeous, baby. Turn around and let me see your ass." His voice had deepened, thickening to a rich honey.

She turned, deeply aware that he was looking at her backside.

"Stay where you are."

She heard him getting up, the couch shifting. His shoes tapped against the floor, but she held still because he hadn't led her wrong yet. He seemed intent on keeping her on the edge, but she was rapidly discovering that it also kept her in the moment. Her thoughts, normally so fast and fractured and going in a million directions, were focused. They were focused on him and on the hum of her body. He'd been so right. She'd tried to push him because she didn't know this place existed. He'd demanded obedience so her rebellious brain would have to shut off.

She closed her eyes, waiting for whatever he intended to do.

A single finger traced down her spine. "I think you're lovely, Avery. I'll prove it to you in the end, you know. It might take a while, but after I've had you a couple of hundred times, you'll have to admit that I want you. You'll have to admit that this body is sexy and fuckable." His fingertips rested at the base of her spine. "I'm going to have you every way a man can have a woman. Do you understand?"

Nope. And she couldn't really think because his hand moved lower, caressing her cheeks, but he wanted an answer. "Yes. You're going to sleep with me."

"No," he corrected. "I'm going to fuck you. Turn around. I want to see my pussy."

She turned again, but when she put weight on her right leg, it faltered.

Lee was right there, holding her up, making sure she didn't find the floor. His arms were around her waist, pulling her lower body against his. She balanced against him, her skin touching the rough denim of his jeans, the hard line of his erection rubbing against her belly.

"I've got you," he murmured. He bent over, brushing their lips together. "I won't let you fall, baby."

But she was falling hard and fast. There was no way to deny it. He was the most exciting thing to happen to her in years, and she wasn't the type of woman to just brush that off. She was setting herself up for an enormous fall, but she couldn't pull away from him. "Thank you."

He smiled, releasing her and dropping to his knees. He looked up at her, dark hair messy and perfect. "That's thank you, Sir, when we're playing."

141

She could give him that. "Thank you, Sir." She touched his hair, felt the silk under her fingertips. "Thank you for everything, Sir."

An arrogant grin crossed his face. "Oh, baby, I haven't begun to earn that thank you, but I think I'll start now. You hold still or I'll stop. This is just a little appetizer to make sure you're damn good and ready. Later, I'll spread you out and eat this pussy to my heart's content, but my dick is dying. I need to get inside you pretty damn quick."

His hands were on her hips, holding her in place while his face went right into her pussy.

She was shocked for a moment, but then he ran his tongue across her clit and she couldn't think anymore. Wet and firm, his tongue slid across her flesh lighting her up and making her squirm. She'd thought she'd loved his fingers playing in her pussy, but they had nothing on his tongue. Fire seemed to lick up her body, threatening to consume her.

She knew it was nasty, dirty. He had his mouth all over her girl parts, and she was wet and creamy and he was licking it all up. She stared down at his dark head moving as he worked her pussy up and down.

"Spread your legs. I need more." He groaned against her skin. She felt it sizzling across her body.

She spread her legs and his tongue speared up inside, invading her pussy like his cock surely would. Soft but strong, his tongue impaled her. He was making love to her with nothing but his mouth. He thrust up inside her pussy and then licked a long path to her clitoris, pressing down firmly.

She couldn't help but cry out.

"That's what I want. Make those little sounds, baby. Let me hear how much you want it." He let go of her hips and parted her pussy with his thumbs, fully exposing her clitoris.

He put his lips right over that little nubbin and sucked it inside.

Avery couldn't breathe. Close. She was so close, she could taste it. Her blood started to pound. Her arms shook.

And he stopped.

Lee got up, moving with a grace Avery wasn't sure she could ever feel, leaving her completely off kilter. She tried to catch her breath, but it was hard because he pulled his shirt over his head and she was assaulted with the vision of the most perfect chest she'd ever seen.

Broad shoulders and perfectly sculpted pecs led down to an eight pack and a lean waist. Even as she tried to take in how beautiful his chest was, he shoved his jeans off his hips and his cock bobbed free. He pulled a small blue square out of his pocket and held it in his left hand.

Yeah, she hadn't seen anything like that before. Long and thick with a plum-shaped head. She'd wanted to turn the light off, but then she would have missed looking at him. Michelangelo couldn't have sculpted a more perfect man.

But he wasn't perfect. He had a lot of scars. A long one ran across his chest, marring the silky-smooth skin there.

He reached his hand out, dragging her fingers to his chest. "Touch it. We all have scars, Avery. Yours don't make you less beautiful. They just mean you survived."

Yes, she'd survived, but only now did she feel like she'd lived. She let her fingers cross the scar that marked his own survival. "This wasn't a nail gun, was it?"

He shook his head. "I was in the Army. I got in a knife fight in Afghanistan. I survived, and I'm happy to be here with you."

She was so close to him, their naked bodies almost touching. "Can I touch you?"

He smiled a little. "You're already touching me. Ask for

143

what you want, Avery. Use those dirty words I taught you. What do you want to touch? Don't be shy. I can still taste your pussy on my tongue. There's no room for shyness anymore. And if you put a polite, sweet little 'Sir' on the end of your request, that would make me very happy."

"I want to touch your cock, Sir." The words were easier now. He'd been right. This was intimacy as sweet and pure as any hug.

He pulled her hand down. "Touch me. Take me in your hand and grip my dick tight. Stroke me. I won't break."

He was so big in her hand. She could barely get her fingers around him. His hand came around hers forcing her to be rougher. He taught her how to touch him, pulling her hand over his cock, stroking up and down from the thick base up to cover the head.

She loved the deep groan that came from his chest as she took over. She didn't have to worry about whether or not she was pleasing him. He would show her how. He would talk to her. There was such sweet freedom in that. A creamy pearl of arousal tipped the head of his dick, and she let it coat her fingers.

"That's it, baby." He growled his approval.

He pulsed in her palm, getting even bigger as she stroked him.

"Stop. I don't want to come in your hand, and I'm going to if you don't stop." He didn't let go of her hand, merely pulled it away from his cock. He backed up to the couch and let his big body fall back so he was sitting down. "I want to be inside you."

She stood there watching him as he tore open the blue package in his hand and rolled a condom on. She was really doing this. He was big and hard and ready to fuck. The word came easily now. It had seemed ugly before, but now she felt the affection behind it.

"Come on. Ride me." He started to pull her on his lap. "Straddle me and take my cock."

"Don't you want to go to the bedroom?" Avery asked.

His eyes hardened. "No. I do not, and if you don't obey me, I'm going to spank that gorgeous ass. I'm going to explain this to you because it's all new, but in the future, you're going to give me what I want or you'll have some discipline coming."

She didn't wait for the explanation. She was being silly and obnoxious again. He'd been perfect, and she was questioning him. He'd brought her more pleasure than she'd ever had in her life, and she still pushed back. It was stupid. She wasn't going to do it anymore. She climbed onto his lap.

"That's what I want." His hand circled her waist. She could feel the head of his cock right at her pussy, teasing her. She put her hands on his shoulders, reveling in the feel of hard steel under soft skin. "I'm letting you set the pace because you're going to be so fucking tight. I don't want to hurt you. You need to control the penetration this time."

His hand went down between them, and he guided his cock. His eyes were down, staring at that place where he'd started to penetrate her. "God, that's so fucking pretty."

His voice was deep, guttural, and it had taken on a lovely musical quality she hadn't heard before. It suited him so much better than the flat cadence of his normal voice. Avery swore to get him to talk like that every time they came together.

She lowered herself on to him carefully, well aware that her whole body was involved. She could feel how slick she was.

"Fuck, baby, you feel so good. Tell me you want me."

Did she want him? How could he doubt it? She looked

at him, trying to find a hint of deception, that he was playing with her, but his face was taut with arousal and desire. For all his beauty, he was just a man and she wasn't giving him credit. She was looking at his gorgeous face and body and thinking he never had a moment's insecurity. It was wrong. He was human, and he was asking her for something.

She leaned forward and touched her lips to his. He needed her, and she wouldn't hold a damn thing back from him. She could taste herself on his lips, tangy, sweet and so intimate it hurt her heart. "I want you, Lee. I need you. I want you like I want my next breath."

He pulled on her hips. "Take more."

He wasn't as in control as he wanted her to think. She could see that, and it made it so much easier to sink onto his cock. He filled her, invading every inch and stretching her pussy until she thought she might burst, but she was determined to take every centimeter of that hard, hot cock. She wanted it. She craved it.

She let gravity do its work, impaling herself on his length. His face was tight, his eyes down. He was such a pervert, watching her pussy take his cock, and she was just as bad, watching his face, glorying in how much he obviously loved what they were doing.

"Do you feel how hard you make me? I'm so fucking hard, Avery. That's all you." Even as he got what he wanted, he still was giving to her.

Tears pricked her eyes because she had no idea what she'd done to deserve this man. He made her brave. He made her honest. "Do you feel how wet you made me? I didn't know I could get so wet. I didn't know I could feel so good, Lee. Your cock feels so good."

Her words seemed to make him lose control. He cursed and his hips swiveled up. "Fuck. Fuck. I need you."

He surged in, and Avery rode the wave. Her hips moved in a rhythm she found utterly natural. She pressed down, taking him in. She wouldn't accept less than all of him. She wanted every inch of that massive cock. She wanted to feel him touching her womb. She forced herself down, every inch a pleasure, an exquisite discomfort because she wasn't just taking some cock. She was taking him. All of him.

She took him to his root. The feeling of him inside her, filling her, made her lust soar. Lust. She lusted. She wanted and it was sweet.

She balanced herself on his shoulders and thrust up. He'd told her to ride him, and that's what she intended to do. She let her instincts rule for once. She brought her hips up and then down and up again, letting every inch of his cock slide along her pussy. Up and down. Up and down. Every moment a pure pleasure.

His hand slipped between them, circling and pinching her clit.

The minute he touched her she went off, pure pleasure coursing through her veins. The orgasm shuddered through her system and she gave over, letting it take her. She didn't bother to cover her moan. Lee wanted it. She gave it to him.

His hand tightened, forcing her down, holding her as he came. She felt him pulse, the tension prolonging her own orgasm. He buried his face in her shoulder as his hips rode up over and over, riding the end of his own pleasure.

He shuddered as she slumped against him.

"Perfect," he groaned against her neck.

She hugged him tight. It had been perfect. Every minute.

* * * *

Liam picked up Avery, enjoying the feel of her weight in his arms. She was dead weight, and he felt an arrogant grin cross his face. He'd utterly exhausted her. Her arms barely made it around his neck as he walked toward her bedroom.

He walked in and laid her down, pulling the covers back. He didn't pull them up right away. She was naked and vulnerable and perfectly happy to be so. He'd gotten her there.

So why was he so fucking restless?

Her pretty blue eyes opened, and she looked up at him. "Hi."

The need to run was riding him hard. He was torn between the need to fuck her again and the need to get as far away as possible.

But he had a job to do. He gave her what he hoped was a gentle smile. "Hey, baby."

He climbed in beside her. She rolled right over and cuddled up next to him, her hand on his chest. She was plastered against him, her hair tickling his skin. She was everywhere. He could feel her skin, hear the breath from her chest, smell the sex that still coated her pussy. His cock twitched even as she started to fall asleep.

He hadn't slept next to anyone in years. He didn't cuddle and have breakfast the next morning. He didn't do the boyfriend thing.

He couldn't go to sleep. *Fuck.* Half the time he woke up screaming. How the hell was he going to explain that? Was she going to buy that he had construction nightmares?

She sighed a little and turned in her sleep, freeing him. He'd thought he would fuck her all night, but this was too much to handle.

He rolled out of bed and got out of her bedroom as

148

quietly as he could. He couldn't breathe in there. She was too close. The sex hadn't felt like a fucking op. He'd forgotten why he was there, his whole being focused in on her body and her pleasure.

She'd been so sweet. She'd fought him, but when she'd decided to submit, she'd done it beautifully. He was pretty sure he'd die one day with the taste of her on his lips, the feel of that tight cunt gripping his cock. She'd been so tight, tighter than he'd ever had before, and once she'd given over, she'd been hotter than hell, her breasts bouncing as she rode his cock.

Liam took a deep breath. The sex hadn't been the problem. The sex had been the best he'd ever had. He wasn't going to lie about that. The sex had been amazing, and he wouldn't wait long to have her again. He would be inside her tomorrow, but not until he'd gotten control of himself. That was the problem. When he'd been inside Avery Charles, all he'd cared about was her. There hadn't been a mission. Thomas Molina hadn't mattered. Eli Nelson hadn't mattered. All that had mattered was getting inside her as far as he could go.

Avery Charles didn't even know his real name. She'd never heard his real voice except those few moments when he'd forgotten and he'd just wanted to be himself.

Scrubbing a hand through his hair, he found his jeans and stepped in. His phone. He needed his bloody phone. He could hear the thing buzzing. A text was on the screen. Adam's code number. He didn't have names on his phone, just code numbers to let him know one of the team was trying to get him.

Open the door if she's secure. Need to talk.

Liam moved carefully after grabbing her keys off the dining room table. He picked up his shirt and shoved his feet into his boots. He needed a good excuse if she got up. He could go grab something from the store down the street. He checked in on her bedroom. Moonlight filtered in. The sheet had slid off her slightly, exposing one breast. Her nipple was pink tipped and erect. She turned as though looking for him, but she settled back down.

If she was his sub, he would make sure she never wore clothes when they were alone. She was worried about some scars? He didn't give a shit. They were just a map of her survival. She was so gorgeous that she needed the scars or she would be too perfect.

He stared for a minute. Why hadn't he seen her beauty from that first moment? Oh, she'd been pretty, but without her clothes she was stunning.

The phone in his hand vibrated again, an impatient thing.

He closed the door to her bedroom and made his way to the outer door, sticking close to the wall so the wood didn't make a sound under his feet. He unlocked the door, and there was Adam leaning against the opposite wall just standing there waiting for him. He put his fist up.

Silent. He wanted Liam to remain silent. What the hell was going on?

Adam opened the door to the apartment he and Jake were sharing and motioned him to come over. Liam didn't want to leave her. Not if something was going down, but he needed to know. And he needed to make a copy of her keys anyway. He locked the door behind him and followed Adam inside.

Jake looked up from the computer on the table. "Dude, shirt?"

"If you wanted me to get dressed, you should have said so. I got out of bed to answer this little call of yours." He tried to play it cool. He pulled the T-shirt over his head.

"That didn't take long," Adam said. "Is she asleep?"

"Yes. She's secure." She was the type who slept at night because her conscience didn't keep her awake. She was the type who deserved a man who didn't run away after he was done fucking her.

"Is she all right?" Adam asked. He held up a hand to stop Liam's immediate reaction. "I only ask because I've spent some time with her. She's very sweet and really naïve. She isn't used to having sex."

He didn't like to hear it described that way, but there it was. It had been sex. Nasty, dirty sex with a woman who didn't even know who she was really sleeping with. Would she welcome Liam O'Donnell into her bed? He doubted it. Liam O'Donnell was cold and he used a woman. He didn't cuddle up to her and protect her.

So why had it been so natural to shield her on the escalator? Why had he already trained himself to know when her leg was going to give so he could catch her? She was a little reckless with that leg. She seemed perfectly willing to take a dive, but she didn't have to because he was there to catch her.

Lee Donnelly was there to catch her. Liam didn't give a shit.

Yeah, not even he was buying that lie anymore. "Avery is fine. Now what's the problem?"

Adam looked like he wanted to argue, but luckily Jake took over.

"I just got a call from Ian, and he's a little worried about Avery's apartment. It looks like we're not the only ones tracking her phone," Jake said.

Fuck. Someone was watching her. "Molina?"

Adam shrugged. "Probably, but we're not sure. I'm

working on it. You understand that if she's involved in this it would make sense that her phone is bugged. Every one of Eli Nelson's contacts probably has an eye on them."

"Or someone's watching her because he's a paranoid freak and he's using her." She wasn't involved. He knew it deep down. He also knew it was stupid. He shouldn't make judgments like that this early in the game. Hell, he shouldn't make judgments at all. Her guilt or innocence didn't really matter. Except it mattered to him. "I want to know who's watching her."

The idea that someone had eyes on her brought a slow roll of anger into his gut.

Adam grinned at his partner. "I told you he wasn't as dumb as you."

Jake's eyes rolled. "Let's not bring that up again. And dear god, don't mention it to Serena. Every time an innocent woman gets wrongly accused I have to sleep on the sofa for a night or two." Jake turned to Liam. "Seriously, Li, if you have a thing for this girl, don't ever let her know if you had a single doubt in your head. Let her think you were always just here to protect her. It goes very wrong if you very gently ask her if she might be involved in something criminal."

Adam gaped, his mouth dropping open. "Are you insane? You gently asked her? I was there, asshole."

And Liam didn't have time for their damage. "I'm not going to let Avery tether my balls to her handbag the way you two let Serena boss you around. She's just a nice girl, and I don't want her to come to harm because she got caught up in a bad situation."

Adam and Jake exchanged a long look. They had a silent conversation. Liam often envied them their weird connection. He'd never had that. Not even with his brother. His relationship with his brother had been strained at times.

He'd always had to try to rein in Rory's anger and his more violent tendencies.

"Okay, you know what you want," Jake said evenly. "So now we have to assume that her whole place might be bugged. You have to be careful when you're in there. The apartment itself belongs to Thomas Molina. His brother bought it ten years ago. If he's the one tracking her phone, he's likely got the apartment bugged."

He needed to move her to his place. It was the only way to make her safe. "I'll get a place, and we'll stay there."

"Or you can stay where you are and use the fact that we know they're watching. Look, Adam is going to make a copy of her keys, and we're going to risk going in. You looked for cameras, right?" Jake held out a hand, silently requesting the keys Liam had in his. He had several small squares of easily pressed clay laid out on the table. The minute Liam handed him Avery's keys, he started to work them into the clay, making impressions so they could duplicate them. To her apartment. Her office. Her boss's office and his files.

While she'd been in the bedroom, he'd made a very thorough study of the flat, looking for cameras. Nothing. Avery kept the place immaculate. There weren't knickknacks or anything in which to hide a camera, but the place could be wired for sound. Luckily, he hadn't said a damn thing he shouldn't. All the bastards could get was some dirty talk and a whole lot of moaning. "No cameras, but you should sweep for bugs so we know for sure. Did you pull up the maintenance records on the flat?"

He'd checked out the building himself, even before he'd approached Avery. It had good security. She had to swipe her key card to get in and out of the building. It was why it was so important to actually have Jake and Adam in the building. There was a concierge who watched everyone. He forced visitors to sign in and out. But would he think of Molina as a visitor since Molina actually owned the flat now that Brian was dead?

"There was an electrician by the name of Howard Pullman," Adam explained. "He spent five hours in the place about a week before she moved in, so we should assume it's bugged. The place came furnished. She just brought her clothes and laptop. She's had two visitors. You and Simon Weston."

Liam felt his gut go cold. Simon Weston. He'd been sniffing around her. Liam wasn't dumb. He'd watched Simon follow her around. The man was interested, but Avery wasn't. What had he been doing in her flat, the fucking blue blood? "Something about Weston doesn't sit right. Has Ian's guy come up with anything?"

"Damon Knight says he's clean. Nothing on his records to make him look bad, but again, he's practically royalty, so that can all be covered up. Being titled means something here," Adam said.

He'd grown up around that shit. "You don't have to tell me that. I know."

Adam laughed a little. "Sorry. I so rarely hear your Irish come out I forget sometimes."

But it had come out tonight. It had come out when he'd been balls deep in Avery because he hadn't been able to think of anything but her.

"Now go downstairs and run out to Tesco and grab something to drink." Jake handed him back Avery's keys after very carefully cleaning them. "It's a good excuse if she's awake when you get back."

She had mentioned she didn't have any beer. He could grab a six-pack. He could drink a couple before he crawled back into bed with her. Maybe he wouldn't scare the shit out of her with his nightmares.

"Okay. I'll do that." The Tesco was half a block down. Maybe a walk would do him good. Clear his head. He headed out. The faster he grabbed the six-pack, the faster he could get back to Avery. He was torn. He wanted to get away from her, but he also needed to protect her.

He nodded to the concierge. Avery had signed Liam in when they'd come back here earlier. Would he be able to get back in? "I'm just running to get some beer. Is that okay?"

The concierge nodded. "Go on then, mate. Ms. Charles signed you in as a person who could come and go for the night. She's a very nice lady, and she seems to like you more than the other one."

That had Liam turning. "Other one? Do you mean Weston?"

The big guy shrugged, one shoulder moving up and down. "He's a prat, that one. Glad to see she found someone nice."

Weston was becoming a problem. Liam pushed through the building's outer doors and turned left, crossing the street. Liverpool station was humming. People poured out onto the street. It would be so easy to get lost, to join the crowd and disappear. He'd done it more than once. He stared out at the throng of humanity that made up London on a Saturday night.

They hustled. They bustled. They slept. They didn't sit around wondering exactly who they were because they just fucking knew. They didn't look a gift horse in the mouth. They took the gift with both hands.

Liam sighed because he knew damn well he was probably giving the people on the street way too much credit. They flooded the side street beside the pub, pints and wine glasses in hand, each one in smart dress. They'd finished their week at whatever bank they worked at and now they were set on forgetting how fucking dull their lives were.

Not a one of them had been balls deep inside the sweetest thing to walk the face of the earth.

He was the only person on earth who knew what it meant to make love to Avery Charles. No other man alive had done it.

That was something to hold on to.

He was crossing the street when he saw him. Simon Weston was walking toward him, his eyes purposeful. He walked like a man who knew exactly where he was going.

Liam swerved down the side street, turning to see where Weston was going. Obviously to Avery's, but he wouldn't be allowed in. Before he'd left, he'd made sure Avery's phone was on vibrate. She was out. She wouldn't wake up and let the fucker in. Would she?

Liam tried to blend into the crowd, but Weston turned down the same street.

He just kept coming. Liam stopped. He was caught, and he'd been fucking right. He'd known there was something wrong with Simon Weston. The big blond man stalked right up to him.

"Are you going to come quietly or do I need to pull my gun?" Weston asked. "I have a few questions about your relationship with Avery Charles. We can go to my safe house or I can take you straight to Scotland Yard, Mr. O'Donnell."

Liam sighed. The fucker was MI6, and he was screwed.

"I'm on an op. I know you won't believe me, but I'm trying to help." It couldn't hurt to try.

Weston gave him a slight smile and didn't reach for his

gun. "Do you know you're working for the CIA?"

Liam stared.

"Yes, I rather thought not. Ian Taggart doesn't tell you a damn thing, does he? Follow me if you want the truth. If you don't then I can have Scotland Yard pick you up. I know some people in Ireland who would love to talk to you about the murders of six university students. I believe G2 thinks you're dead. You can be sent back to Ireland, you know. I happen to believe you didn't have a fucking thing to do with that shit. My car is just up the road."

Liam stood there, thinking about Avery safe and sound in her bed. If she woke up, she would wonder where he'd gone.

He hurried to catch up with her would-be lover. He'd gotten the prize, but Weston knew the truth.

Chapter Eight

Liam sat at the table across from an empty chair. It was a bland, featureless room in a suitably boring house that no one would notice in a suburban neighborhood just outside London. The small room was dominated by a mirror that ran along the opposite wall. MI6. Whoever was watching behind that mirror was MI6, and he was right in the belly of the beast.

He shouldn't have gotten out of her bed, but then he wasn't known for making good choices when it came to women. He sat in the chair, utterly unmoving. They'd offered him food and drinks, but he wouldn't touch a fucking thing. He wouldn't risk the food being tampered with. The very least they would do would be to deny him access to the loo after he'd had a couple of cups of tea. It was the way these things went. Torture could come in small ways.

So he waited.

The door opened, and Simon Weston walked inside carrying a file folder. He was still dressed in his smart suit, still looked every inch the English blue blood even at fucking two o'clock in the morning.

"You're not being held here, Mr. O'Donnell. If you want to leave, you should. I'll drive you back myself," Weston offered, gesturing back toward the door. "I would like to point out that I haven't taken your phone nor was that door ever locked. I merely wish to have a talk with you."

So pleasant. So polite. "You did threaten to hand me over to Scotland Yard."

Serious blue eyes stared back. "I needed a little leverage, otherwise you would likely have told me to fuck off."

"Oh, boyo, I might have done worse than that." It felt so fucking good to just be himself. Maybe he should have kept up the pretense, but it didn't seem to matter. If they knew who he was, the op was blown and Ian was going to have his ass, so whether or not he spoke in his mother accent didn't matter a good goddamn.

Why hadn't he called Ian? Weston was right. Not once had the MI6 agent tried to wrest his phone away. As far as Liam could tell, there wasn't anybody else in the small house. He wouldn't bet his life on it, but he'd also gotten caught without his piece. There were too many checkpoints in London while doing the tourist crap with Avery, and then there had been the fact that he'd always intended to get naked with her. Finding his SIG nestled at the small of his back might have blown his cover.

But he'd still had his phone, and he hadn't even thought about calling in his friend.

Because Weston had a temptation to dangle in front of him. Information. "You said you had information on my boss. My boss is Ian Taggart. I don't work for the bloody CIA."

A little light hit the Englishman's eyes. "You don't, but the question is who does Taggart work for? You know what they say about the Agency. Once an Agency man, always an Agency man."

Liam didn't buy it. Ian had worked for the CIA the same way Liam had worked for intelligence. They were soldiers who got called in from time to time. That was all. Except he'd heard about what Eli Nelson had told Sean just before he'd gotten away, just before he'd nearly killed both Sean and Grace. Sean had told Liam that the rogue CIA agent told him lies about his brother and his Agency status. He'd said Ian did wet work for the CIA. He'd claimed Ian was an assassin. "He got out a long time ago."

Weston waved him away. "We can get back to that in a moment. For now I want to talk about our mutual interests."

And this was the main reason he'd gotten his ass into Weston's non-descript Benz. Weston was working Avery, and Liam needed to know what MI6 knew and whether or not they were going to close him down. "Avery. I take it there's something going on at United One Fund."

Weston frowned. "Yes. Obviously." He studied Liam for a moment. "You aren't here for Molina. You're here for someone else. Who? What do you know that I don't?"

Liam sat back, firmly in the driver's seat now. And he wasn't an idiot. "Tell me what's going on at UOF first. How long have you been undercover there?"

"I suspect you already know, but I'll confirm your intel. I got myself hired on at UOF about a year ago when we started tracking some suspicious shipments going into Africa and traced them back to the same planes that had brought over the UOF relief packages."

Liam's gut took a dive. Suspicious packages going into Africa usually meant one thing. "He's running guns?"

Weston sighed. "Someone is. There's been a surge in high-grade, low-cost weapons showing up in some of the most war-torn parts of Africa. And we tracked some shipments to Pakistan that have us a little concerned."

"If they're in Pakistan, they're going to the Taliban and they can be used against Allied troops," Liam surmised.

"But there are hundreds of arms dealers. Is this one particularly big?"

"He's single-handedly armed both sides of a recent bloody civil war in a small African country. If this is all the work of the same person or organization, they are having a significant effect on the continent, and MI6 doesn't like the idea that the same thing could happen in the Middle East."

He didn't like the idea either. And he really didn't like the idea that Avery was involved in it. "How have you connected Molina to the arms shipments?"

Weston's face told the tale. "I haven't exactly. Don't get me wrong. I can tie the relief shipments to the same transports, but you know as well as I do that Molina can claim ignorance and hide his tracks."

"What the hell is Molina doing in the arms business?" Liam asked, knowing damn well he'd just put a piece together, but he wasn't exactly pleased with the fit. Eli Nelson would be interested in the arms deals. The arms industry would be very tempting for a man with Nelson's connections. His problem was with where Molina fit in.

"I don't know," Weston admitted. "Look, the guy was a recluse for years. He founded UOF with family money, but he ran it out of his house for many years. Then about three years ago, he showed up at a board meeting with his lawyers and his brother in tow, fired everyone, and started over. He claimed it was because of mismanagement of funds."

That was in line with what Liam had read. Thomas Molina and his brother had taken back real control of the Fund, and a few years after that Brian Molina had died of a drug overdose. "How far back do the deals seem to go?"

"I've traced shipments up to three years ago, but again, I don't have the financials to back it up. Without those, it's meaningless. I've been collecting all the data I can, but I haven't cracked it yet. There are some files I can't get into. I need Avery for those."

And that explained the hard press he'd witnessed. "You didn't have a lot of luck in the romance department."

Because that fucker wasn't Avery's type. He was.

Weston frowned. "No, I didn't. You'll have to tell me what kind of approach you used. I tried every bloody charming trick I know."

But she didn't need charming. She needed a man who could protect her, who could claim her. She was submissive deep down. She needed to be needed, and fuck all if Liam didn't need her. "I didn't have the same problem."

"Yeah, I got that. She seems to like arses with dark hair." His eyes had narrowed, frustration evident. So the near royal bastard hadn't liked being turned down. Fucker probably hated the fact that Avery had chosen a common Irish thug to bed down with. God bless Americans and their egalitarianism because if he thought for a single second that Avery had flirted with this bastard, he might have gone over the table and been at the bastard's throat, but he knew the truth. Avery hadn't wanted anyone except him. She'd waited. She'd waited for him.

"She apparently knows a good thing when she sees it." He let his arrogance out. Weston needed to understand that he controlled the flow of information that would come from Avery Charles. If he ended up working with MI6, the team needed to get the fact that Avery was his asset and he would be the one to handle her and make the decisions. "I'm in. I have her right where I want her. Though she'll likely be pissed as hell with me if I don't get back to her before dawn."

Now that he was away from her, he knew it would be a terrible mistake to allow her to wake up by herself. She would assume he'd used her. She would pull away and every inch of ground he'd gained would be lost. He could see it clearly now. He needed to be there.

"I'll have you back before dawn," Weston said, his eyes narrowing. "I wouldn't want to hurt the girl. Though I haven't figured out if she's in on it yet."

Which just proved that he was an idiot, but Liam had no intention of giving anything away. "I'm withholding judgment until I spend a little more time with her. Are you the one who bugged her phone?"

Weston's face went blank. "No. It was that way when I managed to get it out of her bag. I placed a piggyback on the device, but I haven't gotten anything interesting off it. I've heard a whole lot of her talking to her boss, but nothing beyond work and plans to have her walk him through various parks. And she's been talking to some gay guy the last couple of days. Given when he came into her building, I suspect he belongs to Taggart and the Agency."

And Liam suspected that Weston already knew everything. This was a chess game. "Adam. He's been working her from the friend angle. He's been invaluable in getting close to her. Adam knows how to get a woman to trust him."

"Or I went about this shit all wrong. You've been under Taggart's tutelage and everyone knows what that means. Tell me something, O'Donnell, did you tie her up yet?"

He felt a snarl in the back of his throat. "None of your fucking business. Tell me something. Did you bug her house? Did you enjoy the fucking show tonight?"

"Again, we weren't the first. That place had been bugged before she moved in. I suspect Molina, but I can't prove it. And yes, I listened in this evening. It made me utterly certain that if I'm going to get the information I need,

I have to work with you. Or I have to bring you over to my side." Weston leaned forward. "Come back to MI6, O'Donnell. This is where you belong. I'll make all your Irish problems go away. I know bloody well you didn't kill those kids."

"How?" He wasn't sure himself. It was a question that plagued him every day since he'd started to remember. He wasn't completely sure he hadn't killed them.

Weston stopped, his fingers tapping on the folder in front of him. "How much do you remember about the night you lost the bonds? I'm going to forego the recitation of the mission. I suspect you know what you were supposed to do. You and your brother were assets, and according to all records, you did your job. You got in good with the Russian organization that we suspected of terrorism. Leonov gave you roughly ten million dollars in bearer bonds that were intended to purchase a measure of uranium. Your main mission was to discover where the uranium was coming from."

"I remember." He did. Not much more, but he knew that much. "I was drugged at a pub. It was the night before we were supposed to meet with the arms dealer. My brother died that night."

He couldn't get the sight of those boots out of his mind. Even in his sessions with Eve, he got hung up on those boots and the ringing of his phone. And he still couldn't figure out if it was real or a fiction his head had made up because nature abhorred a vacuum.

"Tell me something, O'Donnell. Who were you working for that day?"

He shrugged. He was an asset. He rarely knew exactly who was behind an op. "I was supposed to answer to a high-ranking agent in Irish intelligence, but I always knew MI6 was involved."

"But we were only covering for who had really planned the op. It was all CIA."

Liam went very still. "No. It was a Brit op. You needed someone with an Irish accent and believable IRA ties in order to get into the cell. My mother was IRA. Rory and I gave that up a long time ago. We were loyal to our country and friendly to the crown. The CIA had nothing to do with it."

Liam hated the shit-eating grin that crossed Weston's face. "The CIA is rarely uninvolved, and you shouldn't be so naïve. They planned the op. They selected the SAS assets to use. They had their fingers in every single move we made. Look, this was before I was recruited. I didn't join up until twenty-four months ago, but I've studied the files since I figured out who you are. Did you think you could come here and ruin my operation? I've become an expert on you. And I know exactly who sold you out."

And he was prevaricating. *Fucker.* "Then why don't you tell me?"

He passed the folder over to Liam. "Didn't you ever wonder why Ian Taggart was so willing to take you in? You had run two ops with him three years before that night. Why the hell would he move heaven and earth to save you?"

A cold chill went up Liam's spine. "He's a good guy."

"He's a man with a past you can't even begin to comprehend."

"He's my friend." That word meant something to Liam. He didn't have many friends. He had his crew at McKay-Taggart. That was his little family, and they hadn't steered him wrong. Sure, he thought Adam was an obnoxious prick at times, but he thought of him like a cousin he wanted to punch. He was still his family no matter how much he rolled his eyes.

"Ian Taggart was the agent who ran the op." The words fell out of Weston's mouth like a land mine waiting to go off.

"I don't believe you." Ian would have told him. Ian knew damn well that that had been the op that cost him his brother, his goddamn life. Ian wouldn't betray him that way.

That manila file folder sat between them. Liam's eyes held it. Bare. It had no markings on it, but it suddenly struck him that file folder could change his life. He didn't want to open it. He wanted to be back in bed with Avery. He should have pushed aside all his fears and taken her again. His cock had been ready. It had been his brain that hesitated because he'd been scared of what she meant.

If he was still in bed with Avery, he wouldn't be facing that damn folder.

"Ian Taggart is a brilliant asset." There was a nauseating sympathy to Weston's voice that put Liam on edge.

Ian was his friend. And he knew bloody well what Weston was trying to do. He was trying to drive a wedge between Liam and his team. He was trying to break Liam's loyalty. Manipulation was an art form, and MI6 taught its agents well. "I know Ian Taggart. This isn't going to work. I know he used to work for the Agency. If he's consulting with them again, then he has his reasons."

They were looking for Eli Nelson. Nelson was rogue CIA. It only made sense that Ian would use his contacts. It certainly wasn't a betrayal. It wasn't.

"How well do you know Ian?"

Liam rolled his eyes. This was so transparent, and he was just about ready to test Weston's open door theory. He had some important information. He had the girl. If Ian really was in contact with the CIA, then they probably had some influence and might be able to talk MI6 into leaving him in, although he likely didn't need it. Weston, for all his charm and good looks and obvious money, hadn't gotten into the lady's bed. Liam had done that. She trusted him, not Simon Weston. If they wanted to get close to Avery then they needed to keep Liam around and maybe, just maybe, he would share intel with them.

This was his op. He made the decisions. He might not have any right to run the op on British soil, but he had leverage now. They'd waited too long to call him out.

He made sure his voice was confident even if his brain was running in twelve different directions. "I've known Ian Taggart for years. I've worked with him, trained with him. I know the man."

"Tell me something, O'Donnell, how much does he talk about his wife?"

So transparent. "He's never been married. Don't be ridiculous. Ian Taggart is the man least likely to get married."

The thought of Ian putting a ring on some girl's finger was ridiculous.

Weston flipped that file folder open so casually, as though he wasn't opening Pandora's box. Liam looked down. A marriage license from five years back stating that Ian Mitchell Taggart and Charlotte Marie Dennis had been married in London, England.

"So?" Ian was a deep one. If he had a failed marriage in his background, he wouldn't go around blubbering about it. He wasn't like Sean, and now Adam and Jake, who felt the need to whine about their relationships like they were a walking daytime television show devoted to talking vaginas. Ian would bury it down like a man should.

"So you don't know anything about Charlotte Taggart?

167

You don't know that she was Ian's cover for his last European assignment? That he married her because he needed the cover?"

Liam winced inwardly. He was betting Charlotte Taggart had likely been pissed off. Or more likely she didn't even know that he'd used her. She had probably been quietly divorced and now lived a perfectly boring Middle-American life with three kids and a fat husband who didn't know how to internally decapitate another human being.

Avery would want that life. Avery would move on after he'd used her, and she wouldn't look back at the idiot man who wasn't smart enough to love her.

Did Ian ever think about Charlotte?

Weston's hand flicked the marriage license aside and another very formal-looking document was beneath it. "Does he ever mention that he's the one who put a bullet in her back? Charlotte Taggart was eliminated after her loving husband no longer needed her. Oh, he claimed she was dead when he found her according to Scotland Yard, but it's clear enough to me. And would you like to know what op he was running at the time? Would you like to know why he was 'honeymooning' in England?"

Those pages just kept flipping, an English Intelligence book of horrors. His stomach was a wave of nasty suspicion. Ian had married a woman just weeks before Rory had died, and he'd been in England at the time.

When he'd called Ian that day so long ago, Ian had told Liam he was in Dallas. But according to his passport, he'd been in England. He'd been dealing with his wife's murder.

Had Ian been killing his wife?

"According to all MI6 reports, Ian Taggart was still an active CIA operative at the time of his wife's death. The US government smoothed the way in the investigation of the incident. At the time, he'd been running an op in cooperation with G2 and MI6."

Liam shook his head. "No. I never talked to the CIA."

Weston sighed. "Why would you? You were the grunt, O'Donnell. You were expendable. You've worked intelligence long enough to know that the right hand doesn't need to know what the left hand is doing, and most of the time neither hand even realizes there's a brain behind the actions. Ian Taggart ran the op that killed your brother. It was his baby. It was the whole reason he was in Europe in the first place. He'd tracked those Russians for years. You had worked with him a couple of times. How do you think he managed to get you out of Ireland so easily? Everyone should have been looking for you or your body, but Ian Taggart just bought you a plane ticket to the States? No. The CIA got you out. Taggart made a deal with them. Why the hell would that man risk his newly started company to take in someone who might or might not have killed seven people including his own brother? Even if you discount the potential murder charges, there is no doubt that you fucked up that op. Those bonds are gone because you decided to celebrate with a pint. Why the hell would he bring you in unless he wanted to watch you? He's been watching you for years, O'Donnell, and when he gets what he needs out of you, you'll end up like his loving wife."

Weston revealed a vile photo. A beautiful woman with pitch black hair staring up at the camera, her crystal blue eyes vacant. Charlotte Taggart. Dead and gone.

"Her body went missing from the morgue twelve hours after she was declared dead. I've always wondered what he did with it. We didn't get a chance to do an autopsy. I suspect we would have found evidence against him if we had." Weston sat back, crossing his arms over his chest.

"Taggart is involved in a lot of nasty business. So why don't you tell me why he's come to my island? I need to know so I can form a plan to stop him. He's every bit as dangerous as anything Molina is into."

Liam stared at that girl. She morphed into another girl. Younger, less beautiful, but she'd had her life ahead of her. Had he choked that life away? Had his actions that evening, innocent though they'd been, led that small blonde woman to her death? How many women had died because of that single operation?

How would Avery look on a slab, her face devoid of the life that lit her up from the inside?

Would Avery Charles be one more woman on a slab? He didn't remember the other girl, but he would die with the feel of Avery's arms around him. He would always be able to taste her on his tongue.

"O'Donnell?" Weston's voice seemed to come from far away, but it pulled him out of that very dark place. Somewhere in the background, he could hear a phone ringing. It wasn't real. He knew that. That phone was in his head. In his nightmares. Who had called him? Had it been Ian Taggart? Why couldn't he remember?

Liam forced himself back into the present. He had enough shit to deal with in the here and now. He didn't need to get lost in the past. He schooled his expression. No matter what, he wasn't about to make an emotional decision. He needed time. He needed to sort this out. He'd been played before and people had died. He wasn't going to make the same mistake again.

"I can help you." Weston's voice was smooth, friendly. "I know what it means to be that piece of crap expendable asset. I've had to fight the same shit over here."

Liam doubted that the second son of a duke was really

so fucking expendable. Liam had grown up rough. He knew what it meant to go to sleep with an empty belly and rats skittering across the floor. Whatever worth he'd had in this world, he'd had to fight for.

Weston had no idea what it meant to be utterly expendable.

The door opened abruptly, and his evening was complete. Damon Knight walked in looking utterly different than he did at The Garden. His leathers were gone, replaced with a perfectly cut suit and a frown that could freeze a man from ten feet away. He walked in like he owned the place.

"Do you want to explain this to me, Weston?"

Weston glared back. His eyes had flared, and there had been just a second's worth of panic on the agent's face before he settled back into a calm but annoyed look. And it was brutally obvious they knew each other. If Weston was shocked the owner of a BDSM club had come walking into his safe house, it didn't show. "He's sleeping with my target. I investigated him and discovered he has ties to an American security firm. Not that it was easy to figure that out. They did a pretty good job of trying to hide his true name."

"Yes, McKay-Taggart," Knight shot back. "I am well aware."

Weston stopped for a minute. Yeah, he hadn't known that. It was obvious in the flare of his eyes before the agent moved on. "I had tech pull some CCTV footage of him." He glanced back at Liam. "You were pretty good about keeping your head down, but I found a moment when you looked up at something Avery was trying to show you."

Liam could guess what had happened from there. "You ran my face through facial recognition software and you got a hit from G2."

"From a couple of places, really," Weston admitted.

Knight didn't look like he gave a shit. "Agent Weston, would you please repeat back to me the parameters of your mission. I think you've forgotten. I know damn well you weren't cleared to interrogate this man."

Weston's frustration hardened his face. "He's in her bed. What the fuck was I supposed to do? Was I not supposed to run a trace on him?"

"You didn't just run a trace, did you?" Knight argued. "If you had run a trace, you would have discovered his very solid cover."

Liam looked up at the Dom unwilling to leave it a second longer. "You're MI6. Any reason you didn't bother to mention that to me?"

Knight's shoulders squared. "Talk to Ian."

Well, of course Ian knew. Ian knew everything.

"We're not enemies, Liam," Knight said. "It's precisely why I'm having this fight with junior here in front of you. You'll have to forgive His Lordship. He wasn't given the information because he didn't need to know. He's been a little too thorough, and he does a lot of work on his own. If he'd followed protocol and contacted his handler like he should have, we would have avoided this little scene."

Knight's eyes went to the file folder, flaring briefly before he scooped it up. "What the fuck have you done, Weston?"

"I did my job," the Englishman ground back, and Liam finally understood that maybe Weston did get what it meant to be left out of the information loop like a cog in the wheel that could be easily replaced.

"Your job was to get the information on Molina, not to screw one of our allies."

"I'm not so sure Taggart is an ally. Why is he here? Why is he jumping into the middle of my operation?"

Weston asked, his fists clenched.

"This is not your operation. It's mine and if you don't like it, you can take a nice long vacation, Your Lordship. I will deal with you in a minute." Knight turned back to Liam. "You screwing the girl yet?"

He had the wildest urge to pound the fucker's face until he caught sight of bone, but he shrugged negligently. "Yeah. I'll get what we need."

It looked like he was in bed with more than just Avery. He could walk away. It was an option. He could disappear, but then she would be alone and at the mercy of men who had none. And he would never know the truth. Not about himself or his brother or Ian.

"Good man. Ian's in a car waiting for you. He was very upset when he found out you were in custody. Seriously, I thought he was going to take someone's head off." Knight ran a hand across his face, a weary gesture. "Go on, then. He'll take you back to the girl's place. You need to be with her before she wakes up. Women don't like it when you sneak out of their beds. I'll take care of this one." Knight turned as Liam got up to walk out. "Talk to Ian. This is pile of information is meaningless without the truth behind it. You can interpret this information in a million different ways, but Ian is the only one who knows the truth. I would trust that man with my life."

Liam nodded, giving Knight a smile he hoped was fairly carefree. "Hey, mate, I've known Ian for years. He's protected me. I'm not going to let some papers change that fact."

But he was numb inside as he made his way out of the house. That file did change things, and he needed to get to the bottom of it. The question was how to go about it. He couldn't trust anyone on his team. He had no idea if they were in on it.

He hated this feeling. He'd trusted them to watch his back. He'd fought and bled with these people. How could he think this way? How could he think that Jake and Eve were in on a plot to keep him ignorant?

It was only paranoia if they weren't really out to get him.

Ian was standing beside a black BMW, an annoyed look on his face. "Li, we need to talk. I didn't tell you about the MI6 shit because Damon asked me not to. He facilitated us coming in on their op. He didn't think for a second that Weston would get around your cover and actually try to arrest you."

But Weston hadn't done that. Weston had just tried to show him a ton of information that would have been good to know five years before. "No problem, boss."

Ian didn't know what Weston had shown him. He would know soon enough. Knight would fill him in, but at least tonight Liam didn't have to listen to explanations. He needed time to think.

Ian stared at him warily as Liam hopped into the passenger's seat. "Are you all right? He didn't pull any shit with you, did he?"

Weston had pulled the rug out from under him. He'd unsettled the only world Liam had known for the better half of the last decade. "He didn't waterboard me, boss. He did offer me stale biscuits. That's torture."

Ian sighed. "I'm glad to hear it. I wanted to deal with the little fucker myself, but Damon talked me out of it. You're cleared officially now. Damon saw to it."

"Good." Liam stared forward. "Let's get going. I don't want Avery to wake up without me."

He slipped back into his Midwestern accent like a

security blanket he pulled on to protect himself. He was on a mission, and it had far wider parameters than he thought because now he had to figure out if Ian Taggart had a hand in killing Rory.

Ian turned the ignition and pulled away from the suburban house. "What's going on? Damon just managed to work a deal that officially clears you of all wrongdoing and set things straight with G2. You're clear, Li. Don't you have anything to say about it?"

If Weston was right, Ian could have done that himself at any time. "It's great, man, but I don't exactly have a hankering to head home or anything. I do appreciate it."

Ian's eyes stayed on the road, but frustration dripped from his voice. "Are you sure there isn't something you want to talk about? Are you having mixed feelings about sleeping with Avery Charles? You're protecting her, you know."

"Yeah." How had Ian protected his woman? "I know. It's fine. I'm fine."

Ian drove the rest of the way in silence while Liam's brain raced with a million possibilities.

Unfortunately, not a one of them was good.

Chapter Nine

Avery woke up, blinking in the early morning light. She stretched, her muscles deliciously aching. Every minute of the night before came flaring back to life. She'd made love with Lee Donnelly, big, gorgeous Lee with the broad shoulders and beautiful face and filthy-as-sin mouth.

She'd made love with him in the middle of the night, but now it was morning and time to face the music. She didn't look great in the morning. He probably would stay and have breakfast and be polite because that was the kind of man he was, but he would extricate himself from the situation and she needed to look cool and collected. God, she wasn't cool and collected. She pulled the sheet up, unwilling to turn and look beside her. What if he was already gone?

How did these things work? What made her think she'd be able to handle a one-night stand?

The sheet she clutched was suddenly pulled straight out of her hands and cool air hit her breasts.

"I need you." Lee straddled her, his eyes on her chest. He looked different this morning. Gone was the patient guy who had calmly explained what he wanted, and in his place was a hungry predator. He was boldly naked, his body lean and hard everywhere. The soft light of morning couldn't dull his suddenly sharp edges.

And there was no way to avoid his cock. He was utterly

erect, the thick, bulbous head of his dick nearly touching his navel as he stared down at her.

There was no kindness in him now. There was challenge and a cool distance that frightened her a little. For the first time, she really understood that she was small and weak, and he could likely kill her with his bare hands. Last night had still been civilized for all the dirty talk, but he seemed to demand something different in the light of day.

He leaned over, catching her wrists in his hands. She was trapped beneath his body, their chests touching, his cock nearly throbbing against her pussy. His weight bore her into the bed. His face was slightly cruel as he looked down on her.

"You want me to go, little girl? Last night was for you. If you let me stay in this bed, this morning is going to be for me and it might not be so pretty. It's going to be dirty, and it's going to be my way all the way."

What had happened to him? She searched his face. Yes, he was acting like a dominant prick, but something in his eyes made her wonder. And what he'd said. He needed her.

She'd needed him the night before, and he'd given her everything she could have wanted. She wasn't going to fool herself. She was already half in love with him. She wasn't going to let him scare her off.

And wasn't that what he was trying to do? Push her to see if she could really accept him?

She suddenly wasn't so afraid of him anymore. She brought her head up and touched her nose to his. Her body was already warming up. "It wasn't so clean last night, Sir."

"Fuck." The cold look vanished like it had never been there in the first place, and he slammed his mouth on hers.

He held her in place, and Avery understood what it meant to be inhaled. That was what he was doing to her. He

dominated her mouth, kissing her like he needed her to
breathe. Over and over again he took her mouth, and she
gave it up willingly. When he released her wrists, she
wrapped her arms around him. She let her legs tangle with
his, offering him everything she had. He got her so hot so
fast, as though her body now trusted this man to take care of
her.

He moved from her mouth to her neck, his fingers on
her nipples. "Tell me you're mine."

That was easy. She was beginning to think she'd been
his from the moment he'd caught her in front of the
mummies. "I'm yours."

She wasn't sure why he'd gotten possessive so
suddenly, but he seemed to need reassurance and she was
finding some of her own. He wasn't acting like a man who
was going to walk out on her.

"This is mine. This is fucking mine." There it was
again, that musical tone he took on when he was really
aroused. She loved it. He whispered it across her breasts just
before he sucked one inside his mouth and settled in to
devour her.

She softened, her whole body giving over. She didn't
have to think here. Her mind didn't run away from her. All
she had to do was feel. All she had to do was let the
connection between them flow.

She whimpered a little as he bit her nipple. It was a
short, sharp pain, but seemed to spark something deep inside
her. The pain melted into a thrumming heat.

"Yes, these are mine to torture. You like a little torture,
don't you, love?" He moved to the other nipple and bit down
gently. She didn't flinch. Her chest pressed up, welcoming
him. "Yes, I'm going to clamp these gorgeous tits and run a
chain between them. I can pull on it whenever I like and

you'll feel my bite."

Dark images whispered across her brain. He'd told her what he wanted to do, but it hadn't been real until now. He wanted to tie her up. He wanted her bound and helpless to the whims of his cock. It was so much easier to think that word now. The monster rubbing against her pussy wasn't a penis. It was a big hard cock. It had brought her so much pleasure the night before. She wanted him inside again.

"Fuck, love. I don't want to wait. Tell me I can have you now." He growled against her skin.

Her savage beast. He'd told her it was his way or the highway, and just a few minutes of petting and he was domesticated again. "Please, Lee. I need you, too."

He reared up, his hands pushing her knees apart. He spread her wide and looked down at her pussy. A little of the savage was back in his face, but she could handle him now. "You're going to let me tie you up, aren't you? You're going to let me spank you. You're going to be my submissive."

She was willing to try just about anything with him. "Yes."

"But not now. I need you too much now." His hand went to the end table, and he came back with a condom. He had it rolled over his dick in a heartbeat. "Take me."

He didn't play around as he had the night before. He shoved his cock in. He spread her wide and forced that big dick inside in one long, penetrating thrust. He was up on his knees, his hands on her legs, controlling the penetration. He went at her hard. This was what he'd meant. He was in control, and he would have what he wanted.

And what he wanted was her.

"Fuck, you feel good." He thrust in long passes, his balls hitting the curve of her backside as he shoved his way in.

And he felt spectacular. Despite the soreness she felt, her body was responding, lighting up under him. She could feel the delicious wave of pressure ready to go off.

"No one made you feel this way before." It wasn't a question.

But she only had one answer. "No one but you."

She moaned as he leaned over, and his pelvis started to grind down on her clitoris.

An arrogant smile lit his face, but she was happy. That dumb masculine smile was beautiful and it seemed to have pushed all the demons away. He was Lee again. He leaned down, pressing his body to hers, covering her as he continued to fuck. "I'm glad, love. And I really will do all those nasty things to you. You're mine. I'm yours. We're together now. Do you understand?"

She didn't exactly, but she knew he intended to keep her for a while, likely for his time in London, and that was really all she could ask for. She would explore with him and gather memories to keep her warm when he was gone. "Yes. We're together."

He kissed her again, his tongue surging in just as his cock hit that perfect spot deep inside and she went off. Her whole body tightened and released in a wave of surging pleasure.

Lee's hands tightened on her as he thrust in one last time and gave himself over. His face was so open and honest as he came. He dove into her, giving up everything he had, and finally dropped on top of her, his head in the crook of her neck.

This was what she'd wanted. She wrapped herself around him. This closeness was what she'd longed for but now she knew it was so much sweeter because the sex itself had been deep and intimate.

He didn't roll off her. He nuzzled down, his head in the crook of her neck, his big body pressing her into the mattress. "I didn't sleep last night. I'm so tired now. I want to stay with you."

She didn't want him to go anywhere else. "You can stay as long as you like."

His head came up, those emerald eyes searching hers. "You're not lying to me, are you? You're exactly what you seem to be."

So he'd been hurt before, and that was what the whole possessive thing was about. She gave him a little smile. "I'm boring, Lee. I'm nearly thirty years old and I'm just starting to live. I don't have anything to lie about."

He kissed her, a little touch of his lips. "You're far from boring." He sighed and rolled off her. He walked off to her bathroom and when he came back he was yawning, his hair unkempt but that Greek god body still on full display. She couldn't help but stare.

"Are you hungry?"

His lips kicked up. "Around you? Always. But I need to sleep, love. Is it going to bother you if I bed down for a couple of hours? You can wake me up at noon, and we'll do whatever you want for the rest of the day. We can walk up the Thames and hit the Eye."

She grinned. "I would love that. I've heard you can have champagne while you ride."

He lay down, his face so much softer than before. He reached up and touched her cheek. "Champagne it is." His gaze turned serious. "But while I'm sleeping, I have a job for you."

"Okay."

"I want you to get on the Internet and look up BDSM. I

want you to read up on it because I want to take you to a club in a couple of days, and I need to know if you can handle it. I can keep this vanilla if you want, but I would love to show you my lifestyle."

It was her turn to lean down and kiss him. He looked so perfect laying there, a big tiger among her fluffy feminine bedding. "I told you. I like strawberry."

"Good. Because I intend to get your ass as pretty and pink as any strawberry."

"Now wait a minute," she said with a laugh. "I was talking about the flavor."

"Yeah, I'll get some more of that, too, baby. Though you really taste more like honey." He yawned again.

He was such a dirty man, and she wouldn't have him any other way. She got out of bed, reaching for her robe.

"No." His body was laid out on the bed, but his eyes were on her.

"No?"

"No robe. No clothes. Stay naked for me."

"You'll be asleep."

"And you're alone in this apartment. Stay naked and think of me. If someone comes to the door you can have a pair of sweat pants and a T-shirt to put on but no panties and no bra. Is that understood?"

She bit her bottom lip at the thought of walking around in her birthday suit. It seemed weird. "Is this that BDSM stuff?"

A single eye opened, but it was enough to send a little thrill through her. "Yes. This is that BDSM stuff, love. Obey me or we'll talk about your punishment."

The way he said the word "punishment" made it sound like it wouldn't be such a horrible thing. Still. "All right. But can we talk about the bra?" Her boobs were really too big to leave swinging.

His eyes shut again. "I don't know. Can we talk about anal plugs?"

So no bra then. "I'm good."

"Thought you would be." He sighed and turned, giving her a view of the most amazing backside she'd ever seen.

Ass. It was a gorgeous ass. Her boyfriend had a really great butt.

She quietly pulled her workout pants and a T-shirt out of her dresser and made her way to the shower.

* * * *

Thomas Molina stared at the report in front of him. No pictures yet, just a bunch of numbers and places and dates that made up the seemingly dull life of one Lee Aaron Donnelly. His Texas driver's license photo was so grainy Thomas could barely make it out.

According to everything Malcolm had dug up in the last eighteen hours, Lee Donnelly was nothing. He had a paltry eight thousand dollars in his checking account and twenty in savings. He owned a small company that specialized in customizing kitchens, but he'd left it in the hands of his partner back in the States while he roamed around England.

He was a nobody.

And he was the man who had fucked Avery Charles the night before.

He'd listened in, his cock getting hard even as his stomach rolled. Avery had been quite the whore. He was rather sad that he hadn't wired the flat for video, then he would have been able to watch her slut it up.

"I also got the article to Brandon Charles's parents." Malcolm sat across from him, one eyebrow cocked in

183

obvious curiosity. "Any reason why they care about Doctors Without Borders recruiting newbie surgeons?"

Oh, they would care. They would care quite a bit, and hopefully it would prod them to contact Avery and give her a little hell. She needed to remember who she bloody well was and what she'd done.

He needed her world crumbling so she would remember who she could count on. And when her new boyfriend disappeared, she wouldn't have anyone to turn to except her friend.

"That is none of your concern." Malcolm didn't need to know the whys and wherefores. He only needed to do his job. "Were you able to follow him last night?"

It had been a bit odd. Loverboy Lee had put Avery in bed and then walked around the flat for a few minutes before walking out. At first he'd smiled, absolutely sure that Avery had just gotten what she deserved. She'd fucked some random asshole, and he'd taken what he wanted and walked on her.

He'd actually gone to sleep with visions of a weepy Avery regretting the whole night.

But the bastard had been gone for hours only to come back and get into bed with her again. And fuck her again.

He hadn't sounded like a man who intended to leave. He'd sounded like a pervert who had found a good thing and was going to dig in. He'd fucked her and ordered her to walk around without any clothes. Again, this was where video would have been more desirable.

Malcolm frowned. "No. There was a crowd outside a pub next to her flat. I lost him. I waited and picked him back up. It appeared he'd gone to some sort of store. You know, the kind with brown paper bags. He also had a bunch of flowers. No idea why it took him bloody hours. Guess he had to find one that was open."

Molina could just guess what was in that brown paper bag. Sex toys. Donnelly had mentioned a club, and they had talked about BDSM. Donnelly had given her some fucking hearts and Dom-shaped flowers spiel about taking care of her and how sex was meant for two. Pussy. Donnelly was only playing at being a Dom, and he didn't understand the meaning of sex at all.

Sex was a way for the female to justify her existence. Sex was a way for the male to control and conquer.

She would finally understand what sex meant when he got Avery under him.

"Do you want me to take him out?" Malcolm asked.

"Eventually, but I don't want Avery around when you do it. And get me some pictures of this bastard that aren't so grainy I can't see them. Have you run a trace on Lachlan Bates?" It was time to get down to the real business. He met with Eli Nelson in a couple of days. He wanted to know whether he should kill the motherfucker.

"He's legit," Malcolm replied. "He's got vested interests in that part of Africa. He's attempting to arm the rebels because he wants to control resources there. You'll find his real name and a dossier on his company in the email I sent to your tablet."

Excellent. Then Nelson was providing an actual service. He didn't like the fact that Nelson was demanding fifteen percent, but then this was a big deal. He could afford to be generous. For now. And perhaps Nelson could help him with the Donnelly problem. Something about the man didn't sit well.

"Set up an account. I'll write a report and decline Mr. Bates's donation on the basis that he doesn't fit the criteria. I'll bury it. Avery got wind of this one, but in this case, her new fuck toy will prove an adequate distraction. And let Monica know that the next time she allows one of our donors to go through, I will slit her throat in the middle of the night."

He was still thinking about it. When he had Avery in place, it wouldn't matter. She would obey him or he would kill her.

"I'll make sure she knows." Malcolm said it with a slight smile. He was a man who seemed to enjoy his work. "And I'll set up the shipment. We have a relief package going out soon. I can have the P90s and the C4 ready in a few days. The surface-to-air will take a little longer. And the land mines are already in stock."

"Get those surface-to-air missiles or we're fucked. We need to prove we can get our hands on them. My contact promised me some rich Middle Eastern buyers, but we need the SAMs." He'd made a name for himself. He'd gotten rich, but the Middle East was fucking Broadway to the arms dealer. If he made it there, he could make it anywhere. And it would provide him with enough money to buy a fucking island and kill anyone he wanted to.

It would put him so far from his disgusting, rat-infested childhood.

"I will." Malcolm stood. "And I'll take out Donnelly when the time is right. What do you want me to do about that MI6 agent who keeps sniffing around Avery?"

Thomas smiled. "Well, he's not going to be a problem, is he? He never climbed into her bed. He's got a bunch of nothing, and he knows it. Simon Weston is an idiot. He's a poor little rich boy playing at being James Bond. He's more dangerous if we snuff him out. We know what he is. He has no idea what's happening. Leave him be for now."

Simon Weston was a child trying to play a man's game.

He would die in the end, but not until Thomas didn't have another option. He didn't play a bad hand until he was forced to.

He'd sacrificed too much, fought too hard.

And he was so close to becoming King of the Mountain. No MI6 agent was going to hold him back. And he was going to have his queen. No asshole, shitfaced, nothing construction worker was going to keep him from her.

He would make her pay, though.

Malcolm nodded and walked out. Thomas went back to looking at that file and thinking about just how much he'd like to hurt the bastard.

* * * *

Avery winced as she opened the door and really wished she'd pushed back on the bra thing. She felt like an idiot, but she wasn't about to walk downstairs to meet her guest, and she couldn't exactly turn him away. When the concierge had called and told her Simon was downstairs, she'd thought about it, though. But they were too close to the Black and White Ball, and Simon was crucial to the success.

"Hey."

Her eyes widened as she took in Simon Weston. He was dressed casually in a T-shirt and jeans, but he had his briefcase in hand. God, she really wished she had the bra on. There was no way to hide it. Her boobs were too big. "Hi. What did you need?"

His eyes narrowed marginally. "Are you busy with something? I can come back later."

She was being so rude. "Of course not. Please come in. Sorry, I just wasn't expecting anyone."

He walked in, his big body filling her hallway. "Not a

problem. I just talked to Monica and the string quartet canceled. She's in a panic, and her sister is having a baby. I told her I would bring the CDs of the other options over here and have you decide. The ball is your thing after all."

She sighed. "Thomas wanted me to put it together. I told him that party planning isn't exactly my thing. I hired a party planner, but Thomas didn't like the music he chose. I've been trying to find one he'll like. That's why I've been leaning on Monica. She's into the same kind of music. I really appreciate you bringing them over."

She took the four CDs out of his hands.

"No problem. I wasn't doing anything else this afternoon. Just getting ready for the yearly audit. So much fun, you know."

And she'd been walking around her house naked. It had been odd at first, but then she'd gotten used to it. After her shower, she'd done some laundry and baked a batch of cookies. She'd been deeply aware of everything around her. It had been a freeing experience.

But now she was right back to feeling self-conscious. And why? She wasn't a kid. She didn't have a thing to prove to Simon. She was his colleague. It didn't matter if he thought she looked ridiculous without a bra. Lee liked it. Lee was her lover. In this case, his opinion was the only one that mattered. She could crawl back into her shell or she could start taking herself seriously for once.

"The audit sounds perfectly horrible," she admitted. Simon was a smart man. He probably knew way more about string quartets than she did. "Any way I could convince you to stay and give me your opinion on these? I'm afraid if you leave it up to me, I'll pick based on eeny, meeny, miny, and moe. Actually, that would make a good name for a string quartet."

He laughed, a smile spreading across his handsome face. "Which just shows how desperately you need me. That's a horrible name for what should be a very posh musical group. Don't you know they're all named something like the Bachman-Barnes Quartet or The Buckingham Strings?"

For the first time ever, she felt comfortable with him. "Yeah, I'm more a rock and roll girl. So stay and help me. I can pay you in oatmeal chocolate chip cookies. I put the oatmeal in so I can eat them for breakfast and still hold my head up. Because of the oatmeal."

"So you eat like a five-year-old. I like it." Simon winked at her as she led him into the small room that served as both dining and living room. His eyebrows rose at the sight of a leather jacket draped across one of the dining room chairs. "New coat?"

She wrinkled her nose his way. She wasn't going to hide the fact that she now had a love life. "That belongs to Lee."

Simon chuckled a little as he crossed to her CD player. "So you found a boyfriend?"

"I did. He's asleep." She grabbed the cookies and brought them out. "Do you want some tea?"

"Coffee, please. I got used to it when I went to school in Boston." The smooth sounds of a violin filled the air. "I'm going to turn it up a bit so we can get the full effect."

Lovely music filled the space. And it was a bit loud. She started the coffeemaker. In seconds, it had filled the cup.

"I like it," she shouted over the music. She wasn't sure why he needed it so loud, but he seemed content.

He gave her a thumbs-up and grabbed a cookie. She sat on the couch next to him. He leaned over. "Mozart. They're quite good, but the cellist is slightly out of time."

189

She couldn't hear it. It all sounded nice to her.

"Hey, I was getting everything ready for this audit thing, and I can't find a couple of files." He'd moved close, leaning over to talk in her ear. "Do you know if Molina keeps files in his office?"

"Which ones?" She asked, her voice rising.

"Uhm, let me try to remember. Oh, I wrote them down." He grabbed a folder out of his briefcase and handed it over. "I've been looking for them because I need to reconcile the accounts with the donors."

She looked at the names, a little chill going through her. Bates. Hughes. McMillian.

Hughes and McMillian were donors Thomas had turned down for various reasons. Bates was the current file he was paying close attention to. The three donors he'd met with personally. The only files he kept in his office. Why did those files keep coming up? It was Thomas's company. He could turn down a donation if he wanted to. It wasn't her place to question him. And yet she found herself curious. "I'll check on it for you."

She kind of wanted to get a look at those files. Why had her boss turned them down? When she'd asked, he'd blown her off saying they didn't meet the criteria, but she wasn't sure what the criteria was. Why was there a criteria at all? Money was just money.

Maybe there were tax implications. But the real thing that bugged her was the personal meetings. Molina always met with them personally before turning down their large donations.

And no one else thought it was odd? Molina didn't like to meet with anyone. He often avoided meetings, leaving the department heads to handle the day-to-day business. He preferred to stay in his office or at his house most of the time.

One of the doctors in her study had been disbarred for embezzling funds from the grant. He'd used some interesting accounting practices. He'd filed false receipts for all kinds of medical equipment but pocketed the funds for himself. It had been an enormous scandal. The doctor had a gambling problem and had gotten behind on paying his bets off.

Was Thomas in some kind of trouble?

"Is there a party going on?" Lee walked across the room wearing only his jeans, his big body on display. He turned the CD down and then his eyes were on Simon.

And he didn't look happy about her guest. She'd done as he asked and spent a good portion of the morning researching BDSM and Doms and subs, and one of the things she'd figured out was that Doms tended to be bossy and possessive.

And protective and wonderful.

She stood and walked over to Lee, cuddling up to him. One of the best websites she'd found was a sub's blog where she talked about all the best ways she'd found to handle her Dom. It was a sub's job to soothe the savage beast. Sure enough, his arms curled around her and he hauled her close. "Lee, this is Simon Weston. He's a friend from work."

"And he's brought some work with him." Lee didn't sound like he approved, but after giving her a little squeeze, he held a hand out. "Nice to meet you."

Simon stood up, taking his hand. "And you. I just brought some CDs over for Avery. She's heading the big ball this year. It's coming up in a couple of weeks, you know."

"Oh, I'll be around," Lee assured him.

And she would have a date. She hadn't expected that.

She would have to get Adam to go shopping with her. She'd just planned on wearing her old black dress. She needed something sexy.

A little smile curved his lips up. "Cookies. I like it. Is there any milk to go with these?"

She kind of liked the idea of him enjoying milk and cookies. He was such a big, rough guy. "In the fridge. I'll get it."

"No, baby, I can handle it. You made the cookies." He leaned over and whispered in her ear. "And it looks like you were very obedient." He didn't seem satisfied with her little kiss. He pulled her close and covered her mouth with his, his hands tightening around her. Possession and dominance flowed from him. Avery softened, giving him the lead. He had absolutely nothing to be jealous of. "Be right back."

"Maybe I should go," Simon said. "I didn't want to intrude if you have plans."

"No plans," Avery said.

"Yes, we do," Lee called out from the kitchen. "I have lots of plans, and they don't involve a third."

She felt her whole body flush. "Lee!"

He walked back with a glass of milk in his hand and an innocent look on his face. "I thought we were going to do that Eye thing with the champagne. Does Weston here want to hang around with the tourists?"

Simon shook his head. "Not at all." He reached for the folder he'd handed her and put it on the table. "Go with the Bradford Quartet, dear. And if you don't mind helping me out with those files, I would appreciate it."

"Sure." She was a little anxious about it, but she would rather know. She liked Thomas, but something was off. Surely there was a reasonable explanation, but she wanted to know.

192

She walked Simon out. By the time she got back, Lee was sitting on the couch munching on cookies. He gestured for her to sit in his lap.

It was a long time before she got back up again. It was only much later that she thought to put the folder away. She'd thought she'd left it on the table, but sometime it had gotten moved to the couch.

Avery put the folder in her briefcase. That particular mystery could wait until another day. She had some sites to see and nothing was more spectacular than Lee's body as he walked toward the shower.

"Come with me."

She left all her suspicions behind and joined her lover.

Chapter Ten

Liam rolled out of bed and marveled at the fact that he'd never slept as much as he had in the last four days. He'd slept every night in Avery's bed, making love to her and then falling into a peaceful sleep. Then he would wake up and cuddle close to her. Except he had nothing to cuddle this morning. He frowned and looked around before hearing the shower turn on.

He needed to train her better. She should have woken him up. He liked showering with her. Four days of living with Avery Charles and he'd proven his own fucking words wrong. He'd promised to make her crave him, but he was the one with the addiction. He was addicted to being her Dom. He was addicted to her.

He sighed and scrubbed a hand through his hair. A low vibration hummed, his cell moving slightly on the bedside table.

He was going to have to answer eventually. Avery was going back to work today. She'd used a couple of vacation days and spent them with him. He'd had her close for four days, but she had some sort of meeting today that she couldn't get out of.

Four days of freedom. Four days of paradise. Four days when he hadn't thought of anything except her. He'd ignored his fucking phone. He'd walked away from Jake when they passed in the hall. He'd pretended he didn't know what he knew.

Ian had secrets, and Liam needed to figure out how to handle it. Was he a member of this team or a chess piece Ian Taggart was maneuvering?

He'd avoided the question for days, preferring to dive into Avery. He'd fucked her and taken her all over London. And fucked her again.

He'd started her training. Nothing hard core. Just some light bondage and protocol.

His phone just kept on. He looked down. Eve. *Damn it.* They were sending in the big guns. He picked it up. "Donnelly."

"Can I talk?" Eve asked. What she was really asking was whether she was on speaker or whether someone was close enough to potentially hear her over the phone.

"Sure." He never put anyone on speaker, and his volume was always low.

"Liam, you need to come in. Ian is so concerned." Her soft voice came over the line. "We're all concerned. I know what Weston showed you, and Ian would like a chance to explain."

Damon Knight had looked at the file folder. It had been a good bet he would let his friend know he'd been made. Liam thought quickly knowing that someone, somewhere was listening in to his side of the conversation. He hoped the fuckers had enjoyed the show last night. Avery was turning out to be a screamer. "It's so good to hear from you. Yeah, I'm going to stay in London for a while. I don't think I'll be taking on any new jobs soon."

She sighed over the line. "Liam, this is your family. Are you really just going to drop us because some asshole puts a thought in your head?"

"I don't know. I need some time to think it over."

"He's getting ready to pull you from the op, Li."

A savage rage rolled over him. No fucking way. He kept his voice calm. "That's not a good idea."

"Someone ran a trace on your cover. They're looking at you."

"It's only to be expected." He was going to have to deal with this.

"Please, Liam," Eve pleaded. "Come to the club tonight. Talk to Ian. He's messed up over this."

"I doubt that." But he was having a hard time telling Eve no. She'd helped him so much. "I don't have all the information I need to make an informed judgment."

Because it had been so much nicer to focus on Avery. He'd kept her out of trouble. He'd sent Adam the names Weston had left her to find the files on. He'd done his job. Mostly.

He'd managed to not kill Simon Weston. He'd seriously thought about it when he'd caught the bastard still sniffing around Avery. And attempting to bring Avery deeper into this game. That was what rankled. Weston knew Avery wasn't involved, and he still tried to pull her in. She wasn't a bloody agent. She needed to get out.

"You aren't going to get the truth by staying away. Please, Li. Come to the club tonight."

"I won't be alone. I would need to bring a friend with me. Is there going to be a problem with that?" He wasn't going to leave Avery alone. He wasn't happy about letting her go to work. Something was brewing in that head of hers. He'd caught her staring at those names from time to time, her eyes glassy as she thought. She could sink into her head and get lost for long periods of time. He hated that. He hated not knowing what she was thinking.

"That can be arranged," Eve agreed quickly. "I can talk

to her while you talk to Ian. Li, you need to come in. I've never seen Ian so pissed off and, quite frankly, upset. He damn near threatened that MI6 agent with death for pulling that crap on you."

Yeah, Liam could bet he'd done that. Ian didn't like his plans being upset. "It's always good to know the truth."

"You don't know the truth, Li." There was a little pause. "Can't you talk to him?"

He knew he would have to. "Yes. We'll be there tonight."

A long sigh came over the line. "Thank you."

He hung up the phone. What was he going to do? He was caught. He was trapped. He had to figure out what the fuck he was doing, and he needed to do it fast. Not just for himself but for Avery. Weston had put him in a corner. He'd given Avery names to research. Somehow, those names were connected to the arms dealing, or Weston suspected they were. Weston was pulling Avery further in, and Liam didn't know what to do about that except to bind her up in chains of pleasure and affection so maybe she would obey him when the chips were down and the shit started to hit the fan.

Because he was more sure than ever that it would hit the fan.

She was going back to work, and he was going to figure out just what was going on at United One Fund and how Eli Nelson figured in. According to her day planner, Molina was going to meet with Nelson tomorrow. At least he thought it was Nelson.

The Nelson project might be a done deal tomorrow and then he would focus on Molina. He would need to get into Molina's office.

He had the key to the office, but he wasn't able to copy

the security codes to get into the building. He'd been hamstrung with that security system, but if he was there with Avery, he could get in. He just had to make sure she didn't see him going into that office. That might be a problem.

He might be forced to work with Weston. He would rather see the files without Weston around. He needed to make sure there was no way to tie Avery to anything. It wouldn't be the first time some criminal bastard had set up his assistant to take a fall. Grace Taggart was proof of that.

Bates. Hughes. McMillian. Those were the names on the file Weston had offered up.

According to Avery's day planner, they were the only donors who had met with Molina. There was a connection to the arms deals, but he needed the original documentation to put it all together. A big deal was going down. He could feel it. This was why Nelson was here. The former CIA agent was putting together something, and he was using UOF to do it. He might have been using them for a long time. Even if they got Nelson in custody tomorrow, Liam wanted to take Molina down. It was the only way to make sure Avery was safe.

"Hey." Avery gave him a big smile as she walked into the room.

He couldn't help it. He saw her and he needed. "Is that how you greet me?"

She sank down to her knees, her legs falling apart just as he'd trained her. It was the formal greeting of a beloved submissive to her Dom. It was an acknowledgement of their pact. The sub to support and obey when need be and the Dom to adore and protect.

He'd played at this for years, but it finally hit home with this woman. This was honesty. There was no prevarication. No pretending they were friends and roommates and part-time lovers. They were a Dom and a sub with very delineated roles. She softened him. He strengthened her. It didn't necessarily always follow gender lines. There were plenty of Dommes who lifted up their male partners. But for him and Avery, this was how it was. She showed him that he could sink himself into someone, and he was working on showing her just how fucking right she was.

Her head was down, her knees spread, her hands palms up on her thighs.

She was perfect and his cock responded, but then he was always hard around her. He got off the bed not feeling a damn bit of self-consciousness about his nudity. He hadn't taken a shower. He still had her sweat and arousal on his skin. He would walk around with it all day long if he could. He sank his hand into her hair, giving thanks for her submission. "You know you're gorgeous, love."

"You certainly tell me enough." He didn't have to see her face. He could feel her smile.

She was gorgeous. How had he ever for a moment thought she wasn't? "Have lunch with me today."

Her face came up. Just a few days and she already smiled more. She was so much more confident. "That wasn't a question. Do you need an answer or should you just tell me when I should be ready?"

Brat. Yeah, he loved that. "Noon. I'll be there at noon. I'm crazy about you, you little brat. We're going to the club tonight. Are you ready?"

A sure smile he knew damn well he wouldn't have seen a couple of days ago crossed her face. "Yes. I'm ready. Though I don't have any fet wear. I should have some, right? I read that sometimes clubs don't allow people in plain clothes in."

She'd become an expert in the last couple of days. And

he'd noted that she'd started reading a writer named Amber Rose. Serena would be thrilled that she had a new devotee.

"I'll handle it. You'll wear what I select for you and only what I select." He would have to make a side trip. His first inclination was to ask Eve to find her some clothes. He'd never given a crap about what a woman wore. He'd only cared about how quickly he could get it off her. But the thought of Avery wearing only what he picked out played around in his brain.

"No undies then, huh?" She frowned. "I used to like underwear, you know."

"Why hide that pretty little pussy, baby?" Her nipples had already peaked. He could have her again. Maybe if he impaled her on his cock twenty-four seven he could keep her out of trouble. He wanted to ask about the names on those files. He wanted her to tell him she wasn't thinking about investigating them herself, but he couldn't risk tipping someone off. They were listening in here, and someone had started following them. He'd picked up the tail the afternoon after they had slept together the first time. Someone was watching Avery Charles, and he couldn't be sure whom. Her creepy boss or Nelson? Had Nelson made him? Would Nelson show for the meeting now or would he disappear into the woodwork again?

He was just about to kiss her when he noticed her leg spasming. He pulled her up. "You have to tell me when it hurts."

She held on to him for one sweet moment, her nipples brushing against his chest. "It didn't hurt, Lee. It just does that from time to time."

He didn't like that her leg could give out at any moment. It wasn't bad when he was around because he was always watching and ready to catch her, but what happened when she was alone? "I think you should stay home."

She snorted a little. "Lee, if I stayed home every time something was wrong with my leg, I would never leave the bed."

And that was a problem why? "I can bring you food in bed. We can just stay there."

A haunted look crossed her face as though she was remembering terrible things. "I did that for far too many years."

She needed to be independent in a way others didn't. Of course, her version of independence was just being able to walk on her own. Over the last few days, he'd gotten to really know her. He'd done dumb tourist crap that should have him pulling his hair out, but he'd looked at the world through her eyes and had to admit that he'd had fun.

She'd stood on the beach at Dover, marveling at the cliffs in the distance. They'd gotten something to eat, and she'd talked about how hard it had been in the hospital. He wanted to keep her safe, and she needed a little freedom.

He was walking a very thin line. He wanted to lock the door and never let her out, and it would crush her right when she was starting to find herself.

He stepped back. It wasn't his place to lock her up. Well, not for more than a couple of hours and only for play, but he couldn't do it on a permanent basis. "Lunch it is then, but promise me you're going to do those exercises we talked about."

She groaned. "You are a hard taskmaster."

He'd read up about her leg. She needed daily conditioning to stay strong. He needed her to be strong. "Yes, I am. I'm serious. Daily workouts."

She grinned up at him. Her smile kicked him in the gut every time. "As long as you promise to take off your shirt and work out with me."

"You're going to get spanked for that saucy mouth." He lightly smacked her ass, cupping it afterward. "Go get dressed. I'll take care of everything for tonight. You just have to stay out of trouble today."

Tomorrow was another issue all together. And tonight could prove troublesome. He'd hidden for four days. He'd sank himself into her and forgotten for a brief moment that he was lying to her and manipulating her. And he'd avoided all those nasty questions about the past and about Ian.

He sat down and watched as she started getting dressed. He acknowledged the truth. He'd started to think about becoming Lee Donnelly. He could leave McKay-Taggart and just become the man she thought he was. His cover would hold. He actually was quite good with his hands. He could legitimately work as a contractor. He could be the man Avery was falling in love with.

She hadn't said it, but it was there in her eyes. He wasn't sure he could say the words back, but fuck, he wanted to hear them. He was a greedy bastard when it came to her. He wanted everything.

If she found out he wasn't who he said he was, what would she say? Would she run from him?

Maybe the best way to handle it was to never let her know. Ian would let him go. He was fairly sure of it. If Ian wouldn't then Liam would get enough shit on him that he would.

What the hell was happening to him that he was thinking about leaving behind everything he knew?

Avery slid into her little kitten heels. She rarely wore anything past a one- or two-inch heel. "Hi ho, it's off to work I go."

"Give me a minute and I'll walk with you." He reached

for his jeans.

"Lee, you don't have to do that."

"I want to." He needed to. He needed to stay close. She'd started out as the op, but he was beginning to wonder if she wasn't the only thing worth protecting now.

He dressed quickly and stuck close as they headed out toward Liverpool station. When he dropped her off, he thought seriously about just waiting outside her building for noon to roll around, but his watcher was still close. With a weary heart, he made his way back to Avery's. It was the only place where he wouldn't have eyes on him.

It was time to start figuring out just how screwed he was.

* * * *

Liam nodded to the doorman as he walked through. Avery had placed him on the approved list, and he now had a key card into the building. Once he was back in their flat, he could get on his computer and start trying to find anything he could that would prove or disprove Simon Weston's story.

The elevator doors closed. Like most lifts in London, it was a tight fit. When he was with Avery, she had to stand close. He'd thought seriously about stopping the lift in between floors and having his way with her. He would shove her skirt up and free his cock and fuck her hard and fast. By the time he let the lift free, she would be clinging to him. Pleasure wiped her out. He loved how limp and sated she looked after he'd wrung an orgasm out of her.

The doors opened on the proper floor, but before he could step out, a fist came flying toward his face. He'd been distracted, thinking of Avery, and he barely had time to sidestep the fucker. He ducked, his instincts taking over. He rushed the guy, leaning over and going straight for his gut. Adrenaline started to pump through his system, thrumming through his veins as potent as arousal. Avery wasn't around so he could use a good fight. When he couldn't spend himself on her, he would take a little blood.

He crashed into the opposite wall, his opponent's back slamming into it.

Liam grew up hard. He'd starved half his life on the Dublin streets, and he didn't fucking fight fair. He had the advantage now. He heard his opponent drag air into his lungs. He'd gotten it knocked out of him by the slam against the wall. Liam brought his knee back, perfectly ready to deball the motherfucker.

"Please don't," a familiar voice said. Adam. Liam stepped back. Adam was standing right there in the hallway, leaning against the wall. And Jake. Jake had been just about to lose his balls. "Serena would be so upset if she lost half her chances at getting pregnant. Not that I can't handle the job. I can, but she would be all over him. She's a sucker for a sad story."

Liam growled a little, a predator denied a nice fat meal. "What the fuck was that about?"

Jake's eyes came up. "Adam spoke too soon. I had you right where I wanted you."

Right. "You wanted me to shove your balls up into your intestines?"

"Like you could. I was just about to kick out and shove you back, then I was going to get my hands around your throat and drag you into our apartment and then I was going to beat your ass until you come to your senses," Jake vowed.

"You wouldn't have been able to lift your arms after what I was going to do to you." Jake was high if he thought he had the upper hand in that little fight.

"Or we could all just stop hitting each other and talk this out," Adam suggested.

"Pussy," Jake shot back. He flexed his hand and stretched.

"I'm not the masochist here." Adam turned to him. "Will you please talk to us? You've been a fucking asshole for four days."

He'd avoided them at every turn. And they were his friends, or at least they seemed to be. *Damn it.* Ever since Simon Weston had put that file in front of him, he'd been at odds. "I've been getting in good with Avery."

"I have no idea what the fuck you've been doing," Jake shot back. "I think you might have been sitting on your ass or maybe you got a better deal and decided to start something with the competition."

Anger flared. Jake was just asking for a thorough beating . "You want to explain what you mean by that?"

"What about asking politely do you not understand, asshole?" Adam said to his partner. He turned back to Liam. "We agreed we would just talk to you then the Neanderthal here had to go primeval on your ass. Look, Ian told us what happened. Can we please talk?"

He got the feeling if he didn't they would press the issue. "Fine. But you only have until eleven thirty. I have to meet Avery." He followed Adam inside, Jake hard on his heels. "So I take it Ian told you two to corner me?"

Adam turned, his eyes confused. "No. I'm worried about you."

He really looked like he didn't have a clue. "Ian didn't mention that MI6 is on to us?"

Jake shut the door behind him. "Yes, he and Damon explained what was happening, which you would know if you had bothered to answer your texts and come to the meeting he called."

Liam had ignored it. He'd been at Canterbury Cathedral with Avery. He'd taken a damn bus tour and held her hand when he knew he should be working. "What excuse did Damon give?"

Adam frowned. "Excuse? He needs an excuse to be MI6?"

"He needs an excuse to have not told us."

"Ian knew. Look, Li, the only reason we're still here and haven't gotten our asses shipped back to the States is that Ian is working with MI6. He still has connections, and he's using them to keep us here. We didn't have any idea that MI6 was looking into UOF and Molina. We're only still here for two reasons: Ian's connections and the fact that you've managed to do what Weston couldn't."

"Get into Avery's bed. Tell me something. Why doesn't MI5 take over? They could just pull the records they want." And then Avery would be out of this for good, and she wouldn't have to find out about his involvement.

"You know the answer to that," Jake said, scrubbing a hand through his hair as he sat on the sofa. "God, Li, what the fuck is happening to you? Where is your head?"

"The arms sales are happening on foreign soil. They sent Weston in because his family has done a bunch of charity work in Africa and Asia." Adam's eyes narrowed. He could be brutally intelligent when he wanted to be. "What exactly did you and Weston talk about if you didn't talk about the op? Look, man, something's going on here. You get pulled in by that MI6 guy and suddenly you're acting like you don't know a one of us. What did he say?"

He shook his head. "Weston was kept in the dark, too. He didn't know we had a deal with Knight on the table."

206

"Then why didn't he have you arrested?" Jake asked. "Adam's right. Weston was playing an angle. He was trying to turn you against us. What angle did he use?"

"It doesn't matter," Liam shot back. Now that he was forced to face it, he realized he wasn't going to open his mouth until he'd talked to Ian. "I already talked to Eve. I'm taking Avery in tonight so this is all completely unnecessary, and if things go right tomorrow, we might be home in a day or two. Tell me something. Are we handing Nelson over to the Brits or has Ian got that worked out with the CIA, too?"

"Nelson has been disavowed. He's an embarrassment to the Agency and a potential threat to everyone who works for Langley. What do you think we're going to do?" Jake stared at him, his jaw a harsh line.

So tomorrow was assassination day. "And the MI6 mission?"

Adam shrugged. "Not our problem once we take out Nelson. We had a big sit-down last night with Damon. They believe Nelson is likely attempting to make a buy. At first they thought Molina was just taking kickbacks to allow the weapons shipments safe passage, but those meetings with Molina make me think he's the middle man. He's a dealer."

"How does a borderline agoraphobic shut-in go from running a charity to arms dealing? Something's wrong here." It was a mystery, and he didn't like it. It didn't sit well with him. And if they took Nelson out, where did that leave Avery?

"No idea, but again that's something for MI6 to deal with. We're not going to take Nelson out in front of Molina. We've bugged the restaurant they're meeting at. The Brits agreed to put an agent of theirs undercover as a waitress. We're going to follow Nelson and take him out when it's safe. Molina's operation will continue, and MI6 can figure out just where the arms are coming from and we get to go home and get back to normal." Jake turned, his eyes going a little cold. "Do you have an exit plan for that girl?"

"She's not 'that girl.' Her name is Avery," Liam all but snarled back.

Jake cursed and reached for his wallet. "Motherfucker. I've only got eighty. I'm going to owe you twenty."

Adam smiled, all the tension leaving his face. "Told you."

Liam got the serious feeling he was the butt of the joke. "What?"

Jake suddenly looked more like Jake and less like a disapproving big brother. "I've been a little worried about Avery. She's a sweet girl. I don't believe for a second she's involved in this."

"She isn't. She has no idea what's going on." Though that fucker Weston had planted the seeds. It was up to him to make sure they didn't come to fruition. And if everything was likely going down tomorrow, he had to find a way to stay. He had to convince MI6 to let him stay on.

"And she's in love with you," Adam said, his voice softening and taking on a nauseatingly sympathetic quality.

Liam backed away. "I am not doing this with you guys. Do you understand me? I am not going to sit in some fucking feeling circle and talk about love and babies. You two can screw yourselves."

"But you have thought about love and babies with her," Jake mused.

"No, I haven't." He hadn't. It had been a fleeting thought. It didn't mean anything. "She's a nice girl, and I don't want her hurt, that's all."

"So you're going to leave her?" Jake asked. "I want my

money back."

"I didn't say that." Why couldn't he leave it be? He left everything be. He hadn't said a word about what Weston had showed him. Apart from sessions with Eve, he didn't talk about his past or his brother. So why was he actually tempted to talk about this with Adam and Jake? He needed Sean. Sean would just pop open a beer and sit beside him. After a while, he'd slap Liam on the back and that would be their very manly discussion about feelings. Not a word said. Not a thing worked out because a real man didn't ever really work that shit out. He just did what his wife told him to do.

Holy fucking shit. He'd just thought about marrying Avery.

"Get him a beer," Jake said. "Li, sit down. I'm going to turn on the TV, and we'll find some soccer."

He slumped down into the sofa, the reality washing over him. He didn't want to leave her and not just because he was worried she would get hurt. He liked her. He liked who he was when he was with her.

She'd been hurt. She'd lost everything. She'd lost her home and her parents and her money. She'd pulled herself up and gotten married and had a baby when she was still a baby herself. She'd lost them, too, along with the ability to walk. She'd fought. She'd taught herself to walk again, and she put herself right back out in the world because that girl didn't know how to quit.

He'd quit a long time ago. He could see that now. He'd worked and walked around, but he hadn't really lived since that day in the wharf-side flat. The man he'd been, alive and vibrant and happy, had died and a completely different human being had been dragged out of the water. Shut down, cold, distant. He'd chased pussy that didn't matter. He'd fucked women who couldn't touch him for precisely the reason that he knew damn well they couldn't move him.

Something cold was pressed in his hand, and he took a long swig. The low hum of an announcer's voice filled the room. Jake sat down beside him, not saying a word, and Adam passed him a beer before sinking into the chair and staring at the TV.

Yep. This was what he needed. He trusted Adam and Jake. There was something deep inside that trusted them because in so many ways, they had taken the place of his brother. They annoyed the fuck out of him. He wanted to punch them half the time. And he was happy they were here.

"It's football," he heard himself say.

Jake snorted a little. "Footballs are oval shaped and way more manly than this shit."

"And more interesting. Does anyone ever actually score?" Adam asked.

Fucking plebians. He laughed, his tension dissolving. He would figure out what to do with Avery. He had a little time. Damon Knight wasn't going to kick him out of the country. They would need him, and he would protect her. "It's called football, boys, and we don't need all those pads and shit. This is a man's game."

They started arguing, but the tension was gone. His problems were still there, but he could handle them.

And he would handle Ian. He would listen to him. He owed the man that much and more. He owed them all, and he wouldn't let them down. He'd been sulking for four days. It was time to get his head back in the game and back his people up.

It's what family did.

Chapter Eleven

Avery looked up at Simon Weston. It was so much easier to be friendly with the man now that she had Lee. She didn't feel uncomfortable with him anymore. She'd even caught herself halfway flirting. It was a little perverse that she couldn't flirt before, but now that she had a boyfriend, she was okay with a little harmless repartee. And Simon had eased up so they were finding a very nice friendship.

"How was the time off? I managed to get the quartet scheduled for the ball." He sat on the edge of her desk, a mug of coffee in his hands.

She winced a little. "I'm so sorry I pawned that off on you."

He smiled, a genuine beaming that lit up his face. "Hey, no problem. I'm happy you're having a good time. That Lee guy seems all right. And it's obvious he's making you quite happy." He nodded toward the door to Thomas Molina's office. "I noticed he's been in the office a lot lately. And he's crabby. Aren't you supposed to keep him calm?"

Yep. She'd gotten an earful from a whole bunch of the staff the minute she'd walked in. Apparently Thomas had been a bear to deal with. "I will give it my best shot. Let everyone know that he won't be in tomorrow so they can all take extra-long lunches." She remembered the look Monica had given her. "And I'll buy the first round after work."

"You're going to come and drink with us?" Simon

211

asked, one aristocratic brow arched.

"Sure. I have to warn you, though, I'm a total lightweight and I'll probably get even klutzier than usual."

"I think we can handle that. We would all help you, you know."

She leaned back wondering just how much she could ask him without sounding like a massive moron. "I don't know. I don't seem to fit in here."

"You would fit in just nicely. You're an incredibly likable woman, Avery. Have you ever wondered why you haven't found friends here?"

She wasn't especially good socially. She often felt awkward and out of place. Her twenties had been one long hospital room stay. She could talk to doctors and sling medical jargon around all day long, but she was a little lost when it came to small talk. She liked sci-fi movies and romance novels, two things assured to put a blank look on most people's faces.

But she was more confident now. She had Adam and Jake, and most of all she had Lee. And now she had Simon. And she'd been assured that she would likely find friends at the club Lee was taking her to. He'd laughed a little and said subs liked to stick together.

"I think I've been a little standoffish." She hadn't really tried. She'd asked a couple of the women if they wanted to have lunch, and when they couldn't she'd given up. Why had she done that? Why had she gone into her shell? Because getting close to someone meant deciding just how much to tell them. Because what the hell was she supposed to say if they asked about her past? "But I'm done with that now. I'm going to be more in the present."

It had been easy to view this as a transitory job so she didn't have to open herself up, so she never had to talk about

Maddie. It was easy to be friendly with people on the street because they wouldn't really become part of her life. Even Thomas was easy. He liked to talk about business and news and sports. He rarely delved into truly personal subjects. He could talk with her for hours, but he didn't ask her pesky personal questions.

God, was that why she'd been so comfortable with him?

"You're not standoffish, love," Simon said with a wary little frown. "It was made clear to many people that they should keep their distance."

"By who? Who wouldn't want me to make friends?" That didn't make any sense.

Simon nodded toward Thomas's door. "He was subtle about it, but I understood. We were supposed to be hands off."

"Why would he do that?" One of the things he'd been insistent on was that she would meet new people and see the world.

And he'd asked her to stay with him in his town house. Oh, he'd offered her a separate room, of course, but he'd asked her to stay. It was only when she'd made it clear she would need her own place that he offered her the place by Liverpool station, but he'd been a bit grumpy about it.

Was Thomas trying to be more than her friend? "I'm sure you just misunderstood, but it doesn't matter. I'm here for a little while, and I'm going to enjoy it."

"That boyfriend seems to be good for you." Simon pushed off the desk. "And let me know if you find out anything about our missing files."

She nodded. She was going to look tomorrow while Thomas was out meeting his mysterious friend. The man had never come to the office, but he seemed to be close to Thomas.

Thomas's door opened, and there was a pained expression on his face as he stood in the doorway, cane in hand. "Avery, you're here. I was wondering if you were going to come back to work or if I'd lost you."

He looked like he hadn't been taking care of himself. Guilt rode her hard. She'd been diving into her relationship with Lee, and Thomas had been faltering. No matter what he'd said to the staff, he'd helped her in a huge way, and she couldn't pay that back. He'd given her a chance when no one else had, and they were connected by tragedy. They both knew what it meant to lose a loved one. She'd lost so much, and he'd lost his brother.

"I'm here." She stood up and grabbed her laptop. "I told you I would be back for the monthly board meeting."

"It's being pushed back. Dubai needs a couple of hours to get their numbers together. They had a last-minute donor pull out, and it's changed the budget. Apparently the sheik of some tiny country needs his two million now to put down a coup." He sighed. "We have to completely rethink the Congo shipment. In addition to losing the donor, we have to deal with the fact that the grain we planned on purchasing is more expensive than promised. Something about a goddamn drought. I need this shipment to go through, Avery."

Yes, that would make him crabby. She'd picked a hell of a time to use her vacation. "It's okay. If it's a few weeks late, it will still get there."

His face turned a brutal shade of red. "It will not be late. If it's late, someone's fucking head is going to roll. Do you understand me?"

It was the first time she'd heard him curse, and she took a step back. He'd always been gentle around her. She'd heard rumors that he could be nasty, but she'd discounted them. She didn't question the fact that the man who stood in front of her now could be ruthless.

"Absolutely," Simon said smoothly. "I'll get some of the American liaisons on the phone. We'll find the grain or the money, I promise. This is for the Congo shipment, correct? I heard we had a big donation coming through. A bloke named Lachlan Bates, I heard. We can use that money to buy the grain."

A blank expression went across Thomas's face. He took a long breath, and then he was his sunny self again. "Sorry, dear. I'm in a little pain. My legs are aching today. Weston, you're a legal advisor. Don't worry about this. I'll get Monica on it. The Bates donation might not go through. I'm looking into it."

"Of course, sir." Simon nodded and sent her a small stare before he left the office.

"I'll go talk to Monica myself." Maybe it was a good sign that he was letting himself be real around her. She could handle a little bad temper. The look on his face had been another thing entirely. He'd been righteously angry, but she had to try to calm him down.

"Avery, I'm sorry." He leaned against the door. "I didn't mean to yell at you. It's been difficult to get about on my own. I think you understand that."

She'd struggled for years. Again, guilt welled. "Yes, I understand. I'm sorry. I just wanted a few days to myself."

"But you weren't by yourself, were you?"

There was no way to miss the rebuke in his voice. She wasn't going to feel guilty about Lee. "I was with my boyfriend."

"He's an American, right? A tourist?"

"He's here for a little while."

He hobbled over to her desk. "I hate this. I hate that he's using you."

"He's not using me. He's dating me."

"He's not going to stay around," Thomas said, frowning again. "Are you going back to America with him?"

"No." Lee hadn't even mentioned when he was going back, much less invited her to come along.

"Is he coming to Dubai with us? Are you coming to Dubai at all? I would like to know if you're going to leave me high and dry." He struggled with his cane, walking back into his office, leaving the door open for her to follow.

She had tried not to think about it. She had a good job. It paid well, and she believed in it. And he had a job back in the States that he never really talked about, but she understood it was his company. He couldn't just leave it behind. It was too quick to make decisions.

She'd started out wanting a few weeks with him, but now she knew damn well she wanted more and she couldn't ask for it. She'd known him for a week. She couldn't ask him to make lifetime decisions based on a few days. "I'm going to Dubai."

Unless Lee asked her not to and then she would most likely give up the best job she'd ever had for the chance to be with him. She was so dumb, but she knew she would regret not trying. She could forgive herself if it all imploded, but not if she didn't try. Her stupid, hopeful heart wouldn't shut down no matter what bad stuff happened.

"I'm glad to hear that because I would hate to think I had to go alone." He sat down behind his desk, the cane leaning against the wood. "I'm going to see some doctors in Dubai. They think they might be able to help me with my legs."

"That's wonderful." She knew how much it could change a life. Her phone vibrated in her pocket.

"I just care about you. I wouldn't want you to get hurt."

216

She pulled the cell out, glancing down. Her mother-in-law. Her heart sped up a little. Brandon's mom. She hadn't called in two years. Avery had tried everything to get the woman to talk to her.

"Someone important?" Thomas asked.

"I need to take it. Is it okay?" What if something was wrong? Or what if she finally wanted to talk? What time was it back in the States?

He nodded. "Of course, but I need you with me at that meeting. We'll order in lunch."

Damn it. Lee was going to be upset, but she had to work. She hated to admit it, but while she felt very comfortable with Lee, the truth of the matter was he would likely go back to the States and she would go to Dubai. "I'll be there."

She walked out of the office and immediately answered her phone. "Lydia? Is that you?"

Her hands were shaking.

"Look you little bitch, I told you not to contact us ever again. What do you not understand about that? Did you think sending us that magazine article would change the fact that Brandon and Madison are dead?"

The words lashed at her. "What are you talking about?"

"I don't care what she's doing. Do you understand? I want her dead. I want my son back. You're a traitor. You're a goddamn traitor, and I want you dead, too!" Her mother-in-law, once so sweet, sounded monstrous. "I hate you. I hate you. You killed them, didn't you? You wanted it."

The phone dropped from her hand, nausea rolling in her stomach. Tears threatened, but she was at work. She couldn't break down now. She couldn't cry. She had to stay strong.

"Avery, dear? Are you all right?" Thomas stood in the

doorway, his eyes on her. There was an anticipatory look in his eyes as though he was waiting to see if she would break down.

She couldn't. Not here. This was her little slice of hell, and she wouldn't bring anyone else into it. She picked up the phone and quickly turned it off. She couldn't help the way her voice shook. "It's fine."

"I can see plainly that it's not." Thomas made his way to her faster than she would have expected. He put a hand on her shoulder. "What was that about?"

Avery shook her head. "I'm not exactly sure. It was Lydia."

His face softened, his hand stroking her shoulder. "It sounded as though she was a bit upset."

Her whole body felt weak. "She said something about a magazine article. I don't know what she was talking about. She said I sent it to her. But, I didn't send her anything." A deep weariness threatened to invade her. Would this never end? She'd made a choice that seemed positive, but had caused a complete disconnect between her and the only family she had left. Even her aunt had taken her in-laws' side.

"From what you've told me, she's a bit lost, dear. She could have seen an article that reminded her about Brandon and got it in her head that you sent it her way. She's not someone you can get back, Avery. I know you want a family, but she's never going to forgive you."

She wished he would stop talking. He wasn't saying anything she didn't know. "I just thought she would come around someday."

"No. She won't. Most people wouldn't understand what you did. They would see it as a complete betrayal of your husband and your child. It's why you shouldn't talk about it.

I understand, but most other people won't. Your in-laws prove it." He was close, his body brushing against hers as he pulled her close. "I'm the one who accepts you, Avery. I'm your friend. I'm so sorry you got that call."

She let him hug her. He really had seemed like her only friend for so long. When she'd first taken the job and they'd been in New York, she'd thrown her whole being into her work. Brian had died shortly afterward and she'd stuck close to Thomas, two stunned victims alone on a seemingly endless sea.

She sniffled a little.

"It's all right, Avery." Thomas's hands smoothed across her back. "I can take care of you."

His voice was deeper than before, and she could feel the heat of his breath on her neck. A little shiver went through her. She didn't like being so close. It felt different than before. It felt more intimate, and she wasn't sure she liked it. Maybe it came from being with Lee, but she suddenly didn't want to be so close to Thomas.

"Sir, I needed to talk to you," a masculine voice interrupted.

Thomas's head came up, and there was a little snarl on his face. It was gone so quickly she wondered if she'd actually seen it. "Malcolm, this had better be important."

"I wouldn't interrupt you if it wasn't." Malcolm was the head of Thomas's security. Standing at a massive six foot four, Malcolm was a bit of an enigma. He rarely talked, and he disappeared for long stretches of time. Thomas almost always had a bodyguard around, but Malcolm was the only one who really scared her.

Thomas stepped back, reaching for his cane again. "I'll see you in an hour or so, dear. Please order some lunch for everyone. Use my card."

He stepped into his office, Malcolm closing the door behind him, and she was alone again.

She wanted Lee. She wanted to call him and tell him to come and get her, and she would just go with him anywhere he wanted to go.

And he would ask why and she would have to admit what she'd done. Would he understand? Or would he be like her in-laws and find it to be a betrayal? She wasn't sure she could risk it.

In the end, she picked up her phone and took the coward's way out. She texted him explaining that she couldn't meet him for lunch.

Her phone rang almost immediately. Lee. She couldn't talk to him right now. She would break down. She texted again. *In meeting. Can't talk.*

That's twenty, love. Don't think I'll forget. Pick you up at five.

Twenty. He was going to spank her. She would get upset at the injustice, but just for a moment he'd taken her mind off her trouble.

Yeah, she'd take a spanking for that.

With her hands still shaking, she sat down and got back to work.

* * * *

Molina tossed his cane away with an angry crash.

He hated that cane. It had been necessary for the last several years. He needed it to keep up his pretense, but how he loathed being seen as weak and vulnerable. He should be able to force Avery to her knees, to spread her legs and make her scream, but no, he had to play the pussy role.

One day she would know exactly how strong he was.

"Careful, boss, someone might come running in." Malcolm's voice was perfectly bland as though he hadn't interrupted something intimate. The idiot had the worst timing. She'd been soft in his arms. She'd been ready to accept his lips on hers, and Malcolm had ruined everything. She'd been horrified at her mother-in-law's call. It had been exactly as he'd planned. Now she would compose herself. Now she would gather that seemingly endless supply of optimism around her like armor.

"Give me one good reason I don't fire you this instant." And by fire, he really meant find a bloody gun and take Malcolm's head off. That might start to calm him down.

If Malcolm was affected by his harsh tone, he didn't show it. His face was blank and smooth as always as he took the seat in front of Molina's desk. "You said you wanted an update on Lee Donnelly. I thought I would give you one."

"Do you have a picture of the bastard's face yet?" Molina tossed his body into his chair and then winced at the nasty pain. He was hard, but then being around her always made him hard. The thought of all that innocence for the taking had his fists clenching.

"No, I haven't. It's a little worrisome. It's like the bastard knows what he's doing." Malcolm laid a folder in front of him. He opened it and pulled out four photographs. Not a single one of them had a good shot of Donnelly's face. He was tall and well built, with broad shoulders and arms that looked like they had seen the inside of a gym on a regular basis. "He always wears a baseball cap and tends to keep his head down. He makes sure she walks on the inside. Do you see how he always takes the street side?"

Polite asshole. Unfortunately, he also always seemed to be looking Avery's way so most of the shots were of the side of his head. Avery, on the other hand, was in almost every shot, her face shining up. She held on to her new boyfriend, her eyes constantly looking at him. She looked happy where she always looked so lost and sad before.

He realized in that moment it was her misery that attracted him. She fought so valiantly against it. It was interesting to watch her flail and fight and pretend that her life was all right.

She'd been so brave, and he wondered what could make her cower in fear.

He wanted to be the one who finally broke her. And he wouldn't let this nasty fuck change that.

"Take him out."

"Boss, he moves quite well for a civilian." Malcolm frowned. On him it was practically a cry for help.

"MI6? He can't be CIA. Nelson ran the trace on him," Molina argued.

"And there was nothing in his background that made Nelson worry. But I look at him and I think he's dangerous." Malcolm sat back, his eyes on the pictures. "I've also had the feeling I'm being followed. I can't catch the bastard, though. I don't like it."

Molina sighed. Malcolm was being a worried old woman. "We've known since two weeks after we hired Weston that MI6 was watching. It's not news. They're desperate. They know they don't have a thing on us, and time is running out. They're just trying to justify their continued existence. They won't find anything. I have the files and they're in code."

"Codes can be broken."

"Surely they can. Especially when they look like codes." He was getting too old to argue. "I want Donnelly dead."

Malcolm's eyes held his for a brief moment before he

assented. "All right, but I should remind you that you had a plan concerning Avery Charles and it would be smart to follow it."

"I don't like the fact that she's fucking him." It rankled. She was supposed to be waiting. He'd isolated her so she didn't have any friends, and she'd still found someone to fuck.

"She wasn't a virgin."

But he was sure she hadn't had sex since her boy husband had died. She would be tight. So fucking tight. He could tear her up. He could make her plead and still he would shove his way in. He would spread her wide and fuck her until she bled. That would be a form of virginity. "I wasn't asking your opinion."

"It's my job to make sure this deal runs smoothly, sir, and Avery Charles crying rape to Scotland Yard would be a problem. Wait until we get her safely in the Middle East, and we can deal with her. The house in Dubai is ready, and I have a phalanx of armed guards who will ensure she can't leave. You can have your business, and you can keep her for as long as she entertains you. You've worked very hard, sir. Don't screw it up now."

"I want his head."

"That could prove troublesome. Heads are heavy. How about I cut off his dick? So much easier to transport on the Tube." Malcolm didn't crack a smile.

"I don't give a shit. I want him dead. Make it hurt." He sighed. He really didn't have time for this crap. "Just kill him. Don't do it in her flat. Make it look like a random act. I don't want her thinking this had anything to do with her. Not now."

He would let her know later, when the time was right and she couldn't get away. Avery was the woman he'd waited for. The one he'd sacrificed for. The one who made everything worthwhile. He'd killed plenty of bitches, but they hadn't served his soul the way he thought Avery would.

"I can handle this for you."

After he had the Lachlan Bates deal done, he could head to Dubai and then on to someplace even more isolated and live like a king. He would still travel, but his home base would be safe. Avery would be safe.

All he had to do was get through the next few weeks and make sure that shipment went out. Which meant he needed to find a way to get the cost of that goddamn wheat down or he needed to find a new donor because he wasn't going to bear that cost himself.

He had to pay for too many assassinations anyway. Malcolm didn't murder people for free, which was actually a minus against his continued employment.

"Also, here are the details of your meeting tomorrow," Malcolm slid an envelope his way. It was plain with no writing on it, but he knew who it was from.

Eli Nelson. Another problem he had to deal with. He owed the man. But Nelson had taken his cut, and now he was back for more.

Still, he had connections. He wouldn't have gotten the Lachlan Bates deal without him. Nelson had a real shot at helping him get into the Middle East. Africa was small potatoes compared to the Middle East. And he would dearly love to serve both sides of the inevitable Pakistani-Indian conflict. Nelson was working hard to make that little war happen.

It was worth giving him a cut. To a point.

He opened the instructions and sighed. "Do you have any idea what this shit is about?"

Malcolm shrugged. "I just take notes, boss."

There wouldn't be a second note, no ability to request an explanation for this very strange request. He would either follow it or he wouldn't.

And that rankled, too. Nelson had simply given him his start, his new identity. He'd made it possible to cast off the old one like a snake shedding his skin. When he thought about his old life, it was with a sort of despairing nausea. The things he had done to please his disgusting family, to fit in, to try to show who he was. Nelson had taught him it was all right to follow his instincts, to take care of himself and let the others rot.

Oh, sometimes he missed them. Well, he missed one of them, but that life was dead. He'd eradicated it, and it couldn't touch him now.

And perhaps Nelson had taught him all too well. Sometimes the best solution to a problem was getting rid of it all together.

After he had what he wanted.

"Of course, I'll do as he asks. After all, he's my mentor." He didn't bother to mention that he'd murdered his last mentor.

Malcolm was his liaison with Nelson. It seemed best to keep their meetings to a minimum so they weren't connected. Malcolm had no connections. His cover was so deep Molina would be surprised if Malcolm remembered what his original name had been.

"Should I send Monica in, sir?" Malcolm got up and went to the door.

Sweet, dumb Monica. She thought he was going to marry her. She was good for hiding files and had a remarkably flexible jaw. She could take care of his problem. "Yes."

Malcolm left and Molina found his cane. It was time to

perform again.

Chapter Twelve

Liam watched her. He'd expected a bit more excitement, but Avery was shut down and had been for hours. She'd been waiting for him outside her office building, not inside as he'd planned. He wanted to get a lay of the land, but she'd been standing outside, her face a pale white, her hands on her purse. She'd followed him to the Tube, sat beside him through dinner, but she hadn't really engaged.

It was getting to him. Was she that worried about the evening ahead?

"We could just go home," he said. The last thing he wanted to do was push her and potentially lose her, and it was for reasons that went far beyond the op. He wanted her to enjoy this part of his life. He was finally realizing just how much he needed it. He'd always thought of it as fun before, but now he wanted the responsibility. He wanted the deep ties that came with D/s.

She frowned up at him, her eyes blinking as though she was trying to process what he'd said. "What?"

Or she just hadn't been listening. "I said we could just go home. You seem to have changed your mind."

She seemed to have changed period. Her smile all evening long had been forced, her conversation stilted. She was always so present when she was with him, and now she seemed to be in another place entirely. She shook her head, her eyes going back to the building across the street. "No. I'm fine. I'm looking forward to it."

"I've promised to spank you for disobedience. You're really looking forward to that?" She'd shut down after the threat. Had he really misjudged her? Was she really that worried about an erotic spanking?

A hint of a real smile finally lit her face. "Well, it is a little unfair, you see. I had to work. I don't know that I like being punished for working, but that's not really what it's about, is it? It's play, like you said. It's just a fun game to spark our imaginations. Lee, I'm not afraid of you."

She should be. She would run away if she knew half of the things he'd done under the excuse of protecting people. "Then tell me what's wrong."

He'd been afraid to ask up to this point. He'd been a pussy pansy-ass who wasn't doing his job which was to protect her and comfort her. He might never have had a permanent sub before, but even he knew that was his primary function as a Dom. But he'd been afraid of the answer so he'd let her brood.

She shook her head. "It was just a rough day, Lee. The price of grain is up, and that has everyone scrambling. I'm sorry I'm being distant. I don't mean to be, and I don't want you to think I'm not interested in exploring the club. I want to. I'm rapidly discovering that really nasty sex can be a great stress reliever."

Years he'd used subs for stress relief, but hearing Avery describe it like that cut him to the quick. She wasn't telling him something. She was holding something in, and he hated it. A nasty little suspicion was thrumming through his veins. She'd thought he was a hustler before. What if the perfect little princess was just using him for sex? Had he really thought she was interested in him for anything beyond a little stress relief? She was smart. She'd grown up privileged. Yes, she'd lost her parents and that lifestyle, but did those beliefs ever really go away? She'd married a boy from a good family.

His family was all dead, and he'd had a hand in killing his brother. He'd been born in a slum and still drank cheap beer.

Her hand went to his chest. "Lee? Are you all right?"

He forced his face to go blank. She was his fucking kryptonite. He'd been trained, worked for years, and it all fell away because one passably pretty girl said something to hurt him.

That was the problem. He knew she wasn't beautiful. On an intellectual level, he knew she was rather plain. But when he looked at her all he saw was the sun in the sky, and she was never going to love him. She deserved better.

"Hey, maybe I could use a little stress relief, too." He was well aware the words came out with a nasty little bite. He'd spent all day thinking about her, waiting for her, and she wanted to use him as stress relief. Two could play at that game, and he was the Dom in this situation. She was here for his use. "You'll go into the club, and I have a friend waiting for you. Her name is Eve, and she'll take you back to the dressing rooms."

"You're not going with me?" For the first time in hours, she really looked up at him.

He couldn't help but soften slightly. "You have to change. It's fet wear only once you get beyond the lobby, and men and women have separate locker rooms."

"That sounds oddly normal for a place like this."

"Only because you don't understand a place like this. There are rules to the floor. I can walk you around naked on the floor of the club and everyone understands how to

229

behave. And if they don't they can get their asses handed to them. It's not going to be a sexual free-for-all in there. It's very disciplined."

"You use that word a lot." She started to follow him across the street, her eyes still on the building in front of her as though she was trying to see past the blandness of the outside.

"Discipline is important." He'd been undisciplined for a good portion of his life. It was only when he'd gone into the Army and the SAS that he'd found it. His discipline had been blown away when his brother died, but Ian Taggart had given it back to him. Now the only question Liam had was why.

While Avery changed, he intended to get a few answers from his boss.

"How do you know this Eve person?" Avery asked, a hint of rebuke in her tone.

So she wanted to be a little jealous of her boy toy, did she? It was there on the tip of his tongue to mislead her, to let her think Eve was a lover. Eve was a gorgeous woman. Avery would compare herself and likely find herself lacking and then she would be out of the power position. And he just couldn't do it. He took her by the shoulders and turned her to face him. "She's just a friend. She's Ian's sister, so she's a little like my sister. But she's a perfectly experienced submissive."

She was a whacked-out sub since she would take all the pain and refused any pleasure, but no one seemed to be able to crack Eve's shell on that one. She allowed Alex to scene with her, but pulled away at the thought of aftercare.

"She's Ian's sister? And they play at the same club?"

Yeah, maybe they hadn't thought this part of the cover through. "Oh, I think they try to avoid each other as much as possible, but it wouldn't be safe for her to play anywhere else. Now stop procrastinating. Are you in or out?"

She nodded toward the door. "I'm in. I want to see what's inside."

Ah, sweet curiosity. It had killed many a cat, though this time it might kill him instead.

He opened the doors and escorted Avery into the very posh-looking lobby. Eve was waiting at the desk looking like a woman who often worked the front desk of a sex club.

She smiled brightly as they walked in, but he could hear the disapproval in her voice. "Lee, it's so good to see you. It's been such a long time. I really expected you to come around sooner." Her British accent was every bit as perfect as Ian's had been. Liam often thought that they were a group of people who could have been actors had they not been so bloody good at killing. "You must be Avery."

Avery held out her hand, politely shaking Eve's. She was an inch or two shorter than Eve and even dressed for work, she couldn't match Eve's flair for fashion. There was always something askew about Avery whether it was a button she'd missed or a little tear in her skirt. She was perfectly imperfect, and it just made him want to stay close to her so she never felt the need to change.

"Nice to meet you." She glanced around the lobby. "It looks so normal."

Eve laughed, her face lighting up. "Oh, that is a lovely thought. If only the whole world was normal. I think you'll find we have a slightly different version of normal from most people. Come along, dear. Lee has your clothes set out for you. I'll help you. I don't suppose you've worn a corset before, have you?"

Her eyes went wide. "No."

Eve winked at her. "Then I'll definitely have to help

you. I'll give you a little advice. Breathe now while you can." She started to lead Avery toward the women's dressing room. Her blonde head turned slightly back toward him. "I'll show Avery around. Lee, dear, I believe you'll find Ian is waiting to have a word with you."

He nodded. He could bet Ian was waiting. Ian would be up in his office, sitting behind his temporary desk and ready for to dress Liam down. Ian could be very formal in his own odd way. Liam had seen it happen before, though if Ian tried that *Three Stooges* routine he often ran on Adam, he would find out Liam hit back.

Liam walked through the door to the men's locker room. Ian could wait.

Except Ian wasn't where he was supposed to be. He was pacing the floor of the locker room, already dressed in leathers. Black leather covered his legs and a vest sat on his massive chest.

When he turned, he looked almost human. "Li, I need to talk to you."

Fuck all. Ian looked worried. What the hell was going on? Liam could pretend to not quite understand or he could get right to the heart of the matter. He never had been one to prevaricate. He looked Ian right in the eye. "Did you or did you not run the op that got my brother killed?"

Ian stared right back. "I did and I didn't."

Liam groaned. "I'm not playing games. I want the truth."

"I'm not playing games either, but I'm starting to suspect someone is playing them with us. There are too many coincidences. Those files were buried. Weston shouldn't have been able to find them."

"So you're pissed that Weston got through your wall of protection?"

"Li, I didn't cover the op up. The Agency did, and I didn't even know they had buried the evidence until a few days ago. Honestly, I've always known we would have this conversation. I've been avoiding it for years."

"Why?"

"Because there's a lot you don't know, and honestly I didn't think you needed to know. It was done. And it was a time in my life I don't particularly want to remember."

"Because of your wife?"

Ian's face tightened. "Yes. Charlotte is a part of my life better left buried."

"Did you kill her?" He really wasn't sure he wanted the answer to that question.

"Yes and no."

Liam was ready to punch a wall. "Fuck it, Ian, will you give me a bloody straight answer? I'm sick of this. I'm thinking about walking out of here right now and taking Avery with me."

"Don't you fucking threaten me," Ian snarled.

"Ian, calm down. We talked about this." Alex was sitting in the corner, still in his sweats and a T-shirt.

Liam ran a hand across his hair. If Alex had been a snake, he could have bitten him several times. Liam was losing it. "I didn't see you."

Alex gave Liam a little half smile. "Sorry. I'm here to make sure you two don't beat each other down."

"Like you could stop us," Ian snarled back.

Liam was with Ian on this one. He was starting to think a beat down might be in order. Beating the fuck out of Ian just might make him feel better.

"In that case, I'm here to call the match. Adam and Jake have a hundred riding on it. Jake thinks Ian will kill you, but Adam is counting on the fact that you're awfully mean."

Alex sat back, waiting on the outcome.

"Does everyone know but me?" That was his fear. He was on the outside again. He was the one who didn't fit.

Ian slapped at one of the lockers, the sound reverberating through the room. "No. Alex is the only person on the team who even knew I had ever been married. Adam and Jake and Eve just think I'm talking to you about the fact that you've been an asshole for four days and you're jeopardizing this op."

Ian hadn't told his brother? "What about Sean?"

"My brother has enough problems with me as it is. Even back then, Sean had a love-hate relationship with me. Knowing about Charlie would have put him firmly in the hate camp, more than likely."

"You're wrong about Sean. He would understand," Alex said quietly. "Li will, too. Tell him."

Ian was quiet for the longest time, so long Liam thought he wasn't going to speak. "I was recruited into the CIA through their black ops program. They sometimes recruit active Special Forces members to train as operatives. I was one of them. I had run two or three small-time missions, mostly gathering recon in Afghanistan. I served there for a long time and had very good contacts. That was where I first heard whisperings of an arms dealer selling tainted materials, enough to make a significant dirty bomb or several that when used in a coordinated attack could destabilize the economy of any number of first world countries."

"I know the reason behind the op, Ian," Liam replied. He'd sat through many briefings, boring meetings meant to make him brutally aware of every aspect of the operation. He'd been sure that they were just long to make the agent briefing them justify his job.

Ian moved on. "I started tracking the arms dealer, but I couldn't get close to him. He had ties to the Russian mob. I didn't. I knew it would take more than just money."

"You needed someone with a bad reputation." Liam knew this drill. Someone like Ian would have to be under deep cover. That was hard. The Russian mob had access to many ways to break a cover. They would need real ties, and Liam had them. He had them all over his nasty family tree.

Ian's eyes rolled. "You're going to put the worst spin on this you possibly can. You and your brother had IRA ties."

"I never hid them." He couldn't have hidden them. When he'd gone into the Army, he'd been a dumb kid barely able to wipe his ass much less hide the fact that his mother had seen the IRA as a religion. He hadn't. He never had. It had almost been his way of rebelling.

"I know, and you were so damn good at your job that the SAS took you in anyway. Your commanding officers didn't believe you had a hand in the IRA, but there are always rumors and those rumors can be used for good or bad."

He'd never had a second's misconception why he'd been chosen, and he'd known bloody well there could be a cost. His idiot younger self had practically wanted to sacrifice for the cause. That dumber Liam had believed he'd be a hero. "I knew that going into the mission. I knew there would be fall out. I knew intelligence would put it out that Rory and I were still meeting with Ma's old cohorts."

"Rory did meet with them, Li." Ian's words dropped between them.

Liam couldn't help but reject it. "No. If he did, it was only for the mission." But why hadn't Rory told him? Ian had to be mistaken. Except he was always so cautious.

Ian seemed to choose his words carefully. "He did it

before the mission. He was under investigation, but he convinced your higher-ups that he was just checking in on family. His ties were why I picked you both for the op."

Liam felt the ground shifting beneath him. Rory had gotten in touch with their uncles? Their crown hating, kill 'em all uncles? They'd grown up surrounded with bitterness and bile, and they'd promised to never go back after their mother drank herself to death. "He would have told me."

"We all have secrets, Liam. Even from our brothers." Ian's eyes found the floor.

Liam's head was spinning a little, but it had to be that Rory felt a connection to their family that he didn't. Why the hell hadn't his brother told him? Had Rory thought he would try to talk him out of it? He was right. He would have, but if he couldn't then Liam would have stood by his brother. He would have gone into the belly of the beast with him. Hadn't he always tried to protect Rory? Liam had always been the one to clean up the messes Rory made.

Had Rory died thinking he had to hide from his brother?

"I was coordinating with MI6 and G2," Ian continued. "It was right about that time that I met Charlie, and I lost my fucking head. I was so in lust with that woman. She was gorgeous and sexy and submissive. It was like someone had reached into my libido and pulled out my ideal woman. She was fucking perfect on the outside. She wasn't the type who didn't make you work for her submission. No, not my Charlie. She was a righteous bitch half the time, and that got me panting after her. I let everything slide. My work, my other relationships, everything. I married her ten days after I met her. We were married for exactly 32 days."

Ian went silent again.

"What went wrong?" Liam asked.

Ian chuckled, but there was no humor behind it.

"Everything. I got a call from Langley. The op was ready to go despite my half-assed work. The day you managed to get the bonds, I was supposed to head to Dublin to meet with you and prep you for your final mission. I should have been there the night you went into that pub. I would never have allowed that to happen, by the way. I had a room next to yours, and we were going to spend the evening in a debrief. I was walking in to grab my passport, and that's when I found her."

The idea of walking into a perfectly normal situation and finding Avery's body on the ground sent a chill through him. "You didn't kill her?"

"She was a message to me."

Liam could remember how she looked in those photos. Beautiful. Cold. Soulless. If it was a message, someone had been serious about it. *Shit.* "From who?"

"From whoever hired her to seduce me, I suppose. She had some very nasty ties to the Russian mafia. I didn't bother to look into her past. I was too in lust." Ian ground the words out like every one cost him.

"Call it what it was, Ian," Alex said from the corner. "You were in love with the woman."

Ian's mouth took on a cruel line. "It was lust. I didn't know who the fuck she was. She lied about everything."

Alex sighed as though they had been through this a thousand times. "No, she didn't. She told you her real name. She gave you every opportunity to check her out. You chose not to. I think she was in love with you, too, Ian."

Ian waved him off. "It doesn't matter now, Alex. She's dead and I fucked up Liam's life, and I've been trying to make up for it ever since."

"Did you plant the bomb?" He asked it with a little hesitance. What the hell was going on? Had Ian been the one to eradicate all the evidence? Had he been the one on watch when his brother had been murdered?

"Of course not." Ian sank onto the wooden bench. "I wouldn't blow up my own goddamn assets. I know you don't think a lot of me, but I've never hurt my own men. It's why I didn't sign on as a full-time operative. The Agency uses me on certain ops, but I never fit the profile for a pure agent. I can't sell out my friends. I was talking about the fact that I was too involved in Charlie's death to handle my own op. They brought someone in to handle the operation, and he fucked everything up."

"Who?" Liam asked.

Ian's face hardened stubbornly. A nasty silence filled the air.

"You have to understand he didn't find out until very recently," Alex started.

"Fucking Nelson!" Liam got into Ian's space. Eli Nelson seemed to be everywhere.

"I didn't know who he was when he came to Dallas a while back. He wasn't using his real name, and I didn't know him by sight. It's not like we have an annual Christmas party, but I started to research him after he nearly killed my brother." Ian stood, not giving an inch.

"You know you're both letting Nelson win if you beat each other up over this," Alex pointed out.

"I want to know what happened." Liam didn't back down. "Did you know I was being set up?"

"Fuck, no. I didn't know anything until you called me after the building had blown up," Ian replied. "I was...I was trying to deal with Charlie's death. I was useless."

"We call it grieving in the real world," Alex said, not moving.

"Shut up, Alex," Ian rounded on his best friend.

"I can't. Adam isn't here to lend much needed sarcasm, so I have to. Really, you two are setting a new world record for testosterone levels in a locker room." He got serious for a moment. "I hate watching you two tear each other up when there's no reason for it. Ian was hurting because he loved his wife."

"I didn't love her," Ian ground out.

"Tomato, tomahto," Alex shot back. "Ian's made one mistake in his very long career, and he's felt guilty ever since. It's been worse since he came to give a real goddamn about you. Give him a break, man. He lost his head over a girl. Can you say you're not doing the same right now? I'm not blind. I've followed you for days. You're crazy about Avery."

"She's a pretty girl." He wasn't going to admit it. The last thing he needed was to get pulled off the op because he'd fallen for someone who didn't really want him. A girl who saw him as nothing but an orgasm on two legs.

"Don't be an idiot, Li." Alex shook his head. "You don't want to end up like him."

Ian turned to Alex. "You're supposed to be my best friend."

"I am," Alex replied. "I've also been married to a psychologist for long enough to know that you're in denial about Charlotte, and you can't move on until you at least accept the fact that you loved the woman."

Ian shot Alex the finger as he moved around Liam. "Says the man who still calls himself married years after his wife divorced him. Fuck you, Alex. And Liam, that's the truth. I've told you everything I know. If you don't accept it, you can take a fucking hike. I'm done with this."

Ian stalked out, his boots thudding an angry rhythm over the hardwoods.

And Liam still had questions. He started to walk out after Ian. They weren't done.

Alex got in his way. "Don't. He wasn't ready for this. Please give him a little time."

"He's had years, Alex." Years where he hadn't bothered to give Liam the truth.

"I know. And I know just about everything. Ian didn't know the op had gone south until you called him. He did everything he could to get you out while he sorted through all the shit that was left behind. And as far as we can tell, Nelson claimed to have no idea what happened."

"Did Nelson kill my brother?" Liam felt his fists clench.

Alex frowned. "Possibly, though it's hard to tell. The question would be why. Why bother when it seems like he didn't get any money out of it? The bonds were worth millions. Why wouldn't he spend them?"

"You're right. If he had the bonds, why would he sit on them?" It didn't make sense. Nelson had been in Dallas to steal secrets to sell to the Chinese. Why would he need that money if he had the bonds?

"Nelson's a patient guy," Alex said. "He might have had plans for the bonds. And he was still CIA until a few months back. This seems to be a very long game he's been playing, and I don't like how many of us he's using as chess pieces."

Liam didn't either. So many things didn't make sense. "Did Ian consider that Leonov made me and Rory and this was his version of revenge?"

"Leonov was found dead shortly after. If he found another broker for the deal, the Agency couldn't prove it. No one found any nuclear materials or could even tie him to them in a tangible way. If he had them, he got rid of them and there was no hint of the arms dealer who was selling the uranium again. Ian was left with no weapons, no assets, and no bonds."

And no wife. "Why hasn't he told me?"

"Because he didn't know enough until very recently. After that op he stopped working for the Agency for a very long time. He concentrated on building this business for us. Think about it, man. Eve and I had just gotten divorced. Sean had left the Army. Jake and Adam had been kicked to the curb. I never actually met Charlotte, but I've known Ian for a long time. I've never seen him as dark as he was after she died. We were all lost, and Ian and I decided to try to build a life raft."

"McKay-Taggart." The company had been all that kept him sane for several years. Now he could see they had all really thrown themselves into building the company. It had been what they all had needed. "What the hell is going on, Alex?"

Alex sat back down, his big body slumping as though he couldn't handle just how tired he was a second more. "I don't know, but hopefully it's over tomorrow. If we can't catch him, we'll kill him. We're going to follow him so we don't disrupt the MI6 op by capturing or killing him in front of Molina. They still need to figure out what's happening at United One Fund. It's the deal we worked out with them."

"Where did Weston get that file if not from the CIA?" If Ian was right, then that file really bugged him.

"MI6 kept files. They were classified, but Weston turned out to be quite the pro with a computer. He's not being fired just yet, but I suspect that's because he's too valuable to the op."

He wished he could be there when the bastard got cut loose. "All right. Look, this isn't over. I still have a ton of questions, and you know as well as I do that Adam and Jake should be brought into this."

"I know and they will. Just give him a day. He processes the emotional shit more slowly than the rest of us."

"Do you still consider yourself married to Eve?" It seemed like Ian wasn't the only one who processed slowly.

Alex's face flushed, but he seemed steady. "No. I know that's over. I don't know if you'll believe me, but I was sort of relieved when I thought you were sleeping with her. Oh, I hated your guts, but at least it would have been over."

Liam didn't believe that for a second. "I thought you still loved her."

"I'll die loving her, but she's had me in purgatory for so long, I just want out and I can't until she lets me."

"Six years is a long time without sex."

Alex frowned. "We have sex, Li. We have a lot of sex."

That was news. "Are you kidding me? Then what's your problem, man?" It struck him rather forcefully what the problem was. He'd watched them scene together, a delicate dance of pain and pleasure. It always seemed emotional until the moment Eve got up and refused all aftercare. She used Alex and then walked away, never allowing the Dom the second part of the exchange—the tender part. "She uses you for sex the same way she scenes with you."

Alex looked away. "She hasn't kissed me in six years. What we have is a disgusting imitation of love."

"Break it off." That must be killing Alex.

Alex laughed, a hollow sound. "I can't. I'm the reason she is the way she is. I thought at first that I could get her back, but now I know she's just punishing me. She isn't looking to heal. She isn't looking to move on. She's got me locked in a never-ending cycle, and I don't think she'll ever let go."

"Walk away." As much as he loved Eve, Liam felt for Alex in that moment.

Alex shook his head. "Can't."

"What happened between the two of you?" He'd never had the full story. As far as he could tell, Adam and Jake didn't know either.

"I chose an op over her. I thought I was doing the right thing at the time, but the consequences...god. I'll never forgive myself, Li. And she can't forgive me, either. If you give a damn about this girl Avery, tell her who you are. If you think for one second that you have a shot at a life with her, that you could love her, tell her before the betrayal is too much for her to take."

"I can't. The mission," Liam started. He'd thought about it a hundred times.

"Will go on without her. She doesn't have ties to Nelson. The most she can do is help out MI6 a little. We've already gotten everything from her we can. She doesn't know anything else. She can very quietly disappear, and she'll be out of it." Alex sounded so reasonable.

"Ian would fire me." That argument was having less and less weight in Liam's mind.

Alex waved that thought off. "Ian's bark is worse than his bite. If he didn't fire Adam and Jake, he won't fire you. Look, I can't tell you how to live your life. I just know how you look at her."

"She doesn't know who I am." Liam finally admitted the real problem. "When she finds out, she won't want me. I'm a bastard."

"Yeah, you were. And then you met her. We don't know who we really are until we meet the people we're supposed to be with. They can drag us down or they can lift us up. Maybe you don't know who you are anymore because you're changing. If you let yourself love this woman, you'll be a different person. You'll be the person Avery made you, and you might find you like that man quite a bit. You've already opened up in ways I wouldn't have imagined. Just think about it, okay?" Alex stood up and opened his locker. "I have to get ready. I think Eve and I are going to scene for your girl tonight."

Now that he knew a little about what was going on between them, it seemed like a terrible thing to do. "You don't have to. I'm just going to walk her around for a while and then take her to a privacy room and introduce her to some bondage. Alex, you don't have to do this."

But Alex turned, pulling his leathers out. "It's all right, man. It's only what I deserve."

Liam reached into his own locker, his anger from before easing to low ache. What did he deserve? Certainly not Avery. But he'd never been a man to settle for what he deserved. He was a man who took what he wanted.

Chapter Thirteen

Avery blinked in the low light of the club. The Garden itself was completely different from the posh, traditional lobby. The outer rooms of The Garden looked like any number of hotel lobbies, but the inner room was unlike anything Avery had ever seen. It was a massive greenroom whose plants were all night bloomers. Stone floors were beneath her feet, but the smell of jasmine filled the air. Moonlight streamed into the room from an enormous skylight that seemed to go through the center of the whole building.

It was like she'd stepped into an alien world.

She watched with wide eyes as a diminutive woman in thigh-high boots walked past tugging on the leash of a massive man in leather undies.

Eve moved over, leaning her head close to be heard over the thumping music. "You should really prepare yourself for just about anything in this place."

She was starting to see that. Whatever she'd imagined The Garden would be, it wasn't this lush temple to sensory decadence. She looked around hoping to find Lee. Two steps out of the locker room and she already wanted his hand in hers. She felt weird and exposed without him. Like she didn't belong.

Avery wished she'd taken Eve's advice seriously. She really couldn't breathe. The black and scarlet corset she found herself in was its own form of torture device. And the thong thingee kind of sucked, too. She had no idea why any woman would want to wear undies designed to be shoved between her butt cheeks.

"Are you all right?" Eve asked, her dark eyes lit with mirth.

Avery smiled back. Eve didn't seem like a woman who smiled much. If her discomfort brought Eve a little amusement, then maybe it was a good thing. "I think my boobs are going to come out. Are they really supposed to be around my neck?"

Her boobs were big enough, but the corset took her to epic levels. She didn't look pretty like Eve did. She looked overblown. Eve looked sleek and neat in her corset. Avery felt like she was going to pop out. And Liam hadn't left her any shoes. Eve was taller in the first place, but after she put on her stilettos, Eve's legs looked like they were a mile long. Avery felt like a hobbit someone had stuffed into lingerie.

"You look perfectly scrumptious. Lee picked it out himself. I was sure he would ask me to do it," Eve said.

"Do you often pick out lingerie for Lee's subs?" She couldn't help it. Eve was intimidating. Gorgeous and graceful, Avery couldn't help but wonder why Lee wasn't interested in her.

Eve's eyes widened briefly. "No. I have never done it because he's never had a sub."

"Never? But he talked about how long he'd been in the lifestyle."

"Oh, he's been in the lifestyle for years, but he's never spent more than a night or two with a sub. He's a bit of a manwhore, if you know what I mean."

Avery shook her head and looked around, praying he couldn't hear them. "Don't call him that. He really doesn't like to be called that."

Eve's face lit up, a bright smile crossing her lips. "I heard you had questioned his profession. Oh, my dear girl, you're going to be so much fun. I wasn't talking about him being an actual hustler. I was talking about the fact that he hasn't settled down. He's seemed content with one-night stands and hook-ups. I was very happy when he said he was bringing you here. It's practically bringing you home to meet the family."

The word "family" sat in her gut like a rock. She still couldn't get Lydia's words out of her head. Had she really done the wrong thing? Would she take it back in the hopes of pleasing her in-laws?

"Your Master is on his way," Eve said, gesturing toward the door across the floor. Paths were laid out in cobblestone, weaving their way around the trees and bushes and patches of flowers that dotted the floor along with large areas dedicated to pleasure and pain.

Avery knew the minute she saw Lee that even if she hadn't been wearing a too-tight corset, she wouldn't have been able to breathe. He was gorgeous, six foot three inches of perfectly sculpted male in leather pants and a vest that showed off his chest to perfection. His black hair shone in the moonlight, the crystal of his green eyes making him look like a predator in his natural habitat. He stalked toward her, a panther in a primeval garden.

His eyes caught hers, and she wondered what the hell he saw in her.

"Don't," Eve said.

"What?" They were getting closer. Lee seemed to have found a friend, and they were both walking her way. His friend was just a little taller than Lee. Lee was an elegant panther, but the man with him was a gorgeous tank of a guy.

What was she doing here? Everyone was beautiful.

Eve forcibly turned her, taking her attention away from the men. "Don't start in with the insecurities. I've been watching you all night, and I can tell what you're thinking."

"Well, look at him. Am I wrong to wonder? I don't belong here."

"You don't see yourself the way he sees you. I have very little time to impart something that could make the difference in whether or not this relationship works out so listen up. That man has changed since he met you and for the better. No matter what happens later on, know that. Do not let your insecurities come between you and potential happiness. You make the choice in how you see yourself. You can see your own beauty or you can warp your image until it's so distorted you'll never see yourself the same way again. Don't ask why he's here. He's here and he wants you. He can't fake that."

He couldn't, could he? And why would he bother? Still, Avery felt the nasty bite of insecurity as Lee walked up to her. He was so tall and strong. She was short and couldn't walk for very long without falling on her face.

"Is that the way you greet me?"

Funny how he didn't yell, but she had no trouble hearing him over the heavy gothic rock. It was like that deep, dark chocolate voice of his had a line to her ears that no amount of noise could overcome.

He held a hand out. She'd noticed that Eve had gracefully fallen to her knees, her head bowed in perfect submission. Avery looked at her, every line of Eve's body perfect.

She couldn't even get into position properly without a hand down.

Lee's hand found her chin, tugging it up and forcing her

to look at him. "Don't compare yourself to her. She's been doing this for a very long time."

"I won't ever be able to move like she does."

He leaned in, speaking directly in her ear, his voice full of some unnamed emotion. "Perfection on the outside means nothing to me, Avery. We don't do this like anyone else. This is ours. We're not going to be like them, do you understand me? We're just us. This is just you and me, and we do this our way."

Tears threatened because it was the perfect thing to say. She realized now that he'd been trying to say it all week. He'd talked to her about how he practiced BDSM, but they would find their own way. There was no wrong way or right way. There was only their way.

She put her hand in his and allowed him to act as a balance as her knees found the floor.

"Not for long, love. The floors in the private rooms are better for your knees, but this is symbolic."

Avery placed her hands on her thighs, palms up and spread her legs wide.

"I like the corset, Avery. It fits perfectly."

She couldn't help it. She snorted a little.

Lee's hands tangled in her hair, pulling her head up so she met his eyes. "What was that?"

"Well, it's a little ridiculous, Lee. It's obviously too small," she replied. She wished she'd taken a little thought with her words because his face darkened.

"You didn't tell me she was a brat." Lee's friend stared down at her, disapproval plain on his handsome face.

"That's because I didn't realize she was one."

Brat. *Damn*. She hadn't meant to be. She'd meant to be self-deprecating. "I'm sorry. I was just trying to explain that I'm a little too fat for this corset."

Eve sighed though she didn't move at all.

"Did you just call yourself fat?" Liam asked, his jaw dropping slightly.

She was getting into so much trouble. "I was just being realistic. Tell me you never thought it."

"I don't think it now, and I won't listen to you say it. I bought that corset because I wanted to show off my gorgeous sub, and you are acting like a brat in front of my friends. I told you that your behavior reflects on me. One of my jobs is to make sure you understand you're beautiful and desirable, and you just let another Dom know that I haven't been doing my job. Take my hand and get up."

"I'm sorry."

"I don't require an apology. I require obedience or you can safe word out."

Humiliation swept through her system. She'd just been trying to be funny.

No. No, she hadn't. She'd thought she could distance herself if she called herself fat. She'd been doing it for years. She'd claimed she was being funny or realistic when the truth was it took real actual bravery to see the beauty in her own body because so many people didn't. So many people were waiting to tear her down, but did that mean she should do it first—or should she stand up for herself? Maybe no one could see how pretty she was until she believed it herself.

"I'm sorry," she said with more confidence this time.

Lee wasn't listening. "I told you I don't require your apology."

"I wasn't apologizing to you. I was apologizing to me."

He stopped, his eyes softening. He knelt down. "Are you being honest, love?"

She nodded. Eve had been trying to tell her. She'd lain in a bed for years, and every single day she'd vowed that she would walk. She'd believed, but now she wasn't giving herself the same courtesy she'd given her legs. She couldn't be truly beautiful if she didn't believe, and this man was giving her the chance to find that power. "Yes, I am. And now I'm ready to get up. I'm not going to say my safe word, Lee. I want to be here. I need to be here."

"I need to be here, too," Liam vowed. "Avery, no matter what anyone thinks, I think you're gorgeous and you look amazingly hot tonight. It isn't too tight. It's perfect, and when we're in this club or any other club, you're going to wear what I want you to wear and you're going to understand that I picked it because I want to see you in it. Are you worried about what other people will think?"

"Yes, but I'm trying not to because the truth is you're the only one who counts. You're the one I want to please so no one else matters."

"Thank you, love. That's what I want." He leaned over and brushed his lips against hers.

"So we don't have to do the punishment thing?" Maybe she'd talked her way out of it.

Liam shook his head. "Oh, no, we're absolutely going to do that. We were going to start the evening watching my friends scene, but now I think the shoe is on the other foot. Alex, can you secure us a spanking bench?"

She bit her bottom lip. She'd read about spanking benches. She'd looked them up on the Internet. It looked like she was about to get very well acquainted with one.

"I'm sure I can make that happen," Alex replied. "You can use the space I reserved for Eve and myself."

Eve's head turned slightly, her lips turned up in a little smile. *Told you,* she mouthed.

"Up." Lee stood, holding his hand out.

She took it this time. She'd come here for a reason, and

it hadn't been to put herself down. In the days she'd been with Lee, she'd become so much more confident. Why had she just screwed up royally? She was dressing better, feeling sexy and alive. Why had she just fallen back into that old pattern?

Because of that phone call. Because she was still hiding so much from him. She'd told him about Madison, but she hadn't pulled out the pictures, hadn't made her baby real to him. She was still keeping her distance.

"What's wrong?" Liam asked.

She put on a sunny smile. Baby steps. She'd take baby steps and pray they eventually got her to her destination. "Nothing. I'm good. Well, I'm going to be okay, though I suspect my backside is going to be a little red."

"I think a nice pink will suffice this time." His jaw tightened. "Are you sure there isn't something you're not telling me?"

So much, but nothing she felt secure sharing. She wanted him so badly. She couldn't think about letting him go. She knew he wouldn't stay forever, but just a little while longer. "No. It's good, Lee."

He took her hand, but that tight look on his face hadn't disappeared. Maybe it was just his Dom face.

She walked around taking everything in. Despite having the look of a savage garden, the place was neat and clean. Flowers bloomed on a vine surrounding a scene space. A woman had been tied to a St. Andrew's Cross, her curvy backside on full display as an enormous man dressed in leathers wielded a whip. Avery stopped and stared, wincing a little as the whip cracked through the air.

"It sounds worse than it hurts," Lee said, his arm surrounding her waist and pulling her close. He spoke directly in her ear, lending an immediate sense of intimacy.

Despite the fact that they were surrounded by others, it felt as though they were alone, the scene in front of her being performed only for them. This was how he made her feel when he put his arms around her—protected, adored. "Watch the sub's back. Look at the slump of her shoulders. They've been playing for a while now. She's already found her subspace."

The sub's head was rolled forward as though she didn't have the will or the inclination to keep it up, but there was nothing in her body language that read like pain or weakness. Pleasure. She practically shivered with it every time the whip struck her flesh.

"How can it not hurt?"

"Because Damon's an experienced top. He's worked with a whip for years I would bet. What you hear is the snap of the whip, but depending on where and how hard he lands it, that's what decides the level of pain. Look at the thin lines on her back. They're pink, not red and they aren't welting up. Now that's not to say you won't see some submissives who want welts, who need a higher level of pain."

It was so confusing to her. "I'm struggling with the idea of hurting someone you care about."

"Some people jog and love to work out because they get addicted to the endorphins. Some people get the same endorphins from pushing their bodies."

"But with exercise your body gets something it needs," Avery argued.

"And for some of these people they're getting what their souls need. I'm surprised you're being so judgmental." He pulled her away, taking her toward the back. A frown sat on his face.

She seemed to be very good at disappointing him

tonight. "I'm just trying to understand. I know we've talked about this all week, but seeing it happen in front of me is different."

He forcibly turned her back to the scene. "Look closely. Look past all your pretty notions of how we should treat each other in a perfect world and tell me what you see."

She saw a man whipping a woman. That was what she saw, but she owed it to Lee to at least pretend to look. The scene was coming to an end. The Dom set aside his whip and strode over to the St. Andrew's Cross, his hands working the ties that bound the sub. Her face turned up and instead of the relief Avery thought she would see, the sub gave her Dom a little smile and a wink and slumped into his arms as though all her strength was gone.

But that wasn't a bad thing necessarily, she realized. Sometimes a person had to expend all their strength to get to a place where they could be taken care of. The sub nuzzled the Dom's chest, her affection for him so plain it brought tears to Avery's eyes.

She was being judgmental. Who was she to tell a woman how she should love? How she should get what she needs? Maybe there were as many ways for a woman to love as there were women walking the earth.

"What do you see, Avery?" Liam asked.

"I see a woman getting what she needs and a man who seems happy to give it to her."

"Exactly," Liam replied, relief plain in his voice. "If you don't need this, tell me now because I am not going to be that fucking sadist who abuses you."

She wasn't sure she needed the spanking. Lee had smacked her backside a couple of times during sex, and she hadn't had a problem with that. It had done nothing but get her hotter, more ready, but this was different. She wasn't already aroused. She was disconcerted and a little scared.

But what had he given her? He'd been "topping" her all week. He'd forced her to slow down and be intimate. That intimacy had led to her beginning to look at herself in a different light, to give herself credit she hadn't before. He'd given her more pleasure than she'd ever imagined, and she couldn't discount that part of life anymore. It was important and necessary to her, and she never would have found it if Lee hadn't placed firm boundaries on what was and wasn't acceptable. He'd made her pleasure a necessary act to achieve his own and by doing so forced her to place a value on herself she hadn't before.

How could she find power in submission? It seemed an oxymoron, but she was finding herself by giving up power in certain areas.

"I want to try." She wanted to explore, to see how far she could go, and he was the guide in this new world.

"Why?" The word sounded a little strangled coming out of his mouth.

Why? That was hard and easy. Easy because she could come up with a very logical reason, but it was a lie. And a safe thing to say. "Because I'm enjoying myself."

Such a lie and she was still a coward. The right answer was that she'd fallen in love with him, that he'd brought out an Avery she really wanted to be. She liked herself when she was around him. She felt powerful and strong when she wasn't giving in to her insecurity. She adored him.

But she didn't say it because she was deathly scared about the silence that would likely follow that particular declaration.

"You're enjoying yourself? I guess I should have expected that. Well, I'm glad to hear it." He didn't sound glad. He sounded a little angry.

"What did I do wrong?"

His face cleared. He looked down at her with the polite blank mask she hated. She would rather he yelled at her than stared at her like she was a stranger and there was nothing between them. "Nothing, baby. Nothing at all. Come on. Let's get the punishment portion of the evening done so we can move on to something you'll enjoy."

She followed him wondering all the while exactly what she'd said to put that look on his face.

Ten minutes later, she swallowed as she looked at the spanking bench Alex had directed them to. It was an oddly shaped thing with a long centerpiece that sloped down toward the head and four smaller padded arms and legs.

"I'm going to allow you to keep your clothes on this time. You can keep both the corset and the thong. I'll work around them," Lee said, sounding like he was being particularly magnanimous.

Her backside was going to be in the air and that teeny tiny piece of butt floss wasn't going to cover an inch of it. Her big old cheeks would be right there for all the world to see.

She glanced over and saw Alex grinning a little. What was that about?

"Yes, love, he's excited about watching you get your ass whipped because it means he gets a view of that juicy butt. He's looking forward to it, and I'm thinking about tearing his eyes out." Lee gave his friend a stare that would have caused Avery to run, but Alex just shrugged and kept his hand on Eve's hair. The sub was back in her submissive position, but only after Alex had reminded her. The minute they had gotten to their destination, Alex had put a hand out as though that was their signal. She'd glared at him, too, so it wasn't so surprising Lee's stare hadn't worked. Alex seemed to let it just flow right off his back.

Alex thought he would enjoy seeing her backside? She kind of wanted to ask but decided that would probably set Lee off. He hadn't liked her saying something bad about herself. It was what had gotten her into this position in the first place.

He was doing this for her, she realized suddenly. She'd questioned her own desirability, and now he was putting her on display not for his pride, but for hers.

Her insecurity dropped away, and she looked up at the man who seemed determined to give her everything. "Will you help me get on the bench? I might fall."

A smile lit his face. That pleased him. Helping her pleased him. Over the course of their time together, he'd gotten her into the habit of reaching for him. He held a hand out, allowing himself to be the balance as she lowered herself to the bench. It was thickly padded, but her breasts were bound and it seemed like the bench was meant to split them up in order to assure her comfort.

She would be precariously balanced with the corset on. She tried it and felt a little like a balloon trying to balance on a toothpick. *Darn it.* He'd said he was allowing her to keep her clothes, not that he was demanding it. He was making her choose. Safety and comfort over her own insecurity.

"Is something wrong?" Lee asked, his voice rising in anticipation.

She frowned. He knew exactly what was wrong, the bastard. He'd spent a week helping her to learn how to let go so she could experience pleasure at its fullest and now he was testing her. What side of Avery would win, he was likely wondering. The one who was afraid to show her body off to a bunch of people who really didn't matter or the sexy thing who wanted her pleasure and to please her Master? If she kept the corset on, she might be able to save her pride, but she would just be enduring the experience until she could get back up. Or she could do what she'd come here to do. She could explore and figure out where she wanted to be.

She managed to sit back up, well aware everyone was waiting on her. "Sir, can I please take the corset off? I won't be able to concentrate on the sensation if I'm worried about my balance."

He stared down at her, one eyebrow arching. "It's going to make your boobs hang, you understand that?"

She had large breasts and they would hang like pendulums off the sides of the bench. They wouldn't be perky and petite, but if he wanted perky and petite, then he wouldn't be here with her. If he needed small, lovely breasts to get him hot, he should not have thought about asking her to be his sub. He liked her breasts. He touched them all the time. He couldn't seem to wait to get his mouth on them. That was what she needed to think about, not what anyone else would see. "I think you'll like watching them sway, Sir."

A brilliant smile crossed his face banishing the distant Dom and bringing back the man who cuddled close to her at night. "The girl learns. Come here and let me get that off you."

His hands made quick work of the corset, much faster than Eve had gotten her into it. Her breasts swung free, and she could breathe again. And she was more than half naked in front of a crowd. Liam handed the corset off to Alex, and Avery looked around the space. They'd seemed to be alone, but now at least twenty people were standing around ready to watch the scene, including Lee's big blond friend Ian. He was looking at her boobs, and he didn't look like he was about to barf. "Where did they come from?"

"Hey, word gets around that a hot scene is about to play out. People come out of the woodwork," Lee explained. "I think they'll call this particular scene 'hot little virgin gets her ass spanked and more.'"

"I'm not a virgin, Lee," she corrected.

"How little you know, baby. Your pussy isn't the only place a cock can go. Are you telling me you've had anal sex?"

She shook her head. She should have known this was coming. His fingers had strayed there before, brushing across her asshole and pressing lightly in. It had been a dark, forbidden sensation. "No, I haven't."

"I'm going to claim it, Avery. Your asshole is going to be mine. I'm going to fuck you every way I can and don't think I won't make you love it. Every inch of your body is going to belong to me." His fingers came out to trace the line of her breastbone. "I can punish you in more pleasurable ways. Trust me, Avery. Let me show you off. Let me show them just how hot my sub is."

She was standing in front of a roomful of strangers, and it didn't matter because all that mattered was the pleasure they could find together. Maybe this was for him, too. Maybe he got hot at the thought of showing her off. "Yes, Sir."

"That's what I want to hear." He helped her down again. This time she eased onto the bench, the leather soft on her skin. It wasn't a shiny leather. It was buttery and comfortable, so much nicer than before. This was how it should have been the whole time.

"You don't need these anymore," Lee said, his fingers

delving under her panties and pulling them taut.

She gasped a little as they came off. She turned and saw he'd cut them off her. He handed a small knife back to Alex, who seemed to be serving as his assistant torturer. Lee tossed her thong away. She wouldn't be getting that back. She was naked and on stage, and there was a little part of her that was getting soft and wet and warm. No one had run screaming. No one was laughing. There was a sort of warm appreciation she felt, as though she was surrounded by people who wouldn't judge her, wouldn't toss her out because she wasn't perfect.

She turned her cheek to rest on the bench and looked at them. Besides Lee's friends, they were a rather motley group. Some were bigger than normal, others had somewhat plain faces. An older couple, the man balding with a little paunch to his belly, held the hand of a gray-haired sub. They smiled at her, approval on their faces.

This wasn't about perfection. This was about acceptance. These people accepted themselves, and that seemed to make it easy to accept her.

A sense of peace came over her. Whatever happened, it would be all right because he was right here with her.

"What's your safe word, Avery?" Lee asked. He looked down at her, but she couldn't look beyond the enormous erection he was sporting. It tented his leathers and seemed to block out all the other sights. He chuckled. "Yeah, I've been that way since I first realized I was going to get to smack your ass, baby. Ignore him for now. He'll come into play later. Now answer the question. What's your safe word?"

A safe word, she'd learned, was a word that once uttered by a sub stopped all action. Whatever the Dom was doing, once that safe word was out, he would stop and help the sub. "Telephone."

"Good." He held a length of rope in his hand. "I'm tying you down, but I can have you out in ten seconds if it bothers you."

She wasn't worried. He'd played around with ropes the night before, lightly tying her to the bed before he'd put his mouth on her pussy and made her scream. He made short work of it, binding her hands and feet to the bench. She could wiggle her limbs, but she couldn't escape. She was utterly helpless. He could do anything he wanted with her.

She should be afraid, but all she could think about was the fact that he had the filthiest mind, and she couldn't wait to see what he did.

"It's a count of thirty for talking bad about yourself," Lee said.

She heard a murmur of disapproval go through the crowd. Yep, these were not people who wanted to listen to her complain about her cellulite. She would have to come up with better conversation starters than that.

And then she nearly screamed because his hand met the cheeks of her ass, and it wasn't the little slap she'd gotten before. Fire flared across her skin because that smack had meant business.

"That's one, baby," Lee said, his hand holding the heat to her cheek. "And this is two."

She gasped, the air threatening to leave her body as he smacked her again. Pain screamed along her system, but if he thought she was giving in over that pain, he was insane. She wasn't a lightweight when it came to this. Ten years, seventeen surgeries, each one more painful than the last, and each of those horrible incidents had led to one thing.

Walking. Living. Surviving.

And there hadn't even been a mega orgasm with the world's hottest man at the end of those surgeries. She felt a smile cross her face. Yeah, she could handle him.

Three came like a crack of thunder, but she was more confident now. Her skin was singing, with ache and pain and a weird heat that was starting to build. Sure, some pain was just torture, but some pains, oh, some pains reminded her that she was alive.

Some pains took her away from herself. All the misery of the day slipped away. She didn't have to think about what had happened with her in-laws here. It didn't matter. Here she could be in the moment and not worry about the past or the future. She could be in the present, and the present was all about feeling. Tears slipped from her eyes, but they felt cleansing.

By the time he counted out fifteen, she was sure she'd found something wonderful. Her backside ached, but Lee was careful to never hit her in the same place more than a few times. He peppered the spanking across her bottom, spreading the heat all along her skin.

She concentrated on the sensation. Fire and heat soaked her flesh, sinking in and spreading out. It traveled from the spot he'd struck and seemed to flash across her body, sending out all kinds of signals. Her pussy was wet and soft. Her toes curled. Her nipples peaked and ached for someone to touch her. Her mouth softened, ready for stimulation. She felt each slap from her head to her toes, a sensual dance that started with shocking pain and morphed into pleasure, arousal, peace.

Lee was suddenly on his knees. "Avery, are you all right? I asked you a question, and you didn't answer. Was it too rough? Are you hurt? You're crying. You have to say your safe word."

His eyes were narrowed, concern on his handsome face. He brushed away a tear.

She gave him a frown. Why had he stopped? She'd been in a nice place. "I don't want to say my safe word. Is it already over? I didn't count thirty. That was barely nineteen."

"Little brat likes her spanking." He growled the words with a look of great relief. His fingers came up and skimmed her nipples. "Fuck, Avery. You like it a lot, don't you? How wet is your pussy?"

He didn't wait for an answer. He got up and smacked her ass again before his fingers delved between her legs. It was startling, enticing. She was suddenly thankful for the ropes or she might have fallen off the bench. Her pussy wasn't just wet. It was primed and ready for anything. One little touch made her quiver, want more.

"You're wet, baby." One hand was between her legs, his fingers sliding along her pussy while the other smacked her ass just where her thighs met her butt. Avery squirmed because the dual sensations were bringing her out of that peaceful, almost floaty place. It was bringing her to a place where she wanted so much more. "This pussy is so fucking wet. This pussy is just begging me."

Another slap and she felt a finger slip inside. It wasn't what she really wanted. She wanted his cock, but she would take what she could get. Oh, she wanted to ride that finger, but he'd tied her down and the way the bench slanted made it hard for her to move her hips.

Smack. His thick finger sat just inside her vaginal walls, tempting her, teasing her. "Oh, does my bratty little sub not like her restraints anymore? Tell me what you want to do right now. I see the way you're wiggling." *Smack.*

She kind of wanted to smack him because he was making her crazy. Now every nerve in her body was focused on that finger sitting inside her pussy when it should be moving.

Smack. Smack. Two hard ones that made her squeal. "Tell me. What would you do if you weren't restrained? If you don't tell me, I'll stop what I'm doing to your pussy."

She thought about very politely telling him she would likely attempt to bring herself to a nice orgasm by using his finger as a sexual aid. And that would so get her in trouble. Lee liked it when she talked dirty, and somehow when she was with him even the dirtiest things seemed like caring. "I would fuck your finger, Sir. I want to so badly. Please, I need more."

Another smack, this one softer. "That's my girl." His voice was pure dark chocolate and filled with approval. And his finger slipped inside deeper. "Good girls get fucked, baby. Girls who are brave enough to say what they want get it."

He kept up the smacks, but all of her focus was on her pussy as a second finger joined the first. It still wasn't enough. It didn't come close to how thick and hard his cock was, but she would take it. She wiggled as much as she could, trying to bring him in further. His thumb slipped down and started making long, slow, tortuously good circles around her clit. The pain and pleasure morphed into one gloriously full symphony. It didn't take long before every cell in her body was straining toward orgasm. All that mattered was getting there.

"Thirty," Lee said, his voice deep. "Your punishment is over, but don't think for a second I'm done with you yet."

But it seemed he was done. His fingers came out of her pussy. She heard her own low moan at the loss. She'd been so, so close. This really was punishment of the worst kind.

Lee knelt down and started to work her loose. His hands worked quickly, nearly tearing at her bindings. "Don't get upset, Avery. I told you I'm not done. I just won't do it here. One day we can fuck all you like in public, but I'm not comfortable with it yet. I want you all to myself."

Her backside was sore as he pulled her off the bench, but she let her arms drift up, clinging to him. She cuddled against him. She didn't care if her bottom was sore because her pussy wouldn't be empty for long.

And her heart was completely full.

Chapter Fourteen

Liam gently kicked open the door to the privacy room he'd set up earlier today. He'd had plenty of time to prepare since she'd canceled their lunch date. He could admit he'd thought a lot about punishing her for that. The good news was she'd given him another reason to spank that gorgeous ass of hers.

And she'd responded more beautifully than he could have imagined. Her pussy had been soaking wet. A single slip of his thumb over her clit and she would have gone off like a rocket. He'd been tempted to do it just to see how hard he could make her come in front of an audience.

But he was a greedy bastard, and he wanted her all to himself. It had been a little fun to show her off, but he wanted her alone so those little sounds she made would be all his.

The room contained a king-sized bed, a dresser, and a nightstand. He'd stocked the room himself, making sure he had everything they would need. The bed had a nice firm mattress and several hooks to tie a sub to. The whole room was built for bondage play. Under the bed was stashed a spreader bar that would go between her ankles and keep her exposed for his pleasure. He could keep her here all night and then maybe he wouldn't have to worry about her walking back into the lion's den tomorrow.

"Get on your knees, baby." He had plans for her mouth.

He slammed the door shut behind him. His cock pulsed in his leathers. She'd been so perfect once she'd made the decision to submit. He'd watched her go from timid to a woman who practically demanded her satisfaction and who didn't care who watched or what they thought.

He'd never felt as aware of a woman as he did this one. And he was done lying to himself. He'd never wanted one the way he wanted Avery.

The room was lit with only soft candle-like light. Like everything in The Garden, it seemed to be organic as though it flowed from the walls itself. That soft amber light made Avery's skin look so warm and soft that he was almost sure he could sink into her and never have to come back to the real world. Her dark hair tumbled around her shoulders, curling gently. He stopped and stared for a moment. He'd never imagined he would actually get her naked in front of a crowd. He'd expected her to take her spanking with that corset on. He'd meant to teach her a lesson and had prepared himself to spank her lightly. She would have felt it, but there was no way he would have spanked her hard when he knew bloody well she couldn't find her subspace while she was trying to keep herself balanced. But she hadn't taken his bait. She'd taught him the lesson that she was stronger than he'd imagined. Now he took in the sight of her breasts. So full and round. He'd adored the way her tits had bounced with every slap to her ass.

She was even hotter with a sexy smile on her face as she held out a hand so she could get to the ground.

He was a bastard. She still struggled with balance and here he was practically shoving her to the floor and forcing her to take his cock.

"Are you going to help me, Sir?" She stood there waiting. He'd been trying to train her to wait for his help.

She was reaching for him in a way she hadn't before.

Guilt hit his gut. He was training her for a life he couldn't live with her. What was she doing? Did she really only want him for sex or did she need more? Could he give her more? "Are you really all right? I was rough on you out there. Maybe you should rest."

Even in the dim light he could see her flush, but she stood her ground. "Don't you dare act like that. I'm not an invalid. Don't treat me like I am. I can't deal with you thinking about me that way, Lee."

She wouldn't have found her sexuality without him. He wasn't doing anything to hurt her, and she wasn't weak. She was strong as hell. He took her hand. "You're not an invalid, Avery. Now get on your knees or you'll get another spanking."

She took his hand, seemingly happy with his reaction. "I don't think that's much of a punishment, Sir. I rather liked the spanking part, though I think I'll be sore tomorrow."

And every time she felt that soreness, she would remember how he'd placed the flat of his hand on her ass, how he'd tortured her, worshipped her. "It will be punishment when I withhold your orgasm a couple of dozen times. Think about that when you turn your smart mouth on me. I'll tie you down and get you so hot you can't stand it, and then I'll stop and wait until you calm down and start all over again. I'll have you begging for it."

"That is much worse than the spanking," she admitted, though she smiled as he helped her to her knees. Her eyes lit up as she settled in. "What is it you want me to do, Sir?"

She was staring right at his erection, the little vixen. She knew what he wanted. She knew how much he wanted it. And he was in a mood to shake things up a little. He could deny himself for a few minutes in order to teach her who was in charge.

Because he so wasn't the boss anywhere else. He was rapidly becoming her lapdog, following after her and making sure she was safe. So this was the only real place he had control. He wasn't about to give it up.

He took a step back. "Lean forward. Get on all fours and spread your legs wide."

He loved the way her eyes flared and her mouth became a sweet little *O* before she did as he commanded and got to her hands and knees.

"Stay that way." He walked to the dresser. He'd always known he was going to start training her ass tonight. It wasn't punishment. It was necessary. He pulled out the small plug he'd sterilized and the lube he bought for her.

He turned and was fascinated by the way she waited for him. Even without seeing her face, he would guess that there was a look of anticipation there. It was in how she held her spine and the way her shoulders squared. He got to his knees behind her. He couldn't help himself. He ran a hand down her spine, feeling the scars there. That spine had been broken and splintered and put back together, weaker than before, but the woman who it held up had been made so strong from the incident. He leaned over and pressed a kiss to the base of her spine, silently thanking the universe for whatever had saved her.

He laid the plug on the small of her back. "Don't move, baby. This is going to be a little cool on your skin, but I promise it will warm up fast." He spread her cheeks and dribbled lube right on her asshole.

She shivered but didn't move. "Are you doing what I think you're doing? Because I'm pretty sure you told me that was punishment, and I already took my punishment."

"This isn't punishment, baby. This is prep work."

"You say potato," she began.

He bit back a laugh. "I told you I would take your ass, but not until I've prepared it. I'm going to take care of you." He lubed up the plug and placed it right at the rosette of her ass. His cock jumped just thinking about taking her there. She would be so tight. She would squeeze him. She would try to keep him out, but he would take her and make her love it.

Avery whimpered a little. "It feels weird."

"But it doesn't hurt?"

"No. It doesn't hurt. It just feels weird."

Her asshole clenched, but he played around the rim, teasing her open. He fucked the plug against her ass, gaining an inch and retreating, forcing her to relax and open up to him. Over and over he pressed in and pulled out gently, watching as she settled down and stopped fighting. Her cheeks were already almost back to her normal color. Just a hint of pink. He'd been gentle enough for her first time. Later he could get rougher as they found the boundaries of what worked to send her into subspace or pleasure the fastest.

What was he doing? He was still thinking in terms of the future, and it might all be over tomorrow or next week. He couldn't stand the thought of not being the one to hold her hand as she explored this lifestyle. She needed it. She was naturally submissive and without a strong Dom, men would take advantage of her. She had to be trained to value herself, to stand up for herself even against him. He'd never really thought about it before, but he wanted a partner, someone he could lean on, too. Avery was that woman. He wouldn't find another woman who moved him this way.

The plug slid in, burying itself between her cheeks the way his cock would find its way home one day.

Avery sighed as he let her cheeks go. "That's not bad at all."

"Well, it's a small plug. I'm a little bigger," he admitted. "But we'll work our way up." If he was still here. He leaned over and kissed her cheeks. Her skin was so silky and smooth. "How do you feel?"

Now that he had her alone, he could take his time, reveling in the joy of being with her. The minute he'd closed the door he felt like he'd shed some of his mask, the one he wore every day, even around his friends. Alex had been right. He kind of liked the person he was when he was with her, even if it was temporary and false.

"I feel deeply unsatisfied." Her ass wiggled just a little. She could be such an adorable brat if he let her.

He smacked her ass lightly. "I was talking about your backside."

"My backside is fine, and now it's a little full. I was hoping my pussy would get a similar treatment."

Not just yet. He got to his feet and untied his leathers, setting his cock free. "You're going to earn that, baby. Get on your knees and be very careful. Don't lose that plug. Hold those cheeks together and keep it in while you take care of me."

He helped her up, a little grin crossing his face as she winced, obviously trying to keep the plug in. His cock jumped at the sight of her. She looked primitive and tempting on her knees, waiting for his command. His cock pointed toward her as though the bloody thing knew exactly where it wanted to be.

"Have you sucked a cock before?" He stroked his shaft, forcing himself to go slow when all he wanted to do was shove his cock deep. He could fist his hand in her hair and not stop until he felt the back of her throat, but he waited.

271

"Not for a very long time, and even then I don't know that I was very good at it," she replied.

"I'll teach you what I like. Start with the head. Don't use your hands yet. Just lick me." He felt a pulse of pre-come coat the slit of his dick. He was like a bloody teenager, not a thirty-something who'd done it just about every way a man could. He moved toward her, holding his cock out for her tongue.

Her lips opened and the tip of her tongue came out, and Liam shuddered at the feel of that little butterfly on his skin. His whole body clenched.

"You like that?" Avery asked, her voice a little uncertain.

"I love it." He put a hand on her head. She needed the connection. He stroked her, feeling her getting more and more secure.

She licked the head, rolling her tongue around and playing with the ridges of his cock. She settled in, exploring without reservation now.

"Suck the head into your mouth," Liam ordered.

She licked her lips before sucking his cock head in. He shivered at the feel of her teeth just lightly grazing him. Torture. This was the finest torture ever.

"Don't be afraid. I won't break. You can be a little rough. Play with it." He let his hand tighten in her hair, tugging it lightly. The little pull wasn't meant to hurt, but to be a nice little sensation on her scalp, a way to bring her body into the moment past her mouth. She would be able to feel his hand in her hair, his plug in her ass, his dick in her mouth. He wanted her to feel him everywhere, to surround her with himself.

She leaned forward slightly, pulling him deeper into her mouth. Her tongue made long passes over his cock, awkward at first, but gaining in confidence with every groan he gave her. She licked from the crown of his cock down to the base and then back again. Every pass was a pure pleasure, pushing him further and further, closer to the edge. Her untutored mouth was doing what a deeply experienced one couldn't, threatening to unman him. He could take a blow job for hours and not lose control, but he was close to coming now.

He hissed a little and pulled her head back. Her lips were swollen, shiny. "That feels so good, baby. Now use your hands and play with my balls. I like to have my balls cupped and rolled."

She was delicate at first, one small hand gingerly cupping him. Her skin was so soft, her fingers surrounding him. She tugged and played, rolling them in her palm and pulling lightly until he was in control again. "I want to taste you, Sir."

He wanted to give her everything. "Do it. Suck me dry, Avery. You don't need me to tell you what to do. You're perfect."

She kept one hand on his balls and the other gripped his cock while she sucked the head into her mouth. She was so much more confident. Her tongue laved affection while her hand stroked him up and down, tightening around him like her cunt did. He shook a little as she placed the tip of her tongue right over his slit and delved in like she just couldn't wait another second to taste his come and was trying to tempt it out.

All the while, she played with his balls, her hands and mouth finding a rhythm he couldn't deny. His spine lit up, his muscles shaking as he held her head.

"Take me deep. I'm going to come, and you're going to swallow everything I give you. You're going to drink me down, girl." He heard his accent coming out, but he couldn't help it. When he was so close with her, it was almost impossible to deny.

Her mouth opened, allowing his cock to sink deep. She groaned, the sound reverberating along his cock. Come bubbled in his balls.

He gave up any thought of teaching her. All that mattered was coming. He pulled at her head, forcing his dick in further and further. Her tongue swirled at first and settled into massaging the underside of his dick while she sucked, her mouth fighting to keep him in.

He felt his cock head touch the soft back of her throat, and he was done. The orgasm sizzled along his spine, his cock giving up wave after wave of come.

She took it all, licking his cock long after he'd finished, bringing a sense of sweet peace to him. His hand softened in her hair.

"Thank you," he said. "That was beautiful, and now I want to pay you back."

He lifted her up and tossed her lightly on the bed. He loved the look she got in her eyes every time he lifted her into his arms. A dreamy look crossed her face as though she couldn't quite believe what was happening.

"I liked that," she said with a little smile. "I liked how you taste."

"I like how you taste, too. Spread your legs." He'd wanted to tie her up, but he was too anxious to taste her again, to hear her cry and beg. His cock was already responding to the way she was laid out. "Show me."

She spread her legs for him. Days of training seemed to have worked. He'd kept her naked every night, and at least once a day he required that she spread her legs and show him her pussy. It was a little ritual he demanded. When he gave her the words "show me," she was to showcase that part of her that belonged to him.

He could hear her breathe as she let her fingers slip through her labial lips. She touched herself.

"Who does that belong to?" he asked, his voice rough.

"You, Sir. My pussy belongs to you." Her head came up a little. "Can I see my cock?"

He felt a brilliant smile cross his face as he gave her what she wanted. He stroked himself back to life. "This is your cock, love. No one else's. Now get that hand away from my pussy because if you make yourself come, I will punish you all over again."

Her hand disappeared, going over her head in a flash.

Liam crawled onto the bed. He could smell her. He loved the way she smelled. The dim light couldn't hide the fact that her pussy was coated with arousal. All that lovely juice and he was a thirsty man. He pushed her legs further apart, opening her up more before he took that first long lick.

Her whole body shook. He wouldn't be able to spend hours here like he would prefer. She was too aroused, and he wanted her to come around his cock. But he could play for a moment.

He lightly twisted the perfect pearl of her clit between his thumb and forefinger, eliciting a low moan from Avery. "Don't come until I'm deep inside you."

"Oh, god, Lee, that's going to be so hard."

He growled a little. "Don't. Let me taste you, and then I'll give you what you want."

He speared his tongue up, fucking into her cunt. Her taste coated his tongue, spicy and female, so rich he thought he might drown in it. He worked a hand under her, his fingers toying with the plug in her ass, pressing in and making her writhe under him. Her breath came out in short gasps as he let his tongue run the length of her pussy, sucking at her labia, drawing each side in one at a time. He licked his way up, darting the tip around her clit, never touching her, always teasing.

"Lee, please. Please." Her whole body was quaking, but it was apparent she was trying so hard to follow his commands.

He gave her one long last lick and then came up on his knees, reaching across her for the condom he'd left on the nightstand. Even though he'd come in her mouth just moments before, he was hard and aching for her again. It was the same way every night. As soon as he'd fucked her senseless and thought for sure he was satisfied, he'd catch sight of her smile or her hand would brush across his chest and he would be hard again, as though he just couldn't stop wanting her. He'd fuck her over and over until they both fell asleep, his a sweet dreamless rest that meant the world to him. While he'd been in her bed, he hadn't dreamed about that day, had been able to shove it aside. Every part of his being had been focused on her, on training her, teaching her pleasure.

He rolled the condom over his erection and let his chest find hers. Hard nipples rubbed against his skin, a contrast to the pillowy breast. He kissed her. "This is how you taste to me."

His tongue found hers and slid alongside, tasting his own saltiness there. They kissed, their essences mingling as their tongues played and danced. His cock found her pussy, rubbing against it and foraging in.

Her nails bit into his back as she gasped when he twisted his hips and forced his way in. Her cunt was so bloody tight, nearly strangling his cock. He thrust as far as he could, and then he was the one moaning as the plug dragged against his cock.

So tight. So sweet. So bloody good.

He let her lips go and reared up to his elbows, readjusting her so she could take his full length with every hard thrust of his body. Her legs came around his waist, and he felt the plug slip out, but it didn't matter. All that mattered was the feel of those walls gripping him, her legs and nails digging into him, so desperate to keep him inside.

"Oh, god, Lee. Lee. Lee." She called his name over and over again as her pussy clenched and she came. He fucked in and out, picking up the pace, using her as roughly as he chose because she could handle it. He sank his hands into her hair and let his face bury itself in her neck as he fucked deep one last time and gave up his come.

He let his body slump, covering her and weighing her down. She didn't protest, just wrapped her arms around him and held him close. He breathed in her scent and rested his head on her chest. This was what he'd longed for. Peace. Comfort. The feel of his blood strumming through his body while her heart pounded against his ear.

He could sleep this way. He could sleep and not dream of anything but her.

He was just drifting off when he heard her sniffle.

His head came up, and he was shocked at the sight. She was crying, tears dripping down her face.

"Avery? Avery, did I hurt you?" He tried to think. He wasn't any rougher on her than he'd been in the past. She'd been so aroused it shouldn't have bothered her.

She shook her head as he practically jumped off her. He started looking for bruising or anything that would explain the tears. "I'm not hurt. Not physically."

This was what she'd been holding in all day. He'd felt

it, been afraid of it. He rolled the condom off and tossed it in the garbage before sitting on the bed. "Just tell me."

"I don't want to." She bit her lip, her eyes turning down as though she suddenly found the bedspread deeply interesting.

He reached out, forcing her chin up. "Avery, this can't work if you won't talk to me. I'm supposed to comfort you but you won't even acknowledge that something's wrong. Do I mean that little to you? Am I just the guy who fucks you?"

"How can you say that?" She breathed the question out.

"Because you don't want to talk to me about anything important. You talk about work and what you like on TV and what books you read, but you don't talk about your past. You don't talk about…" He just couldn't say it. He knew he was being a hypocrite, but it didn't matter.

"About Maddie?" The name came out of her mouth in a little puff of air. Delicate. Fragile.

"Yeah. You don't talk about her or anyone you care about. Maybe because I'm not important enough to share her with." He was a rat-fink, bloody, nasty, scumbag bastard, but he wanted everything from her, even if he couldn't give it back to her. He wanted her every emotion. He wanted her history. He wanted her problems and her worries. He wanted everything that was Avery Charles to belong to him.

She sat up, reaching for one of two robes that had been folded on the nightstand. She stood, covering her body, her hands shaking as she tied it around her waist, and Liam realized this was it. This was when she told him he wasn't good enough and that she'd had a good time, but she needed to find a man who was worthy of her. Someone good and kind and better educated. Someone she would want to try to have another child with.

She was quiet for a moment, the air between them stale and hard, but her voice was soft when she finally spoke. "I got a call from my mother-in-law today. It upset me. It was quite horrible. She'd seen an article in a magazine that reminded her of something I had done."

"Go on." He sat on the bed, not wanting to scare her off.

"I still think of her as Mom. I shouldn't. We haven't been close in years, but I keep hoping. For a while, it was because she was the only link I had left to Brandon, but now I think she's the only link I have left to the me I was back then. Everyone is gone. It's hard sometimes to be the only one who knows what it was like to grow up the way I did, who remembers Maddie and Brandon. I've been clinging to the hope that they're going to forgive me someday, and I can have a family again."

A well of despair fed her voice, threatening to cut through him. He wished he'd never asked, but he couldn't make her stop talking now that she was open. He reached out for her. Maybe she could tell the story more easily if he held her.

She stared for a moment, longing plain on her face, but she shook him off. "If you still want to hold me after I tell you the whole story, I'll gladly take it, but you have to listen first."

"What did you do that you needed forgiveness for?" He couldn't imagine Avery doing anything to hurt someone. Did her in-laws blame her because she'd been driving the car? According to the reports he'd read, she'd been blindsided. She'd had the right of way.

"I told you I was in an accident." She'd told him in only the vaguest of terms. "I was driving. Brandon was in the passenger seat, and Maddie was in her car seat behind him. It was late. We'd been at a party but neither of us had been drinking. I was still breastfeeding, and Brandon had never had a drink in his life. We were both pretty straight kids. Besides getting pregnant, I think the wildest thing the two of us did was go to the mall when we were supposed to be at the library."

And Liam had been getting in trouble for as long as he could remember. He'd been in the SAS by the time he was just a tiny bit older than Avery had been when she had the accident. He'd killed more than once by then. His innocent had ended long before his teen years. "Go on."

She took a long breath. "We were hit by a teenaged girl. I told you that much. I remember seeing the light coming at us and trying to move out of the way and then nothing. I went into a coma, and by the time I woke up, they had already been buried. Brandon and Maddie had been buried together, and I didn't even get to go to the funeral. Lydia had to take care of it herself. Later that year, she had to go to the other driver's trial alone because Frank had shut down. That trial was so hard on her, but he wouldn't go. He's never gotten past losing his only son. She was the one who came every week and sat with me. Lydia came to the first couple of surgeries."

"Sweetheart, I am not seeing any need for anyone to forgive you," he said gently.

"A few years passed and that was when she came to see me."

"She?"

"Her name was Stephanie Gibson. By all accounts, she was a good kid. She was only two years younger than me, but I felt so much older at the time."

The room was so quiet, only their voices filling it and even then Avery spoke in hushed, almost reverent tones. Liam found himself nearly whispering his questions. "Is this the woman who hit you?"

She nodded. "The girl, yes. Like I said, she was sixteen at the time of the accident. She was an honor student, graduating early. She admitted to having two beers at the party when the police first interviewed her. In New York, if you're under twenty-one your blood alcohol level doesn't really matter as long as they can prove alcohol is in your system. It could have been a tiny amount, and they still would consider her drunk. But there was a huge mistake at the hospital and her toxicology labs got mixed up with someone else's, and even the cheap lawyer her parents had hired managed to get the whole case thrown out because of it. But I believe her about the beers. I really do. No one at the party saw her have more than two, and she was drinking water when she left according to all accounts. I honestly believe it was the phone distraction that caused the accident."

"That's not an excuse, Avery. She killed two people."

She crossed her arms over her chest, a defensive move. "You're going to be like the rest of them, I can see. Just let me finish. Stephanie came to see me. My mother-in-law was furious because the case had been thrown out."

"Why weren't you angry?"

"I was. I was so mad I could have killed her, but you have to understand years had gone by."

"Years where you couldn't walk." Years where she'd been alone in a string of hospital beds.

"Are you going to let me finish or do you want to judge me now?" She stared at him, her body closed down. What the hell was she going to tell him? Had she somehow killed this girl? She continued when he was silent. "So she came to see me, and she was so utterly different than the girl I'd read about. You have to understand. I was a little obsessed with

281

her for a while. I read all the papers and looked her up on the Internet. She'd been vibrant and pretty. She'd been that girl who volunteered for everything according to the news accounts. She had so many people willing to speak up for her. You know usually when something bad like this happens, people go away, but they stood up for her. They loved her. She'd been very lovable and kind. From her teachers to the volunteer coordinator at the hospital where she worked, no one had a bad thing to say about her. She wanted to be a doctor, you see. But the girl who stood before me that day was so dark. Thin. Like she'd been starving herself. Her mom had sent me a letter begging me to meet with her because she just knew that Stephanie was going to kill herself. The guilt was eating her alive, and her mom thought I might be able to forgive her."

Shit. Had this girl killed herself and Avery couldn't handle the guilt? It wasn't her fault. The girl had killed Avery's husband and child. She didn't deserve forgiveness.

Avery's arms got tighter, like she was attempting to turn in on herself, to hide away. "I agreed because I was going to tell her to go to hell. I was going to tell her that she should do it. She should kill herself and do it so it hurt. I was going to suggest several ways to make it happen. I even saved up my pain meds in case she was a baby and needed to go out easy."

Fuck. What had she done? Liam could have put a bullet through the girl and never thought of her again, but not Avery. Avery would die inside knowing what she'd done.

Her tears had started up again. "And then she walked in and all I could see was my baby. She was just a girl. She wasn't some monster. And I thought about Maddie. What if my baby had lived and she'd made a mistake and had no one to offer her forgiveness? I had to wonder if I would really drag Stephanie's mother into my hell. Into Lydia's hell."

"You forgave her." He let out a long breath he hadn't known he was holding. A deep sense of relief invaded his veins. He could see her doing it. She would say all the right words to save someone else even if they had done her great harm. "And your mother-in-law won't talk to you because of it?"

"It was worse, Lee. I started talking to Stephanie. It was odd, you see, but we were the only two left who had lived through it. We were survivors, and no one else could understand what it meant to be us. In an odd way, we reached out to each other. I got to really know this girl. She had made one mistake in her life. It was an enormous one, but I started to wonder if it really had to be the end for her. Four of us were in that accident. Did we all have to die? I had some money left then. I made a decision. Stephanie's college fund was eaten up with lawyer's fees and she didn't have anything else. Her parents weren't rich. They just got by. Insurance paid for me, so I gave it to Stephanie for her college. For her medical school. I took it out a little at a time so she didn't get taxed for it. I'm ashamed to say, but I took it out in cash because I didn't want my in-laws to see her name on a check. My mother-in-law used to balance my checkbook for me. She found out anyway. She hates me now."

He felt his jaw drop. "You did what? You paid for her medical school? Why the hell would you do that?"

Her words came out in rapid fire, a machine gun he'd primed with his outburst. "Because she owed me a life. She owed me two lives. Can't you see that? Why can't anyone understand? It was so horrible. It was death and horror and despair, and I saw that one good thing might come out of it. I didn't have control over anything back then. Nothing, Lee.

283

But I controlled this. I saw a way to make one thing right and I took it like a lifeline, and she went to med school. She studied so hard. She got through it fast because she was dedicated. She graduated and she's in Africa now doing charity work. She saves babies because I lost mine, and I know no one understands. I know everyone thinks I should want her dead, but her death wouldn't solve anything. It wouldn't bring Maddie back. It won't make Brandon any less dead, but don't you see? Her death would have been meaningless, but her life, oh, her life can mean the world. And I made that choice. Me. I got to do that. For Maddie and Brandon. For me. And when I made that decision to forgive her that was when I knew I was going to walk again because I had made the decision to live."

He didn't understand. He stared at her for a moment, tears streaming down her face and realized that she was a mystery and she always would be to him. He could live forever and not be able to discover the depth of how lovely and amazing she was.

He'd told himself for countless years that he fought for what was right, but it was an excuse. He just liked to fight. When he was a kid, he'd fought whoever was in front of him. In the Army, he'd fought who he'd been told to fight. Now he fought for whoever had the cash to pay his company.

But Avery had done something amazing. Avery fought misery and pain and loss and found a way to make something beautiful in the world.

Avery was worth fighting for. Avery was worth dying for. Avery was worth loving even if she could never love him back.

Liam stood up, his heart pounding, his real voice flowing. "Avery, my name is Liam O'Donnell, and I've been investigating your boss for arms dealing."

Chapter Fifteen

Avery was sure she hadn't heard him correctly. She was emotional, tears still pouring down her face. Sometimes when she got really emotional, she didn't listen well. "What did you say?"

It wasn't just what he'd said. It was the way he'd said it. His accent had changed from flat to a gorgeous, lyrical Irish—the same sounds she sometimes heard when he was making love to her.

He was still naked, his perfectly sculpted body on full display, but his face seemed shadowed, his eyes not quite meeting hers. "I told you. My name is Liam O'Donnell. I work for a security company named McKay-Taggart, and we're tracking a rogue CIA agent. He's been meeting with Thomas Molina. In the course of our investigation into Eli Nelson, we stumbled onto MI6's investigation of the United One Fund."

"What? MI6? What the hell is MI6?"

"It's Britain's version of the CIA. They investigate external threats to the country. They've been tracking black market arms shipments in Africa."

Her head was spinning. All the previous intimacy of the evening was gone in a haze of complete confusion. CIA? Arms shipments? "Why are you saying this? I don't understand."

They were supposed to talk about her day and her in-laws, and he was supposed to have finally understood. He was supposed to reach out and hold her close and make love to her again.

He was supposed to be Lee.

"I'm sorry, Avery." He took a step toward her, his eyes finally coming up, and she read a wealth of guilt in those emerald orbs. His eyes told the tale. He wasn't joking. "I went about this all wrong. I just couldn't let another second go by without confessing."

He reached out for her, but it was far too late. She stepped back as far as she could go, her back finding the wall. "Don't. Don't touch me."

His hands dropped. "Let me explain."

"Explain what? Explain that you lied to me?" He'd lied to her. He'd lied and not about something small and inconsequential. He hadn't lied about his favorite food or whether or not he liked cats. He'd lied about his name. He'd lied about his profession. He'd lied about his whole life. He'd held her, slept with her, fucked her every night for a week and she hadn't even known his name.

"Yes. I lied, but I had reasons, love. This situation with your boss is bloody serious, and I don't want you involved for another minute. I want you out of this. Avery, I want to protect you."

"God, please put on some clothes." She turned her eyes away. He was hard again, his cock jutting out from that perfectly trimmed nest of black hair.

He held his ground, but somehow he made a lack of movement seem aggressive. "What, love? You didn't mind it a couple of minutes ago. Whatever you think, girl, you should know that this was always the truth." He stroked himself with one hand, the other coming out to brace his body against the wall. His hand was planted inches from her cheek, forming an intimate half circle. "Avery, we don't have to do it this way. I fucked up. Let's start over. We'll get in bed and I'll make love to you again, and afterward we'll talk. You'll see that this is a good thing. I'm going to take care of you."

He was even more lethal now that he'd dropped the act. Liam seemed infinitely more deadly than Lee, and she'd thought he was devastating before. He leaned over, his lips almost touching hers. "Come to bed with me. I'll make this right. I'll hold you and tell you anything you want to hear."

She pushed him away with all her might because that was what he'd been doing for a week. He'd been telling her what she wanted to hear and not a bit of it had been the truth. He'd used her. He'd used all that charm and zeroed in on her weakness, and he was trying to do it again. "I am not getting in bed with you."

She had to get out of here. She still wasn't sure what the hell was going on. It was a ridiculous story. The UOF was involved in arms dealing? Bullshit. Thomas was a peaceful man who had dedicated his life to saving people in impoverished countries.

Had she been right that first day? She'd thought he had ulterior motives. She'd thought he wanted money. Was this his way of getting it? Was he a con artist and this whole week had been an elaborate set up?

He sat back on the bed, pushing a hand through his hair. "God, I fucked this up. Avery, you have to listen to me. This is getting dangerous. I want to protect you."

Sure he did. Tears welled up. She'd cried so much today, but it seemed she had an endless well of tears to call upon. Maybe this would be the incident that finally hardened her. Maybe Lee Donnelly was the crack that she finally couldn't heal so she armored up. She had to get out of this place. She had to get home. She couldn't even go home because she'd given him a key. She was the idiot who'd given her conman a key to her apartment.

It didn't matter. All that mattered was getting away from him.

"I want to go home."

He frowned. "I think we need to talk. We can't talk at your place. It's bugged."

Sure it was. Yes. Her apartment was bugged because she was so important. He thought she was a moron, but she couldn't blame him. Everything he'd done had worked up to this point. Why not try a little more? "Fine. Then can you at least get dressed? I can't talk to you while you're naked. I want to get dressed and be civilized about this."

His eyes flared, his mouth lifting in a sexy little snarl. He obviously wasn't hiding anymore, or perhaps it was all just another part of the Liam/Lee show. He invaded her space again. She could feel heat rolling off of him. He was damn good at this part of his act. Every inch of her body lit up when he was this close, and her hormones tried to override her brain. "There is nothing civilized about this, Avery. I know that you're mad right now, but don't think I'll be letting you push me aside. I handled this like a ham-handed idiot, but I'll make it right. There are no more lies between us, and I won't have anything else coming between us either. I'm going to get cleaned up, and we'll go to the bar. You need a drink. God knows I do."

He leaned down and kissed her. No light brushing of the lips. It wasn't an attempt to persuade her. It was outright domination, and she couldn't help but respond. The minute he touched her, she melted like warm chocolate. His tongue invaded, forcing her mouth open and rubbing against hers in a way that immediately got her hot. Her pussy didn't give a crap that he'd lied. All it knew was that he'd trained her to respond. A week of near constant pleasure had done its job. Her arms came up, touching his waist.

"Avery, love, let's not do this. Baby, I just want to protect you." That musical voice sang along her skin as he pressed kisses on her face. His hands wound around her, hauling her close. "You mean everything to me. I won't let you go."

She was opening herself up to him. She was so stupid. "Stop it. You stop it now. I don't want this."

He took a step back, a fierce look on his face. A single finger came out and traced the rigid line of her nipple under the thin robe she wore. "This tells me differently, Avery. I bet your pussy is wet and slick and ready for my cock. I bet your pussy wouldn't lie to me."

"My pussy isn't making the decisions here." At least not yet. If he stayed close for much longer, it just might. "I don't want this, Lee…Liam...whatever your name is. Are you going to rape me?"

His eyes closed, his fists clenching at his sides. "Fine. Like I said, I'll go clean up, and we'll have a drink. But don't think for a minute that this is over."

But don't tink for a minute dat dis is oovver. The way he rounded his vowels and cut off some of his consonants was so sexy. And very likely all part of his plan. He snatched up something that had been on the bed. The plug. God, she'd let him put a plug inside her. What had she been thinking? He turned and opened a door at the back of the small room. A bathroom most likely. She heard the water start to run and realized she had seconds to get out of here. She had zero intention of sitting calmly while he pulled her into some sort of whacked-out scheme meant to do god only knew what.

But the question was where would she go? She needed her clothes. She needed a ride. She needed back up.

Her phone was in the locker room, but Liam's wasn't. It was on the floor. It had fallen out of his leathers. She snatched it up and nearly ran out of the room. Her hands shook as she tried to remember the number she needed. Adam. Adam and Jake could come and pick her up. Adam and Jake were big enough that Liam might think twice about messing with them, and then she would get the apartment rekeyed and she would tell the concierge not to allow Lee…Liam, or whatever he wanted to call himself, in. He would figure out that she wasn't going to be an easy mark, and he would lose interest.

Tears blurred her vision making the hallway a watery mess. She turned down the narrow corridor. The Garden had seemed so lovely and decadent, and now it was just alien and a little frightening. She'd been so stupid. She hadn't known him at all and yet she'd followed him into a BDSM club. She'd let him strip her bare in front of people. God, she couldn't even think about it.

She never stopped walking. She just glanced down and dialed the numbers, grateful she'd always had a good memory. It wasn't more than a second before Adam's voice came over the line.

"Hey, what's up? I didn't expect you to call. Isn't this the big night?"

"What?" Had she told Adam about her date?

"Avery? Shit. Is that you?"

The depths of his betrayal hit her squarely in the gut. Adam had known the number. He hadn't expected a call from this number because he'd known the man it belonged to had a big night.

Adam knew Liam.

291

"Avery? Sweetie? Is Lee with you?"

So nice. So caring. "Liam is cleaning up. I'm afraid your little game is up, Adam. I know everything."

"Holy fucking shit. Avery, I don't know what's going on, but wherever you are, stay there. Don't you dare move. Don't you leave that club. I will be there in fifteen minutes. I will track you down if you leave, do you understand me? It's dangerous for you out there on your own."

She let the phone drop. She had no one else to call. Liam was quite brilliant. He'd seen a lonely woman and managed to give her friends, a lover, everything she could need. Why? She didn't have any money left. She didn't have connections.

Except to Thomas. Who did have money. Lots of money.

She ran toward the stairs. She had to get out. She would just leave in her robe and go straight to the police. That was what she would do. She wouldn't stop for her purse or anything else. She would run until she found a station house, and she would tell them everything.

Except she ran into a brick wall before she could find the lifts. She stopped and stared up into the arctic-blue eyes of Liam's friend Ian.

"Going somewhere, love? Where's Lee? You shouldn't run around without your Dom."

"Liam O'Donnell can go to hell. I'm sure you're in on whatever scam he's running. Get out of my way. I'm not staying here."

She could have sworn the temperature dropped twenty degrees. The look on Ian's face could have frozen fire. For the first time she got really scared. She backed up, only to run into a wall of flesh.

"Don't scare her, Ian. I won't have it." Liam's hand

found her wrist, hauling her behind him, putting himself between her and Ian.

"You won't have it? You won't fucking have it?" Ian seemed to have developed a hard American accent. Well, naturally. She was surrounded by con men. "Tell me she's brilliant and she managed to find out your real name on her own."

"I told her," Liam replied. "I can't lie to her anymore, Ian. And I want her out of this op. I'll take her someplace safe in the morning, and you won't have to see us again. I know I'm fired."

"Oh, you'll be lucky if I just fire you. Get her dressed. I want you both in the conference room in ten minutes. I swear if you take off, I'll find you both. Do you understand me?" Ian stalked off, his boots ringing in a violent rhythm.

Liam sighed, tugging her close. "That went better than expected. He didn't kill me. I'm calling it a win."

She tried to pull away. She hated the fact that all she really wanted to do was wrap her arms around him and pray this was all a bad dream. "Let me go."

"No. You ran. Now we'll do this my way." His hand was gentle on her hair. He smoothed it back. "Come on. We'll get dressed, and you can meet the team."

"Team?"

"Yeah. Ian owns McKay-Taggart along with Alex. Eve's the psychologist. Adam's the communications guy. Jake is pure muscle. Not a brain in his head. They'll all watch out for you now."

"I thought you were taking me someplace safe." She wouldn't go. She would still find a way out. She held herself stiffly in his arms, not willing to give an inch. He hugged her. It was even worse since the embrace was sweet and gentle without his former predatory aggressiveness.

293

"I will if I have to. I'll do whatever it takes to keep you safe. I swear on my life."

"Well, you'll excuse me if I don't believe you since you've lied to me about everything else."

"I won't lie again. Not ever. Not to you."

He was still lying. The whole thing was a lie. It was ridiculous. She wasn't involved in some sort of spy thing. He was playing an angle. "I'd like to get dressed now."

He nodded, brushing his forehead against hers. "Avery, I'm sorry."

But he was too late. She followed him down the hall, determined to shut him out forever.

* * * *

Liam stared at Avery, wishing he'd kept his bloody mouth shut. She looked pale, fragile sitting in her chair still staring at the computer screen in front of her.

He should have planned it out. He should have planned exactly what he was going to say, and he should have made sure she couldn't run until she understood. He should have tied her up, fucked her senseless, told her the truth, and then fucked her some more.

"That was the real live prime minister." Her mouth moved, but her eyes just sat there like she expected the computer screen to talk back.

Thank god for Damon Knight and his connections. She'd been talking about how they were all a group of con artists trying to take her for god only knew what. Knight had made her believe. She hadn't believed Liam, but apparently when the prime minister told her something, it was gospel. She believed politicians. She definitely needed a keeper.

"I told you." Knight was dressed in jeans and a T-shirt,

but even looking so casual, he still radiated authority. And he'd threatened to take Liam's head off for what he'd done. The good news was his head was still sitting on his shoulders, and Knight had managed to get the prime minister on a video chat to convince Avery that they were serious. "This is a real operation. It's important to both our countries." Knight shut the computer screen and pulled it away. "And now you're involved in a way I don't think any of us wanted you to be involved."

"Because we don't have any proof she's not in on it," Ian said as he walked in. He'd changed out of his leathers and wore a dress shirt and slacks. He hadn't changed his attitude. He still looked like an irritable shark waiting to take a chunk out of anything dumb enough to get close.

"She's not involved with Molina's deals." If there was one thing Liam knew, it was that Avery Charles wouldn't hurt a fly. If she'd known anything, she would have come forward.

Ian turned on him. "Yeah, I got no proof of that, but I now have to deal with it because apparently your penis took over. Have I told you lately that your penis is a complete dipshit, and it shouldn't be allowed to make decisions? Did you not get that fucking memo?"

"Must have missed it, boss." He wasn't going to let Ian intimidate him. Ian hadn't had him escorted out of the club and shot. Everything was going to be fine.

"I'm not involved in anything," Avery said, looking from man to man.

"I know, love," Liam replied.

"Which is exactly what you would say if you were a counter agent," Ian shot back, taking the seat across from Avery. He leaned over. "Somehow I don't think you would just walk in and admit 'I like money so I sell black market arms to Africa, and I'm trying real hard to get into the Middle East.' Is that what your Facebook status says?"

Avery shook her head. "I don't have a Facebook page."

"There's your problem. All the best arms dealers are on Facebook." Ian's sarcasm seemed never ending.

Liam would be lucky if he didn't punch his boss tonight. He walked around the conference table and took the seat by Avery. "Sweetheart, no one thinks you're involved."

"I think he does. Do I need a lawyer? Can I have my phone back?" She twisted her hands in her lap.

"So you can call Thomas Molina and let him know we're on to him?" Ian asked.

"Back off, mate," Liam warned.

Avery took a long breath. "He's really doing this thing? He's really letting someone put guns and stuff in our grain shipments?"

For the first time, Liam really understood how hard this was going to be on her. It was just another thing he hadn't considered when he'd broken out and vomited up the truth. She believed in what she did. Finding out she'd been helping an arms dealer was going to kill her. He'd been concerned with Nelson this whole time, but now he wanted to wrap his hands around Molina's throat for using Avery the way he had. It didn't mean a thing to him that the man had physical problems. It would just make the fucker easier to catch.

"You tell me what Molina's putting in those shipments." Ian was that immovable object science talked about. "Did you know your shipments are weighed when they leave the docks here? MI6 pulled the records. They don't match what eventually makes it to the refugee camps."

Her dark hair shook. "A lot of things can happen to grain in transport. Sometimes, if it's not properly stored, it can rot or rats can get to it either in the boat or in the storage warehouse. We also have a lot of trouble with thieves."

"Thieves stole seven hundred pounds of grain from last September's shipment? How about five hundred from December? Did rats eat nine hundred pounds of grain this February? Those are mighty big rats, Miss Charles." Ian passed her the reports.

Avery sat there staring as though she couldn't quite comprehend.

"Nothing to say, huh?" Ian asked.

"Stop it or I'll walk her out of here and I'll find a barrister." It was plan *B*. He didn't particularly want to follow it since it meant taking her out into the real world, and he was pretty bloody sure she would run at the first opportunity.

The door to the conference room opened, and Eve and Alex stepped in. They were both back in street clothes.

Alex took the seat next to his partner and gave Liam a long smile. "Good for you, man."

Ian turned. "Are you fucking kidding me?"

"Hey, I'm a sucker for a happy ending," Alex said.

"This isn't a happy ending. This is a nasty, fucked-up ending. This is months' worth of work down the toilet because Liam over there couldn't keep his dick from making the decisions."

"I think it was his heart, man," Alex shot back, looking at Liam like he was a toddler taking his first steps.

No matter how he felt about Avery, hearing it put like that made him want to vomit. Liam winced. "Jesus, I think I liked it better the way Ian was talking. You're making me sound like a bloody girl."

Avery's hand came out and slapped him across the chest. She gasped. "I'm sorry. I don't know why I did that."

Ah, sweet progress. He gripped her hand and brought it

to his lips. "Because that's what a woman does when her man says something stupid. I'm prepared to be smacked on a regular basis, love."

She pulled her hand out of his, but not before he'd seen her flush. "I'm not your woman."

She could fight it for now, but she needed him.

Eve sat on the other side of the table. Liam couldn't help but notice that she was as far from Alex as she could be. She smiled Avery's way. "I'm so sorry for the deception. We had to be sure you're not involved. I hope you understand."

Ian's hands came up, his head falling back as he groaned in obvious frustration. "Just because Liam's dick likes her doesn't mean she's not guilty. When did Liam freaking O'Donnell become the world's leading authority on judging people? Can I remind you of a few of the choices his cock has made before? Cindy Lou Waitress from hell? She took a baseball bat to his car because he didn't call."

"I never said I would call. I barely knew the girl."

"Ah, but you fucked her, didn't you? I believe it was in the back room of a Hooters."

"Ian, this is unnecessary," Alex said.

Ian ignored his best friend. "How about the twins you screwed and then found out they were secretly taping you and putting up their sex tapes on the Internet under the heading 'Hot Badass With Huge Cock'? Were they innocent, too?"

That was just about enough of Ian. Liam felt his fists clench. "I swear to god if you say one more fucking word, I'll come over the table, Ian. I won't give a shit that we were friends once."

Ian growled right back. "I'm trying to help you, asshole. You don't know a real thing about this woman."

"Like you tried to help Sean?" Eve asked, her voice a calm note in the storm of anger that swirled around the room.

Ian stopped, his face hardening into stubborn lines. "It's not the same."

"It's exactly the same." Eve tapped a manila folder on the desk in front of her. "Right down to the profile I did." She flipped it open and started to read. "'After careful consideration, I would be surprised to discover the subject is involved in anything that would go against her obvious values. It is my judgment that Avery Charles be treated as an innocent asset and all due consideration to keeping her safe should be taken.' I think I said the same about Grace, and you ignored me. Ian, you are allowing your own history to affect your judgment, and it's going to cost you another friend if you don't back off."

"You have a file on me?" Avery asked.

Ian sat back, quiet for once and willing to let Eve take charge. "I do. I'm a psychologist. I've worked for the FBI before. Now I work with these idiots who rarely listen to me. I studied your prior reports. You had a psych evaluation before you were accepted into the medical study that gave you back the use of your legs, and you saw a therapist for years before that to deal with the trauma of the accident."

"That was supposed to be private." Avery reached for the file. "Whatever happened to doctor's confidentiality?"

Eve slid the file to her, a sure sign that she trusted Avery. "I'm so sorry, but MI6 got me the records, and they most likely had the aid and consent of the Agency. This is a very important mission. These are high-grade weapons, and he's moving more and more of them. If he manages to move into the Middle East, those weapons are going to be turned on American and British troops. They can be used to destabilize whole parts of the world we would rather have calm."

"So my privacy is being invaded to fight terrorists, is that it?" Avery flipped through the file. Her face flushed.

"Privacy is something no one really has, Miss Charles." Ian sounded calmer, his eyes steady on Avery. "Privacy is something that's only granted until it intrudes on someone else's right to live."

"You were a crucial piece to this investigation," Alex continued, his voice softer. "We had to ascertain whether or not you were involved in getting the weapons into the grain shipments. You're close to Molina."

"Is there any way this is someone else? Like someone else in the company?" She asked the question in a shaky voice.

Knight slid a black and white photo across the table. "This is your boss with a man named Eli Nelson. Nelson is a rogue CIA agent who by all accounts is rapidly turning into a mover and shaker in the criminal underground. They've been meeting regularly since you and the boss got to London."

"His lunch appointment with a friend." She sniffled a little, and he wanted so badly to drag her into his arms and hold her tight.

"Avery, anything you can tell us will help. Have you noticed anything at all odd about the UOF? Any weird business practices? Something unusual Molina's been doing lately?" Alex asked. He seemed intent on playing good cop.

"I don't think Avery knows anything," Liam replied quickly. He wasn't going to have her brought into this. Simon Weston had asked about some files, but he could be fishing. As long as Avery didn't mention them, he could make a case for taking her out of here, perhaps even back to the States. She would need protection while everything was sorted out. Once he got her back to his place, he could work on reestablishing the relationship, on a proper footing this time.

Crap. He needed a new place. His place was awful. His place consisted of a mattress on the floor, a recliner, and an enormous telly. It would not impress her.

But it might give her something to do. Maybe she would view him as a project. If he could get her involved in fixing up his place, maybe she would start to view it as her place, too.

Or she would burn it down with him in it. He was willing to take the chance as long as he got her out of England and away from Molina and Nelson.

"There are some files I think you should look at," she said quietly.

"Avery, keep your mouth closed. You are getting out of this," Liam ordered.

A stubborn look settled on her face. "No. If I'm in it, then I'm in it. If I did anything to help this gunrunning thing, then I have to try to make it right. I have a friend who works at the Fund. I think maybe he's seeing the same thing I am. There have been several multimillion dollar donors who have been turned down for reasons I don't understand."

"Why would a charity turn down money?" Alex asked.

"For any number of reasons." Eve slipped the file on Avery back into her briefcase as she spoke. "Oftentimes if a charity turns down a donation, it has something to do with the moral view of the donor. A women's group might turn down a donation that was made by a group of exotic dancers who made the money by providing lap dances or a bikini car wash."

"That's stupid. The money is the same, and a lap dance

brings joy to the world," Liam pointed out.

Avery's hand slapped at his arm. She sighed. "That was an accident."

As long as she still cared about how she looked when he said something dumb, there was still a chance. "What I meant to say was, isn't money just money, Eve? From whom I would never accept a lap dance."

That was better, right?

"I think they would say it's a question of public impression. They don't want to run off donors who might be offended. Even if the donation is quite large, it can be smart to keep the smaller, more traditional donors happy because they tend to donate on a yearly basis," Eve explained.

"Does this have anything to do with Simon's theory?" Knight turned to Avery. "Simon Weston is my man on the inside. His last report talked about donors and some files he was trying to get from you. Did you get the files for him?"

Avery paled visibly. "Simon is in on this?"

"Yes, he's the one who will keep you safe on the inside," Knight explained. "I want you to consider him your partner."

Oh, that was not fucking going to happen. "She is not going back to that place."

"She has to." Knight frowned. "If she disappears now, it could put a chill on the whole operation. You're the one who can leave, O'Donnell. Tomorrow your mission is going to be finished, and Simon can handle it from there. You can simply go back to the States like the nice tourist they all think you are."

"I am not leaving."

Knight sat back. He appeared to enjoy having the upper hand. "You will if I kick you out. Don't forget for a second that I can have you tossed into places you don't want to go.

I'll do it without a single qualm if you threaten my mission. I'll shove you so far into prison that no one will remember you even existed."

"Oh, they'll remember when I break him out, Damon. As pissed as I am right now, don't think for a second I'll leave a man behind. You do not want to play that card." Ian stood up. "We can't decide anything tonight. Miss Charles, if I've been hard on you, I apologize. My dick isn't involved in this so I can only go by what my brain tells me and that's to keep you at arm's length. Since I can't do that anymore, I have to trust that Eve's judgment is correct and you're not a supersecret terrorist out to bring down the US military. You should understand that we're not the only ones who have been watching you for weeks. When I took your phone in order to bug it, I found out it was already bugged. Watch what you say and do. If it was up to me, I would pull you in a heartbeat, but it's not. As for you, Li, we'll talk about it when we get back to Dallas. After we bring in Nelson, it's up to you whether you stay or not."

"We're not staying," Liam replied. "Neither one of us. She'll come back with the team because we owe her protection."

Avery shook her head. "I'm not leaving. I'll help out MI6."

Liam gave her his best Dom stare. "You will not. You are not involved anymore. You're out of this."

"She's not out if she doesn't want to be," Knight insisted.

Avery turned to Liam, her eyes bright with tears. "I'm not leaving, Lee. Liam. God, I hate this. I won't leave because he's sending guns in to kill the very people I've been trying to save, that Stephanie is trying to save. What the hell happens when some boy soldier gets it into his head that he can take over the clinic where she works, where she does good? I gave up everything so she could do something good. I will take down anyone who gets in my way. You think I'm so weak, don't you? Well, you watch me now. You watch me. I won't allow you to hold me back."

A sob went through her, her whole body shaking, and he couldn't help it. He pulled her close, his hand soothing down her back. He hadn't thought about it that way. Avery had a stake in this game, a big one. She'd put so much of her grief and pain from the accident and turned it into something good, and she would be devastated if it all went wrong and she had any sort of hand in it.

"It's all right, love. I'm going to take care of it. I'm going to fix this. Do you understand? I'll do whatever it takes to shut this down. I promise."

She pushed away from him after only one sweet moment where she'd softened against him and let him hold her. "You owe me, Liam."

He didn't want this to be about him owing her, but it tied them together and he couldn't deny her this. Her story about how she'd come out of her grief had moved him to tell her the truth. She'd been brave, and now she wanted to protect the world she'd built and he couldn't deny her. She wouldn't be Avery if she didn't try. "I promise." He turned to Knight. "Let me stay, and I'll be a good soldier. Tell him, Ian. Please."

That "please" made his stomach roll. He didn't beg. He didn't plead. He would rather die, but that was how much she'd come to mean to him. It struck him rather forcibly that he'd just gained a huge weakness. Avery could take him apart if she wanted to, and she just might want to.

"He'll do a good job for you," Ian said, no expression on his face. "He'll protect her and get you what you need.

And I want him back when you're done, Damon. Don't get him killed."

It was practically a declaration of love from Ian Taggart.

Ian walked out, slamming the door behind him.

Alex patted Liam's back as he stood up. "I'll keep covering you, man. No matter what happens tomorrow, I'll stay here and back you up. I think you did the right thing. I'm sure Adam and Jake will stay behind, too."

"Great. I need a bunch of yanks hanging around." Knight put a hand out. "Sorry. I'll take all the help I can get, and it really would be optimum if everyone in Avery's life stayed in place. Molina is listening in, and he'll take note of anyone who leaves. The last thing we need is Molina deciding she's on the wrong side. Look, Miss Charles, try to get those files. If Simon is right, they're in some form of code. We'll get you a clean phone with a camera. Don't walk out with the files. Take pictures of them and send them to us. I suspect they're likely in code. We can crack it. If you can do that, we can stop everything."

Or Liam could take all the risks. He would rather he did it. Or Weston. They were trained. Avery wasn't, but he wasn't about to argue with the new boss when Knight had been so close to taking Liam out of the game altogether.

Avery nodded. "I'll get it done. He'll be out of the office tomorrow. If you get me a camera, I'll find the files."

"Excellent." Knight stood up, straightening his shirt. "I know you won't believe this, Miss Charles, but I quite admire you, and I wouldn't see you hurt. My country will be very appreciative of your aid in this matter. If you need anything at all, I'll make it happen."

"Do I have to stay with him?" she asked.

Fuck. He couldn't let her walk out. Not now. "It would

look bad. Everything has to stay the same."

Knight shrugged. "He's right. And you do need a bodyguard. I know you're perfectly angry right now, but I'm going to give you a little advice that you're likely to ignore since I've got a cock and you probably hate all men right now. He didn't have to tell you. It would have been far easier for him to have simply disappeared at the end of this operation and left you without an explanation. It's what I would have done. So you ask yourself why that dumb bloke just risked everything for you. If he'd been on my team, I would have had him shot and disposed of. He'll likely lose his job, and for people in our business, we only have our jobs. So you ask yourself why he would risk everything he has to make sure you knew his real name. Mind that man, Miss Charles. He would die to protect you. He's a bit of an idiot that way."

Liam felt his eyes slide away. What the hell was he supposed to do about that? He was torn between punching the bugger and hugging him. He'd never been as confused as he was right fucking now. The only thing he knew was he had to protect her, and he had to let her take a stand. And those two things were completely counter to each other.

"I understand." Avery took a long breath and stood as well. "I would like to go home now. If I have to go home with Liam, I will do that."

Not the sweetest words he'd ever heard, but he'd take them. He got up and nodded to Alex and Eve before opening the door for Avery. He was going home with her. He had to hope he had a little time to fix the wound he'd opened.

As for tomorrow, that was a fresh hell, and he'd face it when he had to.

Chapter Sixteen

Avery was still shaking as Liam got out of the cab. She almost never took cabs in the city, but Liam had insisted he didn't want to be on the Tube this time. He'd probably thought she would run, but she'd meant what she said. She wasn't going anywhere. She wasn't going to allow all of her hard work to be for nothing because someone was trying to profit off the pain and misery of others.

Still, it would have been easier on the Tube. He'd spent the entire time sitting next to her not saying a damn word. For a man who had so much to say before, he was stubbornly silent now, and they were about to head up to her apartment where they couldn't talk about anything because the whole place was bugged.

Her apartment was bugged, and everyone around her was lying to her. She wouldn't believe it, but it was pretty hard to think the prime minister of England was really on hand to help out a bunch of con artists. Of course, it could have been an actor. One who looked and sounded just like the PM.

She sighed. She kept looking for a way out, and there wasn't one. When she really stopped to think about it, she'd known deep down something was wrong at UOF. Something was wrong with her boss.

"Do you think Brian was in on it?" Brian Molina had been her friend in physical therapy. He'd introduced her to

307

his brother and gotten her the job in the first place.

"Not here." Liam handed the driver the fare and reached in to take her hand and help her out.

She ignored the offered hand. She would have to get used to being on her own again since she had no real intention of seeing him after this mission of his was over. In some ways, it would have been kinder for him to have just left. She would have had a few more days, and then he could have faded away. She would have been left with the memory of being loved once.

"Avery." He was getting very good at making her name sound like a curse word, but she was about to get good at ignoring him.

She managed to stay on her feet. She breezed past him and into the building. He was right behind her. By the time they walked past the front desk, he had an arm around her and she was stuck because she'd promised to keep up the ruse. She smiled at the deskman and managed not to punch Liam when his hand slipped down and cupped the curve of her hip.

How long would it be before she forgot his face? Sometimes she couldn't quite remember Brandon's face.

When the lift doors closed, she started to shove him away, but he seemed to anticipate her move and crowded her to the back of the tiny car, his body covering hers. He leaned over and whispered straight in her ear.

"There's a camera in the left hand corner. Don't give me hell until we get to Adam and Jake's. It's not safe. There are cameras everywhere, and one wrong move could clue your boss in." He tipped her head back and spoke normally. "Are you sure we have to meet your friends for a drink? I just want to get you in bed, baby."

Heat flashed through her. She could hate him all she

liked, but her body didn't care. The minute he started to talk in that deep tone of his, her body responded. The good news was her body wasn't in charge. "I think I'm going to be very tired tonight."

He didn't seem to pick up on her tone. He just winked down as the doors opened. "It's okay. I'll do all the work. All you have to do is lay there."

"Wow. That sounds so charming." She held her temper. Only a few more steps and she could let it fly. She allowed him to lead her out of the lift and down the hall. She glanced up and, sure enough, there were security cameras covering the hallway. She'd never really noticed them before. Someone was watching. Maybe it was the building security or maybe it was someone else. Everything she did and said was being watched and used against her.

Liam pulled her into his arms, his voice low again. "Don't be scared. I'm going to take care of you."

She wanted so much to sink into his strength. She wanted for him to just be Lee and for everything that had happened in the last couple of hours to be a stupid dream.

But it wasn't, and she had to face reality again.

The door to Adam's apartment opened, and he walked out looking like the nice man she'd assumed him to be when he was really some sort of intelligence operative. He was still dressed for the day in a pair of slacks and a button down. "Hey, you two. I was getting worried about you. Come on in. I have a late-night snack ready. Martinis, anyone?"

"Yeah, I want a martini," Liam said, his voice incredulous. "Beer me, man. But my girl here could use a nice stiff drink."

She walked through the door, and the minute it closed, Adam turned. He stood taller than normal, his shoulders perfectly straight and all affectation of softness gone. "Avery, I am very sorry you found out like this."

She hated them all in that moment. Just as she'd thought she was finding some friends and coming out of her social disaster phase, she learned that everyone she'd befriended had ulterior motives, including her boss who she had pretty much bet her whole future on. She no longer had a home in the States. She had no friends there. No friends here. She was alone in a way she hadn't been even after Brandon and Maddie had been killed.

Alone.

"Why am I over here?" she asked. "Can't I just go to bed and get the files in the morning and then I never have to see any of you people again?"

"You people?" Adam asked with a grimace. He turned to Liam. "Wow. You fucked this up."

Jake walked in and tossed Liam a beer with the ease of long friendship. "Catch, man."

"Thanks. Fuck, I need this." Liam had the top off and was downing it in a heartbeat. "I didn't fuck up. I wanted her to know. I had to tell her because I have zero intention of letting her walk into this blind. I won't let her get hurt."

He said all the right things, but then he'd said them before, too. "Since we're here and it seems like the only place I can speak my mind without getting caught on tape, I have a few questions for you, and I want honesty for once."

Liam sobered, his eyes wrinkling into a serious expression. "I won't lie to you again, love. I promise."

"Did you come up with all that 'sex is serious' crap before or after you met me?" She wanted to know if he ran that line on everyone or if she'd gotten special treatment from the jerk who had apparently made a sex tape. Ian's recitation of Liam's sexual history had done nothing to help his case.

"After I met you," he said, his eyes on her.

"Trust me, I've known him for years, and he's never once taken sex seriously," Adam said. Liam growled his way. "Until now, of course."

Liam didn't even flush, but then a man who'd slept with that many women probably had very little that embarrassed him. "My relationships before you have been brief and mostly about getting off, if you know what I mean."

"Whereas this one was about getting off while you worked. The perks of your job are lovely," Avery shot back.

His eyes narrowed. "I deserve that, love, but I want you to remember that I'm the one who came clean, and I did it for your sake."

When he put it like that she almost wanted to give in, but she fully intended to get to the bottom of everything. "Am I your type?"

He stilled, the beer that had been just about to meet his lips stopping in midair before he brought it down and placed it on the table.

"Do any of us really have a type?" Adam asked.

"Go away. Both of you," Liam said, his eyes steady on her.

The last thing Avery wanted was to be alone with Liam. "I'd rather have them here. After all, they've been listening in, too, haven't they?"

Adam's silence was answer enough.

They had listened in while she'd made a fool of herself. "So it doesn't matter if they go. They'll still hear everything. Am I your type, Liam O'Donnell?"

A stubborn look came over his features. "You're female, so yes, you're me type."

He wasn't going to make this easy on her. She

rephrased the question. "Did you take one look at me and decide you wanted to sleep with me?"

"No," he replied shortly.

"What did you think of me?"

The beer bottle slammed against the bar as he set it down. "Avery, this doesn't matter. All that should matter is what I think now. Why does it matter that I looked at a complete stranger and didn't necessarily want to fuck her? I want to fuck you now. I want to fuck you all day, twenty-four hours a day and seven days a week. I'll bloody well prove it to you if you'll just let me take you to bed. I can prove how much I want you."

And she would fall right into his trap. "That would solve so many of your problems, wouldn't it? If I was still the sweet submissive, you could just tell me what to do."

"You didn't exactly follow all of me orders before, darlin'. I don't know if you've been noticing, but you're not exactly submissive outside the bedroom anymore. You've been standing up for yourself more and more this week."

That wasn't the part of the week she wanted to focus on. "Is the BDSM stuff all crap? Because it occurs to me that it's a really good way to get a woman to do what you want."

"It wasn't serious for me until I met you." Liam stood and towered over her, his hands on her shoulders. "I played around with it, but now it feels really bloody serious. I promised I wouldn't lie, and I won't. I wasn't attracted to you at first."

She let a nasty little smile curl her lips up. "You thought I was plain and a little fat, didn't you?"

His eyes closed briefly and those hands on her shoulders tightened as though he was afraid of letting her go. "Why does it matter? I think you're gorgeous now."

"Answer the question, Liam." She really was a

masochist, but she had to hear it come from his mouth.

"Fine, I thought you were a little overweight and uninteresting, but that was my problem. That was coming from a man who barely got a woman's name before he screwed her and walked out the door and started looking for the next warm body that didn't matter. Adam, how many girlfriends have I had in the whole time you've known me?"

"It depends of your definition of the term 'girlfriend,'" Adam began.

"He hasn't had anyone, Avery." Jacob Dean sighed and drank his beer. "He's been utterly alone the whole time I've known him."

"It doesn't sound like he's ever been alone." It sounded like he'd screwed half of the women in the US.

"Sex isn't the same for a man as it is for a woman," Jacob replied. "His emotions weren't engaged. He didn't care. I've never known the man to care about anyone really."

"I don't know that I should listen to you about the emotional needs of straight guys." Avery looked between the two men. Jake and Adam had been in a relationship for years. They couldn't possibly understand how she felt nor could they speak to why Liam had done what he did.

"About that, Avery," Adam began.

"They aren't gay, love," Liam said, letting her go in favor of scrubbing a frustrated hand through his hair. "She's going to blame me for that, too. They aren't gay, but they're damn good at playing it. They're married."

Adam shuddered. "That makes it sound so vanilla. We're married to the same woman. See, we had something freaky to hide."

But she'd been perfectly comfortable with Adam because he was gay. "You tricked me."

He flushed. "I was protecting you."

"Were you protecting me when you helped me buy those clothes?"

"I was helping you and it worked," Adam replied, his voice softening. "You felt better when you dressed better. Avery, it was obvious you didn't have a friend to help you out. You've lived a very sheltered life. I was just doing what a real friend would do. You're a beautiful woman, but you didn't have any idea how to dress. I was helping you find your way."

And it had worked. She did feel more confident in her new clothes. She felt more confident in herself, and Lee Donnelly had a lot to do with that, but he'd been one big lie. Adam had been, too. "Did you enjoy the show?"

Liam's face flushed, and he turned on his friend. "Did you go into the bloody dressing room with her?"

Adam backed off, his hands coming up like he was attempting to ward off an encroaching beast. "I was playing a part, Li. Gay Adam wouldn't hesitate to help a friend with her zipper. By the way, the emerald green undies really do look gorgeous on you, Avery. You have a great ass."

"Jacob, I'm going to kill him," Liam growled.

"Hey, neither one of us have forgotten the fact that you kissed Serena. I think I'm backing him up on this one." Jake turned to Avery as Liam let his fists fly. The two men started to fight, but Jake acted like it was an everyday occurrence. Adam got Liam with a quick upper cut, but Liam had some height on him. "And Adam wouldn't have bothered with that bit of revenge if he hadn't known you meant something to Liam. Liam wouldn't care less if some guy came in and took his place with a woman as long as he'd finished. It won't be that way with you. He's possessive. He's never possessive."

"Shouldn't you stop that?" Avery watched the two men. Liam had Adam in a choke hold.

Jake shook his head and waved the whole thing off. "This is what we do, Avery. We're dumb animals in the end. They'll get it out of their systems and go back to being friends. You women want to attribute all kinds of meaning behind the things we say and do, but we're really simple. We run around aimlessly fucking anything that comes our way until we meet the one woman who can take care of us, who can fix all the shit that's wrong inside, and then we're done, and a man like Liam is done for the rest of his life. He won't fall again."

"He hasn't fallen now." Even before she'd found out he'd lied to her about everything, she'd known it wasn't forever. A man like Liam didn't end up with a woman like her.

"Then why is he over there trying to kill Adam?" Jake asked. "Besides the fact that Adam can be so brutally obnoxious I want to kill him sometimes."

She shrugged. "He feels guilty that he took advantage of the fat, crippled girl."

Jacob's eyes flared, and he suddenly seemed about a foot taller than he had before. "Liam, your girl just called herself something you're not going to like."

Liam came off Adam and turned around, his focus shifting to her. His hand came up and wiped a thin trickle of blood off his mouth. "It better not be something about her size. We've already had that conversation once tonight, darlin'."

When he looked at her like that, she wanted to sink down and beg his forgiveness, but that was stupid. The whole BDSM thing was just as fake as the rest of him. "It's none of your business."

He stalked across the apartment to get to her. "That's where you're wrong. It is me business and it's going to be me business for the foreseeable future, or are you going to walk away from this here and now?"

Walk away? And never see him again? She shook that thought off. It was a dangerous thought and just proved she wasn't really thinking at all. "I'm going to the office tomorrow and you know it."

"I won't have you talking bad about yourself. Not now. Not ever again."

He was just a big old bully. "I want to go to bed now, Liam." She was done with this conversation. She was done with Adam and Jake. She was definitely done with Liam. Except he had to come home with her. "You can sleep on the couch. There are no cameras, so no one has to know. All they'll hear is someone shuffling around."

"No." Liam turned around and pointed a finger Adam's way. "I catch you even looking at her ass again and I'll kill you. I kissed Serena to prove a point, and it worked. It got the two of you working together. I don't need any points proven to me. I'm smarter than both of you combined."

Jake shrugged. "Serena would probably agree."

"Come along. You want to go to bed. We'll go to bed." He tugged her hand into his.

She resisted, pulling back because she knew damn well she couldn't get into bed with him. It would be a complete disaster, and she would look like an idiot. Again. "I'm not sleeping with you."

"Yes, you are."

"I'm not saying yes, Liam. This is rape."

He turned, those emerald green eyes rolling. "I'm not going to fuck you, though we both know damn well it wouldn't be rape. I'm willing to give you some time to see how stubborn you're being. You've had a shock, and you're unsure of things right now, but you'll see that things between us will get back to normal. I lied about my name and why I approached you. I didn't lie about a damn thing else. I want you, girl. I want you so bad that I'm willing to give up the only family I have. That's what I would be doing if Ian fires me."

"Ian's not going to fire you. He didn't fire us, and we probably deserved it more," Adam admitted, holding a bag of frozen peas to his left eye. "And I didn't mean to be a Peeping Tom, Avery. I just couldn't come up with an excuse to not help you. And I told my wife about it."

She wanted to believe them all, but she couldn't. It was too much for one day. She'd rolled around in misery and confusion and pain enough for one twenty-four hour period.

She followed Liam out and was silent as they entered the apartment she'd adored right up until a few hours before. This place had been her fresh start. She remembered the first time she'd walked in and realized that this was a place that held no bad memories, a place where she could make fresh ones.

And she'd spent weeks alone here with someone watching her every move.

Liam locked the door and pulled her along, her feet shuffling against the wood floors, taking the proper steps and, for once, not faltering. She simply followed him, her insides numb. It felt a little like a bad dream that she was being forced to survive until she could wake herself up. He tugged her into the bedroom they'd shared, and he was solemn as he pulled her sweater over her head, reverent as he unclasped her bra.

It didn't matter. If he wanted to fuck her, he would, and there wasn't anything she could do about it except survive.

She almost welcomed it because it would be good to have one more thing to hate him for.

He leaned over and kissed her belly, just a light brush as he got to his knees. His head tilted up, and she would have sworn she saw a glimmer of tears there.

Forgive me. He mouthed the words. *Forgive me.*

She didn't reply, had to look away. She couldn't even think about it. Not yet. Maybe one day in the distant future she could let it go, but not tonight. She was still as he unbuckled her jeans and dragged them off. He sighed and got up, pulling back the covers and tucking her in bed. He didn't give her the comfort of a nightgown. She'd never worn one around him. No underwear and no nightgowns, he'd dictated. Nothing that would come between his flesh and hers. But she didn't need a thin nylon nightie. The truth was a wall between them.

The sheets were chilly against her flesh. She wanted to cry, but she wouldn't give him the satisfaction. She'd known all along that he was too good to be true. He was still playing a game, and she was still his pawn.

Wasn't she?

"Did I ever tell you about my brother?" It was odd to hear him talk in that flat American accent now that she'd heard the lyricism of his real voice. He pulled his shirt over his head and laid it on the dresser. It hurt to look at him, so she turned away.

"No. You didn't mention a brother." He hadn't talked about his family at all.

"We grew up rough, me and my brother. Our mother hung out with, shall we say, a criminal element." He got into bed beside her, and she just couldn't turn away again. It seemed like a declaration of weakness. He climbed into bed, naked as he pleased, lying on his back, one arm behind his head. The sheet covered her, but somehow it only managed to cover Liam to his waist leaving his cut body on display. He turned his head to face her. "He was a rough kid, always getting into trouble, and he was my main responsibility in life. All I heard from the time I can remember being able to walk and talk was to take care of my brother."

What was he doing? Why was he telling her this now?

"I loved my brother so much, but he was a pain in my ass. He had a really thick skull. I don't know. I think I look back with rose-colored glasses. That's the phrase, right? When you lose someone, you tend to try to forget the bad."

She snorted a little. She couldn't help it. Brandon had been the world's biggest slob.

Had Liam really lost his brother or was this another story he was making up? She kept silent, unwilling to be drawn in, but he just kept talking.

"He wasn't a bad kid, at least I told myself he wasn't. I don't know. Maybe I was worse. I got into a lot of fights, but my brother was just very self-centered. He plotted a lot. He stole from the church fund once while we were altar boys. I had to cover it up. He did a lot of other stuff, but I tried to turn a blind eye."

She hadn't had siblings while she was growing up, but she could imagine how hard it would be if one went bad. "That's terrible."

He sighed, his eyes on the ceiling. "We were hungry. I told myself that at the time. Now I wonder what he'd been planning to do with the money. It doesn't matter because in the end, I failed, and I think I've been trying to figure out a way to forgive myself for years. He followed me into the Army. There wasn't any other place for us to go. He rose through the ranks with me, and I lost him on a mission. I failed."

She couldn't help it. She reached out and put a hand on his chest. "You didn't fail."

"Rory died, Avery. I failed. I didn't pull the trigger, but I allowed myself to get into a situation where he died, and I didn't even have a body to bury. I miss him. I can't even imagine how much worse it was for you. I want you to teach me."

"Teach you what?"

"How to live like you. How to be as strong as you are."

"I hardly think you can learn anything from me." She started to pull her hand away, but he held it.

"Please, Avery. Just this much."

She turned on her side. She wasn't sure she could handle the new, honest Liam. He was even deadlier than the liar.

She fell asleep with her hand on his chest, feeling the strong beat of his heart.

* * * *

The man who claimed to be Thomas Molina felt every muscle in his body freeze as Lee Donnelly spoke.

Rory died, Avery. I failed.

The room went cold.

Coincidence. It was just a coincidence. That was all it was. Like the story about the thieving altar boy was just a coincidence. Tension ran down his spine.

He set down his Scotch and walked across the office to where he kept his personal files. He certainly wasn't stupid enough to keep them at UOF Headquarters. No. This was his private office in his privately owned town house. He'd made many modifications to the place since he'd purchased it with all of Thomas Molina's lovely money. That fucker hadn't

320

known how to live. Bloody wanker.

Molina hadn't understood what it meant to be truly hungry. His legs might not have functioned, but he'd never gone hungry. He'd been a sad rich man playing at redemption. Molina had cried when he'd had a gun to his head. He'd bawled and said something about all the good he'd done in the world.

Good meant nothing. What the real Molina had never understood was that all those blighted bastards who ate the food he sent to them would have slashed his throat in a second because they lived in the real world where loyalty meant nothing. Friendship meant nothing.

Brotherhood meant nothing.

Only money mattered, and he'd proven that when he'd killed his only brother in a bomb blast and taken those fucking bonds and made his deal with Nelson.

Teach you what? Avery's voice came over the speaker.

How to live like you. How to be as strong as you are.

He nearly vomited. What an idiot. Avery was weak. Avery was sweet and sugary and all the things that would make her so much fun to break and watch when she finally understood the real world.

Rory O'Donnell's world.

Rory cursed under his breath as he looked at the photos Malcolm had taken. Why wouldn't the bastard look up? Lee Donnelly was a master at making sure no one caught his face.

Lee Donnelly.

The key when you're picking an undercover name, brother, is to find one you won't have trouble answering to. Stick close to the truth. That's the best way.

His brother had always tried to take the lead. He'd always tried to teach him. The truth washed over the man who had been formerly known as Rory O'Donnell.

His brother was alive and in bed with his secretary. His dead brother had managed to show up right before Rory settled the biggest score of his lifetime. Rage shuddered through him. He couldn't tell anyone. Malcolm was already set to kill Donnelly. If Rory was right, Malcolm should be told.

He couldn't do it. It would make him look weak. He'd told his enforcer the story of Liam's death a number of times. He couldn't look weak now. And he couldn't let Malcolm know that Nelson had potentially lied. A man like Malcolm went with the strongest leader he could find. He didn't need to lose Malcolm to Nelson. Hopefully Malcolm would kill the Donnelly chap and no one would know the truth.

Rory looked out over the street. When they'd been children, they had lived in the slums of Dublin, and every night his brother would promise him that one day they would have nice houses and plenty of food.

He'd come so far from that rat hole, but it looked like his past was back to try to reel him in.

He'd killed dear Liam once. If Malcolm failed, he would have to do it again.

Chapter Seventeen

Avery's hands shook a little as she put the coffee down. Even the slight clatter made her want to jump, and she'd made the sound herself. The break room at the UOF building was quiet and the sound echoed. She was jumping at everything today. She wasn't cut out for all the spy stuff. This was her one and only foray into espionage.

She'd woken up with a spy in her bed, cuddled close even though she'd tried to turn away from him.

What the hell was she going to do about Liam? And what was wrong with her? She was in the middle of something serious and all she could think about was a man who had lied to her. A man who had used her. A man who was trying to do something right. She didn't have a problem with his investigation, but did he really have to sleep with her?

"Are you going to get some coffee or just stare at the mug?"

Avery jumped at the masculine voice. She turned to see Simon Weston standing in the doorway, looking cool and collected in his perfectly pressed suit. He didn't have a problem with the spy stuff, but then he was a real live spy. She was surrounded by them all of the sudden.

He looked around the small break room. It was empty, but he still kept his voice low. "Calm down, Avery."

Yeah, she was trying. She'd been told that Simon had

been filled in by his boss, Damon Knight, and would be her MI6 contact. After today, Liam was just a bodyguard if he hung around at all.

I'm not going anywhere, Avery. So stop thinking that I am. I won't leave you alone. Not ever.

He'd whispered the words in her ear as he stood beside her on the Tube, the heavy traffic shoving them together, pressing them until they were nestled like puzzle pieces.

How long would it be before she would stop feeling his hands on her body?

She shook off the thought and grabbed the coffeepot only to have it clatter and shake. Simon cursed and took it from her.

"You're going to get us all killed if you don't stop," he whispered. He poured out a mug of French roast. "It's a normal day, just like any other. When the boss goes out, you go in and find those files. The minute I have them in hand, you're out of this. It's very simple, sweetheart."

She nodded, but there was nothing simple about any of this. Liam was somewhere in the city getting ready to follow a man who was an acknowledged murderer. He was going to follow him and quietly take him down, very likely with lethal force. She'd been sleeping with a killer, and all she could do was pray that he came out of this okay. She wouldn't be able to take a real breath until she knew he was all right. But she wasn't going to let him know it.

"I don't think you should start doing the new reports without me." His voice changed, abruptly going back to the smooth tones he always used.

"Morning, people." One of the women from fund-raising walked in with a cheery expression on her face. Janet. Avery was almost certain that was her name and that she had two small children. Was she in on Molina's plans?

Was everyone in on it? Would they all be watching her?

Simon gave her a little nod. "Morning to you. I was just telling Avery here that we're all going to be able to relax once she and the big boss move on."

Janet sighed. "Oh, how I long for the days of three hour lunches and Ping-Pong battles. And poor Avery is going to have to settle for the drudgery of Dubai. I feel for you, darling. I really do. All that sand and sun and wealth."

It had seemed like an adventure before, but now she wondered.

Janet grabbed a pot and started heating water for tea as she continued on. "I wish I'd known the boss was looking for an assistant. I would have applied for that job. Not that I could have known. I've been working for the UOF for almost ten years, and this is the first time I've ever seen the man in person. Didn't see him much in pictures, either, now that I think about it. The rumor was always that he was a shut-in. You know? One of those people who doesn't go out because they can't stand the openness of the outside. What are they called? There's a word for it."

"Agoraphobia," Avery replied.

Janet snapped her fingers. "That's it. I guess it was just one of those rumors though because he told me the other day that I had to wait on the lift because he couldn't stand cramped spaces. I thought it a bit rude that he required the whole lift for himself and that goon driver of his." She shrugged. "Guess the rich really are different. I don't know. Why don't we ask Mr. Second in Line for the Throne or something?"

Simon rolled his eyes. "I'm not second in line for the bloody throne, love. I'm like twenty-third or something."

Simon and Janet were off poking at each other, but Avery was thinking. Not once in the months she'd been with

Thomas had he had a problem with being outside. Janet had to be wrong, or the rumors were. Just how much did she really know about her boss? When she'd first come to work for him she hadn't really looked into his background. She'd been too happy to have the job, and he was a philanthropist. In her mind, that had to mean he was a good person.

How many secrets did he have?

"Avery? You coming along?" Simon stood at the door, a mug in his hand.

She forced herself back into the present. "Of course."

"And don't forget about what we talked about." Simon turned and started toward his part of the building.

What had they talked about? Reports. She wasn't doing any new reports. She set her coffee mug on her desk and settled in. She could hear Thomas in his office talking quietly to someone. Her computer was right there with all its Internet connections and links to anything she could want to know.

She couldn't help herself. She pulled up her browser and put Thomas's name in it. It was innocent enough. She was his assistant. If she got caught, she could say she was just looking for news articles that highlighted his philanthropy for the ball. There were plenty of UOF promo materials to be made.

But she skipped anything recent, preferring to go deep. There were numerous articles about Thomas Molina and the foundation. He was raised wealthy, but a horseback riding accident left him with weakened limbs and struggling to walk. She knew that story all too well. There were several articles that claimed the multimillionaire philanthropist was a hardcore agoraphobic. One article on a financial website claimed that before he'd started this tour, no one had seen Thomas Molina in person for years with the singular exception of his brother. He'd lived in a small guesthouse on the ground of the mansion he'd inherited. He ran his empire from his computer and rarely took phone calls.

He'd changed. Her heart ached with sympathy for him. He'd had to fight, and it hadn't been easy.

Could Liam be wrong about her boss?

"Avery, sweetheart? What on earth are you doing?"

She gasped a little. Thomas was right behind her, and she'd never heard him move. Usually whatever braces or cane he was using that day made a scratching sound on the floor, but she hadn't heard a thing today. She turned and gave him what she hoped was a brilliant smile. "I was looking for some pictures or articles we could use in the Black and White Ball promo materials. I thought I would put together a bio sheet for the packets we're giving to our donors."

He shuddered lightly. "No one wants to read about me, dear. Focus on the celebrities who are performing and whatever you do, don't put pictures of me in there. We'll scare people off."

"Really? I don't think so. You're quite a fascinating man. I was just reading about how courageous you were after your accident and you were so young."

"I don't like to think about it much. I suppose we have that in common."

She nodded. "Yes, we do. It can be so hard to even get in a car sometimes."

"Well, I don't have to worry about getting on a horse again." He sighed and a sad look flitted across his face. "I'm going to lunch now. I'm meeting my friend. I don't think I'll come back this afternoon. I have a few things to take care of at home."

"Okay. I'll see you tomorrow then."

He shuffled out, a distant look on his face.

Could MI6 have it all wrong? What if Thomas wasn't involved at all? What if he was exactly what he appeared to be? Someone else could be the arms dealer or someone from outside could be using the UOF and no one knew.

She stood up. Maybe the evidence would exonerate her boss. She wouldn't know until she found it. Once she did she could be out of the whole mess and out of Liam's life. She pulled the spare key out of her desk and watched Thomas disappear into the elevator.

She was alone for the moment. She might not get a better chance. Hurrying to get to the door, she tripped, wrenching her knee. Pain flared, combining with frustration. Avery got to her feet. Patience. She needed some patience. Being calm and cool was the only way to be. It was perfectly normal for an administrative assistant to be in her boss's office.

Calm down, girl. Take it slow and easy.

She could hear Liam's voice. He'd lectured her all the way to the building. He'd spoken in her ear while they rode the Tube, his breath warm on her skin.

Act like you own the place. Wait for the right time. It doesn't have to happen today. This thing happens when you make it happen and not a minute sooner.

She wanted him to be here. If she called him, would he come rushing over? Thomas was going to be gone all afternoon. Would he leave his assignment behind and rush to her side? Would he hold her hand and promise her everything would be all right?

With shaking hands, she got the key in the door and straightened up. She didn't need Liam. He had his job to do and she had hers. They couldn't really figure anything out until this operation was over. Deep in the night, she'd decided that if Liam felt anything for her it was likely temporary, an effect of being undercover. It would go away when he wasn't living with her, and she had to prepare herself for that eventuality.

She was in. Thomas's office was pin perfect. There wasn't a file out of place. His desk was clean of the debris that regularly littered hers.

She strode across the room. Thomas had the corner office. A spectacular view of St. James's Park in the distance greeted her when she turned to the windows. He always kept them open. He claimed to love the view of the park. The windows ran from almost the ceiling to the floor, giving the whole office the illusion of being up in the air, the world spreading out in front of her. It was sensational.

It was something that would make an agoraphobic man think twice.

Could someone really get over a deep-seated fear so completely that he would love an expansive view?

Avery turned away and decided to start with his desk. He didn't have filing cabinets. He preferred neatness and minimalism. The files had to be in his desk.

Avery opened the side drawer. Sure enough there were a few files there, but they looked like employment files. Nothing but names and addresses and compensation packages. She dug deeper, but only came up with some proposals and plans for events to benefit the charity and Thomas's most recent stock portfolio.

Where the hell was that file? She'd given him the Lachlan Bates file herself. Was it possible he'd taken it home?

She opened the drawer on the other side and sighed. Nothing but some breath mints and a white bottle of saline and what looked like a case for contacts.

"What are you doing, Avery?"

It took everything Avery had to slowly close the desk. Monica stood in the doorway, her lovely face frowning.

"I'm looking for a list of the donors attending the Black and White Ball. I can't find mine, and I have to finalize the seating chart." Her voice was steady, but she could feel her skin flushing. "What are you doing here? Is there something I can help you with?"

"I was looking for Thomas." It seemed like it was Monica's turn to blush. Her pale skin went pink.

"He's at lunch, but he's not coming back."

Monica nodded. "Fine. I guess I'll just have to talk to him later."

She turned on her heels and left.

Avery drew a long breath. The files weren't here. He had to have them at his place or he'd given them to someone. She needed to get into his town house and search his office there. It was the only answer.

But she could do a little research before then. She had the names of the donors. She could see if she could find them and try to connect them. There had to be connections.

But now she had another question to answer. If Thomas didn't need contacts to see, whose contacts did he have? Why would he lie about not needing contacts?

Avery went back to her desk to start looking for answers. She could only hope that Liam was having better luck than she'd had.

* * * *

Liam looked out from his perch across the Thames. He'd rented the room hoping it would offer the best view of the meeting spot. He'd been right. Through the powerful scope he held in his hands, he had a perfect view of the restaurant. He also had a high-powered rifle, but he probably wouldn't be allowed to use it.

Of course if he really wanted to, he could just take out both targets and Avery would be safe.

And he wouldn't have any answers. He wanted Eli Nelson alive. He wanted to know what had happened to his brother. He'd had the dream again the night before. He'd stood in the middle of that bloody room, bodies all around him and all he'd been able to see was his brother's boots sticking out from behind the couch as his phone began to ring.

Only this time Avery had been in the dream with him. She'd stood behind the couch, her eyes steady on him. *It's only boots. There's nothing of your brother here.*

She'd held the boots up as the phone began to ring. Just before he'd forced himself awake, he'd seen a shadowy figure move behind her, its hands ready to wrap around her throat.

He'd woken up in a cold sweat, shaking.

Why couldn't he stop thinking about those boots?

"Do you have a good line of sight?" Ian's voice came over the small radio link Liam had in his ear. It brought him back to the present. To the outside world, it would look like a Bluetooth device, but it only connected to his team.

"I have a clear line of sight." Alex sounded cool and calm.

"I'm in position," Adam said.

"Me, too. Just waiting on the word," Jake replied.

Adam and Jake were on the ground. They would follow Nelson when he left his meeting with Molina.

And then Liam had a few questions for the man. "How long will we have with the bastard before the Agency takes over?"

"Who said they have to know?" Ian replied. "Damon assures me we can hold Nelson for a little while at The Garden. It seems our MI6 friend's dungeon is also, well, a dungeon."

"Nice," Jake said.

"He was the one who called me." It was the only explanation. "Nelson got me out of that house. Now the question is why. He wanted that mission. He set you up to take it from you."

"I know." Ian's terse reply practically bit across the line, but Liam couldn't give his boss a lot of room here. He had to know.

After he'd woken from his dream, he'd sat up until dawn thinking about every second of the mission. Talking to Avery about Rory the night before had forced him to face some truths about his brother. Rory had been trouble right from the beginning. He'd been selfish and a little mercenary. A lot mercenary, but he'd seemed to be turning it around. The SAS had redefined him.

Or had it? What secrets had his brother been keeping before he died? According to Ian he'd been in touch with their mother's old IRA contacts. Why?

"Do you think my brother was working with Nelson?" Liam was deeply aware that everyone on the line could hear him. He'd kept this secret for far too long. These men and Eve had become his family, and he'd spent far too long being the sarcastic snotty brother who didn't really give anything back. They'd been his friends. They'd protected him. Ian might be a right bastard, but he'd tried his hardest to keep them all together. Had he lied? Maybe, but it had been an omission that Liam just might have made himself under the same circumstances. Liam had made a decision. If he was in, he was in all the way. If he was going to be Avery's man, then he had to be a better version of himself. He had to find a way to trust his family.

The trouble was it seemed to Liam that his blood family might have plotted to have him killed.

"We can talk about this in private, Li," Ian commanded.

"Just a yes or a no. I'm going to fill everyone in anyway. This isn't just my problem anymore. This affects the whole team, and I'm not going to hide it away because I find it embarrassing." And Ian shouldn't either. "Nelson had something to do with the mission that killed my brother, and I worry that he's been playing a long game that we haven't begun to understand yet."

"Just shut it down for now." Ian sighed over the line. "We can talk about this in person, and everyone can be at the table. All right? Can we just take out this fucker first?"

"Right, boss." He settled back into silence, watching the restaurant, but his head wouldn't quiet down. Avery was still in trouble, and there was something wrong with Molina. He needed to get a meeting with the bastard, even if it was just to get an in-person assessment of the man. Something was off about the whole thing, but he couldn't put his finger on it. If Rory had been working with Nelson, what had happened to him? Had Nelson killed him when he was no longer useful?

And he wasn't sure about Simon Weston either. He'd been forced to turn Avery over to Simon when he'd left her at her office this morning.

How the hell had he gotten into MI6 confidential files? Adam might be able to do it, but Adam had been hacking systems since he was old enough to sit at a computer and type. Nothing in Weston's background made Liam think he was capable of it. Ian wasn't thinking. Ian had stopped thinking the minute he'd been forced to think about his wife again. Maybe he'd stopped thinking the minute he'd hit the ground in London.

And maybe that was just what Eli Nelson had planned on.

A cold chill went up Liam's spine. The restaurant was so open. Why had a rogue CIA agent sat outside on the patio in the bright light of day when London had one of the most active systems of CCTV cameras in the world?

"Alex?" Liam asked.

"Yep."

"You have a sight line of where Nelson was sitting in the picture we got, right?"

Alex was set up to scope the front of the patio on the Thames side.

"Where's the nearest camera? The one we caught him on?" The one that had taken the footage that sent them to London in the first place.

Adam's voice came over the line. "I'm standing under it."

"Is it hidden?" There might be a chance he couldn't see it, that Nelson hadn't known.

"No. It's in plain view."

"Motherfucker." Ian's curse burned over the line. "He knew. He had to know. He wanted us to see him."

"Well, he wanted someone to see him. And he's fifteen minutes late," Jake added. "He's moved the meeting. He's not coming."

There was another loud curse over the line as Ian proved beyond a shadow of a doubt that he knew an awful lot of cuss words. He was inventive. Liam had to give him that. Ian went over a number of items he intended to shove up Nelson's bum, and Liam rather thought he would do it without the aid of lubrication. Ian also, it seemed, intended to go medieval on Nelson as there was something about entrails and wrapping the man's intestines around his throat, but only after the aforementioned anal torture.

Liam kept quiet as he packed up his gear. Nelson had drawn them here. Nelson had always known they were here, so why hadn't Molina tried to take them out? What the fuck kind of game were they playing?

"Meet back at the club. We have to rethink everything." Ian sounded tired after his rant. A long sigh came over the line. "Liam, move her tomorrow. Get her out of here. But do it quietly. Nelson will be watching us tonight. Everything has to look reasonably normal. Pick Avery up at work, take her back to your place, and then don't leave until dark. Check in with Adam and Jake at six and they'll get you armed for the night. You and Avery talk about going to dinner and a show. Molina's listening so Nelson is listening, too. Don't say anything that could tip him off. Find the biggest crowd you can and lose yourselves in it. Stay out for the night. I'll have Eve get you both new IDs, and we'll move you in the morning. Meet her in Liverpool station, eight a.m. Do you want this girl?"

He wanted her more than anything he'd ever wanted in his life, but he had questions he needed answered. "Ian, I think Nelson killed my brother."

"You have a decision to make, man. If you decide to stay here, I'll let Adam move her."

"And you will have lost your chance," Alex said, speaking for the first time since the revelation. "Li, do you trust us? I'll do what it takes to find the truth, but you're going to have to choose between revenge and her. I doubt if you walk away that she will ever let you back in."

But Liam knew something about Avery that the rest of

the team didn't. He knew how forgiving she was. She would eventually forgive him, and he could have both. He could find the truth. He'd waited years to discover the truth. He dreamed of it every night—except for those few days with Avery when all he'd dreamed about was her.

She would forgive him, but he would prove that he'd learned absolutely nothing. The past was done. He couldn't bring his brother back, and he couldn't fool himself any longer into believing that his brother had been a good man. Nelson would have needed one of them.

And Rory had been the one to buy the pints. He'd been the one to convince Liam to just have one before they turned in.

Fuck. His brother had very likely slipped him a roofie. He'd been drugged by his own brother and then saved by Nelson. Nelson had known the house was going to blow, but Rory had been the expert in explosives.

None of it made sense unless they were working together, but then why the hell had Nelson saved Liam? The answers were here.

And he was going to walk away from them because he loved a girl. Because she mattered more than anything, and he wasn't going to trust her safety to anyone else. He could get her out tomorrow. He could make sure she was safe. That was his real mission in life. "Tell Eve to get at least two different passports and then send us somewhere warm."

"Will do," Ian replied. "Go pick up Avery and batten down the hatches for tonight. The rest of you get your asses to the club. We have to figure out what this fucker wants."

Liam took a long breath. He was walking away from everything he'd held close for years. For years, all that had mattered was figuring out what had happened to him, but now he had a future. He was going to grab it with both hands and never let it go. Avery would forgive him. She had to because he was going to prove he could be worthy of her.

He pulled the radio off and packed up his gear and left the key card on the bed. He needed to get to her as fast as possible. He'd rather take her away tonight, but Ian was right. There were issues to be settled, and they didn't want to tip Nelson off. Or Molina.

Liam opened the door and out of his peripheral vision caught a flash of metal. He leapt back, shoving his bag up and catching the gun just as it went off with a quiet little ping. Silencer.

Fuck. He'd been followed, and he hadn't even known it. He was losing his edge.

Adrenaline flooded his body. His opponent was caught off guard, and Liam reached out, grabbing the arm that held the gun before the man could aim again. He pulled his attacker inside. The last thing he needed was to get Scotland Yard involved. He brought his knee up, catching the man in the gut while he twisted the hand with the gun. It fell neatly to the floor while his opponent tried to fight back.

Liam let his instincts take over, forgetting everything but the fight. He brought his fist up in a neat uppercut that caught his opponent right on the jaw. A nice crack split the air as the bone broke and blood started to flow. The man fell to the floor but not before Liam managed to get his gun in hand. It was time for a little torture. *Fuck.* He hoped the guy could still talk. Liam looked down at him. Maybe he could just write down all the pertinent information. Liam hadn't broken his hands. Yet.

It was turning out to be a terrible day, but a little interrogation was just what the doctor called for. His inner sadist nearly stood up and cheered.

Until the second bastard invaded.

"Mr. Molina says hello, Mr. Donnelly. He wants you to stay away from his lady friend. Permanently." The second guy was dressed in an immaculate suit and had come equipped for a gunfight.

Liam put a foot on the unconscious, hopefully-wasn't-dead-yet man, though he might have used a little too much force because the bloke wasn't moving. Liam had to admit he might have sent pieces of bone straight up into the git's brain. He could be a little forceful at times, but he wasn't going to tell his current attacker that his partner might be dead already. "How about you put the gun down, and I don't kill your friend here."

The new guy fired once, and Liam was no longer worried that he'd killed the first attacker. The bloke on the floor now had a bullet in his brain. His new opponent simply smiled. "I never liked him much anyway."

Liam got off a shot before he rolled away behind the big four-poster bed. It wouldn't provide much cover, but it was all he had. This bloke wasn't playing, and he was far better trained than the idiot he'd sent in as his first line of fire.

"You aren't what you say you are, Mr. Donnelly. I thought I was shooting a guy who was unlucky enough to be fucking the woman my boss wants, but you're here for something else, aren't you? Who sent you? You're not a bloody construction worker."

And now this guy had to die, too. He couldn't just get away. Liam huddled behind the bed, catching sight of the man moving in the mirror over the dresser on the opposite wall. He stepped over his dead compatriot and had the deeply bland look of a man who had killed hundreds of times.

Liam flattened his body to the carpet and took the only shot he had, splitting the guy's ankle and sending him to the floor, where he promptly proved what a pro he was. There was the briefest glimpse of his body falling and then a shot that went straight under the bed and across Liam's left bicep. Pain flared, fire running over his skin.

And there was not a second to consider the pain. He got to his knees as a second shot grazed his hip. He rolled to the side and let everything but the fight fall away. There was nothing past this moment and this man. He would live or die and everything crystalized. Time seemed to slow down, his vision getting sharper as though he could laser focus.

Breathe in. Move to the side.

Breathe out. See the target, a little spot right between his opponent's eyes. Lift the gun.

Breathe in. Fire.

The man's head jerked back, blood splattering behind him, but on his forehead there was only a neat little hole.

Ian was going to kill him. Liam slumped down, his back to the wall. His left arm ached, but it looked like it had only grazed him. He sighed. He'd fared far better than his opponents. MI6 was going to ream him a new bloody asshole for those corpses.

But Molina didn't know who he was or at least he wasn't telling his people. The would-be killer had called him Lee Donnelly, and he'd done it with the arrogance of a man who thought he was holding all the cards. Either Molina was hiding it from them or Nelson hadn't let Molina in on the fact that they were here.

Very interesting.

Liam forced himself to move, getting to his feet so he could rifle through the dead guy's wallet. Malcolm Glass. Citizen of England. He had a couple of tenners and a bunch of credit cards in several names. Nothing that really told him a damn thing.

Liam picked through his bag. He found his phone and dialed the one person he didn't want to talk to.

"Yeah, you on your way to pick up your package?" It was a cell line. Ian would talk in vague language.

And so would Liam. "Ran into a bit of a problem, boss."

There was a low growl. "The kind we can still ask questions of?"

"Nope. I would say all the questioning is over."

"Fuck. I'm sending someone to you. How bad is it?"

"Just a little. But we might need to call our friends and get the name of a good cleaner." Because someone was going to have to deal with the bodies.

The cursing began, and Liam let himself slide to the floor again. Ian would handle it from here. A sense of peace came over him. Sure it was fighting with the adrenaline that came from being shot at, but it was there all the same. He wasn't alone. He'd fooled himself. He hadn't been alone for a long time. The moment he'd woken up, filthy dock water in his lungs and a blank space in his memory, had been the moment he'd been reborn. For the first time, he understood a little tiny bit of the spark that kept Avery going despite everything she'd been through.

A man wasn't his past. A man was his future, and it was something he had to fight for. And family wasn't necessarily blood. The bonds of friendship could form tight family ties.

Adam pushed through the door. He must have been closer than anyone else, and it was obvious he'd run his ass off. "Holy hell. Jeez, what did you do to these guys? And that's my shirt. Motherfucker. You got blood on my shirt."

Brothers. They could be hell on a man, but he was damn glad to have them.

* * * *

"Why didn't you tell me my brother is alive and well and fucking my secretary?" Molina only waited long enough for the waitress to walk away before he started in on Nelson.

"I didn't realize it myself until about a year ago. I found myself working with his team on the operation that led to my early retirement from the Agency." Nelson leaned over, his face very serious in the gloom of the pub. Unlike the last place Nelson had insisted on, this pub was dark and on a quiet street. The restaurant before had been in the open. "Are you telling me Liam O'Donnell is here in London?"

"Are you telling me you didn't know, ya bloody bastard?"

"Careful, Thomas." Nelson placed emphasis on Thomas. "People might wonder why an American millionaire talks like he should be standing on the docks of Dublin with a pint in his hand."

Molina tried to rein in his emotions. They seemed to be running rampant ever since the moment he'd realized dear Liam was still alive. "How did he get out of that house? I set it to blow the morning after I left. Early. He should have still been metabolizing the drugs I gave him."

Nelson shrugged, a negligent gesture. "He must have had a stronger constitution than you guessed. You never told me why you didn't just kill him like you did the rest of them. Why did you feel the need to kill those kids?"

"I liked it. It was fun." And he'd needed a place to blow up. "I had to be able to disappear, and it had to look good. And I couldn't be completely certain the explosives would go off. Anything can happen. Those dead kids were my backup plan to deal with Liam in case it all went wrong."

"Why not just stab your brother, too? He couldn't come

341

looking for you if he was dead."

It had been a moment of weakness. His brother had fallen into the girl's bed. He'd been so drugged out of his mind that he hadn't noticed when Rory raped the girl and strangled her. That had been a bit of fun. He'd fucked her and killed her, and big brother just slept right on beside them. But when Rory had gone to shove a knife through his gut, his eyes had opened. A stupid smile had come over his face.

We're doing good now, Rory. We're doing good, you and me.

And Rory had stood up and walked out telling himself it was enough to make it out with the bonds. Liam wouldn't live. He wouldn't even wake up. He would never know.

"That was obviously a mistake, but one that's being taken care of as we speak."

Nelson's eyes tightened, his whole body losing its previous casual air. "You're taking out your brother?"

"I sent my two best men to do it." Any minute now Malcolm would text him with the word that his brother was dead and they were safe. "Do you think he was working with MI6?"

"I know he was working with a man named Ian Taggart who still works for the Agency from time to time. They're hunting me, not you, and if you only sent two men to take him down then my guess is your men are dead and Liam now knows you're on to him. You should have talked to me before you pulled a stunt like this."

Rory felt his spine straighten. He didn't like the way Nelson was talking to him. "Since when are you my boss?"

Nelson leaned forward, his voice a low rumble. "Since the day I pulled you out of the SAS and gave you the kind of life you had always longed for. If it weren't for me, you would have ended up getting kicked out of the Army. How long would it have been before your brother found out about your criminal connections? How long before he discovered all the secrets you sold? Do you think he would have helped you out the way I did? No. He would have handed you straight over to the government, and you would be rotting in prison."

The waitress came back smiling a gap-toothed smile. She put two pints in front of them, but Rory wouldn't touch his. He would fiddle with it, but he never drank anymore. He wouldn't allow himself to be out of control for even a minute. But when he was finally able to shed the Thomas Molina guise, he would be himself once more. He would drink and fuck and kill whenever he wanted.

And Avery could watch it all. It would be the perfect punishment for fucking his brother when she'd avoided touching him. She'd treated him like a bloody infant, but she spread her legs as fast as she could once Liam had walked in the door.

The waitress walked away, and Nelson sat back. "I think I should take over setting up the Middle Eastern end of the business. You've done quite well in Africa, but my contacts are better in Asia than yours."

So that was his game. A savage anger started to take hold. Everyone seemed to be trying to get their greedy hands on his property. It was starting to grate on his last nerve, but then he'd been doing a slow burn since he'd come back to England. "No. This is my business. I've been giving you a cut since day one, but that's all you'll ever get."

He didn't owe Nelson more than that. Hell, he didn't really owe Nelson a bloody thing. Now that he thought about it, he was the one who'd gotten the bonds. He was the one who had set the charges. He was the one who had set everything up so no one had looked for him.

Nelson was the one who hadn't even noticed that Liam had survived, and apparently Nelson was the one who had brought dear brother down on his head.

Maybe it was time to get rid of his mentor.

Nelson frowned but his eyes remained cold. "So you don't need my contacts? You're going to be able to move into the Pakistani and Afghan markets without me?"

He would once the Lachlan Bates deal went through. The terrorist cell in Sudan was his way to move into Islamist extremist groups. If he could make sure they were stocked, they would come to him. There were millions to be made and power to be had. And he didn't intend to share a bit of it with Nelson, but he couldn't let the man know that. It would be like announcing he was planning on assassinating him.

"I'm sorry. Of course I need your contacts." Molina hoped he looked sincere. He wasn't. He was thinking about how fast he could put the bastard in the ground. Nelson had been helpful, but his time was done.

Nelson seemed to relax a bit. "I know I can help you. Like I said, you've done a great job with the African markets, but you'll see how much money we can make once you let me in. Have you handled your MI6 problem?"

He wasn't worried about MI6. He was worried about his brother. "They haven't figured out the codes yet." He'd developed them himself, so not even Nelson could get access to his accounts and clients without the cipher, which was in his safe at home. "They won't. They don't even understand that there is a code yet. They've got some weird weigh ins at various ports of call. I just need to find the right people to bribe."

He'd had a couple of breakdowns, but he was getting it cleared up.

"So Weston isn't a problem?"

Molina rolled his eyes. He wasn't worried about that idiot at all. "Weston is an aristocrat playing at being a spy. He's been utterly ineffective, and once I leave London, he won't have a chance to even stumble across something. After the ball is over and the coffers are full, I'll move everything to Dubai. I have a very private compound. Only the most trusted will gain access. I'll run the business from there."

"And Miss Charles will be with you?"

He wasn't so sure about Avery anymore. He wasn't sure he wanted his brother's leavings. It was just a shame that his brother wouldn't know he'd gotten the bitch killed. His brother had always been so moral. His brother had believed in sin and honor when nothing of their childhood should have taught him values. Liam had been stupid. "I think not. I think it's time I found another assistant. This one feels a bit used, if you know what I mean."

She'd been so innocent, but she'd shown her true face. She was a whore like the rest of them, and he'd still have her. He would fuck her and then he'd get his hands around her throat. Then she'd know who her god was. He'd make her pay.

What was taking so long? Malcolm should have texted him by now. He looked down at his phone.

"Something wrong?" Nelson asked.

"I thought Malcolm would message me by now. He should have taken out Liam. He followed him."

Nelson shook his head. "Malcolm is dead. Liam and his crew killed him. I assure you, there's no way you took O'Donnell out with two men. He's been trained by Ian Taggart. Whatever you think of your brother, know that he's a well-trained killer now. He'll be tougher than you imagine.

Taggart is not someone you should underestimate."

He dialed Malcolm's number. Nothing. It went straight to voice mail. *Fuck*. Malcolm had never not answered. What the hell had happened? Was Liam still out there? Did Liam even know he was alive?

"You need help, Rory. I can deal with this for you." Nelson used the same smooth tones that he'd used all those years ago when Rory had made his deal with the CIA's version of Mephistopheles.

"How?" He didn't want to owe Nelson anything, but maybe he should use him one last time.

Nelson leaned in. "I'll tell you."

Nelson started to talk. Yes. This was even better. This way his brother could watch as Rory raped his woman.

And Rory could be the one to kill him. As it should be. After all, they were brothers.

Chapter Eighteen

"What exactly do you mean you couldn't find the files?" Simon ground the words out, his voice low, his face turned down as the elevator started toward the ground floor.

Avery wasn't sure how much she should say. She'd gotten a little paranoid about being overheard. She tried to sound as normal as possible. "I looked and couldn't find them."

"I asked you not to work on the new reports without me." Simon turned, his back to the small red light that came from a camera in one of the corners.

Oh. That was what he'd meant. He'd been trying to tell her to wait for him. It would have made it harder for Monica to catch her. "Sorry."

He turned again, his handsome face in a fierce frown. The elevator doors opened, and Avery stepped out. Despite everything he'd done, her heart softened the minute she saw Liam waiting for her. He leaned against the building, his eyes scanning the street. There was a tight set to his jaw that told her he was worried, but it was his body language that really scared her. Liam was always so graceful. He was tall and lean and so strong, but now his shoulders were slumped.

She forgot about Simon and rushed to get to Li. "What happened?"

He turned to her, and she could see the grim set of his mouth, but he smiled when she reached him. He reached for her with his right hand, pulling her close. "We're getting out of here in the morning."

A little surge of panic hit. "I can't. I didn't find the files."

"That's Weston's problem now." He shot a look at the other man. "She's out."

Weston nodded. "Good for you, mate. Take care of her. And don't tell me anything else. I don't want to know."

"As if I would." Liam slung an arm around her shoulder. "I have one question for you. Where did you really get all that information about Ian? Don't try to tell me you hacked the system. That's not your expertise. I'm surprised Knight bought it."

Only the faintest hint of flush hit the Englishman's cheeks. "I can be very persuasive. Acting is my expertise. I play this part quite well, but I'm starting to wonder if I haven't been duped."

"You got the information from an anonymous source, didn't you?"

"At the time, I thought I was helping," Weston replied. "I was able to verify that all the information was true. Now I have to wonder why someone in MI6 wants to cause trouble with your team."

Liam huffed as though he'd known all along. "Because it wasn't from MI6. It was Nelson. He connects everything. He's the dotted line that we've all ignored. He was the agent who took over for Ian after his wife died, and I'm starting to suspect that he was the one who killed her. He might have been the one to send her to Ian in the first place. I'm almost certain he was the one who killed my brother, and for some reason he saved me."

"What does this have to do with us?" Avery asked, her head ringing with all the twists and turns. "Is this the man

Thomas is meeting with?"

"We need to start walking. Let's head to the Tube. Or do you have a driver meeting you?" Liam started down the street, but there was something wrong with his walk. He shuffled just a bit as though favoring his left leg.

"Sod off," Weston shot back. "I don't have a bloody driver. And I want to know what Nelson's old op has to do with this, too. And what the hell's wrong with your leg?"

Liam shrugged. "Just a couple of bullets. I'm fine. They just grazed me."

Avery nearly stopped in the middle of the street. "Bullets?"

"Keep your voice down, love." He chuckled a little and nodded toward the building they were walking past. "That's Scotland Yard HQ. Let's not talk about bullets or guns."

He'd been shot. Liam had been shot and apparently more than once. Her heart threatened to pound out of her chest. He could have died, and it was very likely that no one would have told her. She would have waited outside the building for him. When he didn't show up, she would have assumed he was done with her. The thought of never touching him again assaulted her. The idea of Liam, his big body cold and dead, was unthinkable.

She was in love with him. She'd spent the last twenty-four hours telling herself that she wasn't, but it was a lie. She was trying to protect herself. There was no way Liam really loved her. He was feeling guilty. From what she could tell, this was maybe the first time he'd been forced to get really close to a woman in a way that didn't involve bondage and video cameras. When things became normal again, he wouldn't want her.

But she was worried that she would always want him.

They walked up Victoria Street and Westminster Abbey

came into view. It wasn't the way they would normally go, but Liam seemed intent on talking to Simon and perhaps it was better to do it in public.

"I'm going to take it you didn't get your job finished," Simon said, walking toward Westminster station.

Liam frowned, adjusting his baseball cap. "No. He didn't show. He's onto us, and he likely has been the whole bloody time. Something's off. I don't know if Molina knows, but Nelson is playing a deep game with the lot of us. That's why I'm moving her out."

"I can't leave. I didn't find the files." Avery struggled to keep up. Even injured, Liam was faster than she was.

He slowed down, his hand tangling in hers. "Sorry, love. I'm anxious. And you will leave with me in the morning. The rest of the team will figure this mess out, but you're done."

The mission couldn't be over. "I think the files are at his house. I can get in there."

"Avery, do you know a man named Malcolm Glass?" Liam asked, ignoring her statement.

Why did he want to know about Malcolm? The files were the important thing here. "Yes, he works for Thomas. He's Thomas's driver."

Simon snorted. Only he could make the sound elegant. "He's Molina's enforcer. He's got quite the history. He's done a couple of stints in prison, but lately he's become smarter. I believe he's Molina's muscle."

"He's dead," Liam said bluntly. "I put a bullet through his skull not two hours ago. He was sent to kill me because I'm sleeping with you. He was quite clear on the subject. Molina wants you, and he's quite angry that I've had you. Do you understand what a man like that will do if he decides to take you?"

A shiver went up her spine. Thomas had sent Malcolm to kill her boyfriend? "It's not like that."

But now she wondered. Thomas liked to touch her. She'd thought it was just affection, but there had been times when he would hug her too long or his hands would slip. And he did seem to be deeply possessive.

"He's the one who made sure you didn't have friends at the office," Simon pointed out. "He's been isolating you. He's actually quite odd, you know. I haven't been able to spend much time with him. Every time I try, he puts me off."

"Because he made you a long time ago." Liam's eyes strayed to the massive cathedral.

Simon stopped. "Bugger. How did he make me? I've been careful."

Liam motioned for Simon to keep up. "Doesn't matter, but if Nelson knew who to send Ian's files to, then you better consider yourself compromised, and MI6 is going to need a new plan. You might talk to MI5 or Scotland Yard. See if you can legally search Molina's town house. I think that might be your only shot or you'll have to work this from another country. Either way, Avery's out. She's not going to be alone with the bastard again."

"Don't I have any say in this?" Avery asked. It was all happening too fast.

"No," both men replied at the same time.

"You're out, Avery. I'll carry you out of this country kicking and screaming if I have to," Liam vowed.

"You're giving up a lot, mate. You really think this Nelson fellow killed your brother? You're never going to know for sure if you run off with her." Simon walked along, a smile on his face like they were talking about the weather and he hadn't just dropped a bomb that might explode in

Avery's face.

Liam was going to leave. He had to. He would need to find the truth. Even when she hadn't known his real name, she'd known the man. He was hard in so many ways. Even though he'd had problems with his brother, Liam would need to find the man who had killed him.

Liam was the one who stopped this time. "I'm done here. Do you understand, Weston?"

"Damn me. I wouldn't have suspected that." Simon pulled away. "This is where we part ways. I think I should probably head to the club. My days of working for the UOF are probably done. Hey, maybe Knight will save me from a formal dressing down and just fire me on the spot. I wish you two the best of luck."

Simon disappeared into the crowd.

"You're not leaving me?" Avery asked, well aware the question came out with a vulnerable sigh.

"I told you I wouldn't leave again."

"But you thought about it."

His hand tightened around hers as though he was afraid to let go. "Of course I did. I thought about it long and hard, and I decided that you're more important than revenge or the truth or anything. Now let's get home so we can very quietly get you packed. I'm going to take a shower and clean up, and then we'll go out for the evening. Just a nice night on the town."

"We won't go back." She would be on the run. It seemed incomprehensible. Just yesterday her biggest worry had been what she would cook him for dinner, and today she was afraid for her life. And his.

"No, we won't go back to your place. I don't know where we'll be. We'll find out in the morning, but wherever it is, I'm going to take care of you. I won't let him hurt you.

The lads will figure this out. I promise. We won't be in hiding forever."

"You're going with me." It sounded dumb. Why would he go with her? Did he feel that sorry for her?

"I am, Avery. You're not getting rid of me. I told you so." His face went stubborn, and he turned to the station. "Let's go. I want to get out of that flat as soon as we can. We need to disappear. I don't like the fact that he wants you."

It made her a little ill. "I'm sorry I didn't get the files, but I did find something. He wears contacts. Why would he do that when he's got perfect vision? At least that's what he told me. And don't you find it weird that he was agoraphobic and now he's fine?"

"Did you see the contacts? Were they colored?" Liam gripped her hand.

"I didn't look."

"And you're sure he doesn't need them to see?"

She should have opened them up and looked. "I don't know. I guess he could have lied, but why?"

"Bloody hell," Liam cursed, shaking his head. "I should have figured that out sooner. Molina never went out before and then all of the sudden, he up and wants to take an up close and personal interest in the business. Simon is right. He should get fired. I would bet money that Nelson planted someone years ago. He needed a way to move the arms around and he needed money to back it up. Even a few million wouldn't really be enough to start this on a large scale. But a few million would set up the scam that could replace Molina with someone else. Molina was a loner."

She was starting to follow his logic. "He only had a relationship with his brother. He didn't even like staff being around according to the articles on him."

"His brother was a drug addict and had gone through the trust fund their parents had left him. They settled the majority of the money on Thomas because they knew Brian would blow through it. Why didn't I see this could be a possibility? What if the man you know as Thomas Molina is someone else?"

That couldn't be true. "There were pictures of Thomas before this started. He looks the same."

"That's what the initial money was for. That's what the bonds were for, to set someone up as Thomas Molina. He would have to be roughly the right height and build, but other than that, plastic surgery can do wonders. But it can't correct the color of a person's eyes. He would need contacts if they didn't match."

"And then he could easily take over the company because he had no close ties to anyone. He wouldn't even have to really answer uncomfortable questions." So much of her life for the last six months had been one long lie. "I met Brian in a rehab facility. For my legs, not drug rehab. He was getting over an injury. He said he'd just come into a bunch of money. He died a couple of months after he introduced me to Thomas." She shook her head, horrified at her own naïveté. "I was surprised that someone like Thomas would want an assistant with so little experience, and then Brian told me he liked to get them while they were still innocent. 'All the better to corrupt them,' he said. I thought he was joking, but he wasn't was he?"

"Probably not. But it doesn't matter now because you're out of this and so am I. Though it makes me wonder exactly who Nelson got to do that little job for him. Who could have hated his life so much that he was willing to do anything to change it?" Liam paled, a tremble going through his body, but he shook it off. "Like I said, it doesn't matter. Come on, love. I need that shower and some Scotch."

He took her hand and led her to the trains. They huddled close, every moment of their time together playing through her head. She followed him, utterly numb. She was a zombie walking where Liam told her to go because she knew she was going to have to make a decision, and she wasn't ready for that yet.

Twenty minutes later, he sat her down on her couch and passed her a couple of fingers of the Scotch he'd bought earlier in the week. "I won't be long." He gestured around the room as though to remind her that someone was listening in. "We need to leave in an hour. The show starts at seven thirty sharp. We can have dinner over in the West End. All right?"

She was supposed to be specific when they could hear her. "Yes. That sounds nice."

He nodded and walked away, leaving her alone for the first time.

He was going to take her on the run. He would be protecting her twenty-four hours a day, seven days a week until the threat was over. There was no way she would be able to stay out of his arms. She would end up in bed with him again. She would submit to him again. She would fall in love with him again.

When would it end? Everything ended. When would Liam O'Donnell end, and why should she even try to take a chance? She'd lost everyone she'd loved. She would just lose him, too.

She shuffled through the apartment, her little London flat where everything had seemed ready to bloom. This was supposed to be her second act, but now she realized that everything before the day she'd met Liam had been a dress rehearsal. He was the real second act. He was her chance, but she wasn't sure she dared to take it.

Tears blurred her eyes, but she couldn't cry. They would hear her. She quietly opened drawers, gathering the few things she couldn't leave behind. Her real passport. A change of clothes. Her medications.

A small book of photographs lay buried at the bottom of her drawer. Pictures of her parents, her husband, her baby. She'd buried it in here, tucking it all away like something that should be hoarded, something that she should hide.

Tears fell as she opened it. Her parents. So loving, so kind. They'd been taken far too soon, and she still missed them every day of her life. Brandon. Would they still be married? Had it really been love or had she been looking for a way out? She'd struggled for so long with questions that didn't matter. He'd been good to her. He didn't deserve to be hidden away.

And Maddie. Her little girl who hadn't gotten to live.

She'd spent so much time worrying about forgiving the girl who had killed them that she'd never forgiven herself for surviving.

This was why she was ready to push away a man like Liam O'Donnell. She'd taught herself to walk, but she was still in that car. She could play at being alive, but she hadn't been forced to really live. She hadn't been forced to put her heart on the line and pray that everything worked out because life could be so hard and cruel. She hadn't chosen between fear and hope yet.

She looked at her daughter, so small and sweet in her father's hands. Brandon looked terrified, but he held Maddie close.

She'd asked what Stephanie owed her, but what did Avery owe these two precious people? What did she owe them? What did she owe herself?

A life. She owed them a life, and not the half-life she'd been living. She'd been a tourist. She'd fought to walk again and then all she was willing to do was watch as life passed her by. She'd spent all her time in museums and art galleries allowing no one to really touch her. It had been easier, but she couldn't do it any longer. She owed everyone who had loved her a real life, with real risk.

With real love.

Liam O'Donnell might come to his senses somewhere down the line. He might wake up and realize she wasn't beautiful enough for him, but no one would ever love him the way she did. She had to take the chance.

She heard the shower running and slowly took off her clothes. She dropped them on the counter. A bloody bandage sat near the sink, a smaller one beside it. He'd obviously torn it off before he'd gotten into the shower. Two fresh ones were waiting along with alcohol and some swabs. He was going to dress it himself? He didn't think she would help him?

She needed to make it plain to him that she would take care of him, too.

She could see him through the glass of the shower. One hand pressed against the wall. His head was down, drooping like he just couldn't hold it up. Her heart ached as she looked at him. He looked weary. How much had it cost him to tell her who he was? She'd taken it wrong, assigned all kinds of dumb motives to his actions, but he'd risked so much for her. What if he'd just done it for the purest reason of all? What if he'd done it because he loved her?

Swinging the glass door open, she stepped in. There was no hiding from this man.

"Avery?"

She put a hand out, touching the muscles of his back.

She loved the way he felt, hard muscle under soft skin. His green eyes touched hers. There was an angry wound on his bicep. God, he'd really been shot. "Are you sure you're all right? Should you be getting that wet?"

He turned, and she couldn't mistake the way his cock hardened like it was a magnet drawn to her. She took comfort in it. Any time he was around, her pussy softened and prepared for him. She belonged to him in a way she'd never belonged to anyone else. Every piece of her lit up when he walked in a room.

A long sigh came from his chest. His arm wasn't the only place that was hurt, and she realized just how much damage she'd done. "I'm fine. It's all right, love. I've had worse. I can still take care of you, no problem. It doesn't really hurt. And it didn't even need stitches, which is good because Adam can't sew to save his life."

She reached out and touched it. It looked more like a burn than anything else. "I want to help you."

He turned back to the showerhead, letting it hit his face. "You don't. You're just feeling bad, Avery. Give me a second and I'll leave you to shower in peace. I want to be out of here in an hour, but we need to stop and check in with Adam and Jake first."

He reached for the soap.

"I don't want you to leave. I want to help you." She reached out for him and was startled when he pulled away.

"It's not enough." He pumped the water up. Heat filled the room.

They could talk here. The rush of the water would filter out the sound of their voices. She stepped back. She wasn't enough? Had she been wrong?

Liam didn't wait for her response. "I don't want you to help me, Avery. I want you to love me. I'm not going to be your good-time guy. Do you understand me? I ain't going to settle when it comes to you. I can make you love me. I know you're mad. I know you think you don't know me, but you know more about me than anyone."

"Liam," she started. He was under some weird mistaken impression.

His hands found the curve of her hips. "No. I ain't listening to you tonight. I know I fucked up. I know I lied, but I ain't lying about this. I love you. I ain't said that to another woman me whole life. I love you, Avery. Maybe my love ain't worth much just yet, but I'm working on that. I'm going to be better. I'm going to be worthy. I'll learn from you. I'll change for you. I'll be a good man. I'll be a man you want for more than an orgasm. I'll be a man you can trust."

Oh, she'd done him such a disservice. Did he honestly think she only wanted him for that gorgeous body? Since she'd decided to look at him with an open heart, she could see how truly lovely he was. He was a man she could trust. He'd offered up his career and a truth he'd been seeking for years, and all he'd asked is that she allow him to protect her. "Why do you think I'm here?"

She was curious. Why on earth did he think she was standing naked in front of him?

His jaw tightened. "You want sex. I taught you to want sex."

Silly man. She let her hand trace the lean muscles of his hips. God, she loved every inch of him. There wasn't a piece of the man that wasn't perfection. "You taught me to want you."

Nothing had ever been as sweet as making love with Liam O'Donnell no matter what his name was. She loved every minute of it, but she'd held back. It would be better now. She would give him everything.

His face contorted, but it couldn't mask his beauty. "Avery, I know you're just saying that, but I'll make you believe it. I'm going to make you love me. It's my mission now."

"You love me?" They were the sweetest words she'd ever heard. He loved her.

"Damn, woman, I'm willing to give up everything to keep you safe. Of course I love you. I love everything about you. I need you, Avery. I need you so bad." His hands tightened on her hips, dragging her forward until his cock touched her belly. "I love you, baby. I love you."

Maybe it wouldn't last forever. Maybe he would die tomorrow or she would, but she would have loved him and that was what mattered. Love mattered. Faith mattered. He mattered. "I love you, too."

Uncertainty clouded his features. "I don't know if I believe you."

His hands moved restlessly on her hips, tracing the lines as his cock nudged her belly. He lowered his forehead to hers, nestling their heads together.

"I love you, Liam." She could say his name here in the shower. Tomorrow they could talk without fear of being overheard, but tonight she still had things she needed to say to him. "I love you, but you should know I am going to need a few things from you."

"I'll give you anything."

"I need a ring and one of those collar thingees."

His hand found her hair, his fingers twisting and tugging gently. It lit up her scalp and brought her to her toes. His mouth, those gorgeous full lips, hovered over hers. "You want to be my sub?"

She was going to be honest with him from now on, even

when it made her vulnerable. "I want to be your wife."

She thrilled to the arrogant, dominant look that banished his previous wariness. "That's a given, love. Wife, sub. It's the same to me, but know that as soon as we can do it safely, you'll stand in front of a judge or a priest or whoever and you'll make your vows in public. But know right now that if you say yes to me, I'm already your husband. And I am absolutely your Master. Do you know what that means?"

It very likely meant she would be sore in the morning. He was a hungry Master. When he got going, he could fuck all night like he was a starving man and she was the feast of a lifetime. It wouldn't mean a thing to him that they were on the run. He'd find a way to have her, and she found deep comfort in that. She was necessary to him. As necessary as he was to her. She brought her hands up to trace the sharp line of his jaw. He was masculine perfection and he was all hers. "Yes, Liam. I know what it means. And I'm saying yes. I'll say it every day."

She knew that every single day with him would be precious.

"Master. You'll call me Master when I'm fucking you, girl."

How did he make the word fucking sound like a declaration of love? It would sound dirty coming from anyone else. She'd actually hated the word before, but now she understood what fucking was. Fucking was down and dirty and sexy and loving. It meant losing herself in him, but somehow she didn't become lost. Somehow fucking Liam made her more Avery than she'd ever been before. She rubbed her belly against that monster cock of his. "Yes, Master."

His face fell, his hands cupping her cheeks. "Avery, this isn't the time, love. We're in danger."

They had always been in danger. She could see that now. "We're stuck here for a while, Liam."

"I need to concentrate, Avery." His hands smoothed back her hair.

"Adam and Jake are across the hall. They can hear what goes on in this apartment. They're keeping watch. We're as safe as can possibly be. And aren't we supposed to act normal?" He'd gone over it on the train. They were supposed to pretend like everything was fine.

"Don't tempt me."

But she wanted to tempt him. "Li, we make love all the time. What were you planning on doing for the next hour? They're listening. Should we play a board game? I don't think so. We should give them a show."

He kissed the top of her head. "Fuck, girl, now you're in for it. Do you have any idea the things I want to do to you? I want you every way. I want to master every inch of you."

He would do it. He would take her every way he could think of, and she would give him everything. And she wanted something back from him. She was finally ready. Her heart was finally open enough. "I want another baby, Liam. It doesn't have to be now, but I'll want it soon."

His face softened, his body cuddling against hers. "I might be a horrible da. I didn't have one meself, love."

His Irish accent went guttural and strong when he got emotional. She held him close. "You'll be great. I'll have to learn it all over again, but we're going to be great."

She could feel his cock pulsing against her belly as his lips found her face. He trailed kisses everywhere as he smoothed back her now wet hair. He kissed her forehead and each eye. He nuzzled their noses together before kissing each cheek. "Mine. You're mine."

Being Liam O'Donnell's was a good thing to be, and

she was ready to prove just how deeply she belonged to him. She went on her toes and ran her tongue along that sexy lower lip of his. "And you're all mine."

He dropped to his knees, putting his face level with her breasts. "These are mine." His big hands cupped her, pressing her breasts together. "These gorgeous tits are all mine."

His tongue came out, licking at her nipple before he bit down gently. Heat flared along her skin, her pussy getting soft and wet. Warm water beat along her chest, but it was nothing compared to the heat of his mouth as he sucked her nipple in. He whirled his tongue around and around before biting her again, oh so gently, just the right side of pain.

Liam moved to her other breast, giving it the same treatment as the first. His fingers played around her nipple. "I want you to pierce your nipples for me. I want you to look so soft and sweet on the outside, just the beautiful mum and wife, but underneath your clothes, you're my naughty little submissive."

It would be a mark of possession just for him. And it would always be a reminder to her that she was a woman, a lover. "Yes, Master. And I want something. I want a tat on your chest, something I pick out."

She wanted her own "property of" sign.

He pinched her nipple hard, making her shake. "You better make it masculine. Nothing girly. No roses or pink hearts."

"I promise."

He sucked her nipple into his mouth again, adoring it with his tongue. He let the nipple pop out. "Tell me something. How wet is that pussy of mine?"

"So wet." She could feel herself getting soft and slippery.

"Show me." He leaned back, his eyes taking in her body, going straight to her pussy. He liked to look at it.

She let her hand trail down her body, past her aching nipples. Her clit was already engorged and wanting. The pad of her finger slipped over it.

"Don't you make yourself come. You will not like how that goes for you. I'll spank that ass red, and then I'll torture those pretty tits of yours. You'll beg me to let you come and I won't."

He was so bossy and a little bit overdramatic. "I'm not going to come from touching my clit."

It was the wrong thing to say. Or maybe she'd used the wrong tone of voice. She was feeling a little bratty, and it seemed to have come out in her voice. Whether it was simply what she'd said or the way she'd said it, Avery found herself turned around, his hard body pressing her against the shower wall.

"That's ten, brat. And you'll let me play with your ass."

She shivered a little. The shower door opened and then he was gone, but she knew better than to leave position. He wanted to spank her. He wanted his hand on her ass. He wanted to know her skin was hot and pink because of him. It was his kink, and she was happy to indulge him. She gripped the handle on the shower wall and spread her legs, thrusting her backside out. The water fell all around her, one more sensation to be had.

The shower door opened, and she heard Liam gasp. "Fuck. That's a beautiful site, love. You aren't afraid of me at all, are you?"

She wasn't afraid of him. She wanted him just the way he was. She wanted him dirty and nasty and oh so loving. "You said you were going to spank me."

The crack of his hand filled the shower, and Avery had

to hold on tight.

"That's right, darlin'. The water's going to make it sting. Wait 'til I take a flogger to these beautiful cheeks." He slapped her ass again. "That might teach you to take that bratty mouth to me again."

Spank number three hit the seam of her ass, and he held his hand there as though he could hold the heat to her skin. His fingers slipped lower and played in her pussy. It felt so perfect, his big fingers running along her pussy. She wiggled a little, trying to get him to penetrate her.

His fingers pulled away, and he smacked her ass again, three times in hard succession. Avery couldn't help the moan that followed. Her backside was aching, and she was shaking with need.

"Bend over, love and I'll make this quick." His voice wasn't even. One hand pressed on the small of her back, pushing her down.

She let him press her down, her limbs stretching deliciously. Two more slaps had her skin singing, riding the perfect line between pleasure and pain.

"I love you, Avery. I love you so fucking much." One more smack. "Tell me you love me. Make me believe it."

"I love you." She wiggled her backside. "I love every filthy inch of you."

He slapped her ass one last time. "I won't ever get tired of hearing you say it. I don't know why you would love a dumb lug like me, but I'll take you, darlin'. I'll take ya. Let me give you what you need so I can have what I want."

She could guess what he wanted. She was nervous about it, but nothing he'd done to her had been less than spectacular. "I want you in every way a woman can take a man."

He turned her around, his hands gripping her ass as he

lifted her in one strong move. "Put your legs around me. I'll show you just what's yours."

She gasped as he impaled her on his cock. He invaded, taking up all the space, but she'd been wet from the moment he'd touched her, the slickness of her arousal facilitating the penetration. Her breasts brushed his chest making her nipples flare to life.

"You feel so fucking good. God, I've never done this. I've never taken a woman without a condom. Only you." He turned, pressing her back against the wall and gaining his balance as he forced another inch in.

Avery held on for dear life, wrapping her legs around his waist, spreading herself wide for him. She wanted every inch he had to give her.

He ground against her, his pelvis rubbing against her clit. Over and over again he thrust up.

"Give it to me. I want to hear it." He slammed into her, his cock hitting that sweet place deep in her pussy. She felt her muscles clamp down as the orgasm raced through her system. Heat and pleasure flooded her veins. This was right. This was perfection. She let it flow, not giving a damn who heard her. She moaned and fought for every minute of her pleasure. She didn't want it to end. She clamped down hard, wanting the come he could give her.

Liam's head fell forward as he thrust up hard, and his moan coupled with hers. His arms tightened around her and his cock swelled. Heat filled her as he came, offering her up his come.

"I love you, Liam. I love you so much." She couldn't ask for more.

He held her close. "And I love you, darlin'. You'll never get rid of me now. And don't think I'm even close to being done."

He picked her up and started to soap her body. Gentle hands washed her clean, and she was ready to start all over again.

Chapter Nineteen

Liam felt a deep sense of peace overwhelm the ache in his body. His arm hurt and his hip had a little twinge, but it didn't matter because his heart was full. Even thinking the words made him want to vomit a little, but he figured he'd get over it. He was just an idiot in love with a girl and that felt good. But he wasn't going to admit it to any of the lads. Not a chance.

He looked down at the woman in his arms. She slumped over, her head against his chest, his strength the only thing keeping her standing. She was so small in his arms, so sweet and vulnerable. The damp heat of the shower made her hair longer, sending it in glorious waves down her back. Her body was curvy, her hips and breasts made for a man's hands and his cock. Everything about her body called to him from her full tits to her rounded hips, and the most gorgeous pussy a woman ever possessed.

But none of her beauty would matter if she didn't have the softest heart he'd ever known. Soft but so damn strong. That was his girl. She'd faced the worst life could throw at her, and she'd conquered it. When her world had gone to hell, she'd forgiven it and made it a better fucking place. It was incomprehensible to him, but also beautiful. He didn't deserve her, but he'd meant what he'd said. He would take her. He would protect her. She was his highest mission now.

Avery Charles was the good fight. Avery was

everything sweet and good in the world, and it would be his honor to protect her with his fucking life. If the world wanted to come at her again, it would have to get through him.

He tilted her head up, brushing his lips across hers. He wasn't finished with her. He wanted her again. And again. And again.

His cock stirred. He shouldn't be hard again so fast, but she was the one. He'd never believed that there was one woman in the world for him, but she was it. She was brighter, hotter, more beautiful than the other women of the world. She shone for him like a beacon. Avery Charles made him want to be a better man, and he intended to make good on his promise.

Liam grabbed the soap and reverently started to wash her body clean.

Her eyes were a little dreamy as she allowed him to soap her up. "Isn't the sub supposed to serve the Dom?"

"Silly girl. Don't you know about aftercare? It's a term we use to make it sound all serious, but it's that time when we Doms get down to the real business of worshipping our subs. Don't let anyone tell you different now." He turned her toward the water. When they were back in the States, he would buy a new house. Every cent he'd saved would be put into buying her the best life he could give her.

And their children.

He was a man who had lived in the past and a whole future was opening up in front of him. It was overwhelming and beautiful. His past didn't matter. The future he could build was all that counted.

His cock was straining, but he ignored it for the time being. He reveled in serving her. This was the beauty of the exchange. She gave him her softness, her trust, and he worshipped her for it. From the outside, a BDSM relationship might look like an exchange of softness for strength, but it wouldn't work if they weren't both strong. Avery was stronger than him in so many ways. She lifted him up and made him better, and he could do the same for her. He could show her just how amazing she was.

"That feels so nice." She leaned back into his strength, her breasts toward the water.

"You feel nice, love." It was so good not to pretend with her. He kissed the shell of her ear, running his tongue along it. He nipped her lobe, loving the way she shivered in his arms despite the heat from the shower. "Tell me again."

Those words fed his soul.

Her lips tugged up. "I love you, silly. I love you a lot."

"I love you, too." It was easier and easier to say those words. They were meaningful. He'd watched Sean and Jake and Adam fall in love and it had seemed so incomprehensible to him, but now he was pretty sure he was better at it than they were. Jake and Adam had needed each other to love Serena enough, and Sean, well Sean was a chef. It was a little douchey. Liam was definitely going to be the best husband. And there was no way in hell he was joining them when they had their vagina talks.

Unless he really needed advice.

A sexy little puff of breath came out of her mouth as he let the soap drift between her legs, gliding over her clit and making a sweet circle. His girl liked it when he played with her pussy. He intended to do it often. The next few weeks would be one long learning session. He would learn every inch of her, discover what made her purr.

"Do you like that?"

"Oh, yes." Her hands drifted back, cupping his hips.

"I'm glad, love. But it's my turn, and do you know what

that means? Do you know what I want?"

Her head fell back, her body open to him. So trusting. He wouldn't let her down. "I know what you want."

He was being a bastard, but he wanted to hear her say it. When they'd met, she'd shied away from the dirty stuff, but he was going to show her how beautiful dirty could be, how hot they would be together. "Tell me."

She only hesitated for a second. "You want my ass, Master."

Yeah, that did it for him. He wanted to shove his cock deep and know that no one would ever have her the way he did. "I want everything. Will you let me have it?"

She turned, her head tilting up. Sleepy, sexy eyes gazed up at him. "Be gentle, baby, but everything I have is yours."

That got his cock really humming again. It swelled against the curve of her ass like it knew exactly where it wanted to go. "Let me dry you off, and we'll go to the bed." He kissed her nose. "I'm going to take care of you, you know? I'll keep you safe."

He was talking about so much more than the sex. He was talking about her life and her heart. She would be safe with him. Always.

Tears filled her eyes. "You're safe with me, too." She put a hand to his chest. "I'll keep you safe."

Her strength was quiet, but fierce. She would fight for him. It was what she did. She fought and she won. She'd taught him a whole new way to fight.

He turned the shower off and led her out, grabbing a towel. She was his to take care of. He hadn't understood what it meant before. He wrapped her up and took his time drying her off. He lifted her arms, running the towel along every inch, making sure she was warm. All the while, he kissed her, his lips adoring her fingers and her elbows, her shoulders and her neck. He rubbed the towel along her hair, pushing it up so he could find that place on the back of her neck that made her shiver and shake. He ran his tongue along her spine and kissed the scars at the small of her back.

"Go and get on the bed. Wait for me." He deepened his voice. This was the place where he was in control. In their bed, he was the Master. He'd always been Sir. Avery was the only one who would ever call him Master.

She winked at him. She'd come so far from the shy girl she'd been when he'd met her. "Yes, Master."

She turned and walked away, that naughty wink letting him know that he only thought he was in control. He was really her slave, but he was going to take command tonight. In a little under an hour, they would be on the run, but he had a little time to show her how much she meant to him. Adam and Jake were watching the building. They were as safe as they could be. He could relax just a bit.

He would lose himself in her. He would forget all his suspicions. They didn't matter now. They were in the past, and Avery was his future. Even if what his every instinct said was true became reality, it didn't matter because he wasn't defined by his brother. He was his own man, and he would claim his own family.

Blood was meaningful, but it didn't necessarily make a family. Love and friendship made families, too.

And lubricant. Lube might not make a family, but damn, it was going to make it so much easier for him to fuck his wife's tight little hole. He grabbed the lube and walked out of the bathroom. He had to be Lee again, if only for a little while. He slipped back into the American accent he would likely use very little after this day. He'd hidden behind it for years, but he wanted to be himself again. He'd finally figured out that he could take what was good about the past, chuck the rest, and move on.

And his almost wife seemed to find his Irish accent sexy. Yeah, he was keeping that part.

"Avery, I think we'll start on your knees."

She frowned a little at the sound of his American voice. Her lower lip came out in an adorable pout. Such a brat. He shook his head and gestured around the room to remind her that Molina was listening in and now knew his plan to take Liam out hadn't worked. Had "Thomas Molina" figured out who he was, yet? Liam rather doubted it. He'd been damn careful to keep his face off cameras, and there had been no mention of who he was when Molina's thugs had tried to kill him.

Avery nodded and sank to her knees, holding on to the bed for support. Somehow her lack of grace made his heart do funny things. He'd had subs kneel before him, their lean bodies a model of perfection and control. Avery's body struggled, but somehow it made her submission more meaningful.

He put a hand on her head. Soft hair, warm skin. Home.

"Touch me, love. I want you to put your hands and mouth on me. Get me hard so I can fuck your ass."

Her eyes widened slightly as she took in the sight of his cock. "Really? You need to get harder?"

He was painfully hard again. He should smack her saucy backside for the sarcasm, but all he could do was smile. "It's a game. Play with me."

Her tongue came out, touching the tip of his dick. Heat shot through him. Fuck all, he loved her mouth. She sucked him inside, just the head. Soft suction pulled at his cock head while her hand rolled his balls.

"More. I want more." He fisted his hand in her hair and pulled gently, feeding her his length. Her tongue whirled around, rolling over his flesh. Yeah, he could get harder. It seemed impossible, but every lash of her tongue made his dick swell.

"I love how you taste," she said before sucking him down again.

"Back at you, baby. You taste so good to me. You're like the best pie I ever had."

She stopped, looking up at him. "Pie? Really? I'm so stupid. That's what they meant by pie. Jake and Adam. Ewww."

He wasn't about to take the time to figure out what she meant by that. He didn't even want to think about Jake and Adam right then. "Back to work or you'll get punished again."

She settled in to her task with a sexy smile, those lips of hers opening up to swallow him. She gripped the shaft of his cock and let her hand glide over it. Teaching her how to suck cock was one of the best things he'd ever done. She'd been so shy at first, and watching her bloom over the last week made him feel ten feet tall. This wasn't the same woman he'd made love to that first night. This woman gave pleasure with the assurance of a lover who knew she would get it all handed back to her.

This woman knew she was loved, and he intended to make sure she always knew it.

He took a long breath and enjoyed the feel of her mouth around his cock. He fucked in long passes, pressing further in and invading her space. "Take it all, baby. You can do it."

Turning his head down, he watched as she struggled to fit him in. Her jaw worked to make room as he pushed inside. She did what he'd trained her to do. She breathed in evenly through her nose, settling into a rhythm. Over and around. Back and forth. Her fingertips tickled his balls. Her hair was still damp, and she used that, too, allowing the soft strands to touch his thighs with every long pass of her mouth.

A shiver began at the base of his spine, and Liam had to pull out. He tugged at her hair. "No more, baby. If you suck me any harder, I'm going to come, and I don't want to do that yet. I want to do that when I'm deep inside that ass. Get up on the bed, and let me have you."

She leaned forward, a wicked little smile on her face as she placed one last little kiss on the head of his cock, her tongue licking up the pre-come that pulsed from his slit. Such a bad girl.

"One day I'll tie you up right and good. I'll tie your hands to the bed and I'll put a spreader bar between your legs, and I'll make you scream for hours, brat."

"Promises, promises," she whispered as she crawled onto the bed. She got on all fours and lifted that hot ass of hers in the air.

He smacked it hard, right on the fleshy part, and loved the way she whimpered. He also loved the way her pussy pulsed with cream, proving she liked it. "I'll promise you everything, baby."

He would do it. The minute they were out of danger, he would have her trussed and tied up and waiting for his pleasure. He would bind her to him in every way a man could bind a woman, and in his head that included just tying her to his bed so she couldn't slip away.

"I don't know that I like that smile, Li." But she was smiling back at him. "I think it might mean I'm in trouble."

Oh, they were both in trouble because he was pretty sure he was about to become one of those pussy Doms who let his sub lead him around by his dick, and there wasn't a damn thing he wanted to do about it. "Stop trying to distract me."

He grabbed the lube and stared at her for a minute. She was in the most submissive position he could think of, offering her Master all of her body for his delectation. There was no tension in her, just a warm willingness to serve and to be pleasured in return. There it was again, that dumb flutter in his heart that the manly side of him would insist was nothing more than a heart attack, but he was beginning to understand it was just the way she made him feel.

He put a hand on the small of her back. "You tell me if it gets to be too much. We'll take this slow and easy. I want you to like it. Spread your knees apart. Let me see you."

"I should be horribly embarrassed. What have you done to me that makes this seem okay?" She giggled a little as she spread her legs wide and allowed her cheeks to part so he could see her asshole.

"Everything's okay when two people love each other." Everything was deeper and more meaningful. Everything took on a sweetness that had been absent before. "And you are gorgeous all over, baby."

She buried her head in the comforter. "You're a pervert."

And he was going to make sure she was a pervert, too. He liked her prim and proper, but he loved it when she got down and dirty. He squirted the lube on her ass, letting it dribble over her tight hole. It puckered sweetly. That hole would fight him, but he would get in. He would be her Master in every way.

"Hold still," he commanded, taking over again. He lubed up a finger and started to play, rimming her rosette, teasing it. She'd taken the plug beautifully. She would take his cock just as well if he prepared her for it. He made circles against her flesh, pressing in a little harder each time.

"It feels weird but it doesn't hurt."

"It's not going to hurt. Not if I do it right." Over and over and around and around. A little more lube. One more circle and he was in, his finger slipping inside like a key that had found its lock. "That's what I want."

She gasped a little, and her ass clenched around his finger. "Is that all?"

He fucked his finger in and out and slipped a second one inside. "No, Avery. I'm bigger than this, but you're going to be all right. We're going to fit perfectly, you'll see."

She wiggled, adjusting to him, her ass opening up and allowing a third finger inside. He stretched her, but she was ready. He pulled his hand away.

"Hey, I was just getting used to that."

"I have to take care of something really fast, baby. Don't you move. Not an inch." He hurried to the loo, washed his hands and returned to find her a very obedient girl. He grabbed the lube again and slicked up his cock. No more playing. He was getting inside his girl. He was going to show her everything he had to offer her. "This is the rough part, Avery. I need you to flatten your back as I ease inside. Don't tense up. Just relax."

His cock jumped like a puppy eager to play. He fitted his dick to her still slightly open hole and immediately gained ground. He pushed in, just the tip, heat surrounding him. It was so different from her pussy. It was tighter. It was a fight.

"Oh, oh. That's so much bigger than the plug." Her breath came out in nervous little puffs.

He smoothed a hand up and down her spine, letting her adjust. It was so fucking hard when all he wanted was to shove his way in, to dominate her, but this was the way to do it. Patience and caring. His hips moved in measured thrusts, easing his cock head in and out, gaining a centimeter here and there. "Relax. The worst is over. Tell me how you feel."

He slipped a hand around her hips and toyed with her clit. Her pussy was soaked and swollen. The minute he slid the pad of his thumb over her clit, she pushed back against him and took him deeper, his cock shifting and easing inside.

"I feel full, Li. So full. It burns a little, but I think I like it." Her back shivered as she rolled her hips, taking him deep.

His skin lit up when he slid inside, his balls nestling against the cheeks of her ass. He had to hold himself still, allowing the heat and tightness to wash over him. His balls were snug against his body, waiting to go off again, to give her his semen. It belonged to her. He never wanted to wear a damn condom again. Nothing between them. She would walk around with his come inside her, and he would never stop feeling her grip his dick.

"Are you all right?" He prayed she was. He was dying.

"I am. It's not bad."

"All right. Then tell me how this feels." He carefully dragged his cock out until just the head was inside.

"Oh my god. What is that?"

"Nerves you never thought you had." He foraged back inside, every centimeter a pure joy. He got to show her just how good it could be.

She slammed back against him. This was the push and pull he wanted. This was the sweet fight. Avery started to move, trying to keep him in, then trying to push him back out. She was beautifully impaled on his cock, and she seemed to love every minute of it.

And it was all happening too fast. She felt too fucking

good, too hot and tight and perfect. He couldn't last. He fucked deep inside and then pinched down on her clit.

Avery's cries filled the room, and she clamped down around his dick as she came, sending him hurling into his own orgasm. Semen shot from his balls, filling her up and sending a wave of pleasure through his spine. He fell forward, utterly exhausted, his body driving hers into the bed. The lavender smell of the soap he'd used to wash her skin filled his nose, and he let his face rub against her damp hair. His arm felt like hell, but he forced it to move so he could wrap her in his arms.

"Mine," he said, twisting so he didn't crush her.

"Has anyone ever told you you're a little possessive?" Avery asked with a happy sigh as her head found his chest.

"Not once." He hadn't been before he met her. He squeezed her tight and kissed her forehead. "I love you, baby. We have to get a move on. Back into the shower with you. I don't want to miss our show."

Worry darkened her eyes. "All right."

The moment was broken, but he promised they would have more. They were getting out. They were going someplace where the past could never touch him again.

Avery got up with a sad little smile, and Liam laid back.

"I put your boots by the door. I almost tripped over them earlier," Avery called out. "We're going to have to talk about your housekeeping skills."

Boots. For just a second, he was back in his nightly dream, looking down at those boots that always seemed so wrong to him. He'd stood there, trying to figure it out all those years ago. Memory was a tricky thing.

It hit like a flash, like a lightning strike that blinded him for a moment.

His dreams had been trying to warn him. Only a silly

man wouldn't listen. He closed his eyes and tried to remember. It was still fuzzy, like a tape that had been slightly warped, but it was still there. The boots had been the key. He hadn't understood why he got caught on those boots every time. He'd imagined it was because those boots had told him his brother was dead.

But he remembered quite clearly now. Rory's boots had been at the edge of the couch in that ramshackle death house, but he hadn't been wearing them.

The boots were wrong because they had been empty, one on its side and sitting straight up as though the owner had simply dropped them after he'd changed into new clothes, a fresh disguise.

Rory had left them behind just like he'd left Liam behind, vestiges of his old life that he'd tossed in an incinerator like old trash.

Bits and pieces of the puzzle started to wind themselves together in his brain. If Rory was working with Nelson, then Nelson had likely had a plan for him. From everything he understood, Nelson hadn't used those bonds to set himself up somewhere comfy. No. He'd used them to start building something. Ten million wasn't enough for a man like Nelson. It wouldn't be enough for Rory either. In the end, what both men truly wanted was power. Nelson was a tricky one. What if he'd kept Rory alive? What if he'd had bigger plans for Rory?

If Rory was alive, then what had he been doing for the last five years?

There was plenty of power and money in the arms business. It would intrigue a man like Nelson, but it wasn't like opening a gas station. It would take time and planning and years of patience to get to the big time. Nelson had the contacts, but he wouldn't have the money to set it up. He wouldn't have an infrastructure to distribute on a wide level.

The UOF had both money a plenty and a way to distribute through their relief shipments. And it had a man at its helm who no one had seen for years before he'd decided to take back over his charity.

Thomas Molina wore contacts when he didn't need them. Unless he was trying to cover green eyes with brown. His brother had always been a good actor, and his accents were impeccable. It was one of the reasons G2 had considered him for training. The magnitude of his brother's betrayal washed over him. He'd suspected it when Avery had told him about the contacts, but now he knew it was true.

The shower started up, and he could hear Avery hum. It was funny how the universe worked. It was even funnier that he was contemplating the bloody universe. If he'd figured it out before, he would have been bitter and cold, and he very likely would have walked out on his own team.

But he'd met Avery. His love. His wife.

He would never forgive Rory for what he'd done, but he could finally forgive himself for letting it happen.

Liam sighed, shoving the past behind him as he went to join his future.

Chapter Twenty

Avery buttoned her sweater while internally debating the wisdom of engaging in first time anal sex before going on the run from a potential killer. On the plus side, she was so madly in love with Liam O'Donnell that she was probably glowing.

On the minus, she really kind of wanted to stay home and sit on a bag of frozen peas.

"Come on, baby." Liam stood at the door. They seemed to have hit some magical time at which he became a serious worrywart. He'd hurried her through the shower that ended with her actually being clean. He'd rushed her through getting dressed. Every moment seemed to be filled with an anxiety to be gone from this place.

She would miss it. Sure it was the place where her creepy ex-boss had listened in on her having sex, but it was also the place where she'd found some peace and love. Liam seemed to think it would be the place where she would be horrifically killed if they didn't get a move on.

"I'm coming," she said, grabbing her purse. She'd selected her big purse. She had her pictures and medications and a single change of clothes. She'd left the undies behind because bossy guy wasn't so into underwear.

What was wrong with her? She was leaving everything she knew behind, and she was making mental jokes. Avery knew it was deadly serious, but somehow it felt like an adventure. Taking Liam's hand, she walked out the door and rapidly discovered that her adventure began in Adam and Jake's apartment. *Very exotic.*

Adam held the door open as Liam ushered her across the hall. Jake stood beside the bar, a grim look on his face. Avery glanced around the formerly cheery apartment. Now it looked like a war room. Maps were laid out and two separate computers were running. Worse, there were a whole lot of weapons on display.

"What is it?" Liam asked after Adam closed the door. "We need to get out of here. We're running late."

"Yeah, we got that. I don't know if that was Ian meant by acting normal," Adam said with a little snort.

Avery felt her skin flush. She'd totally forgotten that more than one set of ears could be listening in. She'd sort of lost herself in the moment. "Can't you stop listening in on that stuff?"

Liam shook his head. "They can now. Up until now, it's been necessary. They've been our backup if something went wrong."

"Yes, we had to make sure Li there didn't slip up during sex. Apparently when he's making love he forgets his accent," Jake said. "Though you did a damn fine job today. Not a single lilt."

Liam shrugged. "Only because you couldn't hear me in the shower."

"Yeah, well, we heard everything else. I think it's safe to say whoever was listening in doesn't think you've been tipped off. Poor girl. She's going to be sore, and you're going to make her run all over London. Do you need some ibuprofen?" Adam asked.

Or maybe they would just be on the run forever, and she would never have to see Jake and Adam again.

383

"Stop embarrassing me girl, Adam. Now, if that's all, we'll head out. Tell Evie to text me if plans change." Liam started toward the door. "And tell Ian I need to have a talk with him. I think I might know who we're up against, but it's complicated. Tell him it all goes back to the Irish operation."

"That's going to have to wait. The plan has changed. Ian got a call from Nelson." Jake pulled on a shoulder holster, settling a nasty-looking gun into the side.

"The bastard just called his cell?" Liam asked, his jaw dropping slightly.

Jake shrugged. "Yeah. He called about thirty minutes ago and asked to meet with Ian. According to him, he has information that could help us out."

Liam shook his head. "He can't think that Ian isn't going to take him down. He put a couple of bullets into Ian's brother and damn near killed Ian's sister-in-law. Nelson isn't an idiot. He's got to know Ian wants revenge."

Adam's mouth was a flat, grim line. "He seems to think that whatever he has is going to convince Ian not to kill him."

She could feel the anxiety in Liam.

"It's got to be some sort of trap." Liam started to pace, his eyes staring at the floor. "This ain't right and you know it. Just before we're set to leave, Nelson up and decides to come in from the cold? No. Ian needs to walk away, and he needs to do it right bloody now. We all need to leave England and regroup when we know what the fuck is really happening here. Leave the cleanup to MI6."

Jake ran a hand through his hair. "Do you think we haven't already tried that line of thinking?"

"Ian thinks he can handle it. Alex is already at the site of the meet up. We've hopefully covered everything. It's in the open so hopefully Ian doesn't just kill the fucker," Adam explained.

"I'm more worried about the fucker killing Ian." Liam's hand drifted up to his arm. Avery had redressed the wound, cleaning it carefully. "Molina already tried to kill me."

"I think Ian's hoping Nelson is turning on Molina. Damon has been informed, and MI6 will be set up, too. Ian's covered." Jake passed Liam a long look. "I'm not worried about Nelson killing Ian. We can watch his back, but I'm with you. There's something else going on here. Something about this spells out FUBAR to me."

"FUBAR?" Avery asked. She didn't know what that was, but the timing of Nelson's call did seem odd.

"Fucked up beyond all recognition. It's a very precise military term." Adam opened a case that was sitting on the bar. Several shiny guns sat inside along with a couple of big, matte black ones. He picked up one and handed it to Liam. "Ian wants you armed. You can give it back to Eve tomorrow, and she'll dump it. There's no way to get you on a plane with it, man."

Liam took the pistol, shoving it into his pocket after clicking some buttons and checking things she didn't have a clue about. He was really competent with a gun. "Give me a couple of knives, too. If I need to do some wet work, I'd rather keep it quiet if you know what I mean."

She didn't know what he meant, but Adam seemed to. He pulled out the top of the case revealing a second layer where he apparently kept the knife store. Liam selected a few, and they started to disappear in various parts of his clothing.

"Are you two going to back Ian up?" Liam asked.

Adam pulled out a wicked-looking knife, and it disappeared into his boot. "Jake is headed to the meet. I've been given clearance to head to Serena's. She's getting on a plane tomorrow, but if Nelson wants to play hardball, taking one of our women would be a good way to go. We're going to hit the town, just like the two of you."

"Are they coming with us?" It might be nice to have another couple with them.

Liam shook his head. "No. We're going to split up. It's harder for someone to trail two of us. The whole team will leave tomorrow. Is anyone staying behind? I'm sure Ian will if he doesn't walk into a trap tonight and get his ass sniped. What is he thinking? There's no bloody way Nelson just decided to talk tonight. He's up to something."

Jake's jaw tightened. "I know, but Ian's not thinking straight. He's a little obsessed with Nelson, and I'm not sure why. I guess because of what happened with Sean."

"There's more to it, but Ian has to tell you that story himself," Liam explained. "I will say that you need to watch him, Jake. He can't be professional about this."

Jake stopped, tension in his every muscle. "Ian is always professional. Ian's a rock."

"Not about this he won't be. He and Nelson have got history, if you know what I mean. I wouldn't say a damn thing if I wasn't so worried about him, but you got to watch his back, mate. He needs you and Alex to make smart decisions for him tonight."

Jake nodded. "I'll do it. Does Alex understand?"

"Yeah. Alex knows more than anyone. He'll watch out for Ian, too," Liam said.

"What's this intel you want Ian to know?" Jake asked.

Liam's eyes narrowed, and he nodded toward the back of the apartment. "Come back here."

They walked off together, Liam speaking quietly.

Adam stared at her, his warm eyes sympathetic. "It

doesn't mean he doesn't trust you."

She stared right back. She knew exactly what Liam was doing. She was going to be the wife of a man who dealt with very sensitive cases. She wouldn't expect him to tell her everything. She would be supportive and let him keep his professional secrets. "He's trying to protect me. I know that."

A smile broke over Adam's face. "You're going to be so much better at this than my wife. She would be trying to listen in right now."

Avery didn't want to listen in. This was Liam's expertise. After this was over, she would find a new job and that would be her thing. Loving Liam was going to be her expertise and part of that meant trusting him. He'd walked away because he either didn't want to scare her or he was worried that what he had to say would hurt her. He was talking about Thomas. He would try to protect her. She might never get the full story out of him.

And that was okay because she knew what Thomas was now. He was creepy and criminal and very likely wanted to hurt her. She'd made her bet. She was with Liam, and she would trust him to the end.

She just hoped the end didn't come any time soon.

"He's going to take care of you," Adam promised.

"I know." She heard the expectation in his voice. "And I'll take care of him, too."

"You're going to get along with my Serena, you know. She's going to like the hell out of you. When we finally get back to Dallas, you can meet Serena and our friend Grace. You're going to fit right into the family."

It sounded lovely, a group of friends. A family. She couldn't ask for more than that. "I would love to meet them."

She would be starting over—again. She'd done it so many times, but this time it felt right. She wasn't alone. Liam was with her.

Jake walked back, his eyes stony. He looked to his partner. Damn but Avery wanted to know how that worked. "How are we handling the clean up?"

Adam slammed the case shut and picked up a small messenger bag on the floor. "I've got what Serena and I need. I think we'll head to Paris tonight and fly out from there tomorrow. I'm going to clear off the computers and leave them behind. Everything else we leave as it is."

Liam stepped up. "Go on. Serena's alone. I can wipe the computers and lock up."

Jake nodded Liam's way. "Thanks, man. We'll see you back at home. Avery, it's been a pleasure, and I look forward to showing you around Dallas." He turned to Adam. "Time to go, brother. Take care of our girl, and I'll take care of our friends."

Adam held out a hand, but Jake pulled him in for a hug, both men giving each other manly smacks, and Avery could see a little bit of how it worked. Jake could handle the rough stuff because he knew Adam would take care of their wife.

Liam shook hands with each as they headed out the door. Liam didn't have a partner. He'd been forced to choose, and he'd chosen her.

"I could go with Adam. Liam, I know you have a big stake in this somehow."

He passed a magnet over the computers and closed the tops. "I had an operation go south a few years back. Nelson was involved. I lost my brother, and I've been looking for answers ever since."

Her stomach knotted. The last thing she wanted to do was be parted from Liam, but she couldn't let him miss this opportunity. "Then let me go with Adam, and you can go meet this Nelson guy. Liam, I want you to find the answers you need. I promise I'll do everything Adam tells me to. I won't put myself in any kind of trouble."

He set the magnet down and turned to her. "You're more important."

"But I'll be okay."

His gorgeous face turned serious as he walked toward her. He stopped in front of her, close so their bodies brushed. His hand came out, tilting her face up to his. "I won't be okay, Avery. I can't walk out without you, and while I love Adam like a brother, I won't leave your safety to anyone but me in this case. Blame yourself, love."

"Why?" She whispered the question because his lips were closing in on hers. She would never get used to the butterflies she felt the minute he came close, his eyes pinning her and letting her know how much he wanted her.

He kissed her, a gentle melding of lips. "You taught me that revenge ain't going to do a thing for me, not really. What we got right here is worth walking away from everything for. I might be a dumb man, but I ain't stupid. I want to know what happened, but I won't let the past wreck my future. Not when I just found out I have one."

She leaned into him, so grateful for his strength. "You always had a future, Liam."

"Yeah, but it involved hot wings and beer. I gotta be honest, love, I was getting a little sick of that." He kissed her again. "Do you have everything? Did you get your pictures? I don't want you to leave them behind."

"I have them." She moved toward him, wanting the comfort of his closeness. He pulled her into his arms. "I only have a little book here. I have a whole storage unit back in the States. It's a small one, but it's got all my keepsakes. Are we going to live in Dallas?"

His face softened. "If Ian don't fire me at the end of all of this." He laughed a little. "He won't, love. If he was going to fire me, I would be dead in a ditch somewhere. Ian's that kind of boss."

Maybe he needed a new career. "Not sure I like the sound of that."

"It's okay. Ian's bark is worse than his bite. You'll see, love. Once we're married, he'll settle down, and he'll treat you like family."

"You're worried about him."

"He's acting on emotion. So am I, so I know just how dumb a man can be when a woman is involved. The man we're tracking had something to do with Ian's wife's death. And don't go spreading that around, love. He hasn't told everyone. His own brother doesn't even know he was married."

But Liam had trusted her with it. "I think I can keep quiet. I feel bad about not getting those files, though. I'll write down everything I know if you can get it to the right people. I've worked for Thomas for long enough to know his habits. If he has the files, he's probably got a backup. He's fastidious about backing data up. He always told me he never knew when he would need something so I had to scan documents for him." A thought struck her. *Damn it.* Why hadn't she thought about it? "He carries his phone and his tablet with him everywhere. Either one of them could have the data."

"We'll let MI6 know, but that's the end of this, okay?"

She was ready for it to end. She wanted to settle down. Maybe she could look at the next few weeks as a sort of honeymoon. "All right."

Liam moved to the door. "This is the last place we can

talk before we're out of this building, okay? Keep quiet until we're in the station. Then we should be able to talk again. We're going to change trains and lines until I'm sure we're not being followed."

She nodded. No talking in the hallways. There were cameras everywhere. They couldn't be sure if Thomas was watching or not.

The door opened, Liam moving out first. He held a hand out to let Avery know it was all right.

The hallway was quiet, almost eerily so. Often she could hear the sounds of the other residents, but today there was nothing, just the squeak of the floor under her feet and the quiet snick of the door closing and locking. Every muscle in Liam's body seemed tense and ready, but there was a bland look on his face.

"Ready for a night on the town?" His flat American accent was back. Now that she'd heard his real voice, she longed for it. The Midwestern tone didn't hold the emotion of the real man.

Still, she flashed what she hoped was a happy smile. "Let's do it."

She took his hand, but glanced back at her apartment, her little flat in London. So much had happened there. This place and the man she'd met here had changed her irrevocably. Despite the bad things, she would always have a fondness for that apartment.

And then she noticed it, a tiny crack as the door she was sure they'd locked began to open.

"Li, someone's in my apartment." Her voice was a whisper, thin and strangled.

The elevator dinged up ahead, signaling the doors would soon be open. They could make it to the elevator and then close the doors. They would be safe in the elevator.

Liam seemed to think the same thing. He glanced back down the hallway. Avery followed, looking behind to see two large men exiting her apartment. She recognized them from Thomas's house. He kept a couple of men around to help move him when he used his wheelchair. They were also trained security guards, though they usually didn't carry really big guns. They were today.

Avery struggled to keep up, her leg weak under her weight and the speed. She nearly tripped, but Liam kept a hand on her, helping her along. If they could just make it to the elevator. Her heart threatened to pound out of her chest. She could hear the men stalking behind them, but the hallway was long and they were almost there.

Liam's gun made an appearance. "When we get to the lift, stay behind me."

The doors were splitting, opening up to reveal their sanctuary.

Liam cursed and stopped, nearly sending her to the ground. His hand circled her wrist.

Two more men walked from the elevator, and one of them was her boss. Thomas Molina was dressed in a well-cut suit, and he wasn't using his cane or the braces or any implement to aid his walking. He strode forth, and despite the fact that she knew the face, this was a completely different man.

Liam's head swung back and forth as though he couldn't figure out which road to hell would take them there the fastest. He covered her body with his own, pushing her back against the wall. "Let the girl go and I'll give up the gun."

That didn't seem like a good idea. "I'm not leaving you."

"You bloody well will," Liam whispered her way.

They were trapped, four against one, and Liam was hesitating. She knew why. Her. He was going to die because he wouldn't risk her getting hurt. She tried to step forward. If Thomas wanted her, then he could have her.

"Thomas, I'll go with you." Her voice shook, but there was no way she could just let them shoot Liam.

"Shut up, Avery." Liam's focus went to Thomas.

"Yeah, shut the fuck up, darlin'." Thomas didn't even sound like Thomas anymore. He sounded an awful lot like Liam. "You'll come with me, but so will your little boyfriend there. I think we should talk, don't you, Li?"

"I definitely think we should talk," Liam said. "But let the girl go. This is between brothers."

"What?" Avery asked. How was Thomas Liam's brother?

A wicked smile crossed Thomas's face. "Figured it out, did ya, brother? I can't leave the girl now, can I? It's a pity, you know. We always did like the same type. Boys, let's take this someplace more private."

Liam cursed, and a shot rang out, splitting the air around her. The floor thudded as a man went down.

"You get them both alive!" Thomas shouted.

A meaty hand pulled her from Liam, and she felt something sharp go into her neck. Immediately the world became gauzy and unreal. Panic welled. Her vision was losing focus. She watched in horror as Liam began to fight. He moved with such grace, but someone shoved a needle in his arm. Even so, he fired again. She began a long fall to the floor, time slowing. Liam was fighting. There was another shot, but it sounded so far away this time. Liam had two men on him, and she saw a flash of something metal before Liam started to go down. He looked at her, the drug obviously hitting his system, but his hand reached out for

393

hers.

Darkness encroached, the world winking out like a candle being snuffed.

* * * *

Rory O'Donnell looked down at his should-have-been-dust-in-the-grave-by-now brother, a little kernel of satisfaction in his gut. Maybe it was better this way. This time he would kill Liam himself. He would prove that he wasn't the weak little brother this time. This time, Liam's eyes would be open, and he would watch as his brother took the victory.

"Angus is dead, boss. What do you want me to do with him?" Colin asked, scratching his head as he looked down at the body.

Good henchmen were so bloody hard to find. By necessity they tended to be incredibly stupid. Malcolm had been smart, but he hadn't been quick enough to take out Liam. "Put the body in the flat, and we'll pick it up later. Hurry. I managed to get this floor clear, but my man at the front desk won't be able to keep them out forever."

Colin helped Brett drag dead Angus toward the flat where Avery had been staying.

Rory looked down at his brother. He probably should have just killed the bastard, but Rory had plans. His brother was into BDSM. It would be good to see how he liked a little torture. Liam had taken him to his first club. Rory rather thought he'd done it to try to teach him some control and to give him a safe outlet for his sadistic tendencies. He pulled a length of rope from his bag. The trouble was, Rory didn't want a safe outlet. He wanted to be able to kill the occasional girl just for grins.

Killing a woman was the right of a powerful man. He would take that right with Avery, and he would make his brother watch.

He hummed a little as he bound his brother's hands behind his back. Liam had always liked a little rope play. Perhaps not like this, but then Liam wasn't calling the shots now.

He turned his attention to Avery. Sweet, dumb Avery. She was going to wish she was dead before he was done. He would certainly kill her eventually, but she would beg for it first.

Should he rape Avery and kill her in front of Liam? Or rape Avery and then kill Liam?

Choices, choices. It was the kind of thing a man had to rely on instinct to decide. He wasn't going to make the decision now. He had a couple of hours. He wanted to play.

"You want me to tie the girl up, boss?" Colin asked.

"No. She's not a threat. I'll keep her in the car with me. The dose we gave her should keep her out until we can get back to my house. You'll drop us off, make sure my brother here has a nice seat, and then I expect you to get to the airport and make sure everything is ready. We're leaving for Dubai tonight."

He'd already shifted money around. Not all of it, of course, but enough to get by until the Lachlan Bates deal came through, and then he would allow Nelson to get his little business into the Middle East and he would be set. It would be safe to kill Nelson then.

Colin lifted Liam up, tossing him over his shoulder.

"Throw him in the trunk." He didn't want to be anywhere near Liam, but Avery was a different story. He lifted her up himself. She wasn't a lightweight, but then he'd never liked a skinny girl. They died too fast.

She really was quite pretty. It was too bad she turned out to be such a whore.

He sighed and kissed her cheek. She was limp in his arms. She would be a bit of fun before he killed her, a way to pass the time until his flight took off.

He followed his men down the stairs and to the waiting car.

The night had just begun.

Chapter Twenty-One

Liam kept his head down as he came to a bleary consciousness. He wasn't sure what his insane bastard of a brother had shot him up with, but he would bet it was ketamine. It was what he would have used. It was a veterinary tranquilizer that wasn't too hard to get if a criminal had the right contacts.

He forced his breathing to stay even, his body to relax. He opened his eyes slightly, thankful he'd let his hair get a bit too long. Carpet was under his feet, and not cheap carpet. It was a rich red and looked to be Oriental. He very carefully tried to move his arms. Rope held him tight. His hands were behind his back, and he seemed to be sitting in a chair. Was anyone behind him? Was it safe to start on the ropes? They were tight, but he could force his hands to work. He just needed to find the knot.

And Avery. He really needed to find Avery. He couldn't see her from here, and he couldn't hear her. Was she still out? How much time had passed?

A deep voice filled the room. "I can see you moving, brother. I haven't completely forgotten my SAS training. You might as well open those eyes wide and see what I have for you."

Dread curled in his stomach. Was she already dead? If Avery was gone, then he would have one job in the world to do. He would make sure his brother suffered. Then he would find and kill the traitorous Mr. Black, Eli Nelson—whatever he wanted to call himself. He would be dead.

Liam brought his head up, the world spinning just a little. Even as his eyes focused, he could feel the knot. Rory had always been lazy. He'd left the knot where Liam could manipulate it. It wasn't a mistake Liam would have made. The pads of his fingers started to work it. "Nelson was a distraction then?"

Rory sat behind a large ornate desk. He'd ditched the contacts, and his deep green eyes showed through. Their mum's eyes. "He's my partner. He has been from the beginning. When we realized you and your crew were here, he obligingly provided me with the distraction I needed to take care of you. He'll take care of your team, of course."

Would he? Nelson didn't have the firepower to take care of Ian and certainly not on the streets of London. Nelson was cool as a cucumber. He wouldn't do a damn thing without planning it out. And why did Rory think Nelson hadn't known about them? Nelson had sent out his calling card and practically invited them to come to England.

Who was the real distraction?

And where was Avery? He couldn't just ask the bloody question. Rory was a sadist of the highest order. Liam had tried to curb the tendencies, but he'd failed. If Rory knew how much he loved Avery, it could mean a long, painful night for her.

"You worked with him on the op that nearly got me killed." It wasn't a question. Liam knew the answer, but he needed to keep his brother talking. He had to get out of the ropes and figure out where Avery was and if he could save her.

"I did. Nelson contacted me. He saw my potential. He

also saw a chance to take over a very lucrative arms dealing market. There was no uranium. That was all a ruse to get Leonov to bite. Nelson came across Leonov and found out about the bonds. Ten million easily transportable dollars, but he couldn't get close. Somehow Taggart heard the stories and started the op before Nelson could get everything in place."

"So Nelson sent along a very handy distraction." Ian's wife had been a means to an end.

Rory shrugged. "I wasn't involved in that part of the business. I just know Nelson took over at the right time, and we got the bonds. Nelson then killed Leonov and together we took over his business. Leonov had a nice contact list going, but we decided we could do better."

His brother, the entrepreneur. "And you became Thomas Molina."

A satisfied smile lit Rory's face. "The trouble is transporting the bloody weapons. So many checks these days, but everyone wants to help poor, starving children. We just needed a well-respected charity to be willing to help stow away our weapons."

Where the hell was Avery? Despite the sedatives still in his veins, he could feel his heart rate speeding up. What the bloody hell had Rory done with Avery? What pain had she already been put through? *Just let her be alive.* He'd help her heal. He'd be with her. He'd hold her and love her and put her back together. She just had to be alive.

And he was losing it. Calm. Cool. Unemotional. He had to stay professional or they would both be dead. And Rory seemed to want to talk. Liam's shoulder was killing him, but he forced his fingers to work without moving his arms. The knot was right there. There was a game they played at Sanctum. Tie up the Dom and see who was best at getting out. Ian was the Rope King, but Liam had come in a close second.

Weapons. He'd been talking about the weapons and the charity. He stared at his brother. Only the eyes were still the same. "How much surgery did it take?"

Lips that weren't his own tugged up on Rory's altered face. "Quite a bit. I was out of pocket for almost a year. I had multiple surgeries and made a careful study of Thomas Molina. Nelson had identified Molina as the perfect target. He formed a sort of friendship with Brian Molina."

Brian Molina had been an addict. Liam could guess just what kind of friendship Nelson had formed. "He became Brian's dealer?"

"Nelson knows many people, and Brian was easy to control as long as he got his fix. Brian kept an eye on his brother while I was preparing for my role and then he coached me on his brother's history and mannerisms. I couldn't simply appear one day. I had to make connections. I had to take my time. The fact that he was perfectly terrified of leaving his house, and he hated talking to people on anything but his computer made it easy. Even after Brian and I took over the fund, I had to keep him around for a bit and bide my time."

"You killed them both?" It was a dumb question, but it kept him talking.

"Absolutely." Rory was nearly purring. "I obviously needed Molina dead in order to take his place, and Brian had outlived his usefulness once I was set up as his brother. I couldn't have him hanging around. After all, he wanted some of my money."

"I bet Nelson wants more."

The first crack appeared, a frown that covered Rory's face. "I'm in control of this business. I have all the power.

Eli Nelson is simply the man who gave me my start."

"Yes, brother, he's such a philanthropist. He just looks for little criminals with hope in their eyes and plucks them from obscurity and sets them up because he's got such a big heart." Pain flared in his arm, but he'd slid his pinky finger under the knot. *Patience. Gain purchase and work the rope.*

Ian had taught him this. Ian, the asshole. Ian, who had been more of a brother to him than the man in front of him. Ian had taught him, and Jake had practiced with him. Adam had sat in the background drinking beer and making sarcastic comments while Sean had timed them. His real brothers were still here with him. The skills they had taught him would come through in the end.

"I can handle Nelson," Rory said, his fingers tapping impatiently along the desk.

"I doubt it. If he put you in a position, it was so he could use you and perhaps get rid of you when he decides to take over. Nelson lost his big payday. My boss took it away from him a couple of months back. He can't go back to the Agency. He needs cash, and he likely needs it bad. Did you spend all the bond money on the surgeries?"

Rory shrugged, a negligent move Liam remembered from their childhood. "Ten million doesn't go as far as you think it would. The surgeries cost money, setting up the infrastructure of the business costs money. The bonds went fast. That's why we had to use Molina. I could easily take over his income and his trust fund, though some of it is tied up legally. I've been slowly shifting money to other accounts. When I leave here tonight, I'll have millions at my fingertips."

"How are you going to explain Avery's death?"

"That is a problem, actually. Maybe I won't kill her. Maybe I'll take her with me to Dubai and marry her. We'll spend plenty of time in Africa and the Middle East. Lots of bad things happen there." He chuckled a little. "Actually, I could make some cash off the little cow. I'll put a good insurance policy in place and then get her killed. Yeah, I like it. Thanks, brother."

Rage churned in his gut. If his brother put a hand on Avery, he would cut Rory's bloody balls off and shove them down his throat. He would tear him limb from limb. But she was alive. She was fucking alive.

"Do whatever you want with the girl. I don't care."

A long sigh filled the room. "Oh, Liam, really? I listened in while you fucked the bitch. Avery, dear, why don't you come in?"

A door opened and one of Rory's thugs shoved Avery inside. She'd changed or been forced to. She was wearing a long white gown, silky and lovely. It showed off her figure to beautiful advantage, and it made her look a little like a bride on her wedding night.

The only problem was she was his bride, and Rory was going to try to take her.

Avery stumbled, her leg giving way beneath her. She hit the carpet, her body crumpling. He wanted to howl. His woman. His to protect and he couldn't get to her because he was bloody tied up. He was impotent and useless, and she was going to pay the price.

"Ah, look, the little cripple seems to have lost her footing. It's all right, dear. I don't need you for your grace." Rory pushed his chair back, standing up. "Colin, you may leave us. Go and watch the door. We'll be leaving in an hour or so, and we might have a guest with us. I haven't decided yet."

The massive thug nodded and walked out, closing the door behind him.

Perfect. Just him and his brother and the rope that bound him.

Avery was on the floor. Her face turned up, so gorgeous, so vulnerable. "Li."

Rory chuckled. "Lee? Oh, dear, do you even know his real name?"

Liam waited, praying she would follow along.

Avery turned from him to his brother. "He's Lee Donnelly."

Good girl. A fierce pride threatened to take over. He had no doubt she had been calling out for Liam, not Lee.

Rory rolled his eyes and got to one knee. Condescension dripped from his mouth. "His name is Liam O'Donnell, you dumb bitch. He's my brother."

"I don't understand any of this. I thought Brian was your brother. Why are you walking so well now?" She turned back to him, playing her part beautifully. Or was she? He hadn't told her his suspicions. Was she shocked that his brother was an arms dealer? Would it affect the way she saw him? "Is it true? Did you lie to me?"

"You were a means to an end, love." She was the reason he was breathing, but he couldn't let his brother know.

"Was she?" Rory asked.

It was time to act a little and to lean on what his brother knew about him. "Please. Do you really think she's me type, Ror? I like 'em a little prettier than that."

Rory shoved a hand into her hair and forced her face up. Liam could see the pain in her eyes. Fuck, he was going to make his brother pay. "I don't know. She's quite pretty in a very innocent 'I never had a cock up me ass' way. Don't you think? Of course, appearances can be deceiving."

He pulled Avery up by her hair, using her weight against her. The little moan of pain that came out of her mouth hit his soul.

"Stop!" Avery struggled, her feet kicking, trying to find the ground.

And Liam had to pretend not to care. If he gave in, even for an instant, Avery would hurt in ways she couldn't imagine. He knew he was likely giving up any hope of a future with her, but he would do anything to save her. "She's got a nice tight ass, brother. You should try it."

Bile rose in his throat but his fingers worked hard, and he could feel the knife in his boot with his foot. They'd taken his gun and another knife, but the stiletto was still there.

"No!" Avery started to fight. Her fists came out, but it was an ineffectual thing against Rory's strength. She hit his chest, but he just laughed and held her away from him.

"Maybe I will, brother," Rory replied. Shrewd eyes slid his way. "I was listening the whole time, you know."

A slippery slope. Another piece of the knot fell free. He had a little room to work now, but he had to be careful. It was also easier to move his arms, and that would give away the whole game. "I was acting the whole time. You've been out of the game for a long time if you think I have a real emotional attachment to her. She was the mark, mate. You remember how that is. I do admit that she was a rather dull lay."

Avery gasped, her face turning to him. Tears fell from her eyes. She was never going to forgive him. He wouldn't be able to explain why he'd turned away from her when she was at her most vulnerable. She would hate him. She would loathe and despise him, and he couldn't take it back. He kept his face cold, blank. Like he didn't love her. Like she wasn't the best part of his soul.

"I wonder," Rory said, twisting his fist in her hair and

forcing her face to his. The gown she was wearing slipped off one shoulder, the top of her breast rounding over the material. "She sounded really hot on those tapes. She loved when you spanked her."

"No," Avery said, her voice tortured as she struggled against him.

"Some subs just say they like it. They're just desperate for a cock. They can't get one so they go along with anything that will get them a man. And when you look like me, well, I can get a girl to do just about anything."

Tears rolled down her cheeks. His heart was breaking, but he had to save her even if it meant he lost her. He would watch over her for the rest of her life, but he meant to make sure that was a long time. He wouldn't take another woman. He belonged to her. If she never touched him again, he would be alone. He would still love her.

Another piece of the rope came loose. *Fuck.* There was still so much rope between him and Avery's life. He was getting close to losing it. How much damage could he do while tied to a chair? He could head butt the fucker, maybe give Avery a chance to run, but how many thugs were out there waiting?

Rory had a gun in his shoulder holster. He could shoot Avery in the back. Liam had to be patient. He had to make sure he could protect her. The pain she endured in the meantime would mean she might live through this.

"Are you desperate for some cock, girl?" Rory's vicious laugh filled the room. "I have some cock for you. Do you know why I hired you, bitch?"

She whimpered, her chest heaving.

"I hired you because you were so dumb and so innocent. You're the stupid bitch who forgave the woman who killed your baby. Do you know how wrong that is?"

Rory was looking down at her, his hand pushing her back to the floor. She fell to her knees. "What the fuck kind of woman are you?"

Avery cried out, trying to get away, but he held her fast.

"They're right to hate you, your in-laws," Rory whispered. "You don't deserve to have a family."

And he did? Rory had fucked everyone who ever cared about him. He wasn't even in Avery's league. He couldn't understand what she'd done. She'd chosen something good over revenge. She'd put grace and love back into the world when most people would have chosen their hate.

Rory kept his eyes on Avery as though trying to drink in her misery. Liam used those minutes to move more freely, working the knot as fast as he could.

"Leave me alone!" Avery put a fist out, proving she was stronger than Rory believed.

"That is not going to happen," Rory growled back. His fist tightened, pulling her back off the ground. Liam hated the way her muscles bunched as she fought him. "I put a lot of work into you, bitch, and I don't buy my brother's little act. I listened in. I heard the way he fucked you. He sounded like a sad little girl telling you he loved you, telling you he needed you. It made me a little sick to tell you the truth. My brother used to be a real man."

He used to be a sad man. He used to be a man who just took what was offered and gave nothing real back. He'd been a pathetic manwhore who slept his way through life not really understanding what he could have, what he could give. He slipped another part of the knot, but he was starting to panic. He still only had an inch of purchase between his hands. He wasn't close yet. He was getting there, but how much would Avery have to endure before he got his act together?

"He's a liar. He isn't a man." The words sounded choked from her throat.

They kicked him squarely in the gut, but he couldn't show it. "Sorry, darlin'. It was me or Ian. We flipped a coin, and I lost."

Rory's eyes narrowed. "So you don't mind at all if I do this?" His hand dug into her hair, pulling Avery's body into his. Her limbs were shaking, but she still tried to get away. "Stop fighting me or I'll gut you here and now."

"He means it." Her fighting would do nothing but piss Rory off. She was strong, but no match at all against Rory's bulk. Rory would let her bleed a little, and then he would still do what he wanted.

"I hate you both." Avery stilled, but he could see the distaste in her eyes as Rory cupped her breast.

And now he had the added problem of Avery being a shield.

Rory's hand squeezed. "She's awfully soft. You're sure you didn't want her? When we were growing up Liam always liked the fluffy ones."

"I like 'em skinny now." Just a little more. His wrists were bleeding now, too. The friction had opened chafing wounds on his hands. All the better. More lubricant to make the bonds easier to slip.

And Rory was a bit preoccupied. Rory's eyes were on Avery's breast. He'd slipped the gown off one shoulder and stared down. "I like a fat girl. They can handle more than the skinny ones can."

Avery stared directly at Liam with tearful eyes, but a stubborn jaw. She was enduring. She was taking it, but she had to hate him for every moment she stood there.

It didn't matter. Nothing mattered until she was safe. One hand slipped free to the knuckles. All he really needed was one.

"I think I'm going to fuck your bitch on the desk. Get on all fours. Liam's a pervert. He'll like the show. It's my final gift to you, brother. After all, you taught me so much. Liam's the one who took me to my first club. He taught me how to tie up a woman and teach her who the boss really is."

"Yeah, you were always a lazy ass when it came to lessons." He moved as fast as he could, slipping one hand free and going for his knife.

Avery went wild, pulling away and punching out. It was perfect because Liam was slower than usual. He bit back against the pain of the circulation starting to flow into his hands again. He forced himself to move, pulling the knife free from his boot.

"Down, Avery!"

Rory slapped her just before she dropped to the ground. Rory reached for his gun, but it was far too late. Before he could even get close, the knife thudded into his chest, Liam's aim utter perfection.

"Li?" Rory stared down at the knife and pulled it out as he started to drop to his knees. Blood bloomed across his shirt.

His brother. He'd been told to protect Rory, but there had been no protecting Rory from himself. Rory had turned bad somewhere along the way, and he'd chosen to remain so. His brother had died a long time ago, and Rory had killed himself with his own dark ambition. What Liam had put down was just another predator.

"Avery?" He got to one knee, a little afraid to touch her for fear that she would fight him. He had to handle her carefully. "Baby, we have to get out of here, and we have to do it quietly."

She sat up, her whole body shaking. "I know. The

window in this room leads to a garden and then out into an alley. We can get out that way."

He helped her to her feet. "Avery, I didn't mean a word of that."

Her face tightened, a quizzical expression in her eyes. "I know that. You couldn't exactly declare your love. Do you really think I'm that dumb? But you're so paying for some of that. I get to be bratty at least twice a day with no fear of reprisals for a year or so."

He pulled her into his arms, reveling in the feel of her. "I was so bloody scared. Fuck, love, I thought you would hate me, but I couldn't let on how much I cared."

"You could have told me I'd been working for your brother," she groused, but her arms went around him. "Liam, you're bleeding. We need to get those files and get you out of here."

"Forget the files." He kissed the top of her head. She was going to look interesting running around London in a silk nightie. He needed to call Ian, but they'd taken his cell along with his gun. Luckily, his brother had died and left him a very nice SIG Sauer. Liam reached down to pick it up. "Ian and MI6 can find the files love."

His hand was almost on the gun when his whole body jerked back and pain fired through his shoulder. *What the hell?* He fell back, agony making him moan.

"I'm afraid I can't allow that to happen, Mr. O'Donnell."

Panic started to crowd out the pain as Liam realized that he'd been the distraction all along—he and Avery, not Ian. Eli Nelson walked through the door dressed all in black, a calm smile on his face.

"Now the real fun can begin," Nelson said.

* * * *

Avery dropped to her knees. Liam had been shot. Again. This time it wasn't a small singe. The bullet had gone into his left shoulder and blood was already staining his shirt. Tears blurred her vision. She looked around. She had to stop the bleeding.

"Avery, get out of here." Liam looked up at the newcomer who bent over and picked up the gun on the floor. If he was bothered by the dead body, he didn't show it. Liam struggled to sit up. "This is between you and me, Nelson."

So this was the infamous Eli Nelson, the man who had been working with her boss.

"Oh, this has never been between you and me, Mr. O'Donnell. You give yourself far too much credit. You were a pawn, nothing more." Nelson sighed as he looked down at her former boss. "Just like your brother was a pawn."

"You saved me that day," Liam said. Though he was bleeding profusely, she could see his eyes looking around, plotting his next move. She just had to be patient.

"I did." Nelson pocketed the extra gun. She should have tried to get it, but she'd rushed to Liam instead, and she wouldn't have been quick on the draw anyway. But maybe she could get the knife. It laid there on the floor, covered in blood. The thought of touching it was revolting, but she would do it if it meant she could save Liam.

"Because you knew I would be good leverage against Rory one day." Liam seemed to be trying to get her behind him, but he was having trouble moving.

"I like to have a backup plan. Never underestimate what a bit of chaos can bring. Rory was proving difficult. I loaned him this business and he'd decided not to give me my fair cut, so now I'm taking it. I realized that your team could be

410

useful to me. MI6 was struggling, you see. So I waved my magic wand, and Ian Taggart followed like I knew he would, and he brought along his team. Now, I couldn't just let you all run around London looking for me, so I sent Weston the files on Ian. Again, chaos is the great equalizer. You didn't like hearing about Ian's past, did you? You shut down and that bought me the time I needed. I knew once Rory here figured out that you were alive, he would lose his concentration and I could take the prize. How's Sean doing by the way? And Grace? I heard she made it out alive. Surprising."

"No thanks to you." Liam gripped her hand, trying to push her behind him. "Avery ain't got nothing to do with this. If you want revenge on Ian, you best be dealing with me and letting her go."

Avery wasn't going anywhere. She looked around trying to find anything that would help.

Nelson's face scrunched into a confused mask. "This isn't about revenge, Liam. This is a fun game between rivals. Ian thinks he's so much smarter, but I am far better at this than he is. I've been playing for years, and he didn't even understand the game was going on. And I definitely am going to need Avery Charles. One of the things your brother did right was to encode everything. I don't even know how to contact my new clients to let them know that management has changed. I made a deal with one of his men to get me the cipher, but I don't have anything to decode. By the way, thanks for killing Malcolm. It saved me the trouble of having to do it myself. I never actually intended to pay him, of course. Miss Charles, if you would fetch the files."

She shook her head. "I don't know where they are."

Nelson frowned. "That's really too bad."

He raised the gun, and Liam's other shoulder jerked

back, taking a bullet. Avery screamed. How many bullets could he take? Neither one of his arms seemed to work, but he was trying to struggle to his feet.

Nelson sighed as though bored with it all. "Don't blame yourself, my dear. I was going to shoot him again anyway. I can't have him getting to that knife. But now it really is up to you. The next shot I take will be lower. I'll take out his right lung and then his left, so you really should find those files."

Anger threatened to take over. Who the hell was this man to think he could just walk in here and take what he wanted? She couldn't lose Liam, but she was utterly helpless. Nelson had the guns, and she doubted she would be allowed to get the knife.

"I'm giving you a chance, dear. If you find the files, I'll walk away. All I care about are those files. Personally I think leaving O'Donnell alive might mean Ian Taggart stays off my ass for a couple of months." He sounded so reasonable.

"Stop moving. You're making it worse," she told Liam, her love, her Master. He was still trying to protect her, but he'd done his job and now it was time to do hers. "Does he mean it?"

"He left Sean alive," Liam admitted.

"Look, I could kill you both and find the files myself. It really would be easier." Nelson looked at his watch.

Avery struggled to her feet. "He kept them on paper. They weren't in his office at work, so they have to be here. I've only been here a couple of times."

"I would check the desk. Hurry along, dear. Time is ticking by." He kept his gun trained on Liam.

She opened the top drawer and rifled through it. Nothing. She checked the side drawers. Everything was neat, and there were no files to be found.

"Okay. I'm going to be merciful. I'll go for a leg this time." A little ping sounded through the room.

Avery screamed as Liam's thigh started to bleed.

"Two more minutes and I'll start on the lungs."

She wanted to plead. She couldn't lose him. Where would he hide the files?

He'd been leaving. He'd scheduled a flight for Dubai.

"It's in his luggage. His briefcase. Where's his briefcase?" Avery nearly shouted the question.

"Clever girl. I think you should look inside and make sure. I wouldn't want to find out you were wrong." He gestured behind her and sure enough, there it was, the designer case he'd carried with him when they traveled. He'd never checked it, always preferring to keep it close.

She got to her knees, her back to Nelson. There was something else he would have kept in here. His phone and his tablet. Nelson would take the whole thing, but she was going to make a play for the backup. She wasn't about to allow this man to just walk away, and if he betrayed them, MI6 would find it and Simon would break the code.

The files were right there in the side pocket beside his tablet.

"Well? Do I shoot Mr. O'Donnell again?"

"Don't give him anything, Avery," Liam growled.

She slipped the tablet out and onto the floor. She grabbed the files and stood. "I have them. There are three here."

"Excellent. I'll take the whole bag."

Deep breath. Stay calm. The tablet was black. If she was careful, he wouldn't notice it. She slipped the files back inside and turned, her hands shaking. She couldn't fight him physically, but she wasn't going to let him win. She tried to walk a straight line so her body hid what she'd left behind.

Nelson took the bag with a wink. "A deal's a deal. I'll leave you two lovebirds here." He started toward the door. "I took care of your brother's goon. You're all alone in the house. Oh, by the way, your brother was very good with explosives, and he never liked to leave anything behind. He wired this whole town house to blow in the event that he wasn't coming back. I set the timer. I believe you'll find you have less than three minutes to get out. I think it will be interesting to see if Miss Charles stays with her lover or runs. And if you do survive, let Ian Taggart know I'm not done with him yet."

He turned and walked out, and Avery ran to Liam. She got to her knees. He was so pale. "Was he serious?"

He'd lost so much blood, but his eyes were open. "He was. Get the bloody hell out of here, Avery. That's an order."

She wasn't losing him. She would rather get her ass blown up in this damn house than live without trying to save him. Death didn't get to take someone else from her. Not one more person she loved. Not today. She would go down with him. She would pray there was something beyond this place because she wasn't staying here without him.

"Come on. Can you walk?" Avery looked down at his leg. She couldn't see his pants for all the blood soaking them. It spilled over onto the carpet. She bit back a cry. He looked so bad.

"I can't walk, love. Get the hell out. I mean it. I'm going to spank you so bad if you don't get the fuck out right this second."

That was a Dom. "You'll have to spank me in the afterlife if you don't get a move on."

His hand gripped hers. "I can't, love. Baby, you have to

run. I love you. You have to live. Please."

Her heart hurt, but she couldn't let begging work this time. She got up and pulled on his arm. She was weak. She knew it, but she couldn't let it stop her. She had to get him out of here. She had to be the strong one now. He'd taken those bullets for her. He could have gotten away at the apartment, but he'd reached out for her. He hadn't left her alone. He would never leave her alone.

"I'm not leaving, Liam. I'll stay here with you," she choked out. "I'll sit right here and hold you until those minutes are up. I won't ever go without you."

"Fuck all, woman. Give me some room." He gritted his teeth and turned over, forcing his knees to move. A low groan came from his mouth as he pushed up and got to his feet. He held on to the desk, his face a sheet of pure white. "Did you find the tablet?"

She nodded and scurried to grab it. She tucked it under her arm.

"Do you have any idea how gorgeous you are?" He swung an arm around her shoulders. "I love you, darlin'. And I will spank you in the afterlife."

She wasn't going to the afterlife. She held on to him and moved to the window. It was the fastest way out. Three agonizing steps and they were there. She forced the window open.

"This is going to hurt, baby." She couldn't imagine the pain he was going to go through.

"Push me out and then follow me." His face was set.

He barely groaned, and she forced him through the window. He hit the bushes outside and rolled. Avery followed. How much time was left?

She started through the window, but a big hand reached out to grab her. She shrieked as she was pulled out of the house and lifted into strong arms. She looked up and saw Ian Taggart's face staring down at her.

"How are you here?" Avery asked.

"When Nelson didn't show up, we figured out something had gone wrong on this end. We found a dead thug at your place and couldn't get Li on the phone. This was the first place we thought to check. Alex? You got him?" Ian didn't seem to even notice her weight.

"I got him," a deep voice shouted. "And if he's not insane, then we need to fucking run. He says the whole place is going to blow, and we need to get him to a hospital ASAP."

She looked over Ian's broad shoulder and saw that Alex McKay had slung Liam over his shoulder.

Ian took off, catching up to his partner and running through the garden gate. Jake was waiting, holding the gate open.

"Fuck, is Li alive?" Jake asked.

"Move, Dean. There's a fire in the hole," Ian yelled as he ran past. "Take cover."

She was suddenly on the ground, Ian covering her with his big body. She couldn't breathe, but she felt another weight on her. Jake Dean lent his own body to protect her. In the moonlight, she managed to move her head, looking for Liam. Alex covered him. Liam reached out, his hand threading among the protective bodies to find hers. He gripped her hand.

She wasn't alone. She would never be alone again.

A loud boom filled the world and the night lit up. Avery held on to that hand as the world exploded around her.

Chapter Twenty-Two

Three months later
Dallas, TX

Liam looked down at the little scrap of humanity wrapped in a pink blanket. It was actually pretty cute, but it was so damn small. Given who her father was, he'd expected more substance to the kid. "Are you sure she's yours, Sean?"

He grunted a little as Avery's hand came out to slap him in the chest. His wife didn't mind telling him when he was being dumb. "That's horrible, Li."

Sean just rolled his blue eyes. "It's not entirely unexpected. Marriage hasn't curbed your sarcasm, man. It's kind of refined it."

Marriage had refined everything. He looked over at his gorgeous wife, his lover, his best friend, his sub. "I'm better at everything now."

He was certainly better at pleasing her. It was his job in life.

Avery laughed, her eyes rolling. He bloody loved that. It was her way of telling him she was amused. He was also very good at amusing her. "Listen to him. He's so arrogant."

He wasn't arrogant. He just knew his place. It was by Avery's side, and she was the smartest damn woman in the world. She was also pregnant. It shouldn't have come as a surprise. He was on top of her most of the time. "Do you think our kid is going to be that wrinkly?"

Grace frowned from her hospital bed. The room was filling up fast. Grace had given birth just twenty-four hours before, but she was already back to smiling and beautiful as she held her tiny girl. "She's not wrinkly. She spent a lot of time in the womb. Give her a little credit."

Serena stepped up. "Baby Carys isn't wrinkly. She's gorgeous. Look at those little fat baby legs."

Adam moved behind his wife, his hand covering her slightly rounded belly. "She is beautiful, sweetheart."

Jake took his place at her side, too. "Our son is going to be gorgeous, too."

Jake and Adam were sure the baby in Serena's belly was a boy, but Liam didn't give a shit. He just wanted a healthy baby. It sort of freaked him out. He still wasn't sure he was father material, but he loved his wife so much he had to try. That baby would be a part of Avery. The baby would get all her goodness. The baby would be the best thing he could put into the world. While he was scared out of his mind, he was also okay because Avery was with him. Avery was his strength. He pulled her close, nuzzling her hair. This was where he lived. Avery O'Donnell was his home.

"She's awful cute, love," Liam offered.

Avery gave him a big grin. "She is."

The door opened behind him and Ian, Alex, and Eve walked in. The gang was all here. Ian had a wary look on his face as he entered the room. He was a little awkward carrying a massive teddy bear.

Sean stood up straighter, his jaw going just a little hard. He hadn't forgiven his brother yet, but he dealt with it for Grace's sake. Liam had talked a little to Sean about Rory. He was kind of hoping that his good-for-nothing, arms dealing, rapist, killer brother would make Ian look good. Sean needed to know that he had it easy when it came to blood family.

Grace gave her brother-in-law a glorious smile. "Do you want to meet your niece?"

"Yes." The answer came out in a rush, Ian flushing slightly. He shook it off. "But she's so…little. I think I might break her."

Big Tag stood over the tiny infant looking utterly helpless. Carys kicked her baby legs and managed to break free of the bunting they had wrapped around her. One tiny fist came free, and there was no way to miss the proud little smirk that hit Ian's face.

"Just pick her up, man," Sean said, sighing. "She's tough. She's a Taggart."

Liam had never seen Ian flush before, but he did as he looked down at that little day-old girl. His big ass paws came out to lift the infant up.

"She's beautiful. I think that's from Grace, though. Not you, Sean," Ian said, looking down at his niece.

A broad smile broke over Sean's face. "Yeah. She looks like her momma."

Liam hated this part, the part that made his eyes water and his stomach roll. Emotion. It still kind of made him want to puke, but he would do anything for these people. His real family. He was a bloody lucky man. He'd gotten to pick his family, and they were amazing. He pulled Avery close. His wife. His better half. He'd lost his brother, but he'd found his soul.

Ian smiled down at the girl. "I'm going to meet all of your boyfriends."

Grace shook her head. "The poor girl. She's never going to date. Sean already has plans."

Ian gave the baby to Sean, handing her over carefully. The baby was precious. He turned to Liam, gesturing to the door.

Liam followed him out. "What's up, boss?"

It had been a quiet couple of months. His marriage to Avery and the birth of Carys had been the big events in their lives. It was a wonderful way to live.

The door closed, and Ian turned to him. "I already told the others, but MI6 just apprehended the first of Nelson's buyers."

A fierce satisfaction flooded his veins. His wife had made that happen. She'd taken down a terrorist with smarts and good sense. She hadn't backed down. She was a warrior, his girl. "Fucking brilliant. Did they get Nelson?"

Ian's face went blank. "He didn't show. He got tipped off somehow. Thanks to Avery, we have the code. Weston broke it, but we can only hope Nelson shows his face soon. He has people inside the Agency. It's obvious. But we've shut his arms dealing down for the moment and MI6 has arrested the UOF employees who helped your brother. Thomas Molina's accounts have been frozen, and MI6 is sure they've tracked down where Rory stashed the cash he'd stolen from the UOF."

Cutting off his access to funds would only make Nelson more dangerous. "He told me this is all a game, and he intends to beat you."

Liam still had the scars. He'd been taken to a hospital and spent the better part of a week there. He had a bunch of new scars to show off, but he was alive because of Alex and Ian and Jake. His wife had gotten his ass up and moving, and his brothers had saved him. His brothers had covered him and Avery with their own bodies as the world blew up around them. Just as his blood betrayed him, he'd found his real family. The old Liam would have pulled into himself and shut everyone else out.

Avery's Liam had opened up. He'd embraced his family. He was a loving husband, a proud brother, a protective uncle. He'd held Avery's hand as they visited the grave of her first husband and her first baby. He honored them because they had such a place in his love's heart.

And he'd visited her in-laws. It wasn't perfect, but they were talking. His wife was too lovable to reject. She'd opened the world for him. She'd taught him to forgive himself.

Ian slapped his arm. "I'll take care of Nelson."

Liam was so fucking worried about his friend. "I think Nelson is planning on taking care of you."

A savage look came over Ian's face. "Then he should bring it on."

"He's going to come after us again." Liam had no doubt.

Ian nodded. "I know. I'll try to take care of it. I'm bringing on a new member of the team, by the way. I hired him yesterday. We've got a bunch of family men now. I need a smart agent who won't get squeamish about handling a dirty op."

"Who? Did Alex approve?" Liam had come to appreciate Alex's opinion.

"Alex is in agreement, and you won't like him." Ian shrugged a little.

Liam groaned. "Not Weston. Please. Doesn't he have a kingdom to run or something?"

Ian's smirk told him he was right. "He left MI6 because he screwed up. I think he won't do it again, and he was the one who figured out the cipher. We shut down Nelson's money because of him. Damon says he's a little haunted because he took Nelson's data. I promised I would take care of him. We've all trusted the wrong people. I think he could be helpful."

He would be a pain in Liam's ass, and if the bugger looked at his wife wrong, he would take Simon out. But otherwise, he was on the team. "I'll show him the ropes, boss."

He owed Ian. He owed them all. Simon Weston would have the chance to prove himself.

"Thanks, man." Ian looked around, his discomfort palpable. "Tell Grace good-bye for me. I love the kid, but I don't know how to deal with her. I have a trust already planned for her school if that makes a difference. I won't have any kids. I figure I can help with Sean's."

"Sure, mate." Liam watched as Ian walked away. Nelson would show up, but they would be ready. They had won this battle, but the war raged on.

He opened the door again. Avery had Carys in her arms, rocking the baby sweetly. She looked up, her eyes bright.

She was his whole fucking life.

"Hey, baby," she said with a smile.

Liam let the door close behind him. It was all right. He was with his family.

* * * *

Deep in the night, Alex turned on his laptop. He would just check his email before going to bed. Hell, who was he kidding? He would be sitting here for hours. The minute he laid down in bed, he would be reminded of the fact that Eve wasn't with him.

Watching Sean and Grace and their baby had hit him squarely in the gut. He was happy for them. He was happy for all of them. Everyone was married and had pregnant wives it seemed. Adam and Jake had wanted to start a family forever. Fuck, even love 'em and leave 'em Liam had settled down. He would be a father before Alex.

That was what churned in his gut. He and Eve should have been parents a couple of times over by now. Two or three kids. They should be in the suburbs with a couple of girls who looked like Eve and a dumbass boy who would act like Alex. They should have had a future.

He'd screwed it all up. He'd thought he was so fucking smart, but Michael Evans had shown him. He closed his eyes, the memories still so fresh in his head like the horror had happened yesterday and not years ago. But then wounds never healed when a man just kept ripping them open again.

A weariness invaded his veins as the screen changed. He'd earned his heartache. He'd gotten out of Eve's bed not an hour before, and his soul was already aching. He'd lain there and just for a moment he'd pretended she wasn't going to kick him out. He'd let himself hope that she would turn to him, lay her head on his chest and they could fall asleep wrapped around each other.

She'd gotten up and taken a shower as though she couldn't wait to wash him from her body. He'd slunk out knowing damn well she was done with him for the night.

Their world was changing, and he was wondering if he wasn't changing with it.

He couldn't handle it. He loved Eve, but he couldn't handle the punishment much longer. He loved her, and he'd destroyed her.

If he couldn't put her back together soon, his life might be over.

He glanced down the e-mails. Work. Work was the only thing that held him together half the time. He could lose himself in work. He answered a few questions about ongoing cases. There was nothing special in the list until about halfway down.

He hit select, his heart skipping a little. His eyes searched the mail, and his blood pressure rose.

Michael Evans was back, and it seemed like he wanted to play a little game.

Eve was in trouble. Eve was in danger. She might not want his help. But she would get it. It was time to protect his wife.

Whether she wanted it or not.

The McKay-Taggart security team returns in 2013 with *On Her Master's Secret Service*:

Her submission fulfilled her

When Eve St. James married Alex McKay, she had her whole life ahead of her. They were the FBI's golden couple by day, but by night Eve gave herself over to her husband's world of Dominance and submission filled with pleasures she came to crave.

His betrayal destroyed her

Worried for her safety, Alex left Eve behind to tackle a dangerous mission. But Alex never suspected that Eve was the real target and her security is destroyed by a madman. By the time he rescues her, his wife has been changed forever.

But when her life is in danger he is her only hope

Unable to heal the damage, Alex and Eve are still trapped together in a cycle of pleasure and misery that even their divorce cannot sever. But when a threat from Eve's past resurfaces, Alex will stop at nothing to save her life and reclaim her heart.

About Lexi Blake:

Lexi Blake lives in North Texas with her husband, three kids, and the laziest rescue dog in the world. She began writing at a young age, concentrating on plays and journalism. It wasn't until she started writing romance that she found success. She likes to find humor in the strangest places. Lexi believes in happy endings no matter how odd the couple, threesome or foursome may seem. She also writes contemporary western ménage as Sophie Oak.

Connect with Lexi online:

Facebook: Lexi Blake
Twitter: www.twitter.com/@authorlexiblake
Smashwords:
www.smashwords.com/profile/view/LexiBlake
Website: www.LexiBlake.net

Other Books by Lexi Blake:

Masters And Mercenaries
The Dom Who Loved Me
The Men With The Golden Cuffs
A Dom Is Forever
Coming in 2013:
On Her Master's Secret Service
Love and Let Die

Masters of Ménage by Shayla Black and Lexi Blake
Their Virgin Captive
Their Virgin's Secret
Their Virgin Concubine
Coming Soon:
Their Virgin Princess

Coming Soon:
Leaving Camelot, Wild Western Nights, Book 1

Enjoy the following excerpt from *Their Virgin Concubine*, by Shayla Black and Lexi Blake, available now:
Copyright 2012 by Shayla Black and Lexi Blake

The country of Bezakistan – renowned for its wealth and the beauty of its deserts…

Piper Glen is thrilled when Rafe and Kade al Mussad ask her to visit their country on a business trip. Madly attracted to both, the virginal secretary knows that neither of her intensely handsome bosses desires her. But every night she dreams of having them both in her bed, fulfilling her every need.

Rafe and Kade have finally found the perfect woman in Piper. Sweet and funny. Intelligent and strong. Before they can reveal their feelings, the brothers must fulfill an ancient tradition. Every sheikh must steal his bride and share her with his brothers. They have thirty days to convince Piper to love them all forever.

The country of Bezakistan – notorious for its danger…

Sheikh Talib al Mussad knows his villainous cousin seeks to take his throne. If Talib and his brothers fail to convince the beautiful Piper to love them, all will be lost. After meeting Piper, he knows he would risk everything to possess her heart.

Khalil al Bashir has long coveted his cousin's rule. Without a bride to seal their birthright, his every wish will come true. If Piper falls for them, he will lose everything but Piper can't love them if she's dead…

428

Chapter One

Kadir al Mussad watched the gorgeous blonde with the swaying, tight ass walk by and wondered if there was something wrong with his dick. She was lovely and obviously available. No ring on that finger. Wearing a gray skirt that barely covered her essentials and red stilettos, she was definitely dressed to attract a man. As she passed, she turned slightly, her eyes widening as she took in his thousand dollar custom-made suit and handcrafted Italian loafers. He could see the hot blonde silently itemizing him, doing her best to estimate his wealth down to the last dollar.

And she would fall short by a few billion.

"Hi." She carried a few folders, but not where they'd hide her breasts. At least a D cup and, from the placement of those large globes high on her chest, he would bet she'd purchased them herself. Like the rest of the blonde, they were magnificently constructed and hard as a rock.

His dick practically yawned. "Hello. I'm looking for Mr. Townsend."

Her painted mouth curled up in a sex-kitten smile. "He recently changed his last name to James."

Good for Dex. A little warmth flooded Kade's system at the thought of his friend finally finding his true place beside his two biological brothers, along with their shared wife, Hannah. "Excellent. Then where is Mr. James this morning?"

Dex was the head of security. He would be the one to talk to about the little problem Kade was having. He needed information on one of Black Oak Oil's employees. Little things like where her office was and whether or not she had all her teeth. All the things his eldest brother, Talib, hadn't seen fit to mention when he'd ordered Kade and their middle

429

brother, Rafe, to fetch this girl and bring her home to Bezakistan. The sheikh could be a bossy asshole at times.

God, if Talib didn't settle on a wife soon, Kade was going to lose his bloody mind—and a lot more. Of course, the problem was that once Talib settled on a wife, Kade and Rafe would have to settle for her, too. One wife for all brothers. God bless Bezakistan.

He had to hope this candidate looked better than the mousy pictures included in Talib's dossier. It wasn't that she was ugly, merely plain and deeply somber. And the photos were grainy, a driver's license picture and a little black and white image that looked like it had come from a school yearbook. Neither had been promising. And her background was so bland he'd forgotten most of it already. Grew up in a small town. Apple of her parents' eyes. Graduated from college with a degree in economics. Yep. He'd gone to sleep just after reading that tidbit.

"He's in a meeting, but you can wait in his office." Her eyes softened, an obviously practiced move. "Or you could buy me a cup of coffee."

Nothing. Not even a stir. His cock was still completely flaccid, despite her less than subtle come-on. Damn it, he was barely thirty. His dick should be standing up and shouting "let's party!" Kade would rather take a nap. He sighed. Maybe his dick's lack of responsiveness didn't matter since he'd likely soon be chained to some boring, dull-as-dishwater intellectual because that was Talib's type.

Maybe he should try to convince his cock to take the blonde up on her offer.

Before he could, a flurry of chaos walked by, her brown hair caught at the back of her head in a messy bun. She quickly rushed down the hall, barely containing a haphazard stack of files in her arms that stuck out this way and that, the edges poking at all sorts of odd angles. She was talking on a cell phone tucked between her ear and her shoulder, her face animated. She plowed right into the blonde, who dropped the two little folders she'd been carrying. The stack in the brunette's arms exploded, paper filling the air like a ticker-tape parade.

"Goddamn it," the blonde cursed. "Fucking researchers."

"I am so sorry, Amanda." The brunette spoke in a soft Texas twang as she dropped to the ground on her hands and knees, phone tumbling across the office carpet as she began wrangling the wild herd of papers. "I was talking and I wasn't looking where I was going. I'm really sorry."

"Here, let me help you," a deep voice said. Rafiq, his brother, always the gentleman, hurried up the hall and got to one knee.

"Thank you," the blonde purred. Then she realized Rafe was talking to the little brunette and frowned down at her. "There's a reason everyone around here calls you Pandora."

Pandora. Goddess of Chaos. The messy bun on the back of the brunette's head looked like it would unravel at any moment, unleashing a cascade of brown curls lit with strands of honey blonde and warm red. She turned her face up, and Kade nearly cheered.

His dick was back in top form now, standing tall and eager. *Oh, yeah.*

There was nothing at all artificial about Pandora. She was soft and feminine, with bee-stung lips and blue eyes that were nearly hidden behind a pair of big glasses that might have been fashionable in the eighties. She wore a shapeless blouse, but as she moved, she popped a button, and he caught sight of creamy white cleavage flushed with a hint of pink. Clearly, she was flustered and embarrassed.

431

"They don't call me Pandora because I unleashed evil on the world or anything," she explained. "I'm just clumsy. I apologize to you, too, sir. So sorry."

Then Pandora bit her lip in a way that made him wonder how she would suck a cock, provided that she'd ever sucked a cock before. Her air of innocence had him wondering. He could teach her how to suck a cock. His cock. His brother Rafe's cock. She looked back at him.

She was far more polite than the blonde, who impatiently tapped her stiletto, palm outstretched, as she waited for Pandora to organize and return her folders. Clearly, Amanda wasn't going to lower herself to help. So the sweet brunette picked up the blonde's folders and carefully placed the documents inside before handing them up to the other woman. Kade watched her every move. Poised on all fours, Pandora's ass stuck up in the air. Even encased in an ugly khaki skirt, there was no hiding those curves. That ass was made to take a cock, her hips perfect for holding on to as a man drove inside and made her howl with pleasure.

There was a vicious swat to his knees, and he looked into Rafe's impatient eyes. "Are you going to help or not?"

Kade heard the unspoken end to that sentence. *Or are you going to stand there and stare at her ass?*

He wanted to stare at her ass. A single grunt from his older brother made him sigh and drop to the floor. Folders were scattered everywhere, paperwork spread out around her like a multi-colored quilt of chaos. Pandora, indeed. She'd shaken up his day. He wondered if she could also rock his world.

"What about that coffee?" Amanda asked him, her voice dropping to a seductive murmur.

He didn't bother to look up at the blonde. "I'm not

432

thirsty right now. I'll just wait for Dex."

She tsked, huffed, and stomped off. He smiled.

"So, once we've cleaned up this little mess, would you like to get a drink?" Kade asked Pandora in his smoothest voice.

His brother's head came up, his mouth dropping open. Rafe's expression silently said "idiot."

Why were Rafe's panties in a wad? Could he not see the bounty in front of them? Now that Kade was close, he could smell her shampoo. Citrus, orangey and tangy. Delightful. He took a deep breath. What the hell would her pussy smell like? He would just rub his nose all over and keep that spicy, feminine scent with him all fucking day long. Damn, it felt good to be horny.

"Are you all right?"

He opened his eyes and stopped sniffing the female. *Fuck.* The good news was she didn't seem to know what he was doing. The bad news? His brother was looking at him like he was the world's biggest moron. Oh, well. Rafe often had that look on his face. Kade tried not to take it personally. "I am very well, thank you."

"He's a bit slow, if you know what I mean," Rafe said with a sharp bite to his words.

Pandora's eyes widened with sympathy. "Oh. Really? Okay. I'll just show you where everything goes. It's so nice of you to help me."

Rafe sat back on his heels, a brilliant smile crossing his face as he held back laughter. Kade wanted to punch the asshole in the face, but it was so good to see his brother smile again that he let his violent impulses go. Still, he had to repair the damage wrought by Rafe's insult. He didn't want pretty Pandora to think he was slow. Except in bed, where he would go very slowly and savor every inch of her.

He caught her hand in his. Soft skin, warm, slightly calloused on the side of one finger where she'd hold a pencil. He flipped her hand over, his thumb tracing the blue lines of her veins before covering it with his other hand. He wanted her to feel surrounded by him, a little taste of what he and Rafe could give her. "My brother is teasing you, *habibti*. I have two degrees from Oxford University. He thinks I am slow because he has three."

That pretty pale skin flushed right up again. He liked that he would be able to tell so much just by looking at her. He would know when she was lying, when she was happy, when she was aroused. He was used to jaded women, but his little Pandora was far from that.

"Sorry. I guess I'm a little naïve. I only have the one degree, and it's from Hale University in West Texas. Go Bullfrogs!" She gave a charming little laugh and seemed unable to stop speaking. "Dumb mascot. Really. You do not want to be in that costume in August in Abilene. Hot. And cramped. It's the only mascot uniform that forces you to hop. They told me it was because they wanted realism, but I think they just wanted to torture me. Terrible way to try to find your school spirit. Though it built strong quadriceps. That's the thigh muscle. Wait. You know that because of Oxford and stuff. I'm going to stop talking now."

"Hello!" A muffled feminine voice called out from the proximity of the floor.

Pandora pulled her hand out of his with a grimace and started shuffling through papers, looking for something. "I dropped my phone. Dang!"

Then she went right back to her hands and knees, frantically searching. Now Kade wasn't the only one looking at her ass. Rafe was practically drooling, his eyes travelling from the graceful curve of her spine to the round cheeks of her backside. Rafe's gaze cut over to his with an interested gleam.

Kade raised his eyebrows and pointed at his watch. It was early, but if they took her to lunch, maybe they could be in bed by twelve thirty. Their condo wasn't far. Feed her a little. Maybe a nice bottle of wine. Then, before long, they'd hopefully sweet talk the glorious little bundle of chaos into getting in between them.

Rafe frowned and held up his folder, the one that contained the name of the woman they had come here to see. Piper Glen. The supposed savior of Bezakistan. Hopefully not some cold-ass intellectual.

Fucking Pandora would have to wait.

Rafe nodded regretfully and mouthed, "Dinner?"

Yeah. If they weren't on a plane home with their future wife in tow. He longed for the old days when no one thought a sheikh should be faithful to one woman. They could have married whoever and kept little Pandora as a treat on the side. But no. Now he had paparazzi and tabloid rags and Sunday news shows commenting about where he put his dick.

Which still hadn't gone down.

He sighed and started cleaning up again.

"Mindy? Are you still there?" Pandora scrambled to put the phone against her ear. "Did you get the check? Good. Buy your books and don't forget to save some. I can't send anything else until next payday. I love you. No. I don't want to hear about him. Unless he's dead. Then I do. Darn it. No, I don't wish him ill. Thank you. You're a good sister." She shut her phone, a ridiculously old contraption that Kade was surprised still worked. "Sorry about all this. I was talking to my sister and I got distracted."

She pushed the last of the papers into a haphazard pile

that would likely make Rafe crazy. His brother was fastidious, but Rafe simply smiled as he handed her the perfectly placed pile he'd gathered.

"We all get distracted at times," Rafe said, the smooth words coming out like he'd never ogled her ass. He bowed politely. "I wish you a good afternoon."

She smiled, pushing her glasses back up. That smile was fatal. Kade just stared because she lit up the fucking room. "Thank you so much. Good afternoon to you, too."

She turned and walked away, her flats shuffling as she tried to balance the papers and her phone.

"Oh, we have got to have that, my brother." Rafe stood beside him, his head angled to one side as he watched her walk away.

Kade silently thanked the heavens because Rafe had been as out of sorts as he'd felt the last few months. "Yes, we do. Let's find Dex and get this over with so we can take Pandora out for happy hour. Then we'll make her even happier. We should find out her name before we fuck her."

An arm slapped around his shoulders suddenly, and Dexter James shoved his six foot five inch, two hundred twenty pounds of pure muscle between Kade and his brother. "Her name is Piper, and I'll kill you both if you lay a hand on her."

"Piper?" *That* was Piper Glen? That gloriously messy little fuck bunny was the drab girl in the pictures that Tal wanted to marry?

Two ideas struck Kade as Dex started to lead them to his office. First, his oldest brother's taste had come up in the world. And second, he better knock out Dex now because he planned to get a lot more than his hands on that sweet woman.

* * * *

Piper Glen managed to make it to her teeny-tiny office without another catastrophe. Except now, she couldn't open the door.

"Allow me." Gina Jacobson twisted the handle with a smile and eased the door open. "Here's your kingdom."

An eight-by-eight cubby hole was hardly a kingdom, especially with its glorious view of a dumpster in the alley behind the building and its location as far from the elevators as possible. The little room had been given to the lowly researcher. Anyone else would have run. Piper merely sighed as she put her files down, grumbling a bit.

"What happened now, hon? Did that guy from the mailroom plow into you? I swear, I can take him. I have two toddlers. One skinny twenty-year-old is no match for me."

Piper slumped down, the last couple of minutes washing over her like a bad horror film. "Nope. It was just me. Pandora struck again."

The employees of Black Oak Oil had christened her Pandora, unleasher of evil on the world, because she'd caused a complete building-wide blackout on her first day. It wasn't her fault that dumb fuse had blown because her coffeemaker was from the sixties. Some days, she was like one big pitfall waiting to happen.

But she was smart and a darn good researcher.

Gina groaned in sympathy and leaned her hip on the side of Piper's desk. "Tell me all about it, hon."

The older woman was a gossip, but a sweet-natured one, unlike Amanda who was a raging... something Piper knew she shouldn't even think because her mom would turn over in her grave. "I was talking to my sister and ran smack into Amanda."

437

Gina waved that off. "Oh, hon, that's inevitable. And I bet you bounced right off those fake tits of hers. I've often thought that she should rent those boobs out as a bouncy house for bored babies."

Piper looked down at her own chest. They were probably as big as Amanda's, but hers were real so they sagged a little. Even at twenty-five. And her clothes wouldn't fit right. She sighed. It didn't matter. She wasn't here looking for love. She was done with that. Johnny Tyler, affectionately known to his friends as Cooder, had proven that men were just dogs with a bone. If she couldn't keep someone like Johnny happy, she probably never would find a decent man. And that was fine. She was going to have a career. See the world. Her female parts had been put into hibernation long ago.

Except they had hummed back to life the minute Hottie Number One had laid a hand on her. Her heart rate had tripled and her skin had sizzled with life. Too bad her mouth hadn't stopped working. She talked way too much when she was nervous. "Hey, do we have a couple of new guys around? Tall, maybe Middle Eastern but talk with British accents?" Hottie Number Two had been just as beautiful as his brother. She was sure they were related.

Gina's eyes widened. "Are you talking about Rafe and Kade al Mussad? Yep. You are. Every woman who meets them gets that glazed look in her eyes. They're here a lot. I'm surprised you haven't met them before." Her voice dropped to a gossipy whisper. "They're filthy rich. They represent all the business interests for Bezakistan. Aren't you working on their green project?"

Yep. And all the paperwork was in a giant heap that she would have to painstakingly reorganize. She could do it tonight. It wasn't like she had anything else to do. This job was her gateway to bigger and better things. "Yes. I'm getting all the numbers ready for the guy on the other end. Tal."

Gina stared at her. "You just sighed when you said his name."

"I did not." Except she kind of had. Tal was her counterpart in Bezakistan. Black Oak Oil was working with the government of Bezakistan to start a green energy project, and Piper was in charge of putting together all the research. She'd been e-mailing and talking on the phone to Tal for several months. "He's just nice."

"Tal, huh? In Bezakistan? I don't think I've heard of him. What I do know is that the sheikh, Talib, is just as gorgeous as his brothers. Have you met this man you've been talking to? You might want to take a look because I've heard they grow them hot over there."

Piper shook her head. Not Tal. Tal was sedate and very polite. His voice was soothing and intelligent. She couldn't imagine him looking like the two movie-star gorgeous men she'd just met, and she kind of liked it that way. "I seriously doubt it. He's really...smart." And organized and creative. And she didn't even know how old he was. Probably older. And married. With lots of kids. But she could dream a little.

Gina hopped off the desk. "I don't need a smart man. Give me a dumb hot guy any day of the week. My Matthew couldn't find his head in his ass, but his chest is a work of art. Are you coming to lunch with us?"

Piper forced a sunny smile on her face. "Can't. I have so much work."

Gina shrugged and walked out, the door closing behind her.

Piper's stomach growled, and she wished she hadn't left her bagged lunch on the train. It hadn't been much. A peanut butter and jelly sandwich and a few baby carrots, but it would have been better than nothing.

She thought about her tiny studio apartment. She'd sent the last of her money to Mindy to pay for her school. There wouldn't be more for another week when her modest check from Black Oak came in. She took mental stock of her fridge. The next week didn't look good.

She glanced at the calendar, her stomach taking a dive. Well, at least she wasn't hungry anymore. Tomorrow was supposed to have been her first wedding anniversary, if she'd managed to get down the aisle. She could still feel the white satin on her skin as she tried on her wedding gown. She'd looked at herself in the mirror and, just for a moment, she'd been a princess.

Tears filled her eyes. Turned out, her prince preferred strippers to nice girls he'd met at church. She'd been left at the altar with a note and the judgmental stares of everyone in her small town. And she'd still had her sister to put through school since Mindy's scholarship had mysteriously dried up the minute Piper was no longer connected to the mayor's family.

Piper took a deep breath. She couldn't go back there. She was here now. Granted, she had a job that paid next to nothing and an office she could barely move in, but this was her kingdom. It wouldn't be forever; it would grow. Until then, she would make it work.

With a deep breath, she put aside thoughts of shattered romances and beautiful men with sun-kissed skin. Piper reached for the stack of papers in front of her. She had a job to do.

Coming May 7, 2013 from *New York Times* Bestselling Author Shayla Black:

Ours to Love, Wicked Lovers, Book 7

Between two brothers...

Xander Santiago spent years living it up as a billionaire playboy. Never given a chance to lead his family business in the boardroom, he became a Master in the bedroom instead. His older brother inherited the company and worked tirelessly to make it an empire. But while the cutthroat corporate espionage took its toll on Javier, nothing was as devastating as the seemingly senseless murder of his wife. It propelled him into a year of punishing rage and guilt...until Xander came to his rescue.

Comes an irresistible woman...

Eager to rejuvenate Javier's life, Xander shanghais him to Louisiana where they meet the beautiful London McLane. After surviving a decade of tragedy and struggle, London is determined to make a fresh start—and these sexy billionaire brothers are more than willing to help. In every way. And London is stunned to find herself open to every heated suggestion...and desperately hoping that her love will heal them.

And inescapable danger...

But a killer with a hidden motive is watching, on a single-minded mission to destroy everything the Santiago brothers hold dear, especially London. And as fear and desire collide, every passionate beat of her heart could be her last.

CPSIA information can be obtained at www.ICGtesting.com
Printed in the USA
LVOW07s1608151014

408902LV00001B/122/P